THE HEART OF LYCAON

ANTHONY COTILLETTA

The Heart of Lycaon

Manufactured in the United States of America

13-Digit ISBN: 978-0-9897301-1-2.

For Chip, Bruno, Booger, and Toni

ONE

The cool night breeze caressed three silhouetted figures in the shadowy confines of the Muttontown Preserve as they snuck closer to their target: the headquarters of the multi-billion dollar corporation, Stumpp Industries. The building stood several yards back from a usually busy street; however, at three o'clock in the morning, the only real activity was that of the individuals approaching the front door.

Donning ski masks to hide their faces, all were similarly dressed in dark outfits, but one had a fanny-pack securely fastened around his waist. Making his way to the well-lit doorway, Robert Mane reached inside his pack and pulled out a security key card. He swiped it through a sensor attached to the door frame and pressed a few numbers on its keypad to gain entry.

"Now what, Bobby?" the shortest of the three asked.

Robert "Bobby" Mane was a young man in his twenties, physically fit and just above average-looking, with dirty blond hair and blue-green eyes. He'd worked for Stumpp for the past five years; and neither his looks nor his exceptional work ethic had gotten him any closer to getting promoted out of the mailroom and into an office—although after this night, he was convinced he would never need to work again. "Just follow me and stay quiet."

"Why are you whispering? I thought you said there was no one here at night."

"What I said, Louis," Mane said, sounding a bit frustrated, "was there were no guards here at night. I didn't say the building was empty."

"If there are no guards in here, then what is?" Louis Falcone had met Mane in grade school, and if one got into something, you could be sure the other wasn't far behind. Slightly overweight at only a hair over five feet tall, with dark brown hair, brown eyes, and some leftover acne scars on his cheeks, Louis wasn't the brightest guy, but he was loyal. Louis had always been more cautious than careless, but if Mane pushed hard enough, Louis eventually gave in.

"Listen, it's no big deal really. I told you the boss don't trust people—"

"How long have you worked here?" Jacob Connors, the group's remaining member, interrupted. He and Mane had pledged the same fraternity in college and bonded through the daily humiliation and embarrassment inflicted by their frat brothers. Standing a little over six feet tall, with light-brown curly hair and prescription glasses over light green eyes, Jacob was never the kind of person to be talked into anything. His college days made him believe life was one big practical joke, and if he benefited from pulling one on someone, then so be it.

"Five years. Why?" Mane answered.

"Whose key card and pass code did we use to get in tonight?"

"I swiped the card and code from one of the daytime security guards. Again, why?"

"I was just a little confused as to why your boss didn't trust people, that's all."

"No one dragged you here, Jake. Don't let the door hit you in the ass on the way out!" Mane pointed to the front entrance.

"Lighten up, man. You always were too serious."

"Umm ... Bobby?" Louis whispered.

"What?"

"You still haven't said what's inside the building with us."

"Like I said," Mane started again, "the boss don't trust people—"

"Doesn't," Jacob said.

"What?"

"The boss *doesn't* trust people," Jacob corrected.

"Dude, seriously, leave or shut the fuck up." Mane pulled off his mask, completely exasperated now. Turning back to Louis, he finished, "He trusts animals. He has guard dogs in the building. I don't know how many, but I know they're on the upper floors; and if we're quiet, they probably won't even know we're here."

Afraid to aggravate his friend, Louis felt compelled to ask one more question. "What if they *do* know we're here?"

"I brought this along ... just in case!" Reaching into his fanny-pack once again, he pulled out a Glock twenty-three compact pistol. "Now, let's go. We've been here for ten minutes and haven't moved twenty feet past the front door. And take off the masks already! I told you there are no cameras in the building, not past the entrance."

"No guards. No cameras. This guy must really trust his dogs," Jacob mumbled.

Using flashlights, all three steadily moved through the sizeable lobby and toward the elevators. Beams of light passed over nicely framed pictures of forest sceneries, an abstract sculpture, and a large table displaying the company directory. Marble tiles reflected light back at its source, and a flash hit Louis in the eye, causing him to recoil, raise his flashlight, and illuminate a Doberman pinscher's snarling face. He yelped, stumbled backwards, and tripped, slamming his head into the sharp bottom edge of the company directory. The loud bang forced the others to center their attention on their clumsy companion cowering on the floor, but his attacker was nowhere in sight. Mane knelt next to his friend and smacked him gently on top of the head with the lit end of his flashlight.

"Ow!" Louis rubbed his scalp. "What was that for?"

Shining his light on the wall opposite them to reveal a painted picture of a man sitting in a chair with the Doberman beside him, he said, "I told you the guy loves dogs. Now, chill out so we can get down to business."

"Guys! Over here!" Jacob lit his own face as he waved to his friends. "I got the elevator."

Louis hoisted his bulk off the ground, leaving behind a few drops of blood and some hair from the cut on his head. But he couldn't turn away from the painting; the dog's eyes seemed to follow him across the room. As the elevator doors closed, Louis let out a frightened gulp while staring one more time into the face of the snarling Doberman.

The trio quietly watched the floor numbers change on the digital display as the car ascended toward the upper floors, and the silence only served to increase the tension and nervousness they were already experiencing. Jacob, who was standing in the middle, started to sniff the air, looked at his cohorts, and wrinkled his nose after taking another whiff. Mane did the same, and both of them inched as far away from Louis as possible, until they were practically flat against the opposite wall. Louis pretended not to notice his two gawking accomplices and continued to watch the floors drift by.

Mane finally broke the silence. "Dude, can't you warn a guy before you do that?"

"Silent but deadly," Jacob chimed in. "So not cool."

"Come on, Bobby. You know I have a nervous stomach, and thinking about some dog taking a chunk out of my ass is making it do some serious flips here."

Upon reaching the thirteenth floor, Louis, who was very superstitious, felt a lump form in his throat. Standing with their backs pressed against the far wall, they eyed each other. Then they watched the doors open and close again, none brave enough to venture out into the darkness.

Shaking off his anxiety, Mane reached for the DOOR OPEN button on the inside control panel. This time, when the doors slid open, he poked his head out. Moving his flashlight right and left, he saw two empty hallways. As the elevator doors shut, he put a hand up to intercept, and they automatically reversed direction. Creeping out of the car and into the hallway, he motioned for the other two to follow and forcibly pulled them out when neither complied.

"Okay, this is what we're gonna do. Louis, you stay here and make sure these doors are open when we get back. We don't need the elevator to leave this floor and slow us down when we have to go. Jake is coming with me."

Jacob glanced at Louis, then at Mane, and said, "Why does he stay with the elevator? I can stay with the elevator, too, you know."

"He already said I stay with the elevator," Louis reinforced the decision.

Jacob began, "All I'm saying is—"

"Will both of you shut up? Jake, don't tell me you're getting cold feet. You're the one who said this would be the best stunt ever, and you didn't even know what we were gonna take. Now, come on." They started down the long, gloomy stretch of hallway, using flashlights to brighten their way.

Gazing back at Louis, Jacob pursed his lips, aggravated that he wasn't permitted to stay behind. He scanned the hall, trying to fight off the fear building inside him. "You sure you know where we're going?"

"Of course I know. I've been bringing mail to every floor of this building for the past few years. So, stay close. I don't want you to get lost."

"Where's his office?" Jacob's eyes couldn't adjust to the darkness.

"Last door on the right."

Both walked on tiptoes, hoping to make as little noise as possible. Passing an intersection with more offices to each side, Mane didn't bother to look around, still focused on his goal.

Jacob tapped him on the shoulder. "Tell me again what I'm supposed to be looking for once we reach his office."

"I've never actually seen it, but I've heard people around here talking about it."

"Wait a minute, Bobby. You told me you knew what we were going to snatch," Jacob's tone rose.

"Keep quiet! I told you already. It's supposed to be really old and the only one in existence. You know what that means, right?"

"Yeah … that we'll be in deep shit once we try to sell it."

"No, it means we'll be freakin' rich when we finally do sell it."

"Are you going to tell me what it looks like, or at least what you heard it looks like?"

"It's called the Silver Heart, so we look for something heart-shaped."

"How do you know it's not locked up? Something that rare—"

"The pompous bastard keeps it on display for everyone to see. Do you think I would even attempt this if I couldn't get at it easily?" Mane shook his head in response to his own statement.

Nevertheless, Jacob replied with another question, "You think he'll come after us when he notices it's missing?"

"It's Friday night—the first night of our two-week shutdown. So we've got a lot of time before anyone even sets foot in the building. And as far as what he'll do the Monday we reopen, well, who cares?"

They made their way quietly down the hall. Jacob looked over his shoulder and was deeply disturbed that his only means of escape was nowhere in sight as the blackness swallowed up the path.

Suddenly, a creaking floorboard caused them to stop in their tracks. Aiming their flashlights in separate directions, neither one found what was responsible. The beams merely revealed potted plants, wood-paneled walls, and an abandoned receptionist's desk, still cluttered with papers from the day before. They proceeded a few more inches until another creak, followed by what could only be described as a low growl, halted them once more.

"Bobby, I know you heard it too. What the hell was that?"

"It's probably the wind," he blurted out, unsure of what to say.

"Why does everyone always say that? We're inside. There is no wind!"

"Don't worry. We're almost there." He firmly gripped the handgun, hoping it would make him feel safe. It didn't.

Four more steps forward and Jacob grabbed his friend's shoulder so tightly that Mane actually winced in pain. Jacob was on the verge of tears. "Tell me something, Bobby," he said, pointing off to the left. "Does the wind have eyes?"

Mane pointed a light at the object in question. "What the hell are you—"

On the left side of the hallway, opposite the office the two were planning to burglarize, sat an animal resembling a large dog.

The flashlight's glow lit its partially opened mouth, exposing the animal's razor-sharp teeth. With the exception of two gleaming eyes, the majority of its body remained camouflaged in darkness. Claws were heard gripping the carpet to achieve the necessary traction to run down its prey, and its shadowed hindquarters slowly lifted off the ground, ready to pounce. Saliva dripped from its teeth as the animal furrowed its brow, narrowing the look of its eyes. It let out a vicious snarl like nothing either man had ever heard.

"W-what the fuck kind of dog is that?" Mane muttered.

"I don't know," Jacob whimpered back. "But I think I just shit myself."

Tilting its head, the animal turned its mouth upward at the corners as if it was amused by the dialogue between the two terrified trespassers.

"Did, did it just … smile at us?" Jacob asked nervously.

"Jake. Listen to me very carefully." Attempting to stay calm, Mane raised his pistol and took aim; however, his hands were shaking so hard, it would have been a miracle if he hit the side of a barn. The animal roared, and Mane squeezed off two shots before turning to his friend, screaming, "RUN!"

TWO

The clock read 4:00 a.m. when the key slid into the door's deadbolt lock. As it maneuvered the pins into position, each clicking noise, followed by a sharp snap, awakened something on the other side. A second lock was penetrated by the key, and two bestial silhouettes skulked across the floor toward the entryway, their nails ticking on the tile floor. The hinges creaked as the door swung open and light from the hallway shone into the room. The silhouettes charged, reared up on their back legs, and pounced on the man entering, slamming his back into the wall. His arm fumbled around, searching for the light switch, while the two dogs, tongues wagging, went for his face. Finally, he found the switch and flicked it on. The room was bathed in artificial light as he was energetically greeted by his pets: a black Belgian shepherd and a brindle-colored pit bull.

"Okay. Okay. I missed you guys too," he said, petting their heads. "Down. C'mon, get down. Down!" The dogs lowered themselves back on the floor, making it possible for him to peel himself off the wall.

After throwing a pile of mail on the kitchen table, he took off his jacket, draping it on one of the chairs. Pulling out a wallet from the back pocket of his jeans, he tossed it on top of the mail, and it unfolded itself on impact to reveal a Nassau County Police Department's gold detective's shield. A cellphone and key ring

9

soon found their way onto the table as well. He quickly shuffled through the mail, checking how much of his salary went toward bills that week, and then looked back at his dogs, who were waiting patiently for him to pay them some attention. Grabbing a bag of dog food from the closet, he shook it at them.

"I guess you guys are hungry." They responded by raising their ears and tilting their heads. "Of course, you're hungry. It's only been ten hours since I've been home." He poured the food into two plastic bowls spaced apart from each other. "There you go."

He opened the refrigerator to nearly empty shelves, containing only a carton of milk, a half-eaten sandwich, and an apple. "At least you guys have food." Retrieving the sandwich and milk container, he noticed a yellow post-it note stuck to the freezer door.

Just wanted to let you know I walked the dogs around ten o'clock. You now owe me for a full week. Leave the money on the table, and I'll pick it up when I come by at six for their morning walk. Thanks, sweetie. ~Rikki

Richard Anderson, the downstairs neighbor who walked the dogs and watched the apartment when no one was home, insisted everyone call him Rikki. Both Rikki and the detective rented different floors in a two-family house. And although Rikki could be a little overbearing, not to mention over-the-top, he was completely trustworthy and one of the only people the dogs genuinely liked, other than their master.

The detective put some money in an envelope and placed it away from the mess on the table, satisfied that Rikki would see it when he came back in a few hours.

Still attempting to rid himself of his hunger, he bit the sandwich and made a face, quickly throwing it into the trash under the kitchen sink, along with the partially chewed bits in his mouth. Drinking what was left of the milk, he disposed of the carton before heading into the living room. He kicked off his black leather shoes, removed his leather shoulder holster, set it on the end table, and sat on the couch. The answering machine blinked, and he pushed the PLAY button as he sank into one of the cushions.

The machine beeped. "Hello again. It's your mother. Why haven't you called me back?"

It beeped again. "S'up? It's Matt. Call me. Later."

The machine beeped yet again. "It's your darling sister. Call Mom—so she stops asking me why you don't call her. Thanks."

One final beep. "Yo, Johnny. It's Bailey. Thought you'd be home by now. Anyway, good work tonight. I didn't think you'd be able to catch that little thievin' bastard on foot. See you in the a.m."

Johnny Mako had been a police officer for seven years, but only made detective eight months ago. Not one to compliment himself too easily, he explained the promotion as merely being in the right place at the right time. Wandering into an all-night convenience store on a routine patrol, he was looking for a quick pick-me-up when three masked gunmen charged in, attempting to rob the place. Either they didn't see his patrol car parked by the side of the building or they just didn't care, but they pistol-whipped the cashier and demanded he empty the register. Quick thinking and superb marksmanship on Officer Mako's part led to a speedy resolution. Two of the criminals were slightly injured from gunfire, another was critically wounded but ultimately survived the ordeal, and the cashier walked away with minor bumps and bruises. It was soon discovered the three teenaged perps were responsible for a string of burglaries in Nassau County, and once the word got out, the media branded the officer a hero. So the department promoted him in the name of good press. Mako accepted, but he knew there were those inside the department who didn't believe he deserved it.

Patting his leg, he called to his dogs, "C'mere Chip." The shepherd walked over, wagging his tail. "You too, Bruno!" The pit bull followed suit.

Even though these two breeds were considered intimidating because of their size and ill-gotten bad reputations, the way they looked at their master through big brown eyes showed only affection and kindness. The slanderous remarks to their viciousness was undeserved and unwarranted. Still, he understood why it would be wise to stay on their good side. He pet the two of them for a while before getting off the sofa and heading into the bedroom. He made sure to take his gun with him and hang the holster off his side of the headboard. He checked the time, then undressed, and had just slipped under the covers when something jumped on the other side of the bed.

Rolling over to investigate, he was met with a face full of white fur as the cat rubbed up against him. "There you are," Mako said, petting him. "I was wondering when you were going to say hello." The cat purred loudly while staring at his master through different colored eyes, one blue and the other yellow. "Okay, Booger, now lie down so I can get some sleep." He turned back to rest on one pillow as Booger got comfortable on the other. Yawning once before drifting off, he hoped the next day would be a little less eventful.

THREE

Mane's breathing was frenzied as he and Jacob ran back toward the elevator to escape the monster chasing them. Frantically looking behind them to see how close it was, their feet maintained an unsteady rhythm, and Jacob's got tangled up in each other. Falling into his friend as they reached the intersection of office hallways, Jacob hit the carpet with a heavy thud. He'd taken Mane down with him. Their flashlights had been tossed a few feet away, along with Jacob's glasses. The pace of the monster following rapidly increased.

"Come on!" Mane said, scrambling to his feet. "It's almost on top of us!" He retrieved a flashlight and started running again, leaving Jacob alone in the dark.

"Bobby, wait up! Don't leave me!"

Mane didn't answer, and Jacob realized he'd been abandoned. Finding his glasses and the other flashlight, Jacob was disoriented and unsure of which way to go. With not much time to decide, he picked a corridor and hoped he'd made the right choice. Sprinting down the hallway, he muttered prayers for his survival, promising the usual terms should the request be answered. He'd change his ways and stop pulling hurtful pranks on others. He'd even be more focused and do something worthwhile with his life. The list went on and on, but he knew in the back of his mind that he'd be hard-pressed to keep any of his guarantees, even if he was to walk away from this. Although, when things settled down, he and Bobby would probably sit back and enjoy a few beers while laughing over the night they were chased out of Stumpp Industries by a dog—a large, ferocious, incredibly terrifying dog, but a dog nonetheless.

Jacob slowed when he noticed something extremely peculiar. Standing still, he wondered where the dog had gone. He had never been a slow runner, but he was no track star either. An animal, even a half-crippled animal, should have caught up to him by now. He thought he should at least have heard something, but there was nothing: no footsteps, no heavy breathing, and no growling, not even any barking. There was nothing except his own panting as he tried to catch his breath.

Recognizing this was the wrong corridor for the elevator, Jacob guessed one of the offices would be open. He could lock himself in until morning when someone would come to the rescue—he figured the animals required daily care. Sure, there would be hell to pay, but he'd still be alive to deal with the consequences, and that was better than dying. Trying each of the doorknobs he passed, he was disappointed that they were all locked. But it was still quiet, and that was good enough for him. He breathed a little easier now, thinking his prayers had been answered.

Reaching the last office at the end of the hall, he twisted the knob. No luck. It was locked like all the others. He held his position, frustrated that no one here trusted enough to have left one room open. While he was formulating a new plan, the floor unexpectedly creaked, and Jacob knew he had not moved since reaching this spot. His heartbeat went from zero to 160 in 2.2 seconds, and sweat beaded up on his forehead. Jacob was uncertain if he really wanted to know what had caused the noise, even though there weren't many possibilities. His prayers had never been answered before, so why should this time be any different?

Like a mouse being pursued by a snake, Jacob's defense was to stay absolutely motionless, hoping the hunter wouldn't see the prey. He contemplated jumping through the window only a few inches away but surmised he would probably knock himself unconscious against the thick glass. But even if he miraculously managed to break through, he was still on the thirteenth floor. It would take a lot of scraping to separate him from the concrete. One creak was followed by another. His knees began to shake, making it harder for him to remain motionless. He sobbed, hoping someone would have mercy and pluck him out of this predicament. The once comforting silence was broken by a low guttural growl, and Jacob suddenly remembered that this trick never worked for the mouse either.

Hot breath on the back of his neck sent a chill down his spine that caused the hairs to stand on end. Shutting his eyes tightly, Jacob gradually turned around until he made a complete one-eighty. Now feeling the breath on his face, he hesitantly opened his eyes but was uncertain of what was directly in front of him. There was a wall of black fur with a small gray patch, expanding and collapsing with every breath. Knowing he'd run out of options, Jacob angled his head upward to get a glimpse of his soon-to-be killer. The light from his flashlight accentuated the daggers within the monster's maw, and it once again gave the impression of a smile before clamping its jaws on the trembling young man beneath him.

Mane, feeling a pang of remorse for leaving Jacob behind, headed back to find him but abruptly halted as the horrific scream of his friend reached his ears. Assuming the worst, he paused for a moment to grieve for Jacob … but only for a moment. He knew he would share Jacob's fate if he didn't get to safety, and fast. As he raced to the elevator, he yelled out, "Louis, get ready! We gotta get the hell off this floor!"

There was no response.

"Louis, you there? You better have that elevator ready to move!"

Again, no answer.

Mane was in range to see his goal but realized something was wrong even before he reached it. Darkness engulfed the end of the hallway where his companion should have been waiting for him in a lit doorway. Reducing his speed, he came to the closed elevator doors, and panic set in. Louis was gone, and Mane wasn't sure if he should be more concerned for his pal or for his own life. He worriedly shouted out to each side of him, cupping his hands around his mouth, "Louis! Louis! Come on, man!" Getting more frantic, he called, "Where the hell are you?"

The shadows held no answers.

His friend was missing, and he was trapped with a ravenous fiend that was out for blood. "Shit, Louis!" He slammed the side of his fist into the elevator doors before leaning forward and resting his head against them. Tapping the call button and pulling his head away from the door, he heard the faint sound of panting. The noise had originated to his left, and he shone the light in that direction; but nothing instantly jumped out at him until a large silver-haired outline twitched in the hallway. It was barely twenty feet away from him, but Mane imagined that if this animal was the same as the first one he saw, twenty feet might as well be twenty inches once it sprang into action.

The animal let out a low growl.

Mane kept the flashlight low, hoping he could fool it into thinking he hadn't noticed it yet. He pulled back the gun's hammer, knowing full well he'd have to make his shots count to take the animal down, but he stopped moving when a second snarl came from behind him in the main corridor. Spinning around to face it, he saw a pair of eyes closing in, and knew it could only be the monster responsible for killing Jacob. The animal to his left started its approach as the other in front of him tensed up, getting a better grip on the carpeting. Terrified, Mane hysterically tapped the elevator call button until a chime sounded, signaling the elevator's arrival. He squeezed through the partially opened doors, as the silver-haired animal to his left lunged forward and tore into his ankle with its enormous front claws. Wailing in agony, Mane stumbled into the elevator. Adrenaline numbed the otherwise searing pain, and after pulling himself away from the elevator car's frame, he simultaneously pushed the buttons marked LOBBY and DOOR CLOSE. He believed an eternity would pass before either choice produced the desired effect.

The doors started to slide shut, but neither animal was about to let its quarry get away so easily. The one in the main hallway used all the muscles in its legs to practically fly through the air, claws and teeth at the ready, closing in on a frightened young man. Mane shielded his face with crossed arms, unwilling to gaze upon his destroyer. He screamed girlishly, but to his surprise, the elevator closed just in time. The fiend slammed into the doors with a thump and howled loudly. Mane watched the numbers on the digital display.

Twelve ... eleven ... ten ... nine ...

As the elevator passed the third floor, he was frightened out of his skin when something massive landed hard on top of the elevator car. Gun in hand, he fired a few shots through the roof.

An angry roar suggested he'd hit his mark.

The animal hammered the metal barrier with its fists, then scratched and clawed as it attempted to tear through the hard shell to get to the creamy human center. The bell sounded and the doors opened. But before Mane entered the lobby, he pressed a few random buttons on the inside panel, hoping to send the elevator rising once again and to put more distance between him and the persistent hunter. Bursting through the main doors, he raced back toward the preserve, but a loud crash from inside the building suggested the animal had accomplished its objective.

Unable to physically maintain his current pace, Mane took one of the nature trails, hoping it would be a shortcut. Every rustling leaf or clicking branch made him flinch, and charging footsteps and excited breathing told him the hunter had returned. "Oh, you gotta be shitting me!" He took off into the woods, intent on finding cover. Heavy footsteps pounded the dirt, and the throbbing pain in his ankle worsened with each impact. Warm blood seeped from the open wound, trickling down to his deadening foot. The area was so desensitized that Mane didn't notice it twist awkwardly in a small depression, and he fell hard into a pile of damp leaves. Scrambling furiously to get to his feet, he tried to evade what was hunting him, but the injury prevented it. Leaning up against a nearby tree, holding his firearm close to his chest, he mustered up the courage and pointed it in the direction of his pursuers.

An uneasy quiet filled the preserve as the young man wondered why his attackers had considerably slowed their pace; but whatever the reason, the prospect of the imminent attack was utterly terrifying. The moonlight permitted him to see an animal's outline creeping toward his position. He pointed the gun at it, but the animal darted back and forth to avoid a clear shot, almost as if it recognized the weapon.

A shuffling behind him triggered his head to whip around in response, and he made out the shape of a man in the darkness. The silhouette was big, slightly hunched over, and partially hidden by the trees. Mane's sea-green eyes couldn't pierce the blackness to get a better idea who or what was approaching. He debated on calling out for help, but then he lost sight of his stalker. *Shit! Where'd the dog go?* he thought.

"Hey, you!" He was desperate. "Can I get some help over here? I'm hurt!" He waited for an answer but none came. "My friends, Jacob and Louis, I think they're dead!" He swore he heard a chuckle. "What are you waiting for? Why won't you answer me?"

The animal returned and circled Mane's position, making him more nervous with each passing moment. With no answer from the stranger, he understood he would receive no help and was about to end up like his friends. He felt the dog bearing down on him and shivered uncontrollably. Out of options, he fired two shots, yelling defiantly, "Come on then! You're just a stupid animal! I'll kill you! I swear I'll kill you!" Tears streamed down his face. "Oh God, please help me."

"A man named Pierre Troubetzkoy said, 'Why should man expect his prayer for mercy to be heard by What is above him when he shows no mercy to what is below him?'" the man-shaped silhouette answered in a raspy voice.

Refusing to die in such a heinous fashion, Mane turned the weapon on himself, but the animal moved like lightning, reaching him before he could squeeze the trigger. Biting into his wrist with immense force, its razor-like teeth sheared through the bone, causing the gun to drop to the ground with Mane's hand still attached. On the way down, the still functioning nerves operated the limb and fired three more shots into the night. Holding his injured arm close to his body, he shrieked, but his suffering had only just begun.

Mane's screams would last for hours before his killer was through with him.

FOUR

Awakened by excited howling and barking, he wanted to continue sleeping, but his pets would simply not allow it. Add the echo of a woman's alarmed screech, and he knew he could not fight the forces conspiring against him. Blurry eyes needed time to adjust to the morning light flooding the room, and the detective slightly lifted his head off the pillow. Listening closely to the distressed call he'd first believed to be female, his opinion soon changed.

"Down! Get down, you monsters!" the voice said. "I'm not on the menu!"

Mako dropped back onto the pillow and threw the covers over his head, hoping to be left alone. First, he heard footsteps coming closer, and then …

"Good morning, Mr. Blue Eyes." The voice was directly above him. "Rise and shine!"

The covers were whipped off the bed, exposing the man underneath, lying in only a pair of boxer briefs. As the exhausted detective reached for the missing sheets with one hand, hiding his face under the pillow, this human alarm clock dragged the sheets even farther away. Mako had to peek out from under his protective cushion if he intended to find them again, but the pillow was ripped from his grasp just as soon as he loosened his hold on it.

"Wakey, wakey! You have a big day today!" the voice continued.

"Go away."

"If you don't get up right now, I'm going to peek under those boxers!"

A snap of the underwear's elastic waistband against his skin compelled him to jump out of bed, the sleep not completely out of his eyes. He pointed at the largest blur in the room, saying, "You know that creeps me out, right?"

"But it always does the trick, doesn't it?"

"The fact that you've done it more than once creeps me out too, Richard." Mako rubbed his eyes trying to see more than just hazy shapes in the room.

"You only call me Richard when you're angry."

"What time is it anyway?"

"It's about nine-thirty, and you have to get to work." Rikki led the barely awake detective to his bathroom. "Your partner called, and you have a breaking-and-entering matter to solve."

"Don't tell me you talked to Bailey." He tried to keep his concern hidden and flipped on the light switch. "That's all I need."

"No need to get your panties in a bunch," Rikki said. "I listened to your voice mail, like a good neighbor. I wouldn't want him to think you've come over to the other side."

"How do you know my password? I changed it since the last time you violated my privacy." He reached for a razor and shaving cream. "By the way, you can talk to me from outside the bathroom, thank you very much." He closed the door after nudging his neighbor out.

"Don't think you're that clever. You use either one of your two dogs' names, and you switch back and forth every so often."

Mako quickly maneuvered the razor around his face, careful not to ruin his moustache and connecting goatee. Once his hair had been all brown, but now the gray was starting to show through on his chin; and he was beginning to sprout a few gray hairs on the top of his head too. Fatigue caused the redness of his eyes to overshadow the blue, and he appeared more pale than usual—but he shrugged it off as he scratched his chest hair. Making sure to throw on a pair of jeans before opening the bathroom door, he found Rikki still standing where he'd left him.

"Don't you look pretty."

"Why are you still here?" Mako's sarcastic nature didn't offend his normally sensitive companion anymore; Rikki pawned it off as part of his charm.

An older man with some feminine features, enhanced by minor cosmetic surgeries, Rikki maintained a manly appearance. Every one of his dark brown hairs, blond highlights included, were expertly styled and held in place with a modest amount of hair gel. Facial hair was almost nonexistent on him, and when he smiled, his teeth practically glowed white. His eyes occasionally changed from his natural shade of brown to whatever color contacts he preferred to wear, and he always looked as if he was going somewhere special—though in reality, he spent more time at home than he would like. The ladies, the ones who couldn't tell right away, were usually disappointed to find he was checking out the same guys they were eyeing.

Moving past his neighbor, Mako picked out a shirt and slipped an arm into it. "Did you take the money off the kitchen table?"

"Yes, and thank you. I see you paid me for this week too."

"Figured I would get it out of the way."

"You must have had some night last night," Rikki commented as he put on rubber gloves and began to straighten up the recently vacated commode. "You didn't even budge when I came in at six to take the dogs out."

"Do I have to feed them now or did you take care of that already?"

"The dogs are good. But I couldn't find the cat, so I figured you'd deal with that one." Making a face as he picked up a pair of underwear off the floor with his thumb and pointer finger, he held it as far away from himself as possible and dropped it into the hamper.

"You know you don't have to do that."

"Well, if you cleaned up a little more, then maybe I wouldn't."

An angry hiss followed by a growl caused Mako to strain his neck when he hurriedly swiveled his head to see the confrontation between Booger and Chip near their food bowls. Rushing into the room, he clapped his hands together to draw their attention away from each other and onto him. "No!" The cat ran under the kitchen table while Chip merely wagged his tail, oblivious to what had just transpired. Bruno looked up from his food bowl momentarily, but quickly went back to eating.

Rikki asked in a concerned manner, "What happened? Are my babies all right?"

"The dogs are fine, but how many times have I told you to leave some food for Booger if you're going to feed them?"

"Booger. What kind of a name is that anyway?"

"When I first got the cat, he was sick and sneezed on me while I was holding him. I noticed a booger on my chest, and that's what I decided to call him." Grabbing the bag of cat food, he poured some into an empty plastic bowl.

"Repulsive. The cat gets snot on you, and you think it's cute."

"What have you got against my cat anyway?"

"Give me dogs any day of the week." He removed his rubber gloves and tossed them into the trash. "I simply don't trust cats."

"You don't appreciate that he doesn't make a fuss over you like the dogs do."

"A woman has needs, sweetie."

"Don't you have a penis?" Mako mockingly inquired.

"Don't go there."

"But—"

"Well, I see my job is done here. Time to take my pretty ass home." Rikki opened the front door, not wanting to listen to whatever else his neighbor had to say. "Bye, babies. I'll see you later."

"Bye, Rikki."

"Was someone talking to me?" He eyed the room, pretending no one was there, and dramatically paused before he finally said, "I didn't think so." Sticking his nose in the air and letting the door close slowly behind him, he returned to his own apartment.

Rolling his eyes at the theatrical exit, Mako took his cellphone from the kitchen table to key in a new password.

Booger brushed his body across his master's legs, hinting that a little affection would be welcome. Mako obliged and rubbed the cat's soft white fur, praising him, "I know. You're a good boy. You just don't take any crap from anyone—even if they are bigger than you." Pulling his hand away, he said, "All right, Boog, I have to go to work now, but don't worry about Rikki. Anyone who tries to hurt you will answer to me."

FIVE

Officer Sanchez doubled over, regurgitating the cheeseburger and fries he'd had for lunch, after taking a good look at a partially disemboweled corpse of a young man. On the job only a few months, he'd never encountered anything like this before. And nothing in his training could have prepared him for the brutality and harshness of the scene in the Muttontown Preserve.

"Hey, rookie!" a detective yelled out. "Don't puke on any of the evidence!"

Two plainclothes detectives walked toward the ill patrolman; one was snickering at his predicament, but the more composed of the two patted the sickly officer on his back. When he didn't respond, the detective signaled for another officer to escort Sanchez away from the body.

"Fuckin' rookies," Detective James Mullins said.

Detective Fred Bailey remarked, "You were there once too."

"I was never that pathetic."

Bailey shook his head, aware that any response would only lead to more boasting and unwarranted commentary on Mullins' part.

A dark gray Mitsubishi Lancer pulled into the parking lot.

"Speaking of pathetic," Mullins said, directing Bailey's attention to the car, "here comes your partner."

"Try to play nice today," Bailey said before walking towards the Lancer.

Stepping out of the car, Mako waved at his colleague. "Hey, Fred. What'd I miss?"

Bailey had been a cop for twelve years. For the first seven he was a uniformed officer, but then he was injured in the line of duty when answering a domestic dispute call. It turned out that a woman who wanted her husband arrested for his constant physical abuse changed her mind in the middle of her husband's capture and thought a well-placed knife to the officer's side would be better than simply dropping the charges in court. Bailey was hospitalized and on disability for months, and upon returning, he was given a desk job. It wasn't something he was suited for, however, and he longed to get back to active duty. Despite years of requesting field assignments, both politely and not-so-politely, he had to ultimately pull the "race card" to get what he wanted. Being of African-American descent, he was able to use that to his advantage and was eventually put back on the streets. Worried that he might stir up more trouble, his superiors promoted him to detective and placed him in a better district. It was more than he had asked for, but Bailey felt like a cop again.

"So? Tell me, what's going on?" Mako asked again.

"A mutilated body was found in the preserve, and it may or may not be related to what we were called in for." Pointing to the Stumpp Industries building, Bailey continued, "Someone broke in there, and we gotta find out who."

"Homicide here already?"

"Yeah, but we don't have to deal with them, so let's investigate our assignment." He tried to focus his partner's attention away from the sanctuary.

"Hey, charity case! Glad you could join us!" Mullins approached.

"Go fuck yourself," Mako responded through gritted teeth. "I don't give a shit how you think I got this job."

"Did I hit a sore spot?"

"Enough!" Bailey interrupted, in his intimidating baritone voice. "We all got a job to do, so you tend to your case, Mullins, and we'll handle ours." He led his partner away from what could have potentially erupted into a bad situation.

Mako wanted to object, but it was hard to argue with a man built like a pro-wrestler. Bailey was older than his partner, but he kept himself in better shape and could easily overpower most opponents if it came to that. With a medium complexion, brown eyes, and black hair trimmed close to his scalp, he dressed conservatively at work; but off the clock, he could be found on the basketball court in sweats and t-shirts. He'd even asked Mako to join him a couple of times and was surprised how well they cooperated on the court.

"I hate that prick." Mako couldn't hold his tongue any longer.

Still nauseated by the gruesome images in his mind, Officer Sanchez remarked, "Mullins is a real asshole."

"You're not the only one who feels that way," Patrolman Higgins answered. "Look over there."

In the distance, Detectives Mullins and Mako exchanged verbal blows as Bailey attempted to control the situation. Sanchez and Higgins snickered, overhearing the vulgarities spewing from one officer to another. But the duo composed themselves once Bailey directed a noticeably irritated Mako past them, just as Mako said, "I hate that prick."

"See, I told you." Higgins lightly backhanded Sanchez on the chest, reinforcing his observation.

Bailey called to Mullins, "Hey, Jim! We need a few guys. Have any you can spare?"

The detective surveyed the area, looking for suitable candidates, and spotted Sanchez sitting with Higgins and two others. Mullins smiled. "Take 'Puke Boy' Sanchez and the rookie brigade! They obviously can't handle real police work."

Bailey waved the four officers over, and they quickly fell in line.

Mako observed Sanchez, very easy to pick out by the unhealthy complexion and the remnants of vomit that stained his shirt collar. "That piss you off?"

Sanchez didn't want to say anything that could be considered insubordination.

"Seriously. Did that piss you off?"

"Leave him alone," Bailey chimed in.

"I'm not trying to start anything," Mako said sincerely. "I just want to know. That's all."

Sanchez gave a slight head bob, but still said nothing.

"Tell him. Go ahead." Mako nudged the officer. "Tell that prick Mullins off."

"I don't think so," Sanchez finally spoke. "I can't lose my job over a stupid comment."

"Smart kid," said Mako, tapping Bailey on the shoulder and nodding in approval. "Well, I have no such reservations." He faced Mullins' direction and cupped his hands around his mouth. "Hey, Mullins! You're a piece of shit! That's from me and Sanchez!" Sanchez immediately became red in the face, and Mako amended his statement, "Mostly from me, though!" The group continued toward the Stumpp Industries building while an agitated Mullins turned away to tend to his crime scene.

"Why do you always have to mess with him like that?" Bailey asked.

"Who, Mullins? Come on. He's a piece of crap and you know it."

"He may be just that, but he has a lot of friends in high places."

"He knows people in high places. I'll give you that. But I doubt they're his friends."

"Well, whatever they are, I'd watch myself if I were you," Bailey warned.

"Let'em talk to my union rep," Mako said, with some annoyance at the threat.

James Patrick Mullins was a bully, always putting people down to make himself feel superior. A chubby kid turned into an overweight adult, Mullins had small, beady eyes disproportionate to the size of his head. He had a hairline that had started receding in his twenties, and that now, in his late thirties, had almost completely vacated his scalp. That coupled with yellowing teeth from years of smoking, and God forbid he shave on a regular basis. It was a surprise he never tried to hide his wretched nature. Friends within the department never clearly explained whether they actually liked him or whether they remained friends because his father was a retired police inspector who was still extremely influential with the higher-ups. Either way, Mullins didn't care.

Walking toward a crime scene investigator who was collecting samples of blood and tissue from the mangled torso that made Officer Sanchez sick, Mullins studied the surrounding area, ensuring that officers painstakingly searched for the rest of the body. He reviewed his mental inventory of what was found so far: a pair of blood-soaked jeans with one leg still inside, a hand with two missing fingers, and the torso.

"I got a finger," an officer shouted in the distance.

Add a finger, hopefully with a print, to the mental file. Despite Mullins' attitude, he was a decent cop. He had to be—his father wouldn't stand for anything else. Stopping by the investigator, he asked, "So, what can you tell me?"

The investigator continued taking a tissue sample, not even looking up, as he replied, "The only thing I can say for certain is, judging by the amount of blood present, this guy was alive when he was ripped apart."

"Sucks for him." Mullins' uncaring tone forced the investigator to scrutinize the detective's face to see if he was really serious. "What else can you tell me?" Mullins asked, with no sign of remorse for the comment.

"Not much until I get these samples back to the lab and the rest of the body is found."

"I found something over here!" another officer shouted from a few feet away. "I think it's an ear!"

"How 'bout that? An ear. Maybe." Mullins chuckled. "I got one more question for you, Samms. Can you tell me anything about who did this, so I can start dredging up suspects?"

Thomas Samms had been a crime scene investigator for eleven years, and if there was one thing he hated, it was to be rushed while doing his job. He preferred to speak when the facts were in front of him. Nevertheless, some very accurate information could be concluded just by looking at the tear marks in the victim's flesh. "Well, Detective Mullins, this doesn't look like the work of a who, but of a what."

"I don't follow."

"The slash marks along the areas of the torso where other extremities have been removed indicate that an animal of some kind was the culprit."

"So, what kind of animal am I looking for, and why did we find two sets of human footprints—one matching the vic's sneaker pattern, and the other barefoot?"

"I obviously don't know who the other set of prints belongs to, but judging by the size of these markings, the claws of this beast are enormous." Samms took a small ruler from his jacket pocket and measured one of the wounds before adding, "I don't know what type of animal could do this except for maybe a tiger or some other big predator."

"Do tigers normally do this kind of thing?"

"I'm not up on big cat behaviors." Samms tried to be comical and succeeded on some level with himself.

"Great," Mullins murmured. "An exotic cat on the loose that decided to use my beat as a hunting ground, and a science nerd who's trying to be funny with me. I don't know which is worse."

"I'll be able to give you some more information once I get these samples analyzed," Samms said in a more serious tone.

"You do that." Mullins lit a cigarette.

The investigator retrieved his satchel of forensic evidence as the medical examiner brought over a body bag to prepare the remains for transport to the morgue. Samms moved to the officer who claimed to have found an ear and began sifting through the ground.

Mako's group reached the Stumpp building and quickly checked the perimeter. Broken glass on the walkway from the front door indicated that something broke out of, not into, the building, and the detective noticed small specks of blood on the glass shards. Hoping it would trace back to the responsible party, he put on a pair of latex gloves, examined some of the pieces, and then motioned to one of the patrolmen present to locate a crime scene investigator to collect the evidence for further analysis. As the patrolman followed orders, the detective placed a marker on the ground so the investigator would know where to initiate the search for clues.

Mako had always been very observant of his surroundings, which was why he'd believed he'd make a good detective, despite some negative opinions in the department by people who glossed over any of his apparent qualifications and condemned him to fail simply because he was never part of the "in" crowd. Being popular was not something he cared too much about. He felt his hard work and exceptional skills should get him noticed, but none of that ever seemed to work in his favor. Consistently an outcast, Mako decided it was better to have a small group of close friends than a large group of fake ones. Nevertheless, he liked to perform his job better than anyone else, and even though that wasn't possible all the time, it only made him try harder.

Ready to move inside the building, he addressed the remaining uniformed officers. "You," he said, pointing at Higgins, "watch the front door. No unauthorized persons are to come inside. We don't want to risk contaminating the crime scene."

The officer nodded and positioned himself to the left of the front door, careful not to step on any of the glass.

"You," Mako spoke to an unidentified female officer, "what's your name?"

"Roman, sir," she answered.

"I need you to go around the building and cover the back entrance. Again, don't let anyone inside who might compromise the scene. And Roman? No need to call me sir. I don't have stripes on my uniform."

"Sorry, sir. I, I mean, sorry." She hurried to the rear of the building.

"Sanchez." Mako waved him over. "Come with us. You're going to help search inside." Speaking to Higgins before going inside, he said, "When the other officer returns with an investigator, send him in." In addition to keen observations, Mako also prided himself on his organizational skills.

Proceeding cautiously into the lobby, Bailey spotted a security room off to the right. The door was locked, but it posed no problem when a swift kick from a strong leg connected with it. He found a few switches on the wall next to the doorway and flipped them up after putting on latex gloves. The fluorescent lights in the lobby flickered on in sequential order from front to back. The two detectives walked on each side of the reception area, checking for trace evidence, while Sanchez remained on the middle walkway, observing from a distance and being careful not to touch anything. Bailey moved along the left side of the lobby until he came to the giant painting of a man sitting next to a snarling Doberman pinscher. The picture, including the frame, was at least fifteen feet high and nine feet wide. He couldn't help but stop and stare. He even needed to step back to take it all in. Sanchez, too, was mesmerized by the sheer presence of the painting and bumped into the large granite table containing the company directory.

In the meantime, Mako was almost at the elevators when he realized his fellow officers were not in the vicinity. Spinning around and finding them captivated by the large picture on the wall, he went back to get a better look. The painting was expertly done, and its massive size was impressive; but the sheer egotism of the man he assumed was the company's CEO kept his attention.

"It's amazing what kind of crap people will hang on their walls, isn't it?" Mako said, startling Bailey, who now realized he wasn't the only one staring at the painting.

Set somewhere in the nineteenth century, the elaborate portrait, and the man in the chair, had a very regal appearance, as if he were a true monarch instead of a wealthy business tycoon. His throne was an eighteenth century Chippendale mahogany wing chair, adorned in red fabric that contrasted the man's dark suit. A small pedestal table was portrayed on the left side with a tobacco jar and a glass of white wine resting on it. The Doberman sat on his right. The slight smirk on the man's face told the detective, even on canvas, that this person thought he was above everyone else. Perhaps that was why he'd commissioned such a large painting, so he could look down on everyone gazing up at him. A tiny, engraved placard next to the portrait stated that the man was Heinrich Stumpp, and Mako reassessed his preliminary judgment about Stumpp Industries' CEO, Peter Stumpp … for the moment.

"It's actually quite remarkable," Bailey stated.

"Tell me about it," Sanchez cut in. "I didn't even notice the directory here because I couldn't take my eyes off of it." He rubbed his outer thigh.

With that, the light bulb ignited in Detective Mako's head. Moving over to the company directory, he explored its surface, studying the waist-high table very carefully. Coming to the bottom edge, he noticed that directly opposite the painting was a small, dried bloodstain with a few stray hairs stuck to it. He took from his inner coat pocket a small plastic container with a cotton swab attached to the cap, and he passed the fluffy tip over the blemish, making sure to get a significant amount for processing. He sealed the container with the bloody swab inside, and then used tweezers to remove some of the hairs, which he placed in a plastic baggie. Satisfied that he'd gotten enough for a good start, he said, "Sanchez, you're a genius."

"I'm sorry?" The police officer was confused at the compliment.

"What did you find?" Bailey at last pulled himself away from the painting to see what his partner was doing.

"Well, Sanchez over here bumped into the directory because he was so involved in this painting, right?" Mako started to explain. "I figure at night, with the lights off, it's gotta be pretty dark in here. If the perp, or perps, became so engrossed in this picture like he did, someone was bound to walk into this thing." The detective held up the plastic tube containing the blood sample. "Apparently, somebody did, and he left something behind for us to analyze."

Just then, rapidly approaching footsteps interrupted the conversation, and the group turned toward another uniformed police officer walking briskly through the front door of the Stumpp building. Mako immediately recognized him as the same officer he'd sent to fetch an investigator. Mako glanced outside, observing an examiner who was vigilantly picking up the shards of glass scattered on the concrete. The detectives returned to their work after Mako left another evidence marker. They made a shocking discovery upon reaching the elevators.

The doors were ripped open, but unlike the main door's broken glass, the metal had several dents in the shapes of two giant fists. It suggested that something had punched its way from the inside out and then tore the doors wide enough to break free. Able to easily fit the top half of his body through the gaping hole, Mako peered inside to get a good look at the elevator car. To his surprise, there wasn't one. Tilting his head upward and using a flashlight to light the darkened shaft, he noticed the car suspended near the third floor. The bottom was ruptured in the same fashion as the doors, and long, deep gouges resembling claw marks in the concrete shaft walls stopped at the lobby.

Without hesitation, he pressed the call button for the adjacent elevator and heard a dull whirring noise as it began its descent.

Mako said to the uniformed cops, "When the elevator gets here, I want you to take it to the top floor and look for any signs of foul play. Bailey and I will finish up here and work our way upward. We'll cover more ground this way and meet in the middle."

Officer Sanchez and the newly arrived patrolman entered the elevator, and as the doors closed, Mako instructed, "Radio us if you find anything!"

Pulling his colleague off to the side, Bailey asked, "What's wrong? You seem frantic."

"I got a bad feeling this break-in ties into Mullins' homicide."

"So? What's the problem?"

"I don't want to get pulled from the case. It's not often we get an assignment that amounts to anything, and I would like to solve this one."

"If this falls through, we'll get another."

"You don't get it. You've been doing this for a while. You get respect." Mako stepped away from his partner. "They think I'm a joke … that I only got this promotion by luck and not because I'm a good cop. I got something to prove."

"To who? Them or yourself?"

Staring Bailey in the eyes, he answered, "Both."

The radio crackled to life. First with static, then a voice, "Detectives, come in."

"Mako here. Go ahead."

"I think we found something." In the background, Sanchez whimpered, "*Ay Dios mio.*"

"What did you find? And tell Sanchez to get a hold of himself."

"Blood … and a lot of it. But no body," the officer replied. Then the sounds of Sanchez heaving the remainder of his meal filled the airwaves.

"Shit!" Mako thought out loud. Pressing the push-to-talk button, he put his lips close to the walkie-talkie and said, "Secure the area, don't touch a thing, and I'll send Forensics up right away." He paced the hallway, trying to figure what his next move should be.

Bailey knew it was hard to say anything to break his partner's thinking mode, but he tried anyway. "You know we have to call this in."

Mako didn't even glance at him.

"Hey," Bailey attempted to get his attention. "Johnny!"

"What?" he snapped back. "I know what we have to do! I just wish I had some more to go on before—" He stopped talking as another inspiration penetrated his brain. "Give me a few minutes before you make the call. I got an idea!"

He sprinted toward the front door as Bailey shouted after him. Mako couldn't make out what he was saying, but it didn't really matter to him at this point.

If he had listened, he would have heard his partner say, "I can't do that. We have to follow procedure." Then he would have noticed Bailey reach into his pocket and grab his cellphone, and after a short pause, say, "Patch me through to Lieutenant Grimes."

Mullins took a few puffs from his third cigarette when he saw a marked police cruiser pulling up to the preserve, but it wasn't until the officer stepped from the vehicle that he realized his C.O. was approaching with urgency.

Lieutenant Casper Grimes was a hard ass, and he demanded respect from his subordinates even if he didn't show it to anyone himself. Rising through the ranks hadn't been easy for him, and

Grimes would be damned before he made it easy for anyone else. A man in his mid-forties with dyed black hair and a dyed black moustache, he kept himself in good shape, visiting the gym four times a week. He said what he thought without regard to anyone's feelings and equated emotions with weakness. A military man before joining the force, he kept his uniform always neat and pressed, his shoes polished at all times, and his medals and commendations shining brightly from being buffed at least once a day. His mirrored sunglasses were more than just a fashion statement—they were a tool for bullying, which was something he liked to do, especially when assuming control of a situation.

"Mullins!"

"Yes, sir," the detective promptly responded. "What brings you down here?"

"I was already on the way when I was informed this murder might have something to do with the break-in over at Stumpp Industries—"

"We haven't found any evidence of that yet, sir."

"I wasn't done," Grimes said irritably. "Can I finish my thought, or are you going to interrupt me again?"

"Sorry, sir."

"I came down here to make sure you and Mako don't have it out if the incidents are related and I have to take him off the case."

"How did you know Mako was here?"

"You think I don't know what goes on in my own precinct? And it's no secret how fond you two are of each other. Now, I also got it on good word that the press will be showing, and I don't need two detectives under my command bickering like morons on the evening news."

"We wouldn't—"

"Don't tell me what you would and wouldn't do! I'll tell you what you will and won't do. And right now I'm telling you I will deal with Mako and Bailey, and you will keep your mouth shut! Understood?"

"Yes, sir."

"Mullins," Grimes said in a more soothing tone, which was possibly more disturbing than when he was shouting.

"Yes, sir?" the detective carefully asked.

"What is that officer doing talking to that photographer over there?" Grimes was still using his softer tone, which told Mullins he'd be in big trouble if he didn't resolve the problem hastily.

Mako had one goal on his mind, and while Bailey was inside the building well out of earshot, he told the investigator—who was sifting through the glass shards at the entrance of Stumpp Industries—about the scene on the top floor, in return for the location of Investigator Thomas Samms. Officer Roman, still guarding the rear entrance, spotted the detective running toward the Muttontown Preserve and attempted to get his attention. But Mako merely gave her a thumbs-up and continued on his way. Spotting Samms several feet away from a mutilated torso while his "favorite" homicide detective went to meet a police cruiser arriving on the scene, Mako made certain to get Samms' attention by invading his personal space.

The investigator jerked back, but then remembered the evidence he'd come to collect, and yelled, "Be careful. There's an ear somewhere on the ground, and I don't need you contaminating it!"

"Samms! Eyes front. I need a favor."

Looking up through his thick black-framed glasses, Samms smiled once he recognized who was addressing him. "Oh sorry, Mako. I didn't know it was you. What kind of favor do you need?"

"I need copies of everything you find here and inside the Stumpp building."

Confused, Samms pushed his glasses back on the bridge of his nose. "When did you make it to Homicide?"

"I didn't. I just don't want to be kept out of the loop on this one."

"I don't know. I don't think I can do that." Samms became nervous.

"Listen, no one will know you gave them to me, and if anyone asks, I'll say I opened Mullins' mail without permission. Okay?"

"I could get in real trouble if anyone finds out ..."

Samms continued talking, but Mako stopped listening as he noticed Lieutenant Grimes speaking to Mullins beyond the crime scene perimeter.

Understanding this meant the end of his participation in the investigation if Samms didn't agree to help him, he was about to persuade the investigator further when he was momentarily blinded by a camera's flash going off near his face. Through little white spots, Mako saw a press photographer nosing around where he shouldn't, and although his first reaction was to haul the guy into custody and reprimand the cop who'd let him in, he decided on another course of action. Directing the photographer's attention to a uniformed officer on the other side of the restricted area, near Mullins and Grimes, Mako pointed out the best way to get there without being seen. The photographer thanked him and followed the path the detective prescribed.

Samms looked skeptically at Mako. "Are you sure you should have done that?"

"Are you gonna help me out or what?"

In a negative tone, Samms started, "I know we're friendly and all, but—"

"Come on, Samms. We're all trying to apprehend the same criminal here."

"I know, but—"

"Listen, you know that redhead down in Records?"

"Mary Ann Murphy?" The drool almost poured out of Samms' mouth as he said her name.

"Yeah, I'm friendly with her, too, and I know about your little crush. How about I get you her phone number?"

"I'd rather have a date with her."

"Who am I? The fuckin' miracle worker? Take the phone number and start from there." Mako wanted that to not sound too cruel. "Think of it like the lotto. You never know."

Samms silently debated the proposition for a minute but finally agreed. "All right. There'll be a folder on your desk first thing in the morning."

"No," said Mako, concluding that he didn't want anyone else, not even his partner, to know about the exchange. "I'll come to you, and we'll swap at the same time."

"Don't forget the number."

"I won't." The detective breathed easy again, feeling his plan would pan out nicely.

"And don't forget the part about not getting anything from me!" Samms shouted out a little too loudly. A stern look was all it took for the investigator to follow up, "Sorry."

Heading back toward Stumpp Industries, Mako noticed that Grimes had caught sight of the photographer talking to one of his officers. Mako guessed the poor sap was going to be thoroughly chewed out, but he still couldn't stop himself from being slightly amused.

Mullins approached the perimeter his men had established upon arriving at the scene, and sure enough, one of them was exchanging words with a member of the press. Accepting that this happened from time to time, he was still extremely distressed that it had occurred while a superior officer was on site. Grimes observed from a distance, folded his arms, and smirked as Mullins laid into the officer. He knew the detective was being harder on the officer because a boss was watching. That made Grimes feel in complete control.

SIX

Jason Brody had a knack of getting the impossible shot. No one was quite sure how he did it, but he claimed it was because he didn't take no for an answer. After intercepting a call on his police scanner about a burglary at Stumpp Industries' headquarters, he was determined to beat out other freelancers to get some front-page photos for whichever paper would pay the most. Arming himself with his state-of-the-art digital camera and a wad of bribe money, he set out to get the impossible shot once again.

Jason passed for someone in his mid-twenties, with his boyish face and short black, spiked hair, dark brown eyes, and a charming smile framed between two dimples. He was pierced through the left ear, tongue, and right eyebrow and had a number of tattoos ranging from his favorite cartoon character to a tribute to his deceased mother. His wardrobe consisted primarily of jeans of varying lengths and styles and of t-shirts, most of which advertised his favorite bands; today he was wearing his Fall Out Boy tee.

After stepping out of his beat-up van, parked several blocks away from any police presence, he made his way through the back parking lot of Stumpp Industries. Immediately detecting the major commotion inside the Muttontown Preserve, he guessed it might develop into an even bigger story than an average B and E.

Officer Roman, stationed at the rear entrance of Stumpp's headquarters, observed the photographer poking around the restricted area but didn't want to leave her post for fear of being chastised. So she used her radio to summon the detectives inside. All she picked up was a lot of static. Soon, however, Detective Mako came jogging past her. She attempted flag him down, but he merely gave a thumbs-up as he passed by. *At least he's heading in the right direction*, she thought.

Jason peered through a wall of bushes and watched the detective approach a uniformed officer guarding an entrance into the crime scene. Displaying his shield, the detective was given access, and once he was out of sight, Jason retrieved some bribe money and confidently walked up to the officer. He flashed two hundred-dollar bills. The officer looked both ways before taking them and permitting the photographer entry into the supposedly secure area.

Walking carefully through the preserve, Jason avoided dried branches and leaves so as not to give himself away. Following the unsuspecting detective, who seemed to be on the trail of something hot, Jason halted when the detective reached his destination. He crept closer while the detective spoke to a crime scene investigator. Jason raised his camera and pressed the shutter release, but either the click of the camera or the automatic flash alerted the detective to his presence. Visibly angry, Mako advanced as if he was ready to rip Jason's head off. Then, unexpectedly, a calmer mood overtook him. Instead of confiscating the photographer's camera and detaining him for trespassing, the detective said, "If you want a scoop, then do exactly as I say." Pointing out an officer who, he said, was very knowledgeable about what had happened, he directed Jason to a secluded path. Jason attempted to hand the detective some money for the information, but Mako firmly refused.

Before he left, Jason asked, "Don't I know you from somewhere?"

The detective shook his head no and then hurried him away.

Along the way, Jason intercepted the medical examiner rolling a stretcher with a body bag resting on it. Determined to get a shot of the corpse, Jason pulled out five bills and offered them to the medical examiner. The examiner momentarily considered calling an officer to arrest the photographer, but decided to profit from this instead. Taking the money, he unzipped the bag to reveal the headless corpse. Jason had no trouble looking at the remains and snapped his potential Pulitzer Prize shots before proceeding onward.

Taking the last of the bribe money from his pocket, he carefully approached the allegedly well-informed patrolman the detective had pointed out. Like the other officers did before him, the cop accepted the money and spilled everything he knew. Jason discovered that the victim's fingerprints would be the only means of identification since the head hadn't been located; and a sickening feeling came over him because he surmised who'd committed the murder.

A snapping twig warned Jason of a second approaching detective, now only a few feet away. Detective Mullins—a moment ago criticized by his superior for not being on top of the situation—was about to take his foul mood out on the photographer, so Jason ran back to his van. The words of the irate detective chased him. Driving away from Stumpp Industries, Jason pulled onto a deserted side street and stepped into the rear of the vehicle, which was loaded with computer equipment, cameras, and radio broadcasting gear. He hooked his digital camera up to one of the computers, and he uploaded the files while making a call. The phone rang four times before Nathan Henry Williams V grabbed the receiver. Nathan wasn't one for formalities, so Jason didn't wait for a hello before saying, "It's Brody."

"What do you have for me?"

"Potentially big troubles." Jason tried not to sound rattled.

"Details."

"There's been a murder." He typed a few commands on the computer keyboard and pressed ENTER before continuing. "I just sent you some photos. I believe he's resurfaced."

Nathan paused, detecting a quiver in Jason's voice. Powering on his computer monitor, he waited for the images to appear. Seconds later, a bloodied, headless torso filled the screen. He studied it closely before asking, "You think one of his did this?"

"No," Jason said confidently. "*He* did."

"I'll assemble a team."

Jason closed his flip phone and detached his camera from the USB port. He sat back in the driver's seat but didn't turn on the ignition. Shaking, he thought, *God, how I hoped I wouldn't have to face him again.*

Nathan left his study, walking out into the hallway of his considerable West Virginia mansion. There was plenty of activity inside his family's estate, handed down through generations, and despite its lavish exterior, his home served a dual purpose. It was also the command center for an underground paramilitary group dating back to the 1800s. There were three floors above ground comprising thirty residential rooms in total, but it was the secret lower levels that contained their communications center, war room, detention center, munitions depot, and garage. Locating his second-in-command, he said, "Bronson, front and center!"

Mark Bronson had the look of a military man with conservative style. Wearing a pair of Ralph Lauren khakis and a black polo shirt over his athletic build, he exhibited his fashion sense without being too ostentatious. He snapped to attention. "Sir!"

Getting straight to the point, Nathan barked, "Gather a handful of our best men, and get them prepped and ready. We leave for New York at fifteen-hundred hours."

"What kind of ordnance will be required?"

"Heavy weapons mostly, containment gear, and all the ammo we can carry."

"What are we going after this time?"

With a dire look, he told his subordinate, "The one nightmare I'd hoped was over. I'll debrief the team before departure. I have some preparations of my own. Dismissed!"

"Yes, sir!" Bronson about-faced and double-timed it to another part of the mansion.

Nathan returned to the study. His expressionless blue eyes showed no emotion as he scrutinized the gruesome photographs, and a hard demeanor gave no indication of compassion for the victim of this heinous act. While examining the picture, his mind recalled the numerous other mutilated corpses he had seen in the past twenty years, but because of the sheer brutality of this killing, he determined that the murderer was sending a message.

Opening his oak desk's middle drawer, he located a file on a man named Peter Stubbe and a handwritten notebook entitled *The Heart of Lycaon*. He put the items in a briefcase, along with twin automatic pistols that boasted a family crest on each of their ivory handles. Nathan, acknowledged for his fearlessness in any situation, was unnerved, knowing what he was up against. Portraits of his male ancestors hung proudly around the study. Standing in front of the painting of his great-great-grandfather, he spoke to it: "Mark my words. This time I will avenge you."

SEVEN

The daylight hours faded, but the Nassau County Police Department's Second Precinct still had a long night ahead of it. The preliminary investigation at Stumpp Industries was completed, and uniformed officers were assigned to secure the scene until interviews with company personnel could transpire. Meanwhile, lab technicians and detectives tried to piece together a picture of the crimes that had occurred there, and despite all the commotion of people talking, phones ringing, and sirens blaring, there was one voice heard above all.

"I promise you," Grimes bellowed, "you'll pay for that stunt!" The lieutenant ground his knuckles into a run-down desk inside his relatively cramped office while his detective sat calmly and silently in the chair directly in front of him, knowing better than to interrupt.

Mako waited for his superior to come up for air before asking, "What stunt are you referring to, sir?"

The mere hint of sarcasm was enough to cause Grimes' head to explode. He looked his lesser straight in the eye through his mirrored sunglasses and rumbled, "Don't think I don't know you had something to do with that photographer poking around the crime scene in the Muttontown Preserve."

Not easily intimidated, Mako, unruffled, answered, "I didn't *allow* him inside the restricted area. Once I saw him, I directed him to a spot outside the perimeter. How was I to know he would find another officer to let him back in?"

"Just tell me one thing," Grimes calmed his tone. "What exactly were you and Investigator Samms talking about?"

Remembering his promise, he said, "I asked if he would like to be set up with a friend of mine." He examined the lieutenant's face for an accurate read on how he would react. As Grimes removed his glasses to reveal angrily squinted eyes, Mako realized he'd forgotten to end with, "Sir."

"You know, Mako." The lieutenant relaxed his face, discerning his next course of action. "I don't like you."

"I'm sorry to hear that … sir."

"I'm sure you are, wise ass." A sinister chuckle escaped him. "You'll be even sorrier when you hear what's coming next." Leaving his subordinate wondering for a moment, the lieutenant stuck his head out of his office. "Mullins! Get your ass in here! Now!"

The detective jumped out from behind his desk. "Yes, sir," he said upon entering.

"You see that, Mako?" Grimes asked as he walked around Mullins, placing a hand on his shoulder. "Mullins here is the ideal soldier. When I order him to do something, he does so without question."

"Does he pee on command too?"

Mullins sneered at his co-worker for the remark but would never speak out of turn.

"That's your problem, Mako. You got a smart mouth, but you're not half as smart as you think you are. You see, even if your little deed with the photographer wasn't going to get you thrown off this case, I just received word that the murder is tied into the burglary at Stumpp Industries, due to evidence found at both scenes."

Grimes smiled when asking, "You do know what that means, right ... smart guy?"

Now it was Mullins' turn to smirk, seeing exactly where the lieutenant was headed.

"That's right, asshole. You're off the case." Grimes patted Mullins' back. "It's all yours, Mullins. Do the department proud."

"Yes, sir."

"Now, both of you get out." The lieutenant returned to his chair and directed his attention to the piling paperwork on his desk.

Mako's feet came to a halt just short of the doorway, and ignoring his better judgment to keep quiet, he declared, "You're making a mistake, sir. I think I deserve to stay on this assignment."

Grimes picked his head up from his papers and gently placed his pen down on the desk. "Oh, you think you deserve it? You think? Well, let me tell you something." He raised his voice, "I don't make mistakes. You don't deserve this case. You don't deserve that shield. You don't deserve shit! You understand me?"

"What the fuck is your problem with me?"

"Is that the way you speak to a superior, boy?"

"Excuse me." The sarcasm surfaced again. "What the fuck is your problem with me ... sir?"

"Get the hell out of my face, and don't ever speak to me that way again."

The detective wanted nothing else but to further aggravate the lieutenant, but this was an argument he could not win. He left the office, and the door was slammed shut behind him. Already fuming at what had happened, his mood worsened when he noticed Mullins staring at him with a comical look on his face.

"So, tell me, Mako, how does your ass feel now that Grimes chewed on it for a while?" Mullins and some other officers around him had a good laugh at Mako's expense. "Need a cushion for your chair?"

Detective Bailey moved up behind his partner and whispered, "Let it go, Johnny. You're already in enough shit."

The laughter hit Mako like a hammer. He despised being made to look like a fool. Bailey spoke again, but rage blocked every sound from reaching his ears except for that of the officers mocking him. Fingers curled into a fist as his temperature streaked off the charts.

Mullins picked up his ringing desk phone, stifling a laugh, and received alarming news. Dropping the receiver back onto its base, he grabbed his coat and motioned to a few of his colleagues. "I need some assistance! There's been another murder in Hicksville! Same M.O. as this morning! Officers are en route to secure the area, but we better move our asses so they don't mess up my crime scene."

Mako unclenched his fist and watched Mullins and the Idiot Parade dash out of the building. Then he snatched his coat and rushed for the door.

Bailey intercepted. "Don't think about it. You're not part of Homicide. Leave Mullins alone."

"Like hell I will. If I can't catch a thief, I'll catch a murderer. I'll show Grimes—and Mullins—exactly what I deserve."

EIGHT

In an underground parking lot sat a dull gray unmarked box truck fashioned with armor plating; two large men, both similarly dressed in dark blue jeans and black sleeveless shirts that showed off their muscular arms, stood beside it. One of the men had long hair tied in a ponytail, with a long goatee held in check by a tiny rubber band, and he wore a thick silver chain around his neck. The other was bald, wore sunglasses, and had a tattoo of a green serpent wrapped around his left bicep and forearm.

Footsteps echoed through the garage as fine Italian shoes clicked on the concrete with every stride. A third man, exceptionally clothed in an Armani suit, approached the truck. He stopped in front of the two men but said nothing. Aware of what he wanted, they led him to the back and unlocked the rear doors. The well-dressed man pulled them open and stared at the cargo inside.

A frightened Jacob Connors was curled up in the corner, shielding his eyes from the light he had been deprived of for nearly twenty-four hours. His clothes were almost completely shredded, exposing most of his flesh, and the dried blood covering them did not appear to be his since there were no visible cuts on his body. Whimpering uncontrollably, he awaited his fate.

The well-dressed man was the first to speak. "Excellent. All your wounds have healed. Have you met Mr. Ball?" He motioned to the bald-headed man. "And Mr. Chainz?" he said, now motioning to the man with the chain around his neck.

The prisoner didn't acknowledge his jailer.

The man retrieved a brown leather wallet from his inside coat pocket. Flipping it open, he pulled out a driver's license and continued, "Look here, Mr. Connors. Or do you prefer Jacob?" A few seconds of silence, and the man moved on. "I really don't care if you speak to me or not, Jacob. You are about to enter a new stage of life."

The broken young man finally looked up.

"Piqued your curiosity, have I?"

"What are you going to do to me?"

Placing the license back into the wallet and throwing it inside the truck, the man replied, "I am not going to do anything to you. You see, when you broke into my employer's office last night, you were blessed—not only by walking away with your life, but also because you have been given a gift. It's a rare gift that most mortals are deemed unworthy to possess."

Jacob was confused, considering the state he was in. "What gift was that? A good ass-kicking?"

The man let out a slight release of air, signifying that he was either amused or annoyed, but no one present could be absolutely sure. "After the … treatment you received last night, you should feel lucky to have survived at all. However, you will never have to worry about mortality again."

"What the hell are you talking about?"

"You'll find out very soon." He shut the door, consigning Jacob to the dark once again. Turning to Mr. Ball, the man said, "Take him to the designated area and let him stretch his legs when the time is right."

"Yes, Mr. Walker. Right away."

"And gentlemen, I'm sure I don't have to tell you to make sure you capture him once he's finished. Our employer will be sorely displeased with you, to say the least, if his new acquisition gets away."

Jenny Hertz checked her watch for the fifth time since the mall had closed. She felt like she'd never finish her closing procedures in order to go home. She used to think managing a Victoria's Secret would be a piece of cake: have everyone else do the hard work, and all she had to do was count the money at the end of the night. The employee discount on perfumes and lingerie had also appealed to her, and to her boyfriend too. But while the money was good, Jenny would prefer leaving while the sun was still shining.

The hands on her watch told her it was almost eleven, and as far as she was concerned, it was quitting time. She placed the money for the morning deposit in the safe and switched the designated circuit breakers off, keeping only the minimum required lights on. She exited through the back of the store, emerging behind Hicksville's dimly lit Broadway Mall. Pulling her jacket tighter to shield herself from the cool breeze, she started towards her car. She'd parked at the rear of the parking lot—a stupid rule her district manager had come up with so customers could park closer to the store. Jenny wished her D.M. could leave at this hour and see how she liked the uneasy feeling of walking through the nearly deserted lot.

Chainz drove the armored car through the populated streets like Jeff Gordon drove his race car on the track. Mr. Ball wasn't worried as they weaved back and forth, narrowly avoiding other cars on the road. The full moon's image reflected off one of Mr. Ball's lenses, and the Broadway Mall filled the other.

As they neared the shopping center, Jacob began pounding the walls of his mobile prison. "Hey, where are you taking me?" He groaned in pain. "I don't feel so good. Pull over!"

Mr. Ball exchanged looks with Chainz and smiled as they both turned to gaze out the front windshield again.

The banging from the rear of the truck became more violent. "I'm serious! I don't feel so—"

Before he finished his sentence, Jacob was wracked with pain and screamed out. Once he was able to speak again, his voice sounded different, raspier than before, and his tone was more aggressive. "Let me out of here before I kill you both!"

Neither man in the truck's cab showed concern over their passenger's threats as the vehicle pulled into the mall parking lot. The commotion continued, but Chainz slowed down only when he saw a young woman walking alone. He parked the truck across a few spaces nearly one hundred feet away, angling it so the rear doors were facing her direction. Both men exited the vehicle. Mr. Ball retrieved a .44 Magnum from where it was tucked in the seat of his pants, while Chainz grabbed a double-barrel shotgun from behind the driver's seat. Another slam inside the cargo hold rocked the truck from side to side, and Jacob's screams had turned to roars.

Taking the keys from his pocket, Mr. Ball was about to insert them into the door lock when something ferociously crashed down on the top of the truck, making it bob up and down. Startled, the two men looked up and raised their weapons, ready to fire on whatever was responsible for the intrusion. Mr. Ball crept to the left of the vehicle as Chainz walked to the right. Whatever took refuge on the roof of their vehicle remained completely still. A few more steps back to get a better look above, but even they appeared to be taken aback when the offender reared its head.

A huge, hairy beast rose into the moonlight and smelled the air, just as the sound of sniffing was heard from inside the truck too. The beast, almost fully upright on top of the truck, was nearly seven and a half feet tall, and had muscles that easily rivaled any body builder's. Its giant head resembled a wolf, and it was covered in dark brown fur. Once the creature noticed the two armed men surrounding it, it bared its razor-like teeth and displayed the massive claws on all its fingers. Roaring loudly in succession at each of the men, the beast used the truck like a springboard, and powerful leg muscles propelled it forward, out of range of their guns.

Moving to the cab of the truck, Chainz asked his partner, "Was that one of ours?"

"I highly doubt it. We better get back and report this to Walker."

The truck shook aggressively as their prisoner grew ever more furious. "What about him?" Chainz asked, getting into the driver's seat.

"His first outing will have to be postponed," Mr. Ball replied. "Now, drive."

Jenny, halfway to her vehicle, spun around when she heard a ghastly howl. Not interested in where or what the noise came from, she made a beeline for her car. But she hadn't gone ten feet when the sound of excited breathing and weighty footsteps approaching at rapid speed reached her ears. She ran, peering over her shoulder to see what was behind, and let out a horrified scream when she saw the grotesque creature pursuing her.

The monster, even though it could stand like a man, ran on all fours toward the terrified female. Its powerfully built form boosted it forward with astounding speed, making any hope of outrunning it quickly vanish. Its tongue dangled in the wind, and the breeze caught some of the saliva dripping off it. Panting hard to take in as much oxygen as possible, the monster showed no sign of letting its prey escape.

Her tears flowed freely; she realized she would not live to see another day. Still, she pumped her legs as fast as she could. But her car, her only salvation, may as well have been miles away. One of her high-heeled shoes had already broken, triggering an awkward limp, and the other eventually tripped her up, causing a painful fall to the ground. Then the beast was on top of her.

Jenny Hertz would be remembered as a kind daughter and loving friend. Those who knew her would grieve this tragic loss. She would be sorely missed.

Eddie Loomis, a veteran police officer, routinely patrolled the Hicksville area, including the malls and local hangouts. Loomis liked the fact that the most dangerous situation he came across was the occasional underage drinking or teenagers fooling around in the back of a car. That was what he expected to encounter when he spotted the lone Toyota Camry parked in the otherwise abandoned lot. Pulling his cruiser around the Camry, he shone a spotlight on the ground near the passenger's side.

The light shimmered off a large pool of blood staining the asphalt. Hesitantly stepping out of his car, he followed the trail to the body of a young woman, dragged several feet away. She was slumped over, facedown. Her clothes were torn and partially ripped from her body. Blood-soaked hair made it hard to determine if she was a blonde or brunette, and there were large scratches and scrapes on her uncovered flesh. The officer's hands shook as he removed the baton from his belt. Extending his arm until the club reached the girl's shoulder, he flipped her over so she faced skyward.

"Holy shit!" Loomis exclaimed, noticing the extent of the damage done to the woman's body. Her insides were torn out, half her face was removed, and it appeared to him that she'd been partially eaten. Fighting the urge to gag, he sprinted back to his car and found the radio receiver inside. He frantically shone his spotlight across the parking lot to determine if her attacker was still in the vicinity. "205! Clear channel! Clear the fucking channel!"

"205, go ahead," an operator responded.

"I need cars, a boss and an ambulance forthwith! I have a fatality in the rear of the Broadway Mall!"

"Is the subject still at scene?"

The officer shone his light around the parking lot again but saw no sign of who or what had done this. "Negative, but notify the squad and have K-9 respond to search the area." Loomis breathed a little easier knowing he'd have company soon enough, but an impulse flashed through his brain, causing him to sound off into his radio again: "And notify Emergency Services for possible animal control! I think we have a wild beast on the loose!"

The operator returned after a momentary silence. "Sit tight, 205. Help is on the way."

NINE

Mako steered slowly past the first police barrier at the south entrance to the Broadway Mall, where it looked as if the entire precinct had responded to Officer Loomis' call. Maneuvering his car around both official and civilian vehicles to get to a better vantage point, he parked a few car lengths away from the main area where most of his colleagues gathered. Exiting his Mitsubishi Lancer, he refrained from taking his flashlight since all the lights on the dozen or so squad cars served to effectively illuminate the area. He smacked his wristwatch a couple of times before checking the time.

"When are you gonna get rid of this piece of shit, Mako?"

The detective spun around to find his number one fan wiping his grimy hands along his Lancer's rear spoiler, and Mako did not like the comparison made between his car and excrement. "As soon as you drop a few hundred pounds."

"Fuck you," Mullins snapped. "What the hell are you doing at my crime scene anyway?"

"The way you bolted out of the precinct, I figured you could use a hand."

Mullins studied his fellow officer, waiting for a hint of sarcasm, but when none was detected he said, "Fine. Make sure no unauthorized personnel enter the perimeter, unlike the Muttontown Preserve."

"You got it," he said, but once his colleague was out of earshot, he finished with, "Douche-bag." Then he wiped Mullins' handprint off his car with his jacket and stepped back, checking at another angle to ensure it was all gone.

Slipping behind one of the wooden police barricades, he snuck over to another familiar face. Investigator Thomas Samms was collecting samples of blood, hair, and fibers from the victim. Most of the corpse was covered by a pale blue sheet so that those with weak constitutions could perform their jobs properly. Samms placed numerous plastic containers, each containing a single sample, into his evidence bag.

Mako observed the investigator for a minute before crouching down next to him. "Hey, Samms, what's up?"

Appearing less than pleased to be up at this hour, with bloodshot eyes, a stubbly face, and a pajama shirt under his coat, Samms groggily answered, "I wish I wasn't. I just got to sleep after a twenty-hour shift, and I get a call to rush over here."

"Why the sheet?" Mako motioned to the body. "Is it that bad?"

"You don't want to know. It's a good thing I'm so tired. I don't think my eyes focused completely, or I might be contaminating evidence with vomit chunks."

Mako was a little surprised to hear that coming from Samms. "Thanks for the imagery. I'll take your word for it."

"Why are you here?"

"Just seeing if I could lend a hand."

Samms did not believe him and said, "Yeah, right."

"So anyway," Mako said, changing the subject, "we still on for tomorrow morning?"

"Yeah, the file's in my desk and ready for you to pick up." He carefully situated a vial of blood into his case. "You have what you promised me?"

Mako was about to tell a little white lie, and since it was for the greater good, he said, "Of course. It's in my desk for safekeeping."

"Come by at ten o'clock. I'll be ready then."

"Hey, any chance of getting the report on this vic too?"

The exhausted investigator responded as politely as possible, "Don't push it, Mako. Now, let me finish up here so I can go back to bed."

"You got it, pal." The detective patted Samms on the back with one hand, and with his other, he reached into the evidence bag, secretly pulling out one of each of the samples he'd watched Samms place inside it. Getting to his feet, Mako put the specimens into his jacket pocket and was startled when Mullins unexpectedly shouted his name.

"Mako! I thought I told you to watch the perimeter! What the hell are you doing over here?"

"Nothing." His brain searched for a viable excuse. "I came by to see if everything was okay with Samms here."

Mullins glanced at the barely awake investigator and then looked back at Mako.

Mako continued, "He looks pretty beat to me. Maybe you should have someone get him a coffee or something. You don't want him missing any crucial evidence, do you?"

"I'm fine, really," Samms tried to interrupt.

Mullins, ignoring the comment, checked the vicinity and snapped his fingers at a uniformed officer nearby. "You!"

The officer hesitantly pointed at himself.

"Yeah, you, numb-nuts. Go get a cup of coffee for Investigator Samms." The officer didn't move fast enough for Mullins, so he yelled out, "Sometime tonight, moron!"

"Well," Mako started again, "you look like you have everything under control here." He took a few steps toward the barricade. "You don't need me hanging around."

Mullins wasn't sure what to make of his colleague's actions, so he merely stared at him through narrowed eye slits, watching him get into his car and drive off.

"Here's the coffee you wanted, sir," the officer said, returning from his errand.

The detective gripped the cup and shooed the officer away. He handed the beverage to Samms, who placed it on the floor next to him. Mullins gazed in the direction the Lancer went, looked back at Samms, swiveled his head up again, and felt he'd missed something he really shouldn't have.

TEN

The familiar snap of the boxer's waistband against his skin jolted Mako from his slumber, and he jumped out of bed before it happened a second time. Rubbing the sleep from his eyes, he gave his "alarm clock" an aggravated look. "How many times have I told you not to do that?"

Not concerned in the slightest with the attitude, Rikki answered, "If you'd get up on your own, I wouldn't be able to sneak a look at your tush."

"You're so disturbing sometimes."

"I mean really," Rikki said, opening the blinds to let some sunlight into the bedroom, "between your alarm, cellphone, dogs barking, and me, you'd think that would be enough to wake you." He fixed the bed and picked up some of the clothes thrown on the floor while continuing his monologue. "But a little tug on your drawers is really all it takes."

Shaving cream on half his face, Mako peeked his head out of the bathroom. "The next time you 'tug on my drawers,' you're gonna get a foot up your ass."

"Promises, promises, sweetie."

He made a face at the thought of anyone's looking forward to that and then went back inside to finish up. A short while later he emerged from the bathroom, sporting jeans and a button-down dress shirt, and moved over to his dresser to spray cologne on each side of his neck.

"Have a hot date?" Rikki was watching from the kitchen.

He entered the room and petted both Bruno and Chip. "Why? You jealous?"

"Maybe." He raised his cup and asked, "Want some coffee?"

"You know I don't drink that stuff."

Finishing what was left in his cup, Rikki said, "Oh, right. Hey, since you're up, can I get a refill?"

Realizing he'd been set up, Mako reached over with the coffee pot and filled the mug, recoiling as Rikki jumped out of his chair and gasped. "What was that on my leg?" From under one side of the table, the cause of the disturbance surfaced.

"It was only Booger. You're such a girl." Mako laughed and carefully lifted the cat.

"I hate that mangy fur ball."

"This cat's cleaner than you."

Sitting back down, Rikki regained his composure. "Only because he licks himself all day long. You'd think that'd get old after an hour or two."

"Lock up when you leave." He placed the cat on the floor. "And Booger," Mako addressed the purring cat, "if he acts like that again, feel free to scratch what's left of his balls off."

"You're a bitch," Rikki commented as the door to the apartment closed.

Driving to the Nassau County Police Department headquarters, Mako finished a phone conversation: "Please do me this one favor. I know, and I'm sorry it's last minute." He stepped out of his car and walked toward the building. "Seriously, it won't be that bad. Okay, make it for lunch. This way you can always say you have to run back to work." Showing his badge to the officers at the Public

Information Office, he was permitted entry. "Okay, I owe you one—but only if you have a horrible time." Disconnecting the call before any further debate, he jotted something down on a scrap of paper.

"Where have you been? It's almost eleven," a frenzied voice shouted.

Mako jerked around to see Investigator Samms urgently heading straight for him.

"What're you so agitated about? I figured I would let you catch up on your beauty sleep."

Looking more official than he had at the murder scene outside the Broadway Mall a few hours before, Samms grabbed the detective by the arm and led him up to his office in the Forensics Evidence Bureau. "I have a lot of things to do today, Mako. With two murders and a burglary on my plate, I don't have the time or the patience to deal with your tardiness."

"Man, are you cranky today." Mako pulled the scrap of paper he'd written on just moments ago out of his pocket. "I think I may have something to brighten your day a little," he teased as he waved the paper in front of the investigator's face.

Samms attempted to snatch it, but Mako's reflexes were too quick for him, leaving him empty-handed. "Give it."

"'Give it?' What are you, twelve?" They entered an office. "Where's the info I asked for?"

Fetching a thick, sealed manila envelope from a desk drawer and handing it over, Samms said, "Sorry, Mako, I'm under a lot of pressure. Everyone wants everything yesterday, if you know what I mean. It was hard enough to put a rush on the Muttontown findings, and now last night's debacle is making things worse."

"Thank you. And here's the phone number you've been lusting after." He held out his arm with the piece of paper at the end of it.

Leaving the investigator to his work, he soon heard Samms yelling out his name behind him.

"1-800, Mako, you son of a bitch!"

As the elevator doors slid closed, Mako stopped them at the last second, laughing, and shouted back at the angry man, "Have a sense of humor, Samms! She said she'd meet you for lunch at Lucy's Steak House! You do know where that is, right?"

"How do I know you're not bullshitting me?"

He shrugged his shoulders. "Come on, a deal is a deal, and I don't let my friends down. Be there at one o'clock and not a minute after. You might not get another shot."

Samms felt like jumping up and kicking his heels together. "You are a fuckin' miracle worker! Thanks, Mako, you'll be invited to the wedding!" He darted away to make preparations for his big date.

"Get through lunch first," the detective mumbled to himself. On the way out of the building, his cellphone rang. The display read MATT D. "Yo."

"Where are you?" Matt skipped any niceties.

Matt DeMarco had known Mako for more than half his life. They first met while working at a store called Cheap Ron's and were inseparable for most of their high school years. Both had similar stories back then, except for Matt's being a few years older. They shared the same interests, found the same jokes amusing, listened to the same music, and had pretty much the same home situations too. They clicked almost instantly. Whether they were arguing or finishing one another's thoughts, the two always had a mutual respect for one another; some people even made fun of them by comparing them to a married couple. Even though life took them on different paths and sometimes strained their friendship, they still managed to stay close.

"Working. You?"

"Finishing a round of golf."

Mako got into his car and opened the envelope from Samms. "Tell me again how nice it is to have your own company."

"Be nicer if I didn't have a lazy shit for a partner and my wife didn't spend every paycheck before I took it in. Did I tell you how she …," he droned on.

Mako haphazardly reviewed the information.

Not realizing his friend wasn't completely listening, Matt asked, "You eat yet? I thought we could get some lunch."

"Not today. I got a lot of work to do." He skimmed through the DNA reports and couldn't believe what he was reading. "What the hell?"

"What's the matter?"

"I'm not sure. It's this new case I'm working on. Something in these reports doesn't make sense." Mako put the information back into the envelope. "I'm going to need some help."

"From me?" Matt was confused.

"Why? Are you a DNA expert all of a sudden?"

Deducing that he wasn't talking about him, Matt asked an obvious question, "Don't you guys have people to do that for you?"

"Yeah, but I need someone who doesn't work for Nassau County. Someone on the outside I can trust."

"Why on the outside?"

Whispering as if someone could hear him through the rolled up windows, he said, "Because, technically, I'm not supposed to be working on this."

"Can't you get in trouble if someone finds out?"

"Yeah, but that's why I need help from someone I can depend on." Mako covered his mouth in case there were any lip-readers around.

"Who do you have in mind?"

"Jacquie," he said with assurance.

"You think she'll help you after—"

"I know we left things on shaky terms, but she'll do it. Let me go for now. I've got some stuff I need to send to her as soon as possible. I'll call you later." Mako hung up, and then contemplated out loud: "I hope I'm right about her, or else I'm gonna need all the luck in the world."

ELEVEN

In the interrogation room, Jacquie Dale reviewed her notes before speaking with Dave Jarvis. At first glance, he thought she was in the wrong career; modeling would have been more suitable. Her long wavy brown hair and slender curves caused him to wonder if he should be scared out of his mind because of the situation he was in, or simply turned on. Starting from the floor up, his eyes traced the outline of long, sexy legs leading to a flat, toned stomach. Her light blue blouse with a few buttons undone revealed ample cleavage that made his mouth water. Her gray skirt and jacket may as well have been nonexistent since he was undressing her with his eyes; but once his brown eyes met hers, Dave realized she knew what he was doing, and her being unaffected by it made it a bit intimidating.

Jacquie had every reason to believe the local police detectives. After all, Dave had motive to kill Pasco. It was a brutal assault on the man Dave knew was treading on his territory. Still, she'd seen too many homicides lately that didn't always prove out where the evidence pointed; one particular instance had been in her hometown, but Savannah was a long way from Boston. The fact that Pasco had lived in Massachusetts his whole life triggered the memory. The whole scenario was simply too neat and tidy, and something didn't feel right to her.

She looked at Dave, who sat with his elbows on the table, his chin resting on his fists, and his wrists in cuffs. "I didn't do this. I swear I didn't do this …," he said, his voice trailing off.

"Dave," she started, "you went out of your way to have your girlfriend followed. Then you had people get to know Jesse Pasco to get information for you. Now the guy's dead, and you have no alibi."

"Yeah. I wanted the jerk dead," Dave whimpered. "That's reason enough to know I didn't do it! Why would I kill him, knowing I'd be blamed?" He seemed to momentarily drift away.

"Stay with me, Mr. Jarvis. I'm trying to find out if you could be responsible for this reprehensible act, and you zone out! Say the word, and I'll leave you here to rot!"

Lifting his head to look at her face-to-face, he said, "I didn't do this. I swear."

She rose up and away from the accused killer sitting behind the table in front of her and examined his expression; he never broke her gaze. Folding her arms and relying on nothing more than uncanny intuition, she said, "I believe you. However, all the evidence we have at this juncture points to you as the guilty party. If there's something the police initially missed—"

A knock on the interrogation room door, followed by an unauthorized interruption by her assistant, Max Hartman, put the conversation on hold for the moment. "Ms. Dale, I'm sorry to interrupt, but I have someone on the phone for you. He said it's an emergency."

Jacquie did not like to be disturbed while questioning a suspect, but something about Max's tone told her this was a call she did not want to ignore. "Who is it?"

"A Detective Mako from New York."

Instantly, her thoughts shot back to her brief stay in the Big Apple and her time spent with Johnny. Still harboring some resentment over the way they'd parted, she almost ordered her assistant to hang up on him, but she knew Johnny would not inconvenience her for something unimportant. "Tell him to hold on. I'm almost finished."

Max departed and followed instructions.

Directing her attention back to the accused, she finished her statement: "As I was saying, Mr. Jarvis, if there's something the police initially missed, and you are, in fact, not guilty of murder, I will find the proof to clear your name."

"Thank you, Ms. Dale." Dave felt more comfortable now that he knew her name.

About to exit the interrogation room, she added, "Better not thank me yet. I'm only doing my job, and I'm damn good at it. So, if I can't find any facts declaring your innocence, then I'll make sure you see nothing else for the rest of your days except the concrete walls that make up your cell!"

Despite the threat, he couldn't help but stare at those legs a few seconds longer until Jacquie was completely out of the room.

She motioned for her assistant to give her the phone. "Hello, Johnny. It's been a long time."

"Yeah, it has. How are things in Georgia?"

Attempting to identify something in his voice that would give away his reason for calling, she decided to get right to the point instead of playing games. "What can I do for you?"

He also got to the point. "Still pissed at me, I see. But I need your help with something I'm working on."

"Why me? Don't they have capable investigators in your department?"

"Of course they do. I simply don't trust any of them to keep this quiet. I need someone unaffiliated with the NCPD, and you are the best at what you do."

Giving in to a moment of weakness, she smiled at the compliment. "You still trust me?"

"You know I do. And besides, I think there's something here you'll have a personal interest in. I can overnight you some reports and some samples to analyze, and all I'm asking is for you to let me know what you make of it."

Intrigued at what personal stake she could possibly have in a case so far from home, she said, "Sure, I'll take a look at them. Send me what you have."

"Thanks. I knew I could count on you. I shipped them out two hours ago. You'll have them first thing in the morning."

"It's Sunday. How did you—"

"Sent it with a courier," Mako interrupted. "Sure, it was really expensive, but nothing's too good for you."

Understanding that he was trying to stroke her ego for good measure, she switched gears so he wouldn't realize it was working. Buried emotions betrayed her as a little flirtation surfaced. "Do you still have the goatee?"

"Yeah, I've gotten used to it."

"I want credit for that."

"For what?"

"For your goatee."

"You want credit for me being able to grow hair on my face?"

"If it wasn't for my suggestion, you wouldn't have."

Detecting the playfulness in her tone, Mako went with it. "I don't know what you're talking about."

"You were clean-shaven when I met you, and I told you that if you had a goatee, you would accent your face better. And I was right. It made your blue eyes stand out."

"So, you didn't notice I had blue eyes beforehand?"

"Stop that. You know I thought—think—you have beautiful eyes. It's my opinion the goatee made you more handsome."

"Okay, so you thought I was ugly when you first met me, and that I should cover as much of my face as I could by growing a beard." Now he was just being difficult.

She could play the same game. "I didn't think it could hurt any."

"Nice of you to say." He was uncertain if she was serious, or if it was her bitterness talking.

A few moments of calm went by before she said, "I still want credit for it."

"Fine," he submitted, to get back to more pressing matters. "So, how long do you think it'll be before you've got something for me to go on?"

"I'll call you when I finish reviewing the information." She was going to hang up to regain the upper hand, but she could not do it before saying, "And you're welcome." Walking down the hallway with Max, she smiled and shook her head. No matter what transpired between them, she still could not say no to Johnny, and she wasn't sure if it infuriated or pleased her that he knew it too.

TWELVE

Ball and Chainz waited patiently inside a private office adorned mostly with modern furnishings; Mr. Ball sat on one end of a long, brown leather couch while Chainz rested partially on a classic mahogany desk with a bowed front edge. The desk was kept immaculate and organized. Nothing was out of place, and there were no pictures or other personal items cluttering the workspace. Instead, to its right, hanging on the wall, were a series of paintings, older than one would expect. The top image depicted a happy family where the husband held his wife in one arm and his daughter in the other, while his son sat in front of the trio. The pictures underneath were solo portraits of his wife and children. Mr. Ball examined the paintings and the lit candles on the small table underneath and thought the arrangement looked like a shrine rather than a reminder of happy times.

Mr. Walker stepped inside and glided across the room toward his lackeys. Appearing to be in his fifties, he was distinguished-looking with gray, almost silver, hair and hazel eyes. Although he was of average height and slight build, he intimidated most men he came into contact with. Ethan Walker wasn't known for being frivolous or friendly, and it had been rumored that he'd ruined a man's life for merely cutting him in line at a restaurant.

Without looking at either man, he asked, "What is so urgent?" He didn't wait for a response before turning to Chainz and instructing, "Get off my desk, you Neanderthal, and use a chair like a normal person."

Mr. Ball stood up, and both he and Chainz positioned themselves in front of the desk their employer now sat behind. Mr. Ball was the one who usually did the talking. "Did you hear about the Broadway Mall killing?"

"Yes, I read about it in this morning's paper." Ethan swiveled in his high-back, brown leather chair to face a set of drawers behind him. "And I have your payment for a job well executed." Opening the faux drawer to reveal a small safe within, he began to enter the combination.

"It wasn't ours that killed the girl."

He stopped entering the code.

"It was a stray," Mr. Ball continued. "We thought you should know about it."

He rotated his chair to face them, rested his elbows on the desk, and steepled his fingers. Again, he didn't look directly at either man and took a deep breath before asking, "And you let it get away?"

"It took us by surprise. Before we knew what was going on, it took off." Fearing for their own safety, Mr. Ball put a hand behind his back and caressed the handle of his pistol while Chainz grabbed the chains hanging around his neck.

Ethan coolly rose from his chair, set the fingertips from both hands onto the tabletop, and leaned over, glaring angrily at his underlings. "Your weapons do not scare me. I could kill you both before either of you could draw them out."

They put their hands in full view to defuse the situation.

"Now, the two of you are to get out of my office and find this stray and contain it. If it cannot be contained, I want it destroyed. Understand?"

"How do you want us to find it?" Chainz asked, even though he already surmised the answer.

"Figure it out for yourself, you clod. That is what I pay you for, isn't it?"

Mr. Ball placed a hand across his partner's chest, and both backed away toward the door, never taking their eyes off their boss.

Ethan took a seat once more and calmly concluded the conversation. "Do inform me of your progress, gentlemen, and please resolve the matter as soon as possible." Once his employees had left and the office door had firmly closed behind them, he hit the speed dial on his company phone.

A voice came through the speaker: "What is it, Ethan?"

"We have a problem."

"I don't like problems. That's why I have you."

Ethan tensed up. He did not fear anyone other than the man he was talking to, and the man on the other end of the phone knew it. "I'm working on it, but it appears we have a rogue lycanthrope."

"Did you take care of the situation in the preserve?"

Hesitating, Ethan said, "The police arrived too quickly. I don't know how they got there so fast, but I wasn't able to—"

"Enough," the man interrupted. "Author Don Wilder said, 'Excuses are the nails used to build a house of failure.' Do not fail me, Ethan. Make these problems go away."

"I will—"

The phone call disconnected before he could finish his sentence. He didn't even get a moment to think how he'd make his troubles vanish before his receptionist paged him. Hitting the intercom button on his phone, he asked, "Yes, Sara?"

"There's a Detective James Mullins on line two for you."

"Put him through," he paused a moment. "And have Mr. Ball and Mr. Chainz return to my office." The light for his private line blinked steadily, indicating that a caller was waiting, but before picking it up, he muttered, "What else will I have to contend with before this is all over?"

THIRTEEN

Digital images displayed on the computer screen changed with every mouse click. The scene at the Muttontown Preserve would cause any normal man to turn away in disgust, but Jason Brody had lost count of how many times he'd viewed photos similar to these; and if he was right about who was behind the killing, he understood firsthand how cruel this monster could be.

Scrolling through the photos of the mauled corpse like a slide show, he paused yet again at the image of one of the detectives at the scene; he was certain he'd seen the man before, but he could not remember where. On the third loop of the show, the detective's face left more of an impression, and with the fourth pass, Jason made the connection. Running over to another desk and pulling out a scrapbook of all the high-profile photos he'd taken, he opened it to a date approximately eight months ago and found the front-page headline that read, "Hero Cop Out of the Infirmary and into a Promotion."

Underneath the heading was a picture of Officer Johnny Mako, his left arm in a sling, shaking hands with the Chief of Police and receiving a detective's shield. Jason also remembered the event surrounding the promotion: a series of armed robberies all over Nassau County were perpetrated by teens targeting convenience stores, hospitalizing some of the staff while making off with the cash. Officer Mako happened to be in the right store at the wrong time when the three teenage boys struck again, and whether it was dumb luck or superb marksmanship, Mako subdued the criminals without killing them and saved the life of the clerk. The officer got away with minor injuries, and the department wasn't sure if they should acknowledge his actions until the media had a feeding frenzy over the case. This also happened to be Jason's first real photo assignment since moving to New York six months prior. However, he didn't remember the officer being promoted to the homicide division; so *why*, he thought, *was he at a murder scene?*

A knock on his front door prevented him from uncovering any answers. Peering through the peephole first, he opened the three locks and removed the chain keeping the door securely shut.

"Afraid of something, Brody?" Nathan Henry Williams asked, once again dispensing with the formalities, and entered the apartment without an invitation.

"I'm sorry, sir?"

Pointing to all the locks on the back of the door, he said, "All these. What are you trying to keep out? Or are you trying to keep something in?"

Knowing what his visitor meant, he glossed over the question. "There's been another murder, sir."

"How many times have I told you there's no need for you to call me sir?" Nathan looked around the dimly lit room for a clean place to sit. "You're not officially part of my outfit even though we cooperate with one another—a courtesy to the memory of my great-great-grandfather."

Circling in place to get a better look at the living conditions his associate had chosen for himself, Nathan spied empty pizza boxes and water bottles littering one corner of the living room and newspapers strewn about the rest. The couch was buried under mounds of laundry, and the coffee table was covered in magazines and empty film rolls, but there was one hopeful spot in this otherwise filthy area—a lone stool, barren of waste, sat a few feet away. Moving closer to the chair, Nathan said, "So, tell me about this murder."

"There's been another since we spoke." Sifting through the scattered papers, Jason found the edition with the facts on the gruesome crime and handed it over. "Take a look."

"Was it *him* again?" He flipped through to find the article.

"No. The girl's head was still attached."

Nathan squinted his eyes, finding it hard to make out the words without the benefit of adequate lighting. Giving up, he folded the newspaper in half, tucking it under his arm. "Are you saying there are more of them?"

"There has to be." A grim thought crossed his mind. "I hope you didn't come alone."

"Of course not," he responded to the completely preposterous statement. "I brought a squad of ten men, including me. We set up a temporary HQ in several suites at the Marriott Hotel near the Nassau Coliseum."

"The Marriott?" Jason didn't think that sounded like much of a command center.

Nathan picked up a wrinkled shirt he found on the floor. "I know it may be hard for you to comprehend, but we don't have to live like the animals we hunt." Tossing the piece of clothing back on the ground, he moved to the exit, stepping over another mound of something he couldn't properly identify in the darkness.

"Where are you going?"

"Back to the hotel. It's late, and I have to prep my team to take down two beasts."

Jason became nervous because if Nathan was unable get the job done, there'd be hell to pay; he'd already missed a previous opportunity, and it'd had dire consequences. Remembering the article he'd read moments ago, Jason proposed, "I know someone who can help."

"A friend of yours?"

"No. He's a cop."

Nathan shook his head in a disapproving manner. "You know I don't like to involve the authorities."

"I know, but this guy has already been poking around the murder scenes. What can it hurt to find out what he knows instead of starting your own investigation from scratch?"

Thinking for a moment, Nathan rubbed his chin and said, "Bring him to the hotel, but tell him as little as possible. Lie to him, if you have to. We'll see if he has any useful information." Opening the door, Nathan was pleased by the sudden rush of the sun's rays, and upon noticing Jason's unkempt living conditions in bright light, he added, "If you decide you need a change of scenery, you are welcome to use the suites. My great-great-grandfather would be appalled to see how you live. Me, I'm used to it." Entering the rear of a black Hummer waiting by the curb, he didn't say another word, and the vehicle carefully maneuvered into traffic.

Jason returned to the darkness, again bolting his front door shut. Finding the paper with Mako's front-page photo, he skimmed through the article and noted where it described Mako's promotion to detective in the Second Precinct. Grabbing his camera and a smaller leather case, he put them both in his knapsack. Come morning, he'd head out to find his quarry.

FOURTEEN

Monday morning arrived and a frustrated Detective Mullins waited outside the abandoned Stumpp Industries building. The preliminary investigation into Jenny Hertz's murder was a bust since his interview of her parents revealed nothing new as to the identity of the killer; however, evidence collected from inside Stumpp Industries and the Broadway Mall indicated a possible connection between the two crime scenes.

Uniformed officers guarded the perimeter, ensuring that no one entered the building. A familiar-looking car pulled up behind the detective's Mercedes, and Mullins was agitated even before its driver exited. Mako headed up the walkway and was greeted with hostility.

"Why are you here?" Mullins stormed over to meet him. "This isn't your case anymore. Remember?"

Mako was hoping to gain entrance into the building without any resistance so he could collect more evidence for his silent partner, Jacquie Dale. Realizing his plan was completely ruined, he attempted politeness to get what he wanted. "This may surprise you, but I'm not here to argue. I didn't even know you were here. I just wanted to take a second look around. I have a feeling something's a little off here."

"If there's anything … off, I'll figure it out." Leading Mako back to his car, he said, "Now, why don't you get going and don't worry yourself with—damn." He interrupted his own thought when the black stretch limousine pulled into the parking lot.

"Expecting someone?" Mako felt someone else's plans were now ruined too.

Knowing there was no choice but to let his colleague stay, unless he wanted to cause a scene by forcing him to go, Mullins said, "Yeah, so keep quiet and let me do the talking. Maybe you'll learn a little something about good police work."

"That's hurtful. Seriously. I may shed a tear."

The rear passenger side door opened, and Mullins, feeling the need to stress his point to keep his colleague's sarcasm in check, muttered through gritted teeth, "Don't act like an imbecile, Mako. This isn't the time or the place!" His heart raced a bit faster as one foot from the man in the rear of the car hit the pavement.

The first man got out of the automobile and both officers were taken aback by the sheer size of him. Standing approximately six foot four inches tall and weighing, what the detectives placed him at, nearly 250 pounds, Mr. Ball was an impressive specimen.

"If anything goes wrong," Mako whispered, "would you mind if I watch him kick your ass?"

The next man exited, and he was just as massive as the first. Roughly six foot three and probably 260 pounds, Mr. Chainz may have even been more intimidating with his long hair and goatee, not to mention the thick, silver chains dangling from his neck.

"Only if I can watch him kick yours," Mullins returned.

Finally the man Mullins was expecting stepped out of the limo, completely offset by the two individuals flanking him, and confidently and leisurely approached the officers. "Which one of you is Detective James Mullins?"

"That would be me," he answered quickly, extending his hand outward to greet his visitor. "You must be Mr. Walker."

Ethan looked at the detective's hand, dismissed it, and then looked at the other man with Mullins.

"I'm Detective Johnny Mako," he said before being asked, and he didn't bother at an attempt to shake hands.

Looking back at Detective Mullins, Ethan said, "I wasn't aware there would be anyone but you here."

Mullins examined the bodyguards and replied, "Neither was I."

"Shall we?" Ethan motioned toward his place of employment.

Mullins comprehended what his guest was hinting at. "Go inside? Uh … we can't. The investigation is ongoing, and we can't risk contaminating the crime scene."

"Nonsense," the well-dressed gentleman said and made his way to the front door.

The detective was shocked that his order was ignored, and he stood motionless as his company continued on their way.

Mako couldn't resist rubbing Mullins' nose in it. "That's telling him."

"Shut up." The comment served to snap Mullins out of his trance, and the two of them followed behind Ethan and his sentries.

Ball and Chainz reached the building first, positioning themselves directly in front of the officers guarding the entrance, towering over them and showing no signs of backing off. The adrenaline rose within both cops as they were silently challenged, but they cleared a path and permitted the trio access inside after Mullins nodded to stand down. He did not want the situation to get violent.

The detectives silently observed Ethan stroll through the lobby, surveying the area. His bodyguards remained close by and glanced over at them every so often to make sure the officers knew they were watching. Mako elbowed Mullins slightly, urging him to take control, but a hesitant Mullins waved him off. Mako nudged him again and was again met with the same response.

"So, I guess this is what good police work is all about," he whispered. "Thanks for the lesson."

Mullins mouthed a profanity to his impromptu partner and approached Ethan at exactly the same time that Ethan noticed the damage to the elevator.

Before Mullins uttered a word, Ethan faced him. "What happened here?"

"I was hoping you could tell me."

"Why would you think I know what occurred?"

"You're high up on the food chain in this company, correct?"

"I am the personal assistant of Peter Stumpp, yes. I take care of all the tasks my employer deems plebian, but that does not mean I am aware of every instance that occurs in my absence. To assume I am only tells me you're a poor detective."

Fed up with the attitude, Mako unintentionally defended his companion. "Well, let's put it this way—"

Mullins tried to stop him but was unsuccessful.

"There isn't one security camera past the front doors, and from what we gathered when we first arrived on the scene, there aren't any night security guards either."

"Is my employer's security preferences something of major concern?" Ethan smugly interrupted.

Mako hated pompous people and believed he might enjoy this confrontation. "Actually, it is, but that's not all I was going to say. You had a break in, but nothing appears to be taken. There's blood on the thirteenth floor, and no sign of a body or what could have caused the trauma. Your elevator looks as if it were blown apart from the inside out; but yet there isn't any residue left behind from an explosive device, and the brakes are still intact which indicates the elevator didn't fall and get damaged on impact. Not to mention the unidentified individual whose mutilated body was left in the preserve behind this facility, who is a prime suspect in this burglary."

Ethan stared but said nothing.

"Now, I ask you, what do you have in this building worth stealing? What the hell type of security do you have here at night to prevent someone from taking it, not to mention pursuing and murdering the alleged burglar? And furthermore," Mako sensed the two bodyguards becoming agitated at his hostile interrogation and saw them closing in out of the corner of his eye. Grabbing Ethan's forearm, he pulled him closer and issued a warning, "tell your goons to wait outside while the adults are talking before I run them in for obstruction."

Ethan seized the detective by the arm with a vice-like grip. The pain that shot up to his shoulder surprised Mako, but he was careful not to show it. Ball and Chainz moved as bouncers in a club would to eject any undesirables.

Mako drew his pistol, shoved the business end into Mr. Ball's face and pulled the hammer back. "Back up, asshole." Turning to Ethan, he ordered, "Remove your hand before I remove it for you."

Unafraid, Ethan studied the detective's face for a moment before complying.

Mullins had had all he could stand, and he took his associate by the shoulders and led him past the two giant henchmen and toward the front door. Mako, knowing his temper had got the best of him, didn't resist and walked away with his irritated co-worker.

"What the fuck were you thinking?"

"Arrogant son of a bitch pissed me off." He holstered his weapon. "I know I should've—"

"I told you to keep your mouth shut! This is my investigation!" Mullins released his hold once the two of them were outside the building and halfway to the parking lot. "If Lieutenant Grimes hears about this, he'll—"

"You're right. Okay? I admit it. I fucked up. Go back in there and tell them I forgot my meds this morning."

Mullins breathed hard and passed his hand through what little hair was left on his head. "Don't worry about what I tell him. You just better hope you didn't completely fuck this interview up for me!"

"Watch yourself with Walker. He doesn't look like much, but he's got some grip."

"Get out of here, before I change my mind about telling Grimes."

Mako recognized he should quit while he was ahead and went to his car. Unknown to him, as he exited out of the lot, he was being watched by a third party from the shadows across the street.

FIFTEEN

Mulling over the confrontation between Walker and his goons, Mako didn't initially spot the faded blue Chevy Camaro following him down Northern Boulevard, making sure to stay an inconspicuous distance away from the detective's vehicle.

He hooked the cell's earpiece onto his right ear and speed-dialed the desired party, but the call eventually went to voice mail, so he left a message while stopped at a traffic light. "Hey, Jacquie. It's Johnny. I just wanted to make sure the courier delivered the package, and ..."

At that instant, he noticed the Camaro in the rearview mirror, a few car lengths back, after its tires screeched to a halt to prevent from rear-ending another car. Suspicion took over, so when traffic began moving, the detective realized the suspect vehicle was trying to keep a constant distance from him. Mako turned south onto Split Rock Road, and a few seconds later, so did the Camaro. He applied more pressure on the gas pedal to put some space between them, but the Camaro accelerated in order to keep up, ensuring that someone was definitely tailing him. Remembering his call, he said, "Call me. I gotta go," then hung up.

Weaving in and out of traffic, Mako kept steady watch in his rearview for his stalker, and sure enough, a faded blue Chevy swerved into the left lane and into the detective's line of sight. He guessed the driver of the Camaro knew he'd been found out but pursued anyway, and although he didn't know who or why anyone would be following him, Mako was determined to find out.

Driving well above the speed limit, the detective veered randomly through each of the roadway's lanes before making a sharp turn at Cold Spring Road, and then he made a sharp right onto another main road. Cruising down the street, he checked his mirrors and believed he'd lost the Camaro, but the Camaro nearly caused an accident while dangerously changing lanes, trying to keep up. Astonished at the driver's persistence, Mako devised a plan to discover who was so unwavering in his chase and headed towards the Second Precinct. The high divider in the middle of the street would prevent the Camaro from making a U-turn, and Mako would be able to get a glimpse of the driver as he passed.

Putting distance between him and his pursuer, Mako made it to the precinct first, parked, and waited. He waited for nearly twenty minutes, but the Camaro never showed. That was when he felt that paranoia had overridden his better judgment, that no one was following him after all.

The detective stepped into the street to see if the vehicle was stopped farther down the road, but he was unexpectedly yanked back by an unknown assailant.

"Detective Mako! You have to come with me right away!"

Startled, he reached behind him, grabbed the man and pulled him in. "You should never sneak up on—You! You're that photographer from the preserve. What in hell do you think you're doing?"

Jason glanced at the detective's fist clenching his coat. "My name is Brody. Jason Brody. Can I have my jacket back now?" As soon as he was released, Jason reached into his sack and retrieved a leather case.

"What are you giving me?"

"Open it."

Mako unzipped it and found an antique dagger inside. The eight-inch steel blade was dangerously sharp, and opposite the cutting edge was a faded engraving of what appeared to be wolves running through a forest by the light of a full moon. The hilt was in pristine condition, like the rest of the weapon, but the material it was made from was unfamiliar. Running his fingers over the hand-painted surface, he came to a howling wolf's head carved at the end of the knife. "Where did you get this?"

Hoping the detective would relinquish the dagger, Jason answered, "A bunch of lowlifes fencing antique artifacts to the highest bidder. I pretended to be interested and made my way inside their operation. But I think they started to get suspicious, so I got out of there—but not before taking a souvenir."

"You mean evidence," Mako corrected.

"Right, evidence," Jason hesitantly agreed. "Can I have the dagger back, please?"

Closing the case, Mako placed it inside his coat pocket. "Where are they set up?"

Jason didn't take his eyes off the spot where the dagger disappeared. "So, you're interested in looking into this?"

"Did you come down here and hope I wouldn't be?"

"No. I just didn't think it would be this easy."

"What wouldn't be this easy?"

Jason ignored the question posed to him and answered the earlier one. "They're working out of the Marriott in Uniondale."

Even though the detective was apprehensive, he could not pass up the chance to prove he was better than what his peers gave him credit for, so the two men hopped into his car and drove away. Minutes later, they arrived at the Marriott Hotel. "What floor, and how many are there?" he asked, to get the particulars out of the way.

"They're in a suite, and the name to give at the front desk is Williams. I didn't count how many."

"Maybe I should call my partner."

"There's no time." Before the detective could question him further, Jason continued, "I heard one of them say they should clear out and move to another location. For all I know, they're gone already!"

Refusing to let an opportunity slip away, Mako forgot about Bailey for the moment and jumped out of the car, with Jason following closely behind. "You do what I tell you when I tell you. You shouldn't even be here with me, but I don't have time to argue about it."

Jason nodded while fumbling with his bag to get his camera ready to go.

"If things get hairy, you bolt. No ifs, ands, or buts! You get out of there, and don't stop until you make it back to the Second Precinct. This isn't in my jurisdiction, but my report will reflect how this sting began on my patrol. Understand?"

Jason agreed, listening to the instructions the detective rattled off. They entered the hotel lobby, and from across a crowded parking lot, a man in a faded blue Chevy Camaro watched and made an important phone call.

SIXTEEN

Detective Mullins adjusted his sports jacket and his demeanor before entering the lobby of Stumpp Industries to continue his meeting with Ethan Walker. Interrupting the man's hushed dialogue with his bodyguards, he said, "Please forgive my colleague. His mouth works quicker than his brain at times."

"You should keep him on a tighter leash."

"I should have him put down," he muttered under his breath.

Ethan pretended not to have heard the comment. "What was that, Detective?"

Mullins motioned to a couple of chairs near the security booth. "I said maybe we should sit down."

Walking by the company directory, Ethan noticed the police marker, and a closer look revealed dried blood and a few strands of human hair stuck to the bottom edge of the table. He ran his fingers over the stain until some of it rubbed off onto them. Mullins spotted his actions and aggressively snatched Ethan's arm away from the evidence. Ball and Chainz closed in to discipline the gutsy detective.

Eyeing their approach, Mullins went for his gun. "You two better stay where you are if you know what's good for you." Turning his attention back to Ethan, the detective said, "And you shouldn't touch anything in here for the remainder of this interview. Do it again, and we can have this talk at the precinct. Are we clear?"

Ethan nodded and took his seat as his giants moved to the front entryway. Mullins sat down, adjusted his jacket again, and mentally put his opening questions together. An impatient Ethan decided to take the reins. "Why did you ask to see me, Detective?"

A little thrown off by the interviewee's lead, Mullins responded, "You are the personal assistant to Peter Stumpp, the owner of this facility. Am I right?"

"I thought I answered this earlier. Get to the point."

The detective understood why Mako had lost his patience, but Mullins had a lot more experience dealing with difficult personalities. "You're here because of the break-in at this site and the homicide which took place in the preserve behind this building."

"Why do you think the two are related incidents?"

Thinking carefully how to answer without revealing too many pertinent facts to a potential suspect, he said, "Actually, I've recently discovered there are three connected incidents."

"Three?" Ethan sounded surprised.

"Did you know Jennifer Hertz?"

"The name isn't familiar."

"Was she or anyone else with that last name ever employed here?"

"Again, the name doesn't ring a bell. Care to tell me why you're asking?"

"You may have heard about a second, similar murder at the Broadway Mall the other night. Miss Hertz was the victim, and there was some DNA evidence at the scene that corresponded to some of the data we gathered from this building and from the preserve. I'm trying to establish the connection."

Ethan tried to discern exactly what the detective knew, but instead initiated a straightforward approach. "Maybe I could be more helpful if I had some detailed information."

"I can't discuss the specifics, but I can tell you we are close to finding out the identity of the victim in the preserve. It's taking a while since his head was never recovered and his fingertips were chewed off by some type of filthy animal." Mullins paused for a second, noticing a slight but distinctly agitated reaction from his guest. "I'd appreciate a list of all employees working in this building and any background information you have on them. It would greatly facilitate the process."

Ethan reverted to his natural unwavering state. "Why would you need those? The office is closed for two weeks. All the employees were gone as of Friday afternoon."

"And yet someone used a security code to enter the building that night," Mullins leaked a fact he assumed his guest was already privy to. "Now, the code could have been swiped or stolen by an outsider, but some, if not all, parties involved may be connected to this company. I want to shorten the list of potential victims and suspects as quickly as possible."

"I don't have to relinquish anything to you."

"True. You don't have to voluntarily surrender anything," the detective said, shifting his position in the seat, "but you will have to hand them over once I get a court order. What do you suppose your boss will think of that?"

"Mr. Stumpp is not a man you want on your bad side," Ethan said in a tone even more serious than usual.

"Speaking of which, where is your employer?" Mullins blatantly glossed over what could have been perceived as a threat. "Don't you think he would want to be here during a time like this? I tried looking up his contact information, but there is none. That's why I called you. Where is he now and where was he the night in question?"

"Mr. Stumpp is a very private man and wishes never to be disturbed outside of his work environment." Ethan leaned back in his chair. "I handle all issues and relay the information as I am the only one who knows how to contact him. As far as his whereabouts, he is on vacation. Every year during our shutdown he travels to the same destination: his ancestors' hometown of Bedburg, Germany."

"And the other night?" asked the persistent detective.

"I cannot say. I assume he was getting ready for his flight, which took off at five thirty in the morning. If you like, I can get you a copy of his itinerary. I made the arrangements personally."

"You can get me a copy of that along with the copies of the employee files, and I'd also like to see the video feed on the night in question from the entryway camera." Mullins cleared his throat in order to issue a threat of his own: "And I suggest you tell Mr. Stumpp to cut his vacation short. I believe it would be in his best interest to be here during the investigation, and let him know I'll want to speak with him too."

Unwilling to prolong this interview any longer, Ethan rose and straightened his suit. "If there is nothing else, Detective, I'll be on my way to retrieve the items you requested. Allow me a day or two to get it together."

"Call me when you have everything." Mullins motioned to the door. "After you."

Ethan exited the building behind his bodyguards.

The detective was the last to leave, and noticed the extra police presence. Apparently, the two officers initially guarding the building had called for backup to avoid another stare-down from Ethan's men. Once the stretch limousine drove away, disappearing in the distance, he thought, *What are you hiding, Walker?*

Inside the car, Mr. Ball asked, "You still want us to take care of the stray?"

"Not yet. Wait for further instructions." Ethan sniffed the dried blood on his fingertips. "I have his scent, and although slightly faded, it's one I remember. He can't escape me now."

SEVENTEEN

Reaching the suites located on the top floor of the Marriott Hotel, Mako inspected his 9mm and returned it to its holster, satisfied that it was in working order if things turned ugly. They crept down the hallway with Jason in the lead.

"Do you know for certain if you blew your cover when you were here last?"

"Not a hundred percent. Why?"

Outside the room the alleged thieves occupied, Mako positioned himself to one side of the door. "Just wanted to see what my options were concerning a cover story, but since anything I make up may be detected as a lie," he started before knocking loudly, "I might as well use the direct approach."

"What are you doing?"

The detective waved him off. "Open up! This is the police," and pushed his companion to the other side of the door while drawing his gun.

Defeated, Jason said, "Oh, for the love of Pete." Taking out a swipe card and passing it through the key lock, Jason snapped the door open and walked inside.

"What the?" Mako felt idiotic, realizing he'd been set up, but soon anger took over, and he followed the fraud with his gun still in hand. "All right, Brody! What's the meaning of this?"

The detective's answer came in the form of nearly a dozen men armed with high-powered rifles and machine guns aimed in his direction as he entered the living room of the suite. A quick scan revealed that the group was something of a military outfit, judging by the weapons, weapon caches, and various types of surveillance equipment spread around. Mako pointed his pistol at the first soldier he saw, but he realized that if anyone started firing, he wouldn't get out alive.

"Everyone, lower your weapons and settle down," came the command from the back of the room. "There's no need for this to get messy."

Mako looked out of the side of his eye and noticed a weaponless, blond-haired man standing next to Jason. No one obeyed the order.

Nathan spoke again, this time a little more sternly: "At ease, soldiers! Put down your weapons!"

With that, the group complied. Mako did not, but instead targeted the blond-haired man he recognized as their leader. Jason flinched when the barrel of the gun passed him by, and one of the soldiers behind the detective pressed his sidearm against Mako's head in case he was inclined to fire on his commander.

"Who the hell are you people, and what do you want from me?"

Nathan sat on a large cushioned chair, unfazed at the notion of having a gun aimed him. "If you lower your weapon, Detective, and have a seat, all will be explained."

"Will that be before or after your goons put a bullet in me?"

"Please, don't be nervous. Sit down and we'll talk."

"Have your man holster his gun first and walk around in front of me where I can see him."

Nathan signaled in agreement. "It's all right, Bronson. Do as he said."

Tentatively, Mark Bronson obeyed. The detective holstered his gun too and cautiously sat on a couch across from his host. Mako's angry eyes drifted toward the photographer, who couldn't look directly at him, and then they landed back on the blond-haired man.

"I can guess how you know me." He glared at Jason again. "But what do you want? Why trick me to get me here instead of simply phoning me at the precinct?"

"First, let me introduce myself. My name is Nathan Henry Williams. It wasn't my idea to bring you here under false pretenses, but my associate thought you would take him more seriously if he lied to you rather than told you the truth." He dismissed his troops with a hand wave.

"The truth about what?"

Bronson returned with a tray of drinks and placed it on the table between the two men. Nathan sipped from one of the glasses and gestured toward the other. "Care for a refreshment?"

"No, thanks. Let's just get to why I'm here."

Nathan sank into the cushions of the chair and crossed his legs. "My apologies for making you wait. I know you must be a busy man. Places to go. People to see. Murders to solve."

"What do you know about the murders?"

"The reason you're here is so I can find out what *you* know about them." Nathan took another sip. "You see, I know a great deal more about what's going on than you ever could; but in order for me to help you, I need to know what you know."

"You're going to help me?" the detective asked. "*You're* going to help *me*?" Mako said again with a slight chuckle. "What exactly are you going to help me with, Mr. Williams?"

Turning to Jason, Nathan snapped his fingers and motioned to the desk behind them. "Fetch me the folder over there, Brody." Jason followed orders, and soon Nathan had a file in his hand. "In this folder, Detective, is information dating back hundreds of years. I am the fifth generation charged with guarding this lore and doing whatever I deem necessary to stop the creature responsible for the situation you have stumbled upon. I know you are not a homicide detective, but I assume you feel the need to demonstrate that you have what it takes to be one; otherwise, pursuing this matter would be a wasted exercise.

"I was once like you, except I desperately needed the approval of my father. I was determined to show him how able I was to follow in his footsteps, but as my father said to me, 'You cannot show what you are capable of until you possess all the knowledge of what you are trying to accomplish.'"

Mako skeptically raised one eyebrow. "Nice story, but can we fast-forward to the part where he smacks your ass, sends you to bed, and you tell me what the fuck you're talking about?"

"Come now, there is no need for profanity. We're both intelligent enough to speak without resorting to such language."

"You're right. I'm sorry. But seriously, can we cut the shit and you just tell me what in the hell you want from me?"

Squinting in annoyance at him, Nathan said, "I see you're a difficult man." Nathan tossed the folder over to the detective. "The information you are about to read must be viewed with an open mind. You will tell yourself none of it can be true; and yet, I'm going to tell you that it is." Mako read as his host spoke. "What you are dealing with is not human. It is, quite literally, a wolf in sheep's clothing. This monster is personally responsible for possibly tens of thousands of deaths throughout the ages. Not all of his victims were treated the same way. Some were brutalized more than others."

The detective observed a tear escape Jason's eye while Jason ground his teeth to fight back any other sign of emotion.

"He has created others to do his bidding, but I hold him responsible for the blood spilt by their hands. He is preparing for war—a war to be waged against humankind and ... others—so that his may be the dominant race. He has been in hiding for many years now; but I believe he was the murderer in the Muttontown Preserve, and I intend to rid the world of his taint."

Mako slowly closed the folder, placed it on the table beside the tray of drinks, sat back in his seat, and looked into Nathan's eyes. He could tell Nathan fully believed everything he said—the tone of his voice bore such conviction that there was no other truth for him. To argue any of this would be completely pointless, but Mako was used to fighting losing battles. "You mean to tell me a centuries-old man—excuse me, wolf—is responsible for these murders?"

"Only one murder directly—so far. And I told you to have an open mind, Detective."

"What about the homicide at the Broadway Mall?"

"I believe that was done by one of his minions, and a fairly new one at that; but as I said, I still hold him responsible."

Mako tried a different approach. "Seriously, I know you accept this as the truth, but a humanoid wolf—werewolf, if I may—is a stretch of the imagination. These things are the stuff of legends and movies—monsters meant to frighten children. How can you expect me to buy what you're selling?"

Nathan studied Mako's face. "As you can guess, I would never normally involve the authorities in something like this. My group and I choose to handle these matters on our own, so I thank you for not laughing and suggesting I belong in a mental institution."

"It's not like the thought hadn't crossed my mind."

Realizing he'd complimented the detective too soon, Nathan proceeded anyway, "This time, however, the circumstances are more grim than usual. If this creature is behind these murders, then it is much too dangerous to let him roam free any longer. Pooling our resources might be our only hope of stopping him before more blood stains your streets."

"I can't even believe I'm entertaining this, but I appreciate what you're saying, so I'll give you a chance to prove that what you're telling me is true."

"How?"

"Show me one."

"How would you like me to do that?"

Mako surveyed the room and pointed out the large stash of military paraphernalia. "You obviously hunt these things. Take me with you, and make me a believer."

Nathan negatively shook his head and hand simultaneously. "You would only get in the way. The Lunar Guardians have been doing this for years. An outsider might disrupt the way we conduct our operations, and one of mine could be killed. I won't risk that."

"The Lunar Guardians? That's what you call yourselves? You're serious?"

"Mock what you don't understand, Detective. But there's more history to this organization than you know, and you have not earned the privilege to have it disclosed to you." Nathan slid the folder toward his guest. "You may take this with you. It's a brief synopsis of some of the information we've gathered for your review, should you reconsider my proposal."

Retrieving the file, Mako was escorted to the front door of the hotel suite. Before taking his leave, he asked, "You're just going to give this to me without asking for anything in return? I thought you wanted to pool our resources?"

"We'll be in touch." Nathan graciously opened the door.

"Wait a minute. You let this guy go out with you," he said, gesturing at Jason, "but an experienced officer you turn your back on."

"There is more to Mr. Brody than you know, Detective. He has been trained by my family to be one of the best snipers in the world," said Nathan, paying Jason a rare compliment. "However, he seldom gets up enough courage to join us on a hunt," he said, following with the insult to specify that the praise was more for his family's name than it was for Jason.

Once back in the hallway, one more question crossed the detective's mind. "One last thing, Williams. Would you mind telling me the name of the werewolf that's plagued the earth for centuries and has now come to my city?"

Staring into Mako's eyes, Nathan said, "The lycanthrope we're hunting is Peter Stubbe, the Werewolf of Bedburg."

EIGHTEEN

The countryside of Bedburg, Germany, appeared quiet and peaceful under the bright midday sky. The farmhouse sat on acres upon acres of land, with not a neighboring home in sight, and the lush green grass extended over every inch of the wealthy farmer's property. The poorer citizens of the community resented his success, which labeled him an outsider; but it was his obsession that caused him to be regarded as evil incarnate.

The farmer was a practitioner of black magic. Conjuring spells and praying to devils, the man alienated himself from most everyone. Only his wife and niece stayed incestuously close to him, and some say they participated in foul rituals like the one going on within the abandoned horse stable even now. Sitting half-naked, legs crossed, on the floor, in the center of an upside-down pentagram that was scrawled in the dirt and meant for summoning demons, with a plain, metal bucket lying at arm's distance with blood sloshing around inside, the man uttered barely audible chants and poured the crimson liquid over his body, exhilarated by it.

An unexpected wind blew through the stable, and the bloodied, half-naked farmer looked out into the fields. Dark, ominous clouds rolled over the once peaceful skies, and the symbol on the floor began to change. Outside, the storm gained in strength, and the wind howled loudly as it shook the wooden building. Abruptly, the farmer was bathed in darkness, but excitement turned to fear as a sharp pain in his abdomen forced him to double over. He jumped when the doors were pounded upon as if something was trying to break them down. Looking back at the floor, the pentagram fully transformed into a more familiar shape: a snarling wolf's head. The doors burst open, allowing the howling wind entry, and the farmer screamed.

Pushing past the pain, he darted out of the stable and ran through the dimly lit woods. He sensed a harmful presence; he weaved in and out of the trees but dared not climb them for fear of being trapped in their branches. Accompanied by the sound of his own heavy breathing, and of weighty footsteps quickly gaining ground, he wished to undo the malevolence he'd wittingly unleashed—but it was too late.

Coming to rest by a nearby tree, he held himself up with one arm and slumped forward, trying to catch his breath. His muscles cramped and his lungs were not able to fill themselves with oxygen fast enough, but his heart raced with an odd sense of anticipation. Glancing over his shoulder, he saw a set of massive jaws about to clamp onto him, and then all went black.

In the darkness, screams of pain, torment, and death were like music to his ears. His own pain vanished, and the farmer started mutilating his own flesh, ripping pieces away, as if stripping himself of his humanity, until finally peeling his face off to reveal another visage behind it. Fingers turned to claws, flesh turned to fur, and where once stood a bloodied farmer, there stood a giant wolf-like creature that howled into the night.

Howling shifted into the sound of a ringing phone, and a dreaming man was awakened from his slumber. Two gray eyes opened, unfazed by the dreadful images, and he reached for the satellite phone lying on his bedside table. After the caller explained his late night disturbance, the man responded, "Yes,

Ethan, I understand. Ready my jet." There was a slight pause in his rejoinder. "Relax. I'll be there shortly. We can't erase what's been done, but remember what Maria Robinson said: 'Nobody can go back and start a new beginning, but anyone can start today and make a new ending.' We will end this our way and emerge triumphant, while all who oppose us will suffer greatly."

Ending the call without giving a second thought to any statement the caller might choose to add, he closed his eyes again. A smile formed on his lips as he drifted back to sleep and resumed his glorious nightmare.

Ethan Walker slammed the receiver of his cordless phone back onto its base and ran his fingers through his short, silver-colored hair, replaying the brief conversation in his mind. With every silent syllable, his agitation grew. "Maria Robinson," he muttered under his breath. "Maria Robinson," he mumbled again. Leaving the comfort of his leather executive's chair, he moved around to the front of his desk and thought for a moment before walking over to the portraits hanging on the wall, studying each of the faces. "Who the hell is Maria Robinson anyway?" he said out loud, as if speaking to those inhabiting the frames. "He thinks just because he has the power of the Heart protecting him, he can make all the rules." Ethan grabbed his jacket and headed toward the office door. Flicking the light switch off, he whispered loudly, "Pompous ass is going to get the rest of us killed."

Sara Ferguson, Ethan's receptionist, vigorously typed on her computer's keyboard but stopped once her boss emerged. "Leaving for the day, Mr. Walker?"

"Yes, Sara," he said. "I suppose you'll be off soon as well?"

She checked the time. "Yes, sir. It's almost sundown."

"Before you go, please inform Ball and Chainz to feed our guest, and have Mr. Stumpp's jet ready for immediate departure."

"Immediate, sir?" she asked, just to be clear.

Ethan's expression showed a certain amount of disappointment when he responded, "Yes, Sara. Mr. Stumpp is coming home."

NINETEEN

"Tense" did not begin to describe the scene at the Marriott Hotel as Mako headed for the elevator and a frustrated Jason had words with the man who'd sent Mako away.

"I think you're wrong for letting him go, Nathan."

Unaccustomed to criticism from those he perceived as beneath him, the Guardians' commander kept his back toward Jason but inclined his head slightly in his colleague's direction, holding back enough to show that he didn't warrant his full attention. "I don't recall asking for your opinion," he said. Doing an about-face from the hotel suite's entrance, he went into the living area, brushing past Jason in the process.

"I don't see why you couldn't take him on a hunt. You'll be going out tonight, and you could've kept him a safe distance away."

Lifting his drink from the coffee table and bringing it over to his desk, Nathan shuffled through some paperwork. "You're only angry because your 'one hope for mankind' isn't what you'd thought he'd be. Detective Mako is too difficult a man to trust with my business. He doesn't like to follow orders, and his information is probably nothing more than we know already. His assistance will not be necessary."

"Look at me when you talk to me!"

Shocked at Jason's outburst, Nathan turned away from his papers and locked eyes with him. Jason's raised tone of voice alerted Nathan's men, and they rushed into the room, ready to

109

defend their leader; but Nathan signaled them to keep back until he could further assess the situation.

Jason continued, "I know what this is really about. You said it yourself when you told Mako that he reminds you of yourself. You're intimidated by him. You don't want him around in case he makes you look bad in front of your men."

Nathan sighed deeply. "What could I possibly be intimidated by? He's crude, obnoxious, somewhat out of shape, and he's tired. You can see it in his eyes. How could he possibly make me look bad?"

"You're afraid he'll catch Stubbe before you do."

Nathan remained silent, and then, shifting his eyes from Jason's, he waved his hand in the air to dismiss the notion. "Please. Even if he did find Stubbe, he'd be killed almost instantly. Mako doesn't know what he's dealing with."

"And that's why you don't want to show him any more than you have to! Because the truth will only strengthen his resolve!" Jason refused to give him a leg to stand on.

Nathan calmly slid into the chair behind his desk, his mind working feverishly to come up with an answer for his combative colleague. And he almost smiled as it rolled off his tongue: "If you're so concerned about Detective Mako knowing the truth, why don't you start by telling him about you? The real you and not this fake persona you've adopted. Tell him that if it weren't for my great-great-grandfather taking you in, you'd still be like some savage living in the wild."

His rage growing, Jason replied through gritted teeth, "You always thought you were so much better than me—than everyone. And yes, if it weren't for your family, I don't know where I'd be right now; but don't think for a second that I didn't treat your ancestor with the respect he deserved. It's a shame the character traits that earned him such admiration weren't passed on to you!"

Nathan slammed his hand on the table in front of him, scattering some of the paperwork onto the floor. The disgust for the man standing before him seethed from every pore in his body. "This meeting is over! My decision is final, and you are not welcome here any longer! Go back to that hovel you call home, and leave me to my work!"

Bronson, Nathan's second, moved swiftly across the floor until he was standing next to the photographer. He placed an arm on Jason's shoulder, giving him an unspoken warning of what would happen should the confrontation escalate.

Nathan was aware that the situation could become ugly, and he regained his composure. "Remember one thing, Brody. Our alliance is only because I, too, show respect for my family's lineage, even if I only know them through stories passed down from one generation to the next. Tread carefully, for you can be disposed of just as easily as the monsters we pursue."

Jason stared at Bronson's hand until he removed it, and then he retrieved his knapsack next to the couch, slinging it onto his vacant shoulder. Looking back, he said grimly, "Since you're so obsessed over who I really am, Nathan, you shouldn't forget what I can do to you if you push me too far."

An uneasy silence filled the room, and Bronson, along with two others, escorted Jason to the door. Nathan didn't leave his position from behind the desk, but he followed their every movement until his visitor was shown the exit and the hotel suite was locked behind him.

In the hallway, Jason's hands shook nervously. He did not like confrontation, and the thought of what could happen if he was provoked frightened him. A war with Nathan's Guardians would be long and bloody, and even Jason wasn't sure what the outcome would be. He looked in his bag to find something to calm his nerves, and his searching became more frantic as he realized an important item was missing. He thrashed wildly through his belongings, and when it didn't turn up, he threw the bag to the floor and fumbled through his jacket pockets. Then he remembered where it was. *Mako,* he thought, and made a beeline for the lobby.

Outside the hotel, Mako noticed the fading sunlight. Still trying to digest all of the information he'd been given, not sure if he should believe it or write it off to bad storytelling, he'd just stepped off the curb of the parking lot when a black limousine pulled up, nearly running over his foot. He jumped back out of harm's way and heatedly smacked the rooftop.

The tinted rear window was rolled halfway down, and a bald gentleman dressed in a black suit with a white button-down shirt and thin black tie leaned forward and said, "My apologies, Mr. Mako. My driver should pay more attention to the road."

Confused, he asked, "Do I know you?"

"No, but I belong to a group that is very interested in your caseload, Detective."

"What's so interesting about it?"

The man paused, his eyes blinking rapidly. "My partners and I believe we can shed some light on why the boy was killed near the Stumpp building."

Mako took some time to surreptitiously look in the limo. It was pitch black, and there didn't seem to be anyone else inside. But Mako was positive he heard breathing from within—it was low and rough and definitely not coming from the bald man. The detective decided to see what he could uncover. "Okay, since everyone seems to be so helpful today, what can you tell me that I don't already know?"

The man wavered again, and this time his eyelids fluttered more noticeably as his eyeballs rolled back into his head. Mako wondered if this was an epileptic seizure of some kind, but just as soon as it began, the spasm was finished. "The victim, Robert Mane, worked for us. He was in that building to take back what was stolen by Peter Stumpp."

The detective mentally noted everything the stranger said. "Why are you telling me this? You've just incriminated yourself in a conspiracy to burglarize Stumpp Industries which led to a young man's death. These charges could get you thrown in jail and ensure that you never get your stolen item back."

Another attack plagued the man for a few seconds, and then he said, "It's your word against ours, and according to our lawyers we've never even met. At least that's what their stance will be. Besides, we have enough money to tie up any motion you might set in place for more years than you have left on this earth, Mr. Mako."

"So, what's your game here?"

The man stammered and then replied, "We only want what's ours. We don't desire any more bloodshed, or complications. The quicker you get to the bottom of this, the better for all parties involved, including that of Mr. Williams' group."

Mako tried to hold back the stunned expression building on his face. *How did they know who I was meeting with?* he thought. But he only said, "And who might that be?"

The bald man smiled. "I know you can't reveal your sources, but believe me, we know a tremendous amount about you and what you do. Robert Mane wasn't the only person on our payroll.

We have eyes and ears everywhere. You may even know some of them."

"All right. I've had enough of the cryptic bullshit. You want to tell me what in hell you're getting at?"

The limo's rear window opened completely, and the man motioned for the detective to come closer. "Come here," he said, leaving Mako no doubt as to what he wanted. "I'll give you what's coming to you."

Cautious about what the man had to offer, yet anxious to get this meeting over with, Mako edged closer to the limo. At that moment, Jason briskly exited the hotel lobby and saw the detective approach the automobile. His eyes widened with fear as the bald man came into view, and again, Jason rifled through his knapsack in search of something important. Once his fingers gripped the handle, he shouted out loud, "No! Get away from the car!"

Startled, Mako stopped short, whipped his head around, and spotted Jason charging the car, pulling an object from his bag. Instinctively, the detective went for his gun, but Jason got his item out first. To Mako's surprise, it was a flashlight. Relieved to have hesitated on his draw, Mako set the pistol back in its holster. Jason aimed the flashlight into the car window, shining it around the compartment; Mako found this strange, but it gave him a chance to investigate his previous hunch. To his disappointment, there was nothing inside but the bald man and a blank, manila folder on the seat opposite him.

The man shielded his eyes as Jason flashed the light into them. "Ah, young Mr. Brody. That *is* what you're calling yourself these days, isn't it? How ... delightful to see you again."

"Get away from him, Harris!"

Harris reached for the folder and held it out the window. "Here you go, Detective. I believe this will help you locate the object in question."

"Don't believe his lies!" Jason told Mako, making a conscious effort to keep his distance from the car.

Taking the folder, Mako backed away to Jason's side. "I'll decide what to believe. And put that thing away before you make an even bigger ass of yourself than you already have."

Harris tapped his door, and the limo pulled away from the curb. "Good day, Detective."

Already heading in the opposite direction, Mako gazed back at the limo and felt a sudden madness come over him: he could have sworn a pair of glowing red eyes in the back seat were staring at him through the darkness. Once the car window was fully shut, and the tinted glass prevented any further spying, the baffled detective dismissed what he thought he'd seen as merely an illusion from lack of sleep. He focused his attention back on Jason. "What is your malfunction, and what's with the flashlight?"

"There's more going on here than you know. I wish I could make you understand, but there isn't enough time."

"Try. And why don't you start with who you really are."

Jason put the flashlight away and slung the backpack over his shoulder. "That's an even longer story. The only thing I can tell you—and I know you'll think I'm crazy—is that the best defense against Harris' group is light."

"You're right. I think you're certifiable."

Jason moved to face the detective, halted, and stuck out his hand. "My knife. Can I have it back, please? My … father … gave it to me."

Mako had completely forgotten about it and reached into his jacket pocket to get it. "Here. I don't need a reminder of how you abused my trust." He gestured to his car. "This is against my better judgment, but do you want a ride back?"

"No, thanks. I'll call a cab," he said, tucking the knife away in his backpack.

"Best idea I heard all day."

"Detective," he called out before Mako got too far.

"What is it now, Brody?"

"Stay by your phone. Nathan may not want to cooperate, but I *will* make you a believer."

"How?"

"Just wait for my call."

"Great." He watched Jason walk away, already on his cellphone to get a ride. Then the exhausted detective placed the new folder with the one given to him earlier, shaking his head in disgust. "I need to get some fuckin' sleep."

"Werewolves; Lunar Guardians; strange, bald Harris; an antique knife; a pair of glowing red eyes, maybe; a centuries-old serial killer," Mako recited his baffling list of clues and suspects. "I hope Jacquie's making out better than I am."

TWENTY

Returning to his apartment, Mako placed the two folders on the kitchen table, removed his jacket, and kicked off his shoes. Gently placing his cell on top of the folders, he then walked over to the cabinet to get food for the dogs, but he spied a yellow post-it note hanging from their dry food box:

I already fed my babies. All you have to do is take care of your evil cat. The little bastard scratched me again today. See you in the morning. Wear those cute, black boxer briefs I love so much! Muahhh! ~Rikki

Mako crumpled the letter, threw it away, and found the cat treats, shaking the container to get Booger's attention. Before the last treat stopped rattling, a familiar purr was heard. Dropping a few of the feline delicacies onto the floor, he stroked the cat's back and said, "Good boy. Don't take any of Rikki's shit."

The tired police detective headed for his comfortable couch, flopped into its cushions, lifted his feet up, and used the remote control to power on the television. Unfortunately, no sooner did he settle into a relaxed position than his cellphone rang. He debated letting the call go to voice mail, but with everything that had happened to him that day, he guessed it was probably a call he wouldn't want to miss. Letting out a grunt, he got up to answer it. "Mako here."

"Is that how you answer the phone?"

Instantly recognizing the voice, he said, "How are you, Jacquie? What can I do for you?"

"Are you being a smart-ass?" she asked, not surprised that he ignored her initial question. "Didn't you ask me to update you on those samples you sent?"

"Yes, I did. I apologize for sounding sarcastic. It's been a really crazy day. What'd you find out?" A tiny beep signaled another call coming in. "Hold on a sec, Jacquie." He clicked over. "Hello."

"Mako, you bastard!"

"I know plenty of people feel the way you do, but which one are you?"

"It's Samms! You stole my samples!"

Knowing exactly what the investigator was talking about, Mako still answered, "What are you talking about?"

"Don't play dumb with me!"

"Wait a minute. All I got from you was what we agreed on."

"Yeah, about that. I haven't heard from Mary Ann after we had lunch!"

"Is that what the hostility is really about, Samms? Hold on." Mako clicked back to Jacquie.

"It's about time," she said, hating to be left on hold.

"Give me another minute. I have to defuse a potentially bad situation."

"But—" she attempted to keep his attention, but the call had already switched.

"Samms, buddy," he said, trying to placate the jilted man, "tell me what's bothering you."

A sigh was followed by muted anger. "I can't figure out why you did it, but you were the only one close enough to take my samples: first at the crime scene near the Broadway Mall, and then in my office. It had to be you."

Dodging the accusation, he said, "Why would I want to steal anything from you? I don't know the first thing about what you do. What's the real problem here?"

Samms ranted, "I take four samples of every bit of evidence I find. Three to test, and a spare set as a control. Only this time my spares have gone missing, and Mary Ann hasn't called. You think she hates me?"

"Why would she hate you?" Mako kept the conversation as far away from his thievery as possible. "As a matter of fact, I'm talking to her right now, and she's wondering why you haven't called her."

"Really?" The heartbroken investigator seemed to have forgotten his stolen property.

"Yeah, but don't let me keep her waiting. She might get pissed at both of us."

"You're right. I'll let you go," Samms said with hope in his voice. "Should I call her now?"

"No. Don't do that. It'll seem too planned, and it might ruin your chances. I'll have her call you tomorrow," Mako said, guessing he'd have time to convince Mary Ann in the morning.

Samms' smile almost burst through the receiver. "You're okay with me, Mako. Still …"

Uh-oh, thought Mako.

"I should probably go to Grimes about the missing samples," Samms continued. "Just so he knows somebody in your precinct may not be on the up-and-up."

"Don't do that either!" Mako blurted out, perhaps a little too excitedly. "I mean, Grimes is not the best person to tell because he'll put the whole county on lockdown."

"Yeah, you're probably right. Let me take another look around here. Maybe I just misplaced them. You'd better get back to Mary Ann."

"Right, I'll talk to you later." He ended one conversation, and swapped the other. "Jacquie? Sorry to keep you on hold for so long."

"It's still me, Mako," said Samms.

Mako's mind went blank. "Uh …"

"You're not talking to her, are you?"

"Uh, her middle name is Jacquie?"

"Don't treat me like I'm stupid! I've got a degree from M.I.T., dammit! I'm smarter than you on your best day! I bet you're lying about the samples too!"

"Nope. Look around some more. You'll probably find them."

"Well, I think I'll mention it to the lieutenant anyway, and we'll see if you've got anything to hide."

"Do what you gotta do." The detective had had enough threats for one day. "Okay, gotta go."

"Mako, you son of a—"

Clicking back to his previous conversation and leaving the rest of what was about to be said somewhere in digital limbo, Mako asked more cautiously this time, "Jacquie? Hello?" There was no answer, but as he was about to hang up, an alert told him a voice mail was left. "Ah, shit," he sighed, knowing this wouldn't be good.

"You're unbelievable," began the message. Jacquie was way too heated for a proper hello. "You ask me for a favor, and you keep me on hold? That pretty much sums up what our relationship was. You never put me ahead of anyone, and you still don't! All I had to tell you was that I was running the samples again because the first batch appeared contaminated. Was it too much to spare five minutes? For that, I may scrap the next batch of results too and let you fend for yourself. I'm sure you'll have some time for me then, won't you? You're such an asshole sometimes!" Voice mail disconnected after that.

He knew she was really angry. Jacquie didn't like to curse, and from the tone of that message, Mako knew he was going to get an earful the next time they spoke. Figuring he might as well take advantage of some peace, he grabbed the folders off the table, lay back on the couch, and skimmed through the information.

Chip rested on the floor next to him, and Mako draped a hand over the sofa to brush his thick, black fur. Bruno got comfortable on the reclining chair off to the right. Booger climbed onto the back of the couch and stretched out; his purring calmed Mako, helping him fall asleep.

His last thought before losing consciousness was that dealing with a killer would be easier than facing the wrath of Jacquie Dale.

TWENTY-ONE

The black Hummer rolled to the designated position around half past midnight, and Nathan was the first man out of the vehicle to survey the area. Bronson and one other went to work. Nathan didn't have to say a word: he and his team had been doing this a long time, and it was almost second nature to them.

The full moon hung high in the night sky, lighting up the parking lot of the Broadway Mall where Jenny Hertz had lost her life. Nathan had never been to New York before, much less Nassau County, Long Island, but his unfamiliarity with the surroundings didn't lessen his confidence that he would catch his prey. As Bronson and the other soldier opened the back, fold-down door of the Hummer and pulled out a large, heavy caliber Gatling gun, bolted to a sliding metal plate, Nathan knew the other two teams were also getting ready for the night's activities in the exact locations chosen for them. Together, the teams formed a triangular pattern so the three could combine forces if needed.

The soldier took position behind the heavy gun mounted to their automobile while Bronson stood silently next to his commanding officer, rifle resting on his shoulder, waiting for instructions. Nathan saw a tiny glimmer on a rooftop of one of the taller buildings in the vicinity and snapped his fingers to notify his second-in-command. Without delay, Bronson radioed the second team—which was positioned there—to alert them that the moonlight was reflecting off their gun's scope. Nathan hated sloppy preparations, and if *he* saw the reflection, the monster they were hunting could also spot the trap. Feeling he'd noticed it in time to correct the situation, he ejected the clip from his sidearm, noted the full load of silver bullets, and snapped it back in. There was nothing more to do now except set out the bait and wait.

The two-man sniper team parked next to the tallest building in the neighborhood; but the streetlights shone too brightly for proper concealment, so they shot them out with silenced pistols. Using knotted ropes attached to grappling hooks, the men scrambled up to the roof in record time, understanding their commander wouldn't accept anything but the best. A third rope tied to two duffle bags was rapidly hoisted upward until a black-gloved hand reached over the ledge and grabbed them. The snipers moved swiftly and silently to the edge of the building overlooking the target area. Setting their bags beside them, they unzipped them in unison. After assembling their large, high-powered rifles inside in just under thirty seconds, they were in position and waiting for their mark to show its face.

Sniper One flipped open the lens cap on his scope to adjust its magnification, not realizing as he did so that his gun moved into a moonlit area. Before he was done, he received Bronson's radioed order to get back under the cover of night. He immediately shut the cap, shifted to avoid exposing himself again, and muttered to his partner, "How do they expect me to get a clear shot if I can't see what I'm shooting at?"

Sniper Two shrugged. "Relax. You know how careful Williams is."

"I don't know what he's so worried about. It's dead out here. No one would have spotted us in that split second."

As the sniper team got back into position, a lone figure, shrouded in darkness on the far end of the rooftop, watched and waited for his time to act.

While rummaging through the garbage, looking for food, the sound of clacking heels on hard concrete rang loudly in the werewolf's ears. Lifting its nose, it inhaled deeply, and a sweet smelling perfume filled its nostrils. Even though the noise and aroma were coming from at least ten blocks away, it was as if she was only ten feet away. Drooling, the werewolf tossed the empty garbage can aside and lumbered toward its next meal.

The streets were uncharacteristically abandoned since most were afraid to be out this late so soon after the murder at the mall; the werewolf had no trouble wandering the locale without persecution. Continuing to sniff the air, it followed the potent scent, and then, as instinct kicked in, the werewolf's pace quickened. Darting through the back alley of a store, it unintentionally knocked a few metal trash cans over as its massive body brushed up against them, and the loud clang the containers made against the pavement startled it, causing it to stop and investigate. Satisfied that there was nothing to be alarmed about, it snorted at the mess.

Ducking through a second alley, it stopped at the end, knowing its prey was just around the bend—even though it couldn't see her. The footsteps pounded loudly in its ears, and the fragrance overpowered its sense of smell. Saliva dripped faster from the corners of its mouth, and the stray could hardly contain its excitement. Yet, as with all predatory animals, it did not act rashly. It peeked from behind cover and investigated until it spotted its quarry—tall and slender with a tan trench coat flowing behind her, she had her back to the werewolf. Intuition told the werewolf that it was time to strike, and it crept out of hiding, onto open ground, with thoughts of murder running through its mind.

Nathan was not recognized for his patience, but during a hunt, he tolerated much. Some believed it was because he was content ridding the world of a deadly menace; others thought it was because he'd adopted the nature of the beasts he sought to exterminate. According to his watch, it was a little after 2:00 a.m., and there was no sign of his target. Watching the woman walk through the street, he did nothing to warn her of the impending danger.

Suddenly, the crash of what could only be garbage cans slamming against concrete echoed through the otherwise quiet night. Concluding that the force was too strong for a smaller animal to muster, Nathan raised an arm at a right angle and curled his fingers into a fist.

Bronson took a knee on the driver's side of the Hummer, rested the stock of his rifle against his shoulder, and aimed into the target area. He, too, saw the woman as she flinched from the unexpected noise.

Lowering his arm, Nathan put the radio to his mouth and whispered, "Sniper Team, we have a green light. Keep your eyes open and shoot on sight."

The soldier sitting behind the modified Gatling gun looked for orders from his commander, and Nathan used his pointer and middle finger on one hand to point at his own eyes, then at the target area, indicating where the gunner should look for their mark. Removing his pistol from its holster, Nathan prepared for war.

His unit covered a fifteen-block region, and about six blocks away from his team, he spotted a large, clawed foot edging out from behind a closed clothing shop. It would not be long now.

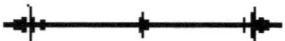

On the rooftop occupied by the sniper team, the solitary figure, standing in a dark corner opposite the soldiers, disrobed, neatly folded his suit jacket, and placed it into an open briefcase at his feet with the rest of his clothes. He was left totally naked. He was confident he'd taken all the necessary precautions to remain undetected, but part of what made him so effective was the fact that he rarely underestimated his opponents.

Without warning, the clang of garbage cans toppling onto the street informed him the werewolf he was searching for was nearby. He closed his eyes, lifted his head, and breathed deeply. A smirk formed on his lips as he rotated his neck in a semicircle. Opening his eyes, Ethan Walker focused on the men he must eliminate before his true objective could be achieved. Over their radio he heard Nathan's instructions: "Sniper Team, we have a green light. Keep your eyes open and shoot on sight."

Ethan could not allow that to happen. As he skulked toward the unwitting soldiers, a startling transformation began to take place. His face quivered as canine teeth turned into fangs too long for his mouth to contain—until his muzzle grew large enough to accommodate them. Ears elongated into funnel-like openings, and a wave of sound poured into them. His eyes immediately amplified the subtle light surrounding him—different spectrums, denied to him when he was in human form, now registered against his retinas. His neatly groomed, silver-colored hair grew longer and spread all over his body, while his toenails and fingernails lengthened to dagger-like extensions on each digit. Bones broke, realigned, grew larger, and re-formed as muscles stretched to abnormal proportions and became like steel cables. He endured what would be agony for any normal man, but he never even missed a step along the way. When the change was complete, Ethan Walker was unrecognizable inside the man-monster that had taken his place.

The two snipers lay quietly on the ground, waiting for the perfect opportunity to execute their mission, but a low growl disturbed their concentration.

Moving faster than the human eye could detect, Ethan used one of his finger-knives to separate Sniper Two's head from his body. The soldier didn't have time to react and was dead before ever glimpsing his attacker. Sniper One managed to roll onto his back to face his partner's killer, veering his massive rifle toward Ethan, but Ethan's enormous, clawed hand caught the rifle mid-swing. As a werewolf, Ethan's strength was far superior to even the strongest soldier, and he held the gun effortlessly at bay. He raised his free hand above his head, and he drove it down into the sniper's chest. So much force was put behind the blow that Ethan's hand tore a hole completely through the soldier's body, embedding his claws into the hard surface of the roof; the soldier's still-beating heart was in his palm. The second sniper's suffering was swift, but his death did not go unnoticed.

Peering over the ledge, Ethan saw a woman on the street below staring up. He realized the last shriek of the soldier must have alerted her; but he was not worried. She would soon have her own troubles. Two blocks away, behind her, was the reason why Ethan had come—the stray.

The stray, an impressive specimen in its own right, also stopped momentarily when it heard the sniper's death cry. Its dark brown fur rippled down its muscular back, and it hesitated. Instinctively feeling that all wasn't right, it shifted its large brown eyes to each side, searching for some form of danger; however, the need to feed was strong, and it could not ignore its animal nature.

Darting out of the alleyway, the werewolf ran on all fours as considerable muscles propelled it forward at tremendous speed. Slobber spilling out of its mouth was carried on the wind. Although she tried, the woman had no chance of escape, and her faint whimpering only served to excite the stray. Almost on its victim's heels, it secured a good grip on the roadway and launched itself skyward.

The woman crossed her arms, inserting both hands inside her trench coat, and pulled out two six-shot revolvers. To the stray's surprise, she spun around and rolled onto her back in one graceful motion, evading its killing blow as it sailed overhead. As she fell, she fired, squeezing each trigger in succession. Fear spoiled her aim, but she wounded the creature with a silver bullet to the shoulder.

Landing awkwardly, the stray fell onto its side and held its injured arm with its other hand. Werewolves have an incredibly high tolerance for pain. Nearly as soon as it felt the round pierce its flesh, the sting was gone; and seconds after, the slug was pushed out of its body. Standing at full height on its hind legs, the stray lifted its arms high and roared angrily, towering over the defenseless woman. Both emptied guns were at her sides. Its next blow would shatter her.

From the moment the stray set foot on the prearranged battlefield, Nathan focused on its every move and watched it stalk the bait. A sense of pride overcame him, observing his subordinate execute a backward roll to avoid otherwise certain death, and he waited for the werewolf to fall from a silenced silver bullet shot from one of his sniper's guns. Yet, the stray did not fall, and Nathan wondered why. Now he watched as one of his own was about to be reduced to a bloody pulp on the street in front of him.

Suddenly, his mind flashed back to a few moments before the attack, remembering how the female soldier stopped to stare up at the rooftop where his snipers were stationed. He had questioned why she would potentially give up their position, but once the stray rushed her, he'd quickly dismissed the incident. Now Nathan determined he shouldn't have disregarded her actions. Calling to his second, "Can you take the shot?"

Bronson knew the powerful arms of the werewolf were about to slam down on his fellow Guardian and replied with great regret, "Negative. The target is out of range."

Nathan immediately grabbed his two-way radio. "Team One, fire on the beast!"

The crackling of static momentarily filled the airwaves, followed by a voice. "Are you sure? Sniper Team is in a better—"

"Sniper Team doesn't have a shot! I repeat. Sniper Team is blind! Take the shot now before the creature mauls Winters!"

Team One was set up similarly to Nathan's team: two riflemen in a black Hummer with a modified Gatling gun in the hatch of the vehicle. The soldier sitting behind the heavy caliber machine gun squeezed his finger on the trigger, and the barrel of the gun spun around with a hum, preparing to fire. The first bullet was ejected, and the echo of a mini-explosion filled the air.

Nathan turned to his gunner and ordered, "Fire on Sniper Team's position!" The gunner was puzzled, but Nathan insisted, "NOW!"

Moving his Gatling gun into position, the soldier squeezed the trigger. Mere seconds after Team One fired, the sound of thunder rang out from Nathan's position as well.

Soon the entire area was flooded with gunfire and adrenaline.

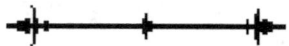

Ethan, still in wolf form and standing over the two lifeless snipers, heard Nathan over their radio and stared at the street. Though he knew the stray below had no clue what was about to happen, a strong sense of self-preservation prohibited Ethan from signaling it. He reasoned that the stray would have to find a way to survive if it was to figure into his plans; and if it didn't, there would always be others to exploit.

The resonance of combat rapidly filled the air, and the buzz of gunfire rang loudly in his ears—a little too loudly even. It only took Ethan a second to realize his foes weren't as simple-minded as he'd initially considered them. Jerking his head to the side, the massive silver werewolf observed a hail of onrushing bullets headed straight for him. Leaping out of their path, Ethan escaped death by a hair—literally—as a patch of fur on his rib cage was singed. Fleeing became his only recourse; after undergoing the painful transformation back into human form, he grabbed his briefcase and retreated into the stairwell of the building to get dressed and slip away unnoticed.

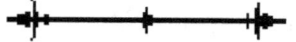

The stray perceived a soft whirring noise, and it spun around in time to see the first projectile fired from a large gun in the distance; one bullet was followed by another, then another, and a few more in rapid succession. Forgetting the helpless woman beneath it, the stray used the steel-like muscles in its hind legs to thrust itself out of the way of imminent doom.

The gunner's aim was tested as he attempted to keep the fast-moving werewolf in his sights, while keeping clear of his teammate who lay facedown on the ground, shielding her head with her arms. It spoke to the stray's speed and agility that although the modified Gatling gun fired nearly three thousand rounds per minute, not one even nicked it.

It sprinted on all fours, weaving left and right, and the bullets narrowly missed its massive bulk. It lunged at a building, dug its claws into the brick, and ran vertically up the wall without slowing.

Adjusting his aim, Team One's gunner fired at the building, but the gunfire did little to hinder the stray's escape. Jumping to a nearby structure, it zigzagged upward until it disappeared over a rooftop ledge.

Bronson was mesmerized by the werewolf's actions and only snapped out of his trance when he heard a voice coming over the Hummer's police scanner. The gunfire was deafening, so he put on a headset to hear the transmission more clearly. Throwing the earphones down, he called to Nathan. But whether it was because of the sound of the firing Gatling gun or the bloodlust that was clouding his judgment, the leader of the Lunar Guardians didn't hear Bronson's words. Seizing his commander by the shoulders, Bronson spun Nathan around; but he was taken aback when he saw the crazed look in Nathan's eyes. Bronson snapped his fingers in front of his commander's face to focus him on the intercepted message.

Disappointed, Nathan tapped his gunner's shoulder. Still firing on Sniper Team's position, the soldier swerved his head to look behind him, only relaxing his hold on the trigger when Nathan gave the signal to cease fire. Not waiting for the gunner to dismount, Bronson slid both gunner and gun inside the Hummer.

"Team One, cease fire," Nathan ordered. "CEASE FIRE!" he bellowed, after his words went unheeded the first time. "Make sure Winters is uninjured and get to Sniper Team's position to recover their bodies, weapons, and vehicle. Local law enforcement was dispatched for a 'shots fired' call at this location and will be here in minutes. We'll rendezvous back at the hotel."

Team One's ranking officer responded, "We'll need more time. I repeat: there's not enough time. We can retrieve their equipment, but we won't be able to secure the bodies for transport."

"Negative, Team One. There's nothing we can do. Leave the bodies. Take their tags and get the hell out of there!"

"With all due respect, sir, I refuse to leave our men in the hands of the enemy."

"Do not endanger the mission! Grab their identification, and make your way back to the hotel! We'll retrieve our comrades at a later time. Williams, out!"

The officer retrieved the dog tags from around Sniper Team's necks and searched their fatigues for personal effects. Becoming alarmed by the approaching sirens, he rappelled down the building. He and his team exited the scene in one direction as the Nassau County Police pulled up from the opposite.

Climbing over the building's ledge, the stray escaped certain death, but another obstacle blocked its path to freedom.

"Now, where do you think you're going?" said Jason. He'd waited out of sight so he wouldn't be disturbed by the Lunar Guardians. He fired two tranquilizer darts into the stray's neck.

It sprung forward, eager to rip Jason's throat out. But the powerful sedative coursing through its system quickly took effect, and the massive werewolf wobbled slightly before falling unconscious on its side.

Jason dialed his cellphone.

"Second Precinct. How can I assist you?"

"Patch me through to Detective Mako," Jason said. A few minutes later, he had the desired party on the line. "It's Brody," he said. "I'm ready to make good on my promise."

TWENTY-TWO

The hot water rushing over his shoulders and down his back slowly brought Mako back to life. He had a lot to accomplish this day. Shutting the water off, he reached around the shower curtain to grab a towel, and when one was handed to him, the groggy detective automatically replied, "Thanks."

It took a moment for the idea to sink in, but when he realized someone was in the bathroom, his body jerked to full alert. Wrapping the towel around his waist, he threw the curtain open to see who was on the other side. Unsurprisingly, Rikki sat on a closed toilet seat, reading the morning paper, legs crossed and quite relaxed.

Looking up, Rikki smiled. "Good morning, bright eyes. I was going to wash your back for you, but you already turned off the faucet."

"Get out," the less-than-amused detective responded, holding the towel firmly in place.

Rikki folded the paper in half and set it on his lap. He wanted to continue teasing his homophobic friend, but he knew better than to push his luck when Mako wasn't fully awake. Instead he said, "It's such a shame."

"Seriously. Get out. I have a busy day ahead of me."

Ignoring the order and continuing his previous thought, he asked, "Did you hear about the two dead bodies your brothers-in-arms found last night near the Broadway Mall?"

Mako gritted his teeth. "Do I really have to—wait—who was killed?"

Rikki displayed the front-page headline. "It's right here." The big, bold letters seemed to smack the detective right in the middle of his forehead: "Broadway Mall Killer Claims Two More."

"Can you get out so I can finish up?" Mako went back behind the curtain.

"Go right ahead. I don't mind."

Mako's arm shot out from behind the curtain, pointing at the bathroom door.

"You have no sense of humor," Rikki said. "I'll go have my coffee."

A short while later, Mako joined his neighbor in the kitchen and flipped through the pages to find the full story. "I hate the news," he grumbled.

"You should be more in touch with the world around you. I never met anyone who didn't read a paper or watch the news on television."

"It's always bad," Mako said, examining the article. "I see enough shit every day at work. Why would I want to bring it home?" As if on cue, his two lovable dogs bounded into the room and greeted him. He answered his own question: "I don't. This is what I need when I leave work—a nice distraction from those who are genuinely happy to see me." He felt a gentle nudge against his leg from what he instantly knew to be the cat; he lightly scratched Booger under his chin, and then brushed his pant leg to remove the white fur now clinging to him.

"Go away," Rikki shooed the cat, "before I go all *Fatal Attraction* on you for scratching me yesterday."

Mako got defensive. "Do you *want* me to hurt you?"

Rolling his eyes, Rikki said, "Oh puhleez. Don't be such a tough guy all the time."

"What makes you think I won't?"

Rikki gently tapped him on the cheek. "Because you like me."

"Bitch."

In as stern a tone as he could muster, Rikki said, "Watch who you're calling bitch, Bitch. Now, go earn that paycheck."

Mako stepped out of his apartment, and Rikki closed the door behind him before any more words were exchanged. Rikki then went back to the kitchen table to finish his coffee. Noticing Booger getting a little too close to him, he waved the cat off again. "Back off, kitty. I don't want you messing up my clothes. I'm too pretty for your fur."

Booger hissed at him and scampered into another room.

"Bitch." Rikki's epithet followed the cat as he took another sip from his cup.

After a brief stop for breakfast at a local deli, Mako pulled up in front of the station house. He had his phone to his ear and he carried the folder that strange, bald Harris had given him. "So, do you think you can do that for me?"

"Yeah, but I don't know exactly when. I have the kids this morning, but after I drop them off, I'll have some free time."

Tired of hearing the same excuses, he said, "Matt, this is important. I need to know if you're going to flake out on me again."

"You don't trust me?" he said, sounding surprised. "When have I ever not come through for you?"

"Do I need to take out the list?"

"What do you mean? I always help you out."

Silence.

"Usually?"

More silence.

"Sometimes?"

No response.

"Come on, you gotta give me sometimes."

Knowing his friend wouldn't stop until Mako recognized his past efforts, Mako said, "I'll give you sometimes, but seriously, let me know if you can't do it. I would do it myself, but I'm behind schedule. And I can't have anyone here do it for me. Remember?"

"I'll Google it and find out everything I can by tonight," Matt declared confidently. "Just spell it for me one more time."

"It's L-Y-C-A-O-N, or look up Silver Heart."

"Cool. L-Y-C-O-A-N. Got it."

"No. Are you even listening to me? It's A-O-N. Write it down so you don't forget."

"Don't worry, I got it." His bickering children got louder in the background. "O-A-N. How do you pronounce it?"

"I think the A is silent, or maybe it's the O."

"Well, which is it?"

"Matt, who gives a shit?" said Mako, his frustration surfacing. "And look up a guy named Peter Stubbe. He lived a few hundred years ago in Germany—in a place called Bedburg. He was supposed to be a, well, you tell me what you find, and I'll tell you if it's what I heard."

"You wanna spell that for me?"

"Forget it! I'll do it myself."

"I'm kidding. I gotta go." Matt hung up while yelling out to his kids to stop fighting.

Mako prayed Matt wouldn't screw this up, hopped up the steps to the front entrance, and held the door open for an exiting visitor while putting his phone away.

The Second Precinct was buzzing with activity after the incident near the Broadway Mall, and the lieutenant was in a foul mood. His officers had recovered two bodies and nothing else except indiscriminate bullets and shell casings. So far there weren't any witnesses to question or suspects to interrogate, and that would not sit well with the lieutenant's superiors. Mumbling under his breath, though loud enough for those outside his office to hear, Grimes was trying to calm himself. He detested having to be the one to call his captain to deliver the bad news.

Mako sat at his desk and schemed about how he could work what he knew about the previous night's incident to his advantage. His partner took a seat opposite him. After placing a hot cup of coffee and a bag from his favorite donut shop next to his computer monitor, Bailey glanced around the screen. "I know what that look means, and I gotta warn you again. Stay away from the murder investigation. Mullins may not be much more popular than you, but it's safe to say the friends he has can screw you; and the friends you have, well, you don't have any in the department, so you better watch yourself. And Grimes has been waiting to burn you, so—"

"Oh, look who bothers to show up after disappearing for a few days," Mako interrupted without looking at him. "And always quick with the advice."

"I had some personal business to attend to. My family comes before the job. Remember that." Bailey's baritone voice always made his statements sound sterner than intended, but it got his point across.

"I didn't ask where you were."

"We haven't been partners that long to where I think you should know everything that goes on in my life."

"That's why I didn't ask." Mako sounded sarcastic but he sincerely felt the same way. "And you'll excuse me if I don't follow your advice." He headed for his C.O.'s office.

"Your call. Even if it is a bad one," Bailey muttered.

"Excuse me, Lieutenant," Mako said, refusing to cross the threshold until receiving permission.

"Shut up and get in here!" Grimes cut him off.

"Did I miss something?"

"You've stepped in it big time!"

"I'm sorry, sir, but I don't know what—"

"I said shut up. Or don't you understand English? I'll do the talking. You just stand there and look stupid!"

Mako's blood pressure rose, especially when he heard some of the other officers outside the lieutenant's office snicker, but he decided to stay quiet for the moment.

Grimes pressed on, "As if I didn't have enough shit on my plate right now, you have to add to it! I ordered you not to interfere with the homicide at Stumpp Industries, but you don't know how to listen! I know you almost screwed up a vital interview for Mullins, who's in charge of the investigation, in case I need to remind you again. And what the hell were you doing at the murder scene at the Broadway Mall?" His face was beet red as the anger spewed out of him. "You are NOT a homicide detective! You aren't even a detective in my book! You are the poster boy for what it means to luck-out into a cushy job!"

Mako didn't feel so lucky right now. "I may not be much to you, but I *am* a good cop and I'm just doing my job."

"Your job?" the lieutenant asked angrily. "Your job?" he repeated. "Your job is to do whatever I tell you to do! Why can't you get that through your head? Why can't you be like your partner? Bailey will push whatever pencil I tell him to! Isn't that right, Bailey?" Grimes directed his voice to the detective still at his desk. "I know you can hear me!"

Mako interjected, "I think you need to calm—"

"Don't tell me what I need, Mako! I'll tell *you* what you need, and *you* need to stay the fuck out of my way!" Grimes was now standing with his finger in his subordinate's face. "I got a call yesterday from your supposed buddy down at Forensics, Thomas Samms. He's accusing you of potentially stealing samples of evidence from him."

Samms! thought Mako. *That bastard!*

"I'm opening an investigation into the matter, and if the allegations against you prove to be true, I'll have your ass in a sling!"

All was quiet inside and outside the lieutenant's office until Mako evenly asked, "My ass, sir? Did you say you want my ass?"

Now it was Lieutenant Grimes' turn to hear the officers laugh at him; and his recently flushed face became redder than it was before. "GET THE FUCK OUT OF MY OFFICE, MAKO, AND CLOSE THE DOOR BEHI—"

Holding back his own laughter, Mako exited the office with Grimes still spouting profanities.

Mullins shouted, "Hey, Mako. I can see you're going to go far in your career!" Some of the detective's fan club openly expressed their amusement at the dig.

Spinning around, Mako was about to exchange witticisms with the portly detective when he noticed a list of names on Stumpp Industries letterhead sitting on top of Mullins' desk. At first he tried to figure out how to sound clever when asking about it, but then he decided his time was better spent on other things. He put the question to Mullins directly: "What's that?"

Mullins followed his colleague's eyes to the paper he was reading, and then, as a schoolboy would prevent one of his classmates from cheating, Mullins covered it up. "You really are ignorant. Didn't anything Grimes said penetrate that thick skull of yours?"

"Humor me for a minute, since my career is dying anyway. Is that an employee list for Stumpp Industries?"

Now it was Mullins turn to be curious. "Yeah, why?"

"Is there a Robert Mane on the list?"

Mullins attempted to read his co-worker's face but didn't find a clue as to where he'd gotten the name. Mullins' finger slid down the first page and stopped moving halfway down the second. "How did you know?"

About to answer, Mako was summoned by another. "MAKO!" The closed door did nothing to reduce the bellow that came from behind it.

Everyone who heard the call looked up, except for the man who was being summoned. Instead, he lowered his head and thought, *What could he possibly want now?*

The door flew open. "Mako, get your ass in my office!"

"Yes, sir, what can I—"

"What were you coming in here for before I told you about Samms' claim?"

Hoping this might be his chance to shine, he said, "I was going to tell you I may have something to offer on last night's double murder."

"Are you for real? You must be the dumbest cop I've ever had under my command. How many times do I have to tell you that you have nothing to do with homicides?"

"Nevermind, then. Sorry to have bothered you." He was going to follow up on his own regardless.

"Don't you move from that spot."

"Excuse me?"

"'Excuse me' what?"

Recognizing he'd forgotten Grimes' favorite acknowledgment, he said, "Sir."

"Finish what you were saying."

"It was nothing ... sir."

"Why don't you tell me, and I'll have Mullins decide if it's useful."

Mako did not want to divulge his information only to have someone else get the credit for the discovery, but he didn't have a choice at this point. He'd worked the kinks out of his story prior to arriving at work, not wanting to expose Jason or to explain how a supposed werewolf was killing people. "I received news last night from an informant who claimed to have knowledge of the incident, stating he could ID a witness on the scene and would take me to him today."

Grimes was skeptical. "Why you?"

"I've worked with this informant before, and he trusts me."

"Does this informant have a name?"

Tired of the questions, Mako pushed for a resolution to the issue. "No disrespect, sir, but would you rather play twenty questions or have something to investigate? As much as my informant trusts me, he may not wait if he feels it isn't safe. I'd like to get to him before he changes his mind."

The lieutenant weighed his options, and even though he hated to involve Mako, he wanted to leave a good impression of himself with the captain. "Go. But take Mullins with you." Grimes wasn't taking any chances.

Shit! Mako thought. But there was no way around it. Any further confrontation and he could be forced to reveal Jason and his highly improbable tale. "I'll get Mullins," he turned to leave, nearly forgetting to add, "sir."

Grimes huffed and grabbed the receiver of his phone.

Pissed, Mako had to devise a way for Jason to deliver the package without Mullins catching wind of what was truly going on. Finding a secluded spot, he grabbed his cell. "It's me. Change of plans. I have to bring the lead homicide detective with me." He paused. "Yes, I had to tell my C.O. What else was I going to do? Bring a potential serial killer back to my home?"

"I have it contained," Jason said. "I wanted you present last night when the change was upon it."

"You woke me at 3:00 a.m. I got there as fast as I could, but you were gone already."

"I couldn't risk it waking up."

"And why didn't you tell me he killed two more people last night?"

"Because it didn't. That was … someone else." Jason didn't want to disclose too much. "I think we have bigger concerns since you involved your entire department. I don't like this. I should take it to Nathan and be done with it."

"You sound like my mother, always worrying. Pay attention. Here's what we're going to do …"

TWENTY-THREE

The roar of the jet engine drowned out all other sounds, and Peter Stumpp was unfazed by the turbulence. Safety belt undone, Stumpp sat quietly sipping wine. The flight attendant attempted to fasten it for him, but a warning look spurred her to beat a hasty retreat. Checking his watch, he nodded approvingly that the flight was on time and hoped his car would be waiting when he landed. Peter Stumpp hated to be disappointed.

Pulling up in a black limousine in front of the airport gates, Ball and Chainz exited from opposite sides. The driver remained inside as security guards made their way toward the vehicle. "Wait here," Mr. Ball said. "I'll get Stumpp." He walked inside the terminal as the head security officer tapped the passenger side window to get the driver's attention.

"Move along, Buddy. You can't park here."

Chainz moved around to the curb and confronted the security detail. Going face to face with the lead man, he growled, "Hands off." In case the threat was not clear, he grabbed and twisted the large steel chain around his neck.

The security officer gulped hard, took a few steps back, and in a last effort at bravado, said, "You got ten more minutes. On my next pass, I don't want to see you or this car. Let's go, boys." The guards left Chainz and the limo driver alone and proceeded to harass other parking offenders.

The plane's landing gear locked into position, and the aircraft hit the landing strip; the screeching tires on the asphalt grated against the ears of those onboard. The plane bounced slightly until it was firmly traveling on the concrete. The pilot applied the brakes, and the noise was almost deafening as the jet came to a halt. Stumpp might have applauded if not for a small drop of wine that splashed on his expensive designer shirt when the plane touched down. His facial expression reflected his displeasure. He would make sure the pilot paid for his sloppy landing.

Mr. Ball marched through the airport, looking for his employer. Those who weren't terrified enough to notice and get out of his way were impolitely bumped aside. One man who started to yell at the giant quickly closed his mouth and scurried away when Mr. Ball stood unswervingly in front of him, staring down through black sunglass lenses. Then Mr. Ball continued on his way to the international gates.

Stumpp didn't bother with luggage. He knew someone would attend to it—or else. He ruminated on the circumstances forcing him back to the United States prematurely: the murder close to his company's facility, followed by a second murder that, although miles away, could still cause serious trouble for him. He'd believed his trusted aid, Ethan, could deal with any and all matters concerning the incidents. But it appeared he would have to address the situation directly. He understood how it could escalate, like before. He'd be sure to handle things more discretely this time.

Brushing a few more people aside before coming face to face with Stumpp, Mr. Ball stood a few inches taller than his employer. Mr. Ball had a much more massive build, but he never felt as apprehensive as when he was in Stumpp's presence. He looked around before asking, "No bags, sir?"

"They'll be sent to my home," Stumpp stated, inwardly pleased at how uneasy he made those around him, "along with the pilot."

Mr. Ball wasn't sure why the pilot would be visiting his employer's home, but he really didn't want to find out either. Mr. Ball had gone by the name Timothy Green before he was sent to prison for burglary; but in prison, he committed some necessary evils to stay alive—like crushing another inmate's skull with a medicine ball—which earned him the moniker Mr. Ball. As bad as that was, it was nothing compared to what he'd heard about Stumpp, and even though he didn't go by Timothy Green anymore, the man he used to be pitied the pilot who displeased his boss.

Stumpp eyed his hired muscle until he stepped aside to let him pass. The bodyguard walked a few feet behind, and the two strutted through the crowd, shoving all others out of their way.

Once they were in the limo, the driver asked him, "Where to, Mr. Stumpp?"

Pouring himself a fresh glass of wine, he replied, "To my second home, of course." The driver automatically headed to Stumpp Industries.

Ball and Chainz sat quietly across from their superior and watched his every move.

"Please, gentlemen," Stumpp said, understanding how both felt, "don't be worried. You haven't done anything to disappoint me, have you?" He chuckled as the car steered onto the expressway, headed for Long Island.

From his top floor office, Ethan Walker utilized his amplified eyesight to see his employer's limousine arrive in front of the main entrance. He knew exactly when Mr. Stumpp entered the building. He adjusted his tie and put on his navy blue suit jacket.

He stepped past the repairmen, who were still fixing the mangled elevator door, to the undamaged elevator car, and went down to meet him in the lobby.

Escorted by Ball and Chainz, Stumpp observed the cleanup crews and the contractors working industriously to put his business back in order. He admired the giant wall-sized painting of a powerful man seated in a chair with his loyal Doberman beside him. He then regarded the woodland paintings scattered throughout. He remembered why he chose this location.

Stumpp Industries was headquartered in Boston, Massachusetts before he decided to move close to the "city that never sleeps." The most appealing aspect of relocating to Nassau County was the surrounding terrain next to the structure, the Muttontown Preserve: a nature center on 550 acres that included ten miles of hiking trails. Some thought it to be a strange location for an industrial venue, but Stumpp said being close to nature exhilarated him. He would often quote Claude Monet when explaining his decision: "The richness I achieve comes from Nature, the source of my inspiration." There must have been some truth to the quote, since Peter Stumpp was a very successful man.

The elevator doors slid open, and Ethan emerged with a forced grin and an outstretched hand. But his employer dismissed the gesture with disgust and stepped past him to enter the car his subordinate had just vacated.

Furious at being humiliated, Ethan angrily followed. Ball and Chainz dared not utter a word, noticing his tightly clenched fist. Ethan ordered, "Leave us. I'll call when I need you." The henchmen didn't need to be told twice and stayed put. Once the elevator doors closed, Ethan asked coldly, "Would you like to go to your office, sir?"

"Please, Ethan," Stumpp began, "first you make a pathetic gesture to welcome me back, and now you show your ignorance by asking me something you clearly know the answer to."

"My ... apologies." He took a key from his inside coat pocket and inserted it into a keyhole located under the numbered buttons on the panel next to the door. A hidden plate opened, displaying three more buttons numbered S-1, S-2, and S-3. Ethan pressed the third, and the elevator began its descent, feeling slower than usual. He'd rather not be with his present company any longer than necessary. True, he'd worked for Stumpp for a very long time, but he'd despised the man almost from the beginning.

"I'm sorely disappointed in you, Ethan. I would have thought you could handle this situation on your own, but I see I have given you too much credit."

Ethan's fist clenched even tighter.

"After all, you have worked for this company for how long now? Decades? Centuries? I would think you'd have learned a thing or two by this point."

Ethan's nose wrinkled, and he gritted his teeth.

"Well, they say if you want something done right ...," Stumpp said. He sighed and left the thought unfinished. "Besides, this isn't the first time you've shown how inadequate you can be when it comes to these affairs. Maybe you don't have the stomach for it anymore. Once this is finished, we may have to discuss your future within this establishment."

He wanted to lunge for his boss' throat, but as luck would have it, the elevator doors slid open. The brightly lit hallway of Sub-basement 3 was revealed.

Stumpp led the way through the maze-like corridors, coming to a halt at an unbefitting solid steel door. He held his hand out for an oddly shaped gold key his assistant carried, and then he fit it into a strange-looking keyhole. Upon turning it, two panels were exposed: one was waist-high, consisting of a pad with an outline of a human hand; the other was eye-level and resembled a peephole on a residential home's front door. He placed a hand on the pad and pressed his eye to the peephole, and a few seconds later, a computer voice said, "Identity confirmed. Welcome, Mr. Stumpp." The heavy metal locks clanked, and he stepped aside so his subordinate could open the door for him.

The door was pulled back with little difficulty, and Ethan permitted his employer to enter first. He followed him inside to a plain gray observation room, complete with a one-way window and a second steel door that had a digital combination lock at its center. Ethan went to punch in the code, but Stumpp placed a hand in front of his assistant's chest to stop him. Stumpp entered the code himself. The lock snapped open with a hiss, and the door swung out automatically.

As he stood in the middle of the doorway, it took only a moment for Stumpp's eyes to adjust to the darkness inside. The light from the adjoining area illuminated a path. At the back of the highly secure space sat a frail-looking Jacob Connors, disheveled and depressed, slumped onto the floor, reminiscent of a broken doll. Stumpp made his approach, spying several decomposed body parts littering the place, most of which were not easily identifiable—except for an aged hand, separated from the arm it once belonged to. He studied it for a brief moment, then kicked it aside like yesterday's garbage and knelt beside Jacob. He carefully retrieved a pair of eyeglasses just inches from the young man's hand. "These must be yours, although I'm sure you don't have a use for them anymore."

Jacob didn't reach for them and mumbled back, "I did this."

"Yes," Stumpp replied, looking around the room once more. "I believe you did."

"I'm a monster."

"There are very few monsters who warrant the fear we have of them," Stumpp said, getting to his feet. "That's not mine. It's a quote from a French author, Andre Gide, but I don't suppose you've heard of him."

Baffled by his coolness, Jacob looked up and asked, "You're not afraid of me?"

"Why? Should I be? Come now. Stand up." He helped the boy to his feet, and Jacob was surprised by how easily the stranger lifted him off the ground.

"Look around you!" Jacob yelled, gesturing to his gruesome surroundings. "Look what I did! I'm a monster, and you should be running for your life!"

Stumpp laughed heartily. "My young man, I have been around monsters, and you are nothing of the sort. Not yet anyway. You have been thrown into a situation you cannot fully appreciate, but I am here to help you with that."

"How?"

"First," he said, leading Jacob out of his prison, "we'll get you cleaned up and into more pleasant surroundings. And you," Stumpp addressed Ethan, who had been waiting outside the whole time, "I can't believe you would treat our guest in such a manner." Turning back to Jacob, he finished, "I hope you'll accept our apologies."

"I guess so," Jacob felt compelled to answer.

"Splendid. You will join me and my associate here at my home for a proper dinner, and then I will explain to you exactly how fortunate you are."

"But how can you help me?"

"All your questions will be answered in due time, but for now I will tell you one thing: I am very well versed in taking care of your like." Stumpp gave Jacob a reassuring pat on his back.

"Are you like me?"

"Oh, no. You and I are nothing alike. Now, you and Ethan here," he said, motioning toward his assistant, "have something in common, and you can learn much from him."

"Really?" Jacob asked Ethan. "You're a monster too?"

"I prefer to think I have more self-control than most of our kind," Ethan said. "Self-control, after all, is what separates us from mere animals."

"Aren't you afraid to surround yourself with monsters?" Jacob asked Stumpp.

Shaking his head firmly, he confidently reassured him, "Absolutely not. As I told you, I have much experience in dealing with persons having your … unique characteristics. I know you at this moment better than you know yourself."

"What if you don't?" Jacob's inquiries were starting to sound like a child questioning his parent.

"If that is the case," Stumpp started eerily, "then I'll simply kill you."

Jacob gulped in fear.

"Ah, I'd say your curiosity has been satisfied for now. Let's leave this place and go to my home."

Ethan opened the weighty door for a second time, allowing them to leave. He then moved to the intercom on the wall, waiting until Mr. Ball's voice came through the speaker: "What can I do for you, sir?"

"We're coming up. Have the limos ready to take us to Mr. Stumpp's home in Sands Point, and get a cleanup crew down here immediately. The smell is starting to bother even me." He didn't wait for an answer and left the room to join Stumpp and his new charge.

TWENTY-FOUR

Mako drove while Mullins sat quietly in the passenger seat, but every so often he caught his colleague glance at him out of the corner of his eye. "Something wrong?"

"Besides this cramped shit box you call a car?"

"Why don't you try *not* being a dick for once?"

"As soon as you learn your place," Mullins said. "I have to tell you, you're a moron. Either this is total bullshit or you're disobeying a direct order."

"What?"

"You've been told to stay out of my way, but you keep gathering information on my case. How do you think this is going to end for you? Don't answer. I'll tell you. You're going to get shit-canned."

"But—"

"There are no buts. Don't you think I know what you're doing here? Trying to get on Grimes' good side so he'll write a recommendation for you to get into Homicide? It's not going to happen. This is exactly how it's going to go down. If your lead isn't total bullshit, like I think it is, he's going to hand it over to me. I'm going to proceed with my investigation, and you're going to get assigned another shitty assignment without so much as a thank you or any recognition. Then he'll find some way to burn you for your unsolicited involvement."

Mako disagreeably smirked. "How do you know that?"

"I've seen it happen to too many guys." Mullins let a bit of emotion surface. "Listen, Mako. You may be a decent cop. I don't know, nor do I care, but you're your own worst enemy. You're going to fuck yourself in the long run. Learn to get in line, and remember, it's just a job. Don't try to be a hero. You're not going to change the world."

"Then why do you do it?"

"Same as everybody else. It's a steady paycheck." He looked away. "And can we hurry this up? I've got a schedule to keep, and the medical examiner is waiting for me at the morgue to give me his report on the two stiffs that showed up this morning."

Wanting to hear the news too, Mako suggested, as candidly as he could, "I can go there first."

"Sure," said Mullins, figuring it couldn't hurt at this point.

Pulling up to the Nassau University Medical Center, they headed straight to the morgue where the medical examiner was waiting. "Hey, Jim. I was just going to call you."

"Sorry, Lenny. I'm carrying some extra baggage today."

Mako knew the comment was directed at him but said nothing, recalling that the medical examiner was a good friend of Mullins'. He'd prefer the meeting to go as smooth as possible.

"I understand." Lenny gave Mako a look. "Follow me. I'll fill you in on what I've got." Lenny led them down the hall to a room full of freezers where the cadavers were stored. "Is it okay to show you-know-who?" he said, as if Mako didn't warrant a name.

"Go ahead," said Mullins. The medical examiner opened two side-by-side drawers and pulled out the slabs. The bodies were completely covered, and Mullins signaled the medical examiner to wait before removing the sheets. "Grimes doesn't hear about this. You understand?" He expected Mako's secrecy.

"Like I need him any further up my ass."

"Since I'm allowing you to participate, answer me something, Mako. How did you know Mane was on Stumpp's employee list?"

Initially unsure how to respond, Mako decided it would be in his best interest to tell the truth. "Here's the deal. Some guy approached me and gave me the name, identifying Mane as the murder victim. He also told me Mane was trying to steal something that Stumpp had previously stolen, and he gave me a folder with information on the item. I figured he was a crackpot, until you partially confirmed what he said."

"Are you playing me, Mako?"

"That's how I found out. Honest."

"We compared DNA from the Muttontown Preserve body to some of Mane's first hair clippings kept by his now distraught mother, and we're waiting to see if they're a match. We should know in twelve hours. But what I'd like to know now, is what he was looking for inside the Stumpp building." Mullins moved closer to intimidate him.

"I can't tell you."

"You can't, or you won't?"

"All I know is it's a heart made out of silver. I can make you a copy of the information, let's say right before you invite me to go down to Stumpp Industries to interrogate the big boss."

"You didn't listen to a word I said on the way over here!" Mullins forcefully poked a finger in his associate's chest.

Mako brushed the chubby digit away. "All I said was you could invite me along to ... further strengthen my interviewing skills."

Mullins mulled the proposition over. "We'll see." Turning back to the examiner, he said, "Show me."

"Brace yourselves."

Once the sheets were removed, Mako was sickened at the grisly sight of one man's head lying slightly apart from his decapitated body. The skin where the head and neck would meet appeared to have been torn with a serrated knife. Several scrapes and lacerations on both men's features indicated that they were dragged facedown along the roof's surface; but the lack of blood indicated that those wounds were made post-mortem, possibly to make identification more difficult. The second body wasn't in better shape, considering there was a hole punched through the chest in the exact place where the heart would have been. Both victims seemed familiar, and after studying them a few moments longer, Mako remembered where he'd seen them.

Mullins detected an involuntary facial tick his colleague made upon seeing the bodies. "What's wrong? You know these guys?"

Upset that he hadn't held it together at first, Mako nonchalantly glanced over one more time but shook his head negatively. "No. I feel a little queasy. That's all."

Mullins understood the sight could be harsh to someone inexperienced in such matters, so he bought the explanation. "Here," he said, tossing a couple of individually wrapped peppermint candies to Mako. "Eat these. They should help your stomach."

"Thanks." Surprised at the gesture, he put one in his mouth and the other in his pocket.

"All right, Lenny, give me your report. I'll read it later. We've got to get going."

Exiting the building, Mako observed a memorable light-blue Chevy Camaro parked a few yards away. The engine was silent, and the recently tinted windows prevented him from seeing inside. But Mako was sure it was the car from the other day. "Hey, you know whose car that is?" he asked Mullins.

Not giving it much thought, Mullins answered, "Never seen it before." Changing the subject, he said, "I hope your guy is waiting for us. We can't afford to go back to Grimes with nothing."

"I'll call him." Mako dialed Jason. "It's me. We're on our way."

Arriving at the predetermined address, Mako looked around for any sign of Jason, but as per their discussion, Jason remained out of sight. "Over here," he called to his temporary partner and took point as they entered the run-down tenement. The dimly lit foyer added to the ambience and the validity of his "informant's" cover story. Retrieving his flashlight and pistol, Mako climbed the stairs to the second floor.

Mullins copied his actions and followed close behind.

If Jason adhered to the plan, he was to dose the captive suspect again, and leave him sleeping in a corner room away from trouble. "You sure this is the right place? There's no one in here." Mullins said after passing the third empty room.

"This is what my guy told me. He saw someone flee the scene last night and hide in here, and he hadn't seen him leave since." Mako hoped he had not beat Jason here. After two more rooms and another flight of stairs, he spotted a pair of bare feet sticking out from under a flattened cardboard box. "Over here." He approached the potential suspect, lifted the box, and tossed it aside, revealing the naked man underneath.

The sleeping man wasn't aware that anyone was with him until Mullins went to check for a pulse. The light touch of the detective's fingers against his neck startled him, and he thrashed about wildly. Inadvertently connecting a right cross to Mullins' chest, the naked man tossed him halfway across the room. Jumping to his feet, the man saw Mako aiming a gun at him and immediately threw his hands up. "Wait! Stop! I didn't do anything!" Upon realizing he wasn't wearing any clothes, he repositioned his hands to hide his privates as best he could.

"Down on the ground with your hands to your side!" Mako ordered.

The man complied without argument.

Mullins staggered over, a little dazed from the altercation, but kept his gun trained on the man. "What the fuck did he hit me with?"

"I think it was his hand."

"Couldn't be. No one is that strong."

"Maybe he's on something," Mako said. He couldn't tell Mullins the other possibility. "Either way, be more careful when cuffing him."

"Fuck you. You're cuffing him."

"Fine. Watch him." Mako inched closer, holstering his weapon and retrieving his handcuffs. "Listen to me. I'm going to cuff your wrists one at a time. You resist, and my partner is going to shoot you. Nod if you understand."

The man nodded.

Mako knelt beside him and restrained both arms behind his back. Once secured, Mullins moved to the other side, and both detectives lifted the suspect to his feet. Mako removed his jacket and tied it around the naked man's waist, leaving the remainder of the man's dignity intact. As they walked him to the exit, Mako asked, "What's your name?"

Embarrassed, he answered, "Louis. Louis Falcone."

Locked alone in a holding cell, Louis was given a hospital gown to wear and a bologna sandwich to eat. He hadn't been in the precinct long, but he wondered what he'd done to get there and when he would be released. No one had spoken to him since his arrival, and that worried him even more.

In the lieutenant's office, the detectives waited for further instructions. "Well, Mako, looks like you kept your word. My superiors will be pleased."

"Glad I could—"

Grimes moved past him, ignoring his comments, and stopped in front of Mullins. "When you're ready, I want you to interrogate this Falcone and find out everything he knows. I've already cleared Interview Room Two."

"Yes, sir. I'll let him sweat it out a few more minutes in his cell."

"Do what you feel is best, but make sure he talks." Grimes turned his back on his officers. "You're both dismissed."

Mullins headed to the exit but noticed Mako was not behind him. Looking back, he shook his head, realizing Mako was about to question the lieutenant.

"Sir?" Mako started.

"Didn't I dismiss you?"

"I brought you Falcone. I think that warrants—"

"What?" Grimes cut him off. "You want me to pin a medal on you for doing your job? Did you think I was going to let you assist on the case? You are thickheaded. This is the last time I'm going to say this to you: you are not to involve yourself any further in the homicide investigation or I will burn you for disobeying a direct order! Is that clear enough for you?"

Mako remembered what Mullins had told him in the car. "Yes, sir."

"Now, get out of my sight."

Leaving the office, Mako saw Mullins eyeing him. "So, you were right. Whatever."

"It was friendly advice. Maybe next time you'll listen."

Mako returned to his desk to finish some overdue paperwork. He heard Mullins tell one of his cronies, "I'm heading to Room

Two. Give it ten minutes, and then bring in the guy who's wearing the hospital gown in Cell Three. Time to see what he knows."

TWENTY-FIVE

The drive to Sands Point was long, and Jacob was concerned about the time, knowing his humanity was going to vanish with the sunlight. Although he'd washed the filth off his body and put on a fresh change of clothes, he still felt sullied due to his recent actions—even though he could not fully remember them. Staring at the barren road out the chauffeured automobile's back window, he got a sinking feeling that something terrible was going to happen. He was always up for a good prank, but it appeared this time the joke was on him.

As Ethan sat beside him in the limousine, the stench of Jacob's fear was overpowering to Ethan's sensitive nose. He could hear the pounding of Jacob's heart. He tried to calm his companion, but Jacob recoiled when Ethan touched his knee. "No need to be afraid. You're one of us now."

"You lock everyone in your little club in a dungeon and send them helpless victims to dine on, or am I special?"

Ethan strained a grin. "It was necessary. You weren't very cooperative, and you did need to keep up your strength."

"Why not feed me a steak or some other normal food? Why turn me into a, a cannibal?" He unsuccessfully held back a tear, thinking of the nightmare his life had become.

"Our kind has not been treated with kindness by regular humans, and we must learn to be strong in times of need. Steaks and sit-down dinners are a thing of the past. You need to learn to live off the land. And unfortunately for humans, they are below us on the food chain."

"What if I don't want to?"

Ethan folded his arms across his chest. "I know you'll want the normalcy you've been accustomed to all your life, and you will have it for three weeks out of the month. However, for one week, when the moon is full, you will transform, and you will give in to your animal instincts."

Jacob huffed indignantly. "This is fucking great. You tell me I have a supernatural menstrual cycle ahead of me for the rest of my life that makes me crave human flesh, and I'm just supposed to accept it. Un-fucking-believable."

Amused at the analogy, Ethan said, "Let me assure you. This 'supernatural menstrual cycle' has many more benefits than disadvantages, as you'll soon find out."

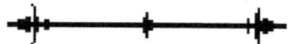

Peter Stumpp emerged from his bedroom, prepared for company in a custom suit. He walked over to a large hallway mirror, preening. Standing over six feet tall, he was strikingly handsome with salt-and-pepper-colored hair that was neat and shiny without one out of place. He admired his physique since it was that of a much younger man, although his chiseled features were flawed by a small scar that dissected his left eyebrow.

"Your guests have arrived," the butler announced from the foyer.

"Thank you, Charles. I'll go and greet them." He went to the front door. "It's about time. I was beginning to think you'd reneged on my offer. Please, come in."

Jacob stared at his new surroundings, having never been in a house with its own reception area. In awe of the mansion, he could not say anything other than "Wow."

Ethan had been here on many occasions, so the enormity of the house, and its décor, had less of a mystique for him. He was merely waiting for what was to come next.

Stumpp moved over to the boy and placed his arm around him, and for the first time, Jacob truly noticed how much bigger his host was than he'd first perceived. "Jacob. I need to speak with you. Today when we met, you seemed quite distraught over your situation. I hope our conversation and a change of atmosphere served to change your mind, but I need to hear it from you first, if we are to proceed further." He moved away to face him, shrugging his shoulders. "Now, I can't decide for you, but it's time for you to choose. Either embrace your new life, or turn your back on it. It's entirely up to you."

Something in Stumpp's mannerisms seemed threatening to Jacob, forcing him to weigh the supposed benefits of his new life against what he guessed would be the consequences if he disputed it. He would never tell which influenced his decision more. "Well, with your help, I'll figure out a way to adapt. Just tell me what I have to do."

"You've made me proud, young man. And do not be afraid of your darker side. The Swiss psychologist Carl Gustav Jung said, 'The most terrifying thing is to accept oneself completely.' Now that you have, I have something to show you." He led Jacob back toward the living room and said, "Ethan, excuse us for a moment."

"Of course." Ethan sighed deeply, carefully releasing the hammer of the gun he was holding behind his back, relieved that Jacob had made the smart choice.

Jacob followed Stumpp through the tremendous mansion, passing through a billiards room into the study where several portraits of men resembling his host hung around the room. His art history background informed him that they were all painted in different time periods, and he concluded that the portraits were Stumpp's family tree. But the resemblances were uncanny.

Moving to the large mahogany desk, closest to the wall directly opposite the doorway where Jacob waited, Stumpp stood beside a pedestal with a box-shaped object sitting on it, covered by a dark cloth. "Come closer."

Bookcases lined the walls along with the various pieces of artwork and artifacts in a display case off to his right. He was not sure what they were, but Jacob could tell some of the items in this room must have cost a fortune to obtain.

"Please, don't be intimidated by mere trinkets. These petty things are nothing compared to what I want to show you."

"I find that hard to believe. What could possibly be more extraordinary than all this?"

"How about the very item that has brought about your current predicament?"

Jacob wasn't entirely sure what Stumpp was talking about, and it showed.

"Come now, don't tell me you don't recall what it was you were looking for the night you and your associates broke into my office building."

"It was a heart-shaped thing. Bobby called it the Silver Heart. It was supposed to be on display in your office. Bobby said we'd be rich since it was a one of a kind item."

"It is a unique piece, that much is true, but I can't fathom how Mr. Mane figured he would sell such a high-profile item without one such as myself noticing."

"That's what I told him, and he said not to worry about it. He had it covered."

Stumpp understood that Jacob had been duped.

"What? What's wrong?"

"Your friend was not upfront with you, I'm sorry to say. He never intended to sell the item and make you a rich man."

"How do you know? You didn't know Bobby." Jacob sounded angry at the accusation.

"No. I didn't know him, but I know men like him," Stumpp said, trying to put it as sympathetically as possible. "Jacob, the Silver Heart, or the Heart of Lycaon as it is originally known, is not something of great value to anyone save a few. Its true importance is only to those who dabble in the occult and the supernatural."

"So, why are you interested in it?" It was an honest question from an innocent mind.

Stumpp sighed. "A wise man named George Bernard Shaw once said, 'No question is so difficult to answer as that to which the answer is obvious.'"

He continued, "Let me tell you a story, Jacob. Some centuries ago, a man came across a tale of an evil king named Lycaon who was turned into a wolf-like creature by Zeus, lord of the Greek gods. Because he was something of a sorcerer, Lycaon turned the curse to his advantage. Not to bore you with the gory details, but Lycaon was eventually cornered and killed, and his heart was encased in silver. Hence the name."

"That's clever," Jacob broke in.

"Yes." He noted the boy's sarcasm and was prepared to deliver some of his own. "Now, be clever enough not to interrupt me again." Continuing his narrative, he said, "The Silver Heart was said to have magical properties, but the ignorant paupers who owned it were not interested in its significance other than as a paltry trophy.

"That is why it was so easy to acquire for a few pennies. The money was worth more to them than the power the Heart could bring. The Heart of Lycaon has been in my family for generations, and I have amassed enormous wealth because of it, as you can see. But there have been those who have tried to take it away to fulfill their own selfish desires. Your friend Robert Mane worked for someone who sought my prize.

"Once I discovered Mane was inquiring about the item, I had to be sure of his intentions. I began a rumor that the Heart was in my private office for all to see, in hopes that the actual traitor would come forward. It was not my objective for you to be caught unaware by your friend's treachery, but I simply could not allow him to steal what was rightfully mine. Now, as a gesture of friendship, not deceit, I want to share with you the very item you were going to take from me." Moving behind the pedestal, he took hold of the ends of the black covering. "Please excuse the theatrics, but I wanted the first time you laid eyes on my most prized possession to be memorable," he said, simultaneously pulling the sheet off in one fluid movement.

The fabric appeared to be moving in slow motion, and when Jacob's eyes finally focused on the object within the glass case, it didn't look anything like he thought it would. He was expecting something resembling a Valentine's Day heart, despite the story he just heard. He couldn't imagine who would sheath an actual heart in silver, but that was what it was: a human heart covered in bright, shining silver. The fatty tissue around the heart shone with a bluish tint, but the rest was a giant, pure silver mass. It even had portions of the once blood-pumping arteries still attached. It disturbed him to think this was once a life-giving organ that now simply sat in a container on display.

The Silver Heart rested in the palm of a golden clawed hand, and Jacob wondered if the hand belonged to King Lycaon too, even though Stumpp hadn't mentioned it in his story. The hand seemed real enough, as real as a golden hand with razor-sharp fingernails could seem, but it could just as well have been man-made. Equally fascinated and disgusted by the object, he subconsciously stretched his own hand outward until his fingertips lightly brushed against the glass, but he pulled it back in fright when the golden hand tightened its grip around Lycaon's heart.

"Remarkable, isn't it?"

"This is bullshit!" Jacob yelled out, but heaven only knew if it was because he was embarrassed from imagining that a supposed inanimate object came to life or because his life had been changed for this item he had no interest in. "This, this thing is what Bobby lied to me for? This fucking thing is the reason why I'm a monster now?"

"I thought you had come to terms with your new situation. You're not telling me you're having second thoughts again, are you?"

"I don't mean any disrespect, Mr. Stumpp. You've been cordial to me, but because of Bobby's lies, my whole life has to change. And that pisses me off!"

"Not only Robert's lies," Stumpp interjected, "but also the dishonesty of his employers."

The rage built up inside Jacob to the point where he was ready to unleash it on anyone who crossed him, and he was not afraid to voice it. "Well, show me who these others are, and I'll rip them apart."

Stumpp was pleased. Recognizing that the boy was completely his, he was ready to oblige this request—until Jacob placed another thought in Stumpp's head.

"You know, he didn't only lie to me! Bobby lied to Louis too. But that fat fuck got away! He ran like the scared blob of shit that he is!"

"Yes. The third boy with you that night. I've been meaning to ask you about him. You wouldn't happen to know where to find him, would you?"

TWENTY-SIX

Mullins stared at Louis, who sat in a chair behind a wooden table; Louis' handcuffs were shackled to the floor of the interrogation room to prevent any violent outbursts that could injure either one of them. The detective did not say anything. He just stared.

Louis sporadically looked up but promptly returned his gaze to the floor every time his eyes met the detective's. The nervous energy churned the bologna sandwich in his stomach to the point where he gagged without vomiting.

Mullins figured he was ready to talk. "Do you know where you are?"

"Yes," Louis mumbled.

"Louder."

"Yes, I know where I am. When do I get to make a call?" He made sure the detective could hear him.

"When I say so." Mullins slid a second chair out from under the table and sat across from Louis. "You said your name is Falcone, correct?"

"Yes."

"What were you doing in that building, Mr. Falcone?"

He hesitated. "I don't know."

"Don't make this any more difficult than it has to be."

"I'm not trying to. I don't know how I got there."

Mullins rubbed under his nose with one finger, then passed his hand across the stubble on his face. "Okay. Let's try this. What is the last thing you remember before I woke you?"

Sighing, he said, "I was home. Watching TV. Nothing special. I started to feel sick and went into the bathroom to puke. I must have slipped and fell and hit my head because I don't remember anything after that."

"Is that so?"

"I'm telling you the truth."

"So, you mean to tell me you weren't in the vicinity of the Broadway Mall last night?"

"I just told you where I was."

Mullins rapidly lunged forward, kicking the chair out from under him, and nearly touched noses with Louis. "You haven't told me shit!" he yelled, spraying Louis' face with spittle. "You'd better tell me something I want to hear! And don't jerk me off this time! What the fuck were you doing in that derelict tenement I found you in?"

His eyes beginning to water, he said, "I, I don't remember."

"Shit." Mullins composed himself, picked up the overturned chair, and left the interrogation room. Pacing for a few moments, he called over to a nearby office. "Get this asshole a soda, wait for him to finish, and then get it to the lab for prints and a DNA sample. Have them run it through the database to see if he pops up anywhere. And give him his phone call."

"Were you able to locate your friend?" Stumpp asked.

Hanging up the rotary phone in the study, Jacob answered, "His mom said he called her an hour ago from the Second Precinct. She didn't know what time he would be back."

"Did she say why he was there?"

"I don't think she knew."

"Ethan," Stumpp said to his assistant, "do you have any idea what Jacob's friend would be doing with the police?"

"None." He understood his employer wanted the matter handled swiftly. "I'll send Mr. Ball and Chainz to inquire."

"I think that would be best."

Ethan left the room to make the arrangements.

Nine hours had passed since Louis had been taken into custody, and Mullins was no closer to getting any answers than when he'd first begun his interview. The fingerprints they lifted from the soda can revealed no criminal behavior in Louis' past. The DNA wouldn't be processed for at least another few days, but Mullins wasn't hopeful that it would turn up anything either. Knowing they couldn't hold him for much longer, the detective had no recourse but to inform his lieutenant of the bad news. He knocked before entering the office.

"Come," Grimes said without looking up.

"Sorry to bother you, Lieutenant."

Putting his pen down on the pad he was writing in, he lifted his head. "What do you have for me? Did he know who was responsible for the murders, or better yet, was he responsible?"

"That's the thing, sir." The detective cleared his throat. "He doesn't remember anything."

"Excuse me?"

"He said he doesn't remember anything about last night."

"It's your job to *make* him remember."

"Believe me, I tried. Every time I push, he looks like he's going to break down."

Grimes rubbed his forehead in frustration. "Then you push. And push hard! If he breaks down, you push harder. I want answers!"

"I've done everything I can to get them for you, sir. I've run his prints and saliva, but so far, nothing. I've even given him a phone call, and he used it to dial his mother. I don't think this guy is capable of killing anyone, and if he saw who did it, he's too scared to tell."

"Do I need to talk to him?" The lieutenant's question almost sounded like a threat.

"I don't believe that's necessary, sir."

"So, what do you suggest we do with him?"

"Technically, Falcone isn't under arrest, so he can leave whenever he wants. I don't think he knows that though. The best I can do is finish up some more paperwork and let him stew for a few hours longer. Maybe it'll jog his memory. Other than that, we have to let him go, or possibly face the consequences of a legal shit storm later on."

"Let him go?" Grimes asked as if he did not fully understand what his subordinate was saying. "Just like that." He thought about it some more. "Do what you need to. I should've known Mako's lead would be nothing but bullshit anyway."

"With all due respect, I don't think it was Mako's fau—"

"Finish that sentence, and I'll have you demoted down to custodian."

Mullins knew the lieutenant didn't have the clout to make that happen, but he could still make life difficult while the detective was under his command. So Mullins didn't finish that sentence. "I'll get Falcone processed for release after I find him some clothes to wear out of here."

"Dismissed."

Mako looked up from his mound of reports and saw Mullins shake Louis' hand and send him on his way. Walking over to his colleague, he asked, "What's going on? Why are you letting him go?"

"Don't worry about it. It's not your business."

"Did you at least learn anything?"

"Not. Your. Business."

"You're a dick, you know that?"

"And you're a stubborn asshole who doesn't know when to quit!"

"I'm only trying to help."

"No, you're a glory hog who thinks this case will make your career if you solve it first."

"You don't know me at all."

"And I don't care to. Now, I got some real police work to do. Why don't you go find your partner and make yourselves useful? I think the toilets need scrubbing." Mullins shoved Mako aside as he passed.

The spurned detective felt his anger growing, but instead of letting it loose on the target of his aggression, Mako chased after Louis. Despite wanting to do the right thing, he figured a little glory wouldn't be so bad, especially if he took it away from Mullins.

TWENTY-SEVEN

Waiting across the street from the Second Precinct, Ball and Chainz saw Louis emerge onto the street and let him get half a block away before pursuing. They pulled their armored truck past Louis and turned down a nearby alley. Mr. Ball got out, stood by the alley's opening, and snatched Louis off the sidewalk, gripping him firmly by the collar of his hand-me-down flannel shirt.

"What do you want from me?" Louis asked in high-pitched voice.

"Shut up." Mr. Ball backhanded Louis across the face. "Speak when spoken to."

"O-okay. No! I'm sorry. I didn't mean to. P-please let me go."

Mr. Ball slapped him again, this time on the other cheek. "What did you tell the police?"

Louis remained silent.

"Here's the part where you answer."

"I didn't tell them anything. I don't even know why I was there."

The driver's side door slammed shut. "I think he's lying," Chainz said.

"I, I'm not." Louis' stomach rumbled. "Why would I lie?"

"What did I tell you about that?" He punched Louis in the body, with horrendous results. It didn't take long for the smell to reach him. "What is wrong with you, kid?" He punched him again.

174

Louis doubled over, and Mr. Ball threw him to his partner, who in turn slammed him into the side of a dumpster.

"I'll ask again," he said. "What did you tell the police?"

Cowering, Louis answered, "Nothing. I swear."

Mr. Ball nodded and Chainz kicked Louis in the ribs. "This is gonna be a long day for you, if you don't start talking," he added.

"Maybe the boss could get him to talk."

"You know what, Chainz? I think you're right. Get his legs." Mr. Ball reached for Louis' arms. "Oh well, kid, you had your chance."

Mako exited the precinct, looking up and down the street for any sign of Louis, but it appeared he'd gotten away. There were plenty of ways to get his address or phone number but all would alert Mullins and Grimes to his continued, unwanted involvement—and that was not something he was willing to do at present.

Hearing a commotion coming from the nearby alleyway, Mako sprinted to it with his gun drawn. He heard someone yell, "Help!" Turning the corner, he saw Louis struggling to escape from two familiar-looking giants who were trying to heave him into the back of their vehicle. "Drop the kid, and back away from him now!" The detective aimed his weapon.

Both heavyweights were not scared. Instead, they tossed Louis in the truck, slammed the doors shut, and directed their attention to Mako.

Chainz said, "Isn't that—"

"The cop who shoved his gun in my face the other day?" Mr. Ball finished his partner's thought. "Yeah. I was hoping I'd get a chance to tell him how I felt about that."

"Now seems like a good time to me."

"You said it, Chainz. Let's go talk to him."

They were speaking loud enough for him to hear, and Mako's situation grew more serious the closer they got to him. He shouted another warning. He didn't wish to open fire in broad daylight with civilians walking near his location. There were so many variables of how a shootout could go horribly wrong. But the detective wasn't sure how to avoid one as the two men were not complying with his orders. His mind racing, he was unable to come to a solution.

A patrol car pulled into a space in front of the precinct, and the officers inside the vehicle spotted Mako by the alley with his gun drawn. Unsure who the detective was or what he was aiming at, they assumed he was simply another perp with a loaded weapon who needed to be hauled off the streets. Exiting the car, they moved into flanking positions, pulling their firearms and aiming at Mako. "Put the weapon on the ground slowly and take two steps back!" the lead officer yelled.

Doing a double take, Mako saw the cops approaching and tried to identify himself. "Officers! I'm a detective with the Second, and I need some help over here."

"Sir, I'm warning you," the officer answered. "Put your weapon down or we will open fire!" He maneuvered around scattering civilians to keep Mako in his sights.

"Here's my identification," the detective said, reaching for his shield on a chain around his neck.

"Don't do it, sir! Put the gun down now! This is your last warning!"

Mako had no choice but to obey. Setting his pistol down in front of him, he took two steps back with his hands raised high in the air. He was seething because the officers prevented him from helping Louis, still trapped within the truck.

"Face down on the ground with your hands out to your sides!"

Mako hesitated.

"Do it! Now!"

As he knelt down to get into position, Ball and Chainz hustled back to their truck before the cops got too close to arrest them next. In their haste to deal with Mako, neither one had locked the rear doors after throwing Louis inside. As they drove off, Louis shoved the doors open and fell out of the truck. Rushing out of the alley, he ran into the two officers who detained Mako, and they tackled him to the ground too.

At least they didn't get Louis, Mako thought.

Moments later within the precinct, Grimes' voice bellowed so loudly the walls practically shook from his fury. "Are you shitting me? How the fuck can you not keep this asshole under control?"

Mullins and Mako stood side by side within the lieutenant's office, and neither was sure who he was more pissed at.

"Do I need to take you off this case too, Mullins?"

"No, sir."

"Well, you had better show me you can handle things. Because one more fuck up, and you're gone!" Grimes shifted his gaze and stuck his pointer finger in Mako's face, nearly touching the bridge of his nose. "And you! You're like a pimple on my ass that won't go away! I don't understand how many times I have to say the same thing before you understand that I don't want you working on this! Get it? I. Don't. Want. You. On. This."

"But, Lieutenant, if I hadn't gone after Louis, he would have been taken."

Grimes made a motion with both hands, implying he wanted to strangle Mako. "Do you realize how close you were to being shot by your fellow officers? Do you know the giant cluster fuck that would have made for me? If my cops didn't know enough not to fire on one another, I'd have been torn a new asshole by the commissioner."

"I was only trying to—"

"Did I ask for your input? Shut your mouth, and get out of my face. But don't leave. I want a letter from you right now that I can hand to my superiors, explaining why you did what you did. And it better say how *I* had absolutely no involvement in your asinine actions!"

The detectives turned to leave the lieutenant's office.

"Not you Mullins. We still have business to discuss." When Mako was out of earshot, Grimes continued, "Have a seat." The two men sat opposite each other; the lieutenant was behind his desk. "You have any inclination that the kid was in danger when you released him?"

"I wouldn't have let him go if I did, sir."

"Do you have any idea who those men were in the alley, based on Mako's description?"

"I have a pretty good suspicion. But I don't know what they'd want with Falcone."

"Pretty ballsy of them to try and nab him this close to a building full of cops," Grimes said, thinking out loud. "I imagine they'll try again."

"That crossed my mind too."

"I guess we only have one choice, then."

"I guess so, sir."

"Give me an hour to set it up. In the meantime, see if you can get Falcone to shed some light on what that was all about. I'll let you know when everything is ready."

Mullins rose from his chair and made for the exit, but a thought compelled him to ask, "What about Mako, sir?"

Stroking his moustache, Grimes said, "Leave that to me. I know how to deal with Mako."

TWENTY-EIGHT

At Stumpp's Sands Point mansion, Charles set the huge rectangular dining room table, easily able to accommodate twenty people, for only four. He used some of the finest china and silverware in his master's collection. Oak paneling ascended halfway up each wall and decorative antique light fixtures surrounded the perimeter. Although the room was bright, there were three lit candelabras evenly spaced over the table. A large painting of a man resembling Peter Stumpp, depicted in a much earlier time period, hung on the far wall above the paneling.

The sound of his shoes tapping on the tile floor signaled to the guests that their host had arrived, and the expectant couple turned to meet him. The man extended his hand in friendship, and Stumpp did likewise. They gripped one another's hands firmly. As the host of this event, Stumpp was the first to speak. "Thank you for coming. I assume this is your lovely wife."

"Yes. Yes it is," the man replied. "Anna, meet Mr. Peter Stumpp." He stepped to the side so his wife could shake hands.

"It was very nice of you to invite us," she said.

The man nodded in agreement. "Yes, thank you. I was under the impression you were angry with me after we landed. I was very surprised when I got the call to come to your home. You've never invited me here in the six years I worked for you—not that I expected you to. But I thought this was going to be—"

180

"Relax," Stumpp said, offering his most sincere smile. "Accidents happen, and after all, it was only a shirt. The wine stain should come out, and if not, I have more."

"Hi," a tiny voice piped in, and a small child standing nearby with her teddy bear waved hello. "My daddy flies planes."

"Yes, I know," Stumpp answered with a condescending tone.

The pilot knelt down next to the little girl and placed his hands on her shoulders. "Please, forgive me. This is my daughter, Rebecca." He addressed his child, "Becca, this is Daddy's boss, Mr. Stumpp."

"I four years old," she said proudly, struggling to hold up the correct number of fingers.

"Good for you," Stumpp responded with a tone between sincerity and mockery.

Before another word was uttered by anyone in the room, Charles returned with a rolling cart carrying several serving dishes. "Dinner is served," he said. The pilot and his family took their seats. As Stumpp moved to the head of the table, Charles motioned to his master, forestalling him from sitting, and whispered, "Mr. Ball and Mr. Chainz have returned, sir."

Looking around the table, he said, "Let Ethan deal with them. I have … other business to attend to here."

Charles admired the modest-looking family and reminisced on his younger days. Their attire was simple, but the joy they gave to one another was written plainly on their faces. The pilot lifted his little girl into her seat, and he and his wife sat on either side of her. A gentle kiss to Becca's forehead reminded Charles of finer times, and his lips quivered with sadness. Anna turned and smiled at him, and he quietly wished they would have declined his master's dinner invitation.

Ethan and Jacob were in Stumpp's training room on the mansion's lower level. The room held various types of conventional gym equipment and free weights, along with some eccentric apparatus. "This is where you will begin your schooling. I will show you the benefits your human form will be afforded now that you are so much more."

Glancing at the equipment, a certain amount of doubt plagued Jacob's mind. He'd never been particularly strong. What did they expect him to accomplish by proving that openly? His insecurities coupled with a sudden bout of nervousness forced him to speak up. "Look, I don't know what's going on, but I can't stay out in the open. It's getting late, and I need to be locked away before … before I change with the full moon tonight. Aren't you even worried?"

"No," Ethan answered coldly. "It's true our transformations are controlled by the phases of the moon for a time, but eventually you will be able to make the change at will." Displaying a portion of his own control, Ethan opened his mouth to reveal the razor-sharp fangs within, and then placed a hairy, clawed hand on Jacob's shoulder, causing his cowardly student to flinch. Ethan returned to normal, demonstrating how easily the change was reversible. "That is the type of power that control will grant you, except when there is a full moon. You may be able to delay the transformation, but even the strongest of our kind will succumb to it," he finished.

"What if I don't want control, or power? What if I just want a normal life again? Can I have that?"

"If you value your life, do not repeat those words in front of Mr. Stumpp."

"Why not? He wouldn't really kill me, would he?"

Ethan merely replied, "Let's begin with strength training."

Lying on the bench press, Jacob's muscles were shaky as he tried to keep the barbell steady. The weight on it was a little over 300 pounds, well over what a person his size should be able to lift. But he was lifting it with relatively minimal difficulty. "I ... can't believe ... I'm lifting this," he said through strained grunts.

Ethan spotted Jacob in case the weights fell, but he knew it would only be Jacob's lack of confidence that would cause him to drop the load. "That's only the beginning. I decided we would start small. As you become more confident, your strength will increase, as will your other attributes."

"What do you mean?"

Using one arm to lift the bar out of Jacob's hands and place it back on the rests, Ethan answered, "Strength is not the only gift you've received. Yes, you'll be stronger than ever—plus your speed, stamina, and durability have been increased to superhuman levels—but there is so much more."

Mr. Ball entered the room. And as Chainz waited near the doorway, Mr. Ball whispered into his employer's ear about how they'd botched Louis' capture.

"You did what?" Ethan asked him. "You tried to take Falcone practically in front of the police precinct?" The more the thought encircled his brain, the angrier he grew. "Do you realize how stupid that was? It would be smarter for me to kill you both and replace you with intelligent employees."

"If it wasn't for that detective, we'd have had Falcone and been gone before anyone noticed," Mr. Ball defended his actions.

"Yes. Detective Mako has become more of a problem than I anticipated." Ethan momentarily forgot his subordinates' bungle. "He *will* have to be dealt with."

Looking to atone for their mistake, Mr. Ball offered, "You want us to take care of him?"

"What makes you think I'll trust you not to make a debacle of that too?" Ethan wasn't sure what to do. He could kill them for their ignorance, but finding and training new help would not benefit the situation at this stage. Not many humans could handle the idea that monsters existed, and even fewer would be able to hunt and restrain them as these two could. No. He wouldn't kill them, but they didn't need to know that. Perhaps the fear of death would keep them on their toes, for a little while anyway. "You buffoons have caused me great pain by failing to procure the target, and I would be justified in expressing my displeasure. But I have more pressing concerns, such as delivering the news to Mr. Stumpp. I hope for you he doesn't feel the need to express *his* disappointment."

They didn't openly display emotion, but Ball and Chainz were frightened at the thought. And Ethan could smell their fear. But that wasn't all he smelled. Moving closer, he detected a familiar scent on Mr. Ball's shirt. Uncharacteristically nervous, the bodyguard took a step back from his employer, but Ethan moved with lightning-quick reflexes and clawed the shirt off Mr. Ball's body. It happened so fast, the henchman wasn't aware that he was topless until he saw the shredded tee held firmly in Ethan's deformed grip. Ethan sniffed the shirt intently. Mr. Ball also didn't realize that there were several slash marks across his chest until Chainz silently pointed them out to him. The blood trickling from the wounds didn't worry him as much as making it out alive.

"Leave me," Ethan said. "I need to inform Mr. Stumpp."

Mr. Ball started, "Should we—"

"I said leave me. I'll summon you when I have a simple task for you to perform."

"But Falcone."

"You services won't be required." Ethan swiveled his head to look at them, his face partially transformed into the wolf. "I'll be taking a more personal role in securing Mr. Falcone." Going over to the intercom, he paged his boss. "I'm sorry to disturb your supper, but I have urgent news I believe you'll want to hear."

"Please excuse me. I'll be right back," Stumpp said to his guests.

"Of course, sir. If you'd like us to go, I'd understand." The pilot started to rise.

Stumpp hindered the man's movement by placing a hand on his shoulder and shoving him back into his seat. "Stay!" Taking a calmer tone, he said, "I insist."

Even though he was visibly shaken, the urge to be polite overwhelmed the pilot's common sense. "O-Okay. We'll stay. Thank you."

Joining his assistant in the weight room, Stumpp said, "This had better be important."

Ethan didn't know how to sugarcoat the bad news, so he spit it out: "The police still have Falcone. The detective I told you about stopped Ball and Chainz from taking him."

"Are you testing my patience? Because I assure you, it is running out. I want you to resolve this personally. And this time, do not fail."

"I intend to, but there's nothing that can be done while he's in police custody. I'll have to wait until they move or release him."

"Once you secure Falcone, find out what he told the police and kill him."

"Wait a minute," Jacob interrupted. "You're talking about murder. You can't do that."

Stumpp's annoyance turned to rage. "Your incessant droning is beginning to infuriate me, boy! You broke into my offices and attempted to take what is rightfully mine! Your life belongs to me for as long as you draw breath, and you will learn the order of things! Never question me again!"

"It was a mistake," he said. "I'm sorry. I want to forget that night ever happened."

"Fellow countryman Richard von Weizsaecker said, and I happen to agree with him, 'Seeking to forget makes exile all the longer; the secret of redemption lies in remembrance.' And your curse will make you remember what you did for a very long time!" Before exiting, Stumpp stopped briefly to speak to his assistant. "Ethan, if he does not wish to train voluntarily, make him do so by force."

"There are laws against this kind of thing, you know," Jacob shouted after Stumpp.

"If I were you," Ethan said, "I wouldn't anger him any more than you already have."

"With everything you told me I'm capable of, I'm not scared of him."

"You should be."

Stumpp stormed down the hallway, back to the dining hall, and bumped his servant aside as he passed.

"Is everything all right, sir?"

"No, Charles, it is not. I am tired of the imbeciles I surround myself with, and I am repulsed by the level of incompetence humans possess. I am at my wits' end. The earth would be a better place if humans simply ceased to exist!" His voice traveled throughout the corridors to the ears of the pilot and his family.

"Anna, sweetheart, let's go," the man said, putting down his fork and hurrying his family out.

Stumpp's abrupt appearance blocked the exit and startled the couple. "Where do you think you're going?" he asked in a sinister tone.

The man tried to hide his panic. "I, it sounds like you have enough to deal with without us being here. I thank you again, but we should leave."

"You're not going anywhere." Stumpp didn't budge an inch, and the fury in his eyes told the pilot all he needed to know. But Stumpp explained anyway. "You're a poor excuse for a human and an even worse pilot."

Anna stood up to the bully. "Who are you to talk to my husband that way?"

The pilot tried to restrain her. "I'm sorry, Mr. Stumpp. It won't happen again."

"You are entirely correct!" As Stumpp slammed the dining room doors closed, Charles exchanged glances with the child, Rebecca. Then the doors were sealed tight and locked from the outside.

Charles gripped his master's arm, and Stumpp spun around, staring at his manservant's hand until it was removed. "Sir," Charles began, "is this absolutely necessary?"

"Are you questioning me?" Something about Stumpp's voice didn't sound natural.

"You know I have been loyal to you for many years now, but I must protest this current course of action. The little girl is innocent. There is no need to—"

"Would you like to share her fate, Charles?" Stumpp spat out. "It can be easily arranged! Besides, you should be relieved that I

won't allow his family to suffer the burden of living without him."
The servant remained silent, and the master took his leave.

Looking back at the door, he mumbled, "She reminds me of the daughter I once had."

If Stumpp heard the comment, he didn't deign to reply.

Inside the room, the couple pulled furiously on the door handles, hoping something would give so they could flee this place. Rebecca stood by their side and hugged her teddy bear tighter. She didn't understand what was going on; but she knew her parents were upset, and that frightened her.

At the rear of the room, one of the large wood panels slid open, revealing foreboding darkness. The faint sound of breathing was heard, and slowly, a large bestial hand with claws at least six inches long emerged and rested itself on the floor. It was followed by a second hand, attached to a muscular, hairy arm, and then the creature's snout. The werewolf was huge, but it moved without making a noise. Its prey remained unaware of its presence. Its lips were parted, revealing interlocked razor-sharp fangs and saliva dripping through the canines. It stayed low to the ground while stalking its unsuspecting quarry. The family was still pulling at the locked doors. The werewolf crept across the floor until it was behind the family, and then it rose up on its hind legs. At full height, it stood nearly ten feet tall. It spread its arms apart, so its shadow engulfed the two adults.

The pilot noticed the immense outline hanging over him and swiveled his head to see what was causing it. His terrified eyes grew wide, and he grabbed his family, holding them close.

"Daddy, I'm scared," Rebecca sobbed.

The pilot rested her head on his chest and said, "Close your eyes, baby. Close your eyes."

The monster roared.

"Now, where were we?" Ethan asked. "Strength. Senses. Yes. We'll continue with your enhanced senses."

Jacob sat up to listen more closely to what his teacher had to say.

"Your vision has been increased tenfold. Not only won't you need glasses, but you can see incredibly far with ease, even in almost pitch darkness."

"It'll be nice to get rid of my dorky glasses."

Ethan overlooked the childish remark. "You'll begin to detect aromas previously denied to your inferior human nose, pick up a scent miles away, and smell the blood of your prey from the tiniest of wounds."

Jacob made a face that told his teacher to switch gears before he repulsed him.

"Try this with me, Jacob," Ethan started. "Focus on the sounds around you. I want you see how your hearing has improved to the point where you can hear a butterfly's wings flap in the breeze."

"Really?" He sounded as if he was excited at the possibilities his new abilities would afford him. He closed his eyes, attempting to follow instructions.

"Drown everything out and try to focus on a single sound far away from here. Try to listen to something, anything, outside these walls."

Struggling, he faintly heard a truck's reverse warning beep near the front door of the mansion, but a bloodcurdling roar rocked his concentration. And then the sounds of a family dying an unimaginable death caused Jacob to cover his ears, hoping to stop the screams from flooding in.

Ethan heard them too and knew he'd lost the boy. "Oh, hell," he said and speed-dialed Mr. Ball. "Come and get him. We're done here."

Jacob ran out of the room and sprinted up the stairs.

"He's heading your way," Ethan said into the phone. "He knows his strength has increased, but an unexpected blow should be sufficient to stun him. I'll be along presently."

Scrambling around a corner, Jacob frantically searched for the way out but didn't pay attention to where he was going. A muscular arm swung out from around a second bend, and Jacob was clotheslined square in the jaw; the impact lifted him off his feet, and he landed hard on his back. Before he could regain his footing, two electrodes from Mr. Ball's stun gun pierced his chest, and a jolt of electricity brought Jacob dangerously close to blacking out. Chainz wasted no time in tying his massive chain around the boy's ankles and dragging him to the armored truck parked outside.

Ethan strolled down the long hallway. "Keep him locked and unfed overnight in the truck. Tomorrow you'll take him somewhere where he'll learn to appreciate his new abilities. If that doesn't work, nothing will. You then have my permission to put him out of his misery."

"But I don't think Mr. Stumpp would—"

"Don't hurt yourself. I'll do the thinking from this point forward. You handle him," he said, pointing to Jacob, who was now being loaded in the back of the vehicle.

"Yes, sir."

Ethan watched the truck pull away, and then walked to the area of the house where the screams had originated from. Outside the dining area, the manservant was waiting alone. "Something on your mind, Charles?"

"It's been silent for a few minutes, but I'm still afraid to open it."

Ethan took the key from him and unlocked the door. "Allow me." He pulled the flaps toward him, looked inside the room, and gazed upon the bloody horror that was once a lavishly decorated dining hall. The table was overturned; food, blood, and flesh had been intermingled and smeared everywhere. The distorted bodies of a man and his family lay on the floor, partially devoured. Ethan had witnessed this type of carnage many times, but he now centered on the remains of a child's plaything: a small, brown teddy bear, once loved by a little girl, soaked in blood and torn apart, with the stuffing falling out of it.

"That poor child," Charles cut into Ethan's thoughts.

Ethan nodded, knowing what the butler was thinking. "We all had families once."

"I think of mine often."

"As do I," said Ethan, a bit of humanity seeping through his otherwise insensitive nature.

"What we do isn't right," said Charles.

Placing a hand on the butler's shoulder, Ethan said, "Right or wrong has nothing to do with it. Self-preservation is a natural instinct in all animals."

"This wasn't self-preservation."

"Do you forget, Charles?" Ethan headed toward the exit. "We work for a monster."

TWENTY-NINE

"This is a load of crap!" Mako said loudly, and the surrounding diners started to stare at him.

Mullins leaned in; his stomach flowed over the table's ledge. "Keep it down. Making a scene won't help matters." Sitting back, Mullins ripped open two sugar packets and poured their contents into his coffee. "You said you wanted to help, and this is what Grimes wants you to help with. Should I tell him you decline?"

"Don't treat me like I'm some kind of asshole, all right?" Mako slapped the booth's tabletop hard.

A waitress immediately rushed over. "Is everything all right? Can I get you anything else?"

"We're fine," Mullins said, then turned back to his company. "Listen, Mako. I don't have time for games, so here's the deal. You either do this or you don't. I don't give a shit either way. I told you this was going to happen, but you didn't want to listen to me."

"What did you tell me? That I was gonna get stuck babysitting while you do the 'real' police work?"

"You know what I said. I'm not repeating myself since it didn't do any good the first time. But the lieutenant wants you and Bailey to sit on Falcone to make sure nothing happens to him. I don't see what the big deal is."

Mako took a bite of his sandwich, swallowing most of it prior to speaking through a partially opened mouth. "You wouldn't. The only reason Grimes wants me to protect Falcone is because if I'm holed up in some motel room, I can't investigate the case at the same time."

"Which you shouldn't be doing anyway." Mullins sipped his drink. "But maybe you'll get lucky, and someone will try and kill you both. Come to think of it, maybe I'll get lucky for the same reason."

"Up yours."

"You screwed yourself, pal. But here's a bit of advice." He took another drink. "If you do decide to do this, you had better not mess it up. I can almost guarantee Grimes will nail you to the wall if you do."

"Did you ask Bailey yet?"

"No need to. Bailey will do what he's told. Unlike *some people.*" Mullins implied that his last words were directly associated with Mako: a point Mako didn't miss.

"It's still a bullshit assignment, but I'll do it. Just tell me when and where."

Later, Mako packed an overnight bag with all the essentials to survive a few nights in a motel room with his partner and their witness. He'd phoned Rikki earlier to ask him to care for his pets during his short absence, but his neighbor felt the need to discuss the matter in person.

"What do you mean you don't know how long you'll be away?"

"It's not like I'm going on vacation. It's work. I have to stay until I'm told."

"Why a motel?"

"It's the way they do things." Mako tossed a couple of comfortable shirts into his bag, along with a hairbrush and some socks. "The witness' house isn't safe. We can't keep him locked in a cage until this blows over. And he's not staying here!"

"But motels are filthy."

"I doubt that. Besides, I don't think the taxpayers want to pay for a suite at a five-star hotel."

"Well, be sure to sterilize the room before touching anything." Rikki searched for writing utensils, and then he asked, "What's the number there in case I need to reach you?"

"Really?" Mako sarcastically said. "Didn't I already tell you no one can know where we are?"

"So? I'm not just anyone."

"I hope you're kidding."

"Somewhat."

"I would hate to think a stone cold killer found out you knew where the witness he was looking for was stashed and came here to get the information. Think you can handle physical torture or worse?"

"I can take care of myself. My kickboxing instructor says I'm the best in the class."

Mako zipped his bag closed. "Well, I'm not willing to bet your life on that claim. Now, can you watch the animals or not?"

"Of course. You don't even have to worry about your cat."

"Thank you," Mako said, leaving the apartment.

Once outside, his cell rang. "I didn't even get in the car yet. What did you forget?"

"Mako. It's Jason."

"Oh, Brody. Sorry."

"Where's the lycanthrope now?"

"If you're talking about the young man named Louis Falcone, I'm on my way to babysit him for the night," he said, loading his bag into the trunk.

"You can't do that."

"Why is everyone telling me what to do all of a sudden?"

"I'm serious. There are only a few more hours of daylight, and if you are with him when the moon rises, he'll kill you and anyone else around."

Starting the car and switching his phone's speaker on, he said, "That kid is no killer. I had to save him from Walker's goons earlier today. They tried to kidnap him."

"Ethan?" Jason paused. "You definitely cannot do this! Tell me where you'll be. I'll take Falcone from you and put him somewhere he won't be able to hurt anyone."

"Relax. You said you were going to show me a werewolf, but all I saw was a frightened kid who can't even defend himself."

"That's because you saw him in the daylight, and he obviously doesn't realize what he is yet. But trust me. If you're with him when he changes, you will die!"

"Thanks for the concern, but I'll take my chances." Mako hung up on Jason and thought, *Werewolves. How stupid does he think I am?*

After parking his Lancer in the Second Precinct's back lot, away from passersby, Mako grabbed his duffel bag and loaded it in an unmarked car. He waited with Bailey until three uniformed officers brought Louis out in shackles. The lieutenant accompanied them with Mullins in tow. The officers loaded the prisoner in the unmarked car's back seat.

Bailey already had the keys, so Mako walked to the passenger side.

"Wait a minute," Grimes said. "I want to speak to you."

The detectives approached.

"I want you to remember you asked to be part of this case, so I expect you will perform your duties admirably and to the letter." He eyed both through his mirrored sunglasses.

"Yes, sir," Bailey answered, even though all present knew full well that he wanted nothing to do with the homicide investigation. "We understand."

"Dismissed." As they entered the car, Grimes added, "And Mako, don't fuck this up. I'm warning you."

Sighing heavily, Mako answered, "I'll try not to … sir."

At a nondescript motel, on the Nassau/Suffolk border, Mako found the room key in the car's glove box. Everything appeared to be taken care of to limit the amount of people Louis could potentially come into contact with. "Hang out a sec," he said to Bailey, and he entered the motel room alone to ensure that the area was cleared of unauthorized individuals and audio/video equipment. He drew the thick curtains and returned to the car. "We're good. Let's bring him in, then get the bags." He wasn't taking any chances.

Bailey helped Louis out of the back and rushed him inside, sitting him down in a chair away from the windows. Uncuffing one wrist, the detective fastened the steel shackle to an armrest, ensuring that Louis wouldn't get far should he try to escape.

Mako hurried in with all the bags and bolted the door shut behind him. "I didn't see anyone nosing around. You?"

"Nah. We're good," his partner replied.

Their witness appeared extremely nervous, so Mako sat on the bed, facing him, and said, "Take it easy, kid. I promise if you trust me, I won't let anything happen to you. By the same token, if you run, there'll be no place you can hide from me." Then Mako went into the bathroom, closing the door behind him.

Not sure what to think, Louis asked Bailey, "Is he for real?"

"I can tell you that for as long as I've known him, he's been true to his word," Bailey said.

Reemerging, Mako asked, "Who's hungry? I'm buying."

"With departmental money," Bailey added.

"Does that mean you're not eating?"

"I didn't say that."

"That's what I thought. You know what you want?"

"I know what I'd like," Louis spoke up.

"You eat what we eat," Bailey said. "Give me the cash. I'll go get the food."

Mako handed over the money-filled envelope. "Make sure to get a receipt. Don't want Grimes any further up our asses than he already is."

"Wouldn't be that way, if you could've minded your own business."

"Let's not get into that again."

"You don't listen anyhow. I'm only reminding you that I didn't ask for any of this, so if it doesn't go right, I'm holding you responsible for any shit he gives me."

"Whatever," Mako unpacked his toiletries and put them in the small bathroom. Sticking his head out, he said, "Are you going to get the food, or do we go hungry tonight?"

"Lock up behind me." Bailey took the car keys and left.

Mako returned to Louis' side and removed the handcuffs, allowing him to move freely about. "Now that we have some time alone, you and I are going to talk."

"About what?"

"Can you tell me where you were Friday night?"

Louis didn't speak.

He tried a different approach. "Do you know someone by the name of Robert Mane?" There was still no response, but Mako noticed that Louis' eyes watered up at the mention of his friend. He went with it. "Did you know Robert Mane was brutally murdered Friday night in the Muttontown Preserve?"

A tear rolled down Louis' cheek.

"Were you there?" Mako asked, attempting to sound sympathetic. "Do you know what happened?"

"I, I don't know anything," he whispered, shame sounding in his voice.

The detective had questioned many individuals, both as a police officer and as a civilian, and he knew when someone was lying. Under normal circumstances, this would be the time he would try to strong-arm a suspect who was untruthful, but there was something about Louis that unsettled him. "Listen, if there's anything you want to tell me, now would be a good time."

"I have nothing to say." He couldn't look the detective in the eye.

Mako's patience was being tested, but before he did anything about it, his cellphone rang. The name displayed was MULLINS, and Mako moved away to answer it.

"I hope our boy isn't giving you any trouble," a gruff voice came through the speaker.

"Did you call to just break balls?"

"I didn't want to tell Grimes I knew the two goons who tried to kidnap Falcone, or I'd have to give away that you crashed the interview I had with Stumpp's assistant. But I have a meeting with the big boss tomorrow. I'll see if I can find out if he authorized the failed hit."

"Did you think about my offer?" Mako asked, referring to the offer he'd made to exchange information if he could participate in that interview too.

"My answer is no. You just sit on that kid, and don't let him out of your sight."

"Why call then?"

"I wanted you to know I'm not a rat. That's all."

"Is that supposed to make me feel warm and fuzzy?"

"Go to hell, you unappreciative jerk." And Mullins hung up on him.

As soon as Mako hit the END button, his anger rose. He had to get something out of Falcone, if only to prove that he could be useful in the investigation. Rushing the pudgy witness, Mako rammed his forearm into Louis' neck. He grabbed Louis' bicep, in case he decided to resist. The detective's unexpected thrust served to knock Louis off balance and slam him into the mirrored closet door behind him. Mako pushed hard on his throat, subconsciously taking out some of the anger he felt toward Mullins on Louis. "All right, you little bastard. I tried to play nice with you! Now, you better start talking. What the hell happened that night at Stumpp Industries?"

Louis' facial expression was strained: squinted eyes and a clenched jaw made it seem as if he was trying to hold something back. Then a look of mortification overcame him, and the smell soon followed.

"What the hell?" Mako gasped as the aroma overwhelmed him. "What crawled up your ass and died?"

"I'm sorry," Louis said through a partially crushed windpipe. "I have a nervous stomach."

"You should get that checked." Mako eased off, so Louis could talk easier. "Are you going to talk now?"

Louis saw no point in keeping quiet any longer, already humiliated. The faster he got this over with, the better. "I was there. Bobby and me were friends since we were kids. It didn't take much for him to convince me to help him out with anything, and that night was no different. I knew I shouldn't have let him talk me into it; but he always knew what to say to make me feel guilty about, well, about almost everything," Louis said, with regret apparent in his voice. "He wanted to steal something, and he'd heard it was in his boss' office. Bobby thought it would be a cakewalk. It's called the Silver Heart or something like that."

The Heart of Lycaon flashed through Mako's mind. "Why did Mane think it would be easy?" he asked, still covering his nose to avoid breathing in the noxious odor.

"Bobby said his boss didn't trust men to keep his stuff safe. That he only trusted his animals, dogs to be specific. I was scared shit to be in that place, but I still went with him to the thirteenth floor. Bobby told me to stay by the elevator and keep it open so it wouldn't leave. It was fine by me. He was so stupid to think we'd get away with it."

Before Louis went off on a tangent, Mako interrupted. "At what point did you leave them stranded?"

"How do you know?"

"If you had waited like you were told, you would've most likely left the scene the same way your buddy did: in a body bag."

"Yeah, I left. But believe me, it was hard to do, even when the screams started. I tried to stay and wait. I was even debating going to see if I could help Bobby; but then out of the corner of my eye, I saw it staring at me," Louis said, catching his breath. "It was huge." The fear in his eyes told the detective that he was reliving the moment. "The security lights gave it away, and the fucking thing was huge! Never seen a dog that big before. It jumped at me, and I hit the son of a bitch in the nose with the flashlight, hard. I fell back into the elevator, got to the lobby, and ran the hell out of there as fast as I could. I called the police once I was far enough away, but they weren't able to save Bobby."

Mako was undecided about what to do next. Technically, Louis was involved in a breaking-and-entering, but he didn't actually steal anything. He could still charge him with third-degree burglary, but Louis might have other vital information leading to the capture of a killer.

Louis was merely hoping the air had cleared—literally.

Making his choice, Mako said, "I appreciate you being honest with me, so I'm going to try and make life a little easier for you from this point on. I have to speak with my superiors, but if you're willing to make an official statement, I'll see if they agree that any involvement on your part will be shown leniency because of your cooperation with the Nassau County Police Department. How does that sound to you? Would you like this nightmare to finally be over?" Just then, his cellphone rang, and he stopped Louis from answering his questions. "Mako."

"Johnny, it's me," Jacquie said. "I have some news."

"Hold on." He cuffed Louis to the chair again and went to the door, looking around before stepping outside. "Don't move," he warned.

Unable to extend his arm any significant distance from the armrest, Louis said, "Where am I gonna go?"

"Everything okay?" Jacquie asked.

"Wonderful." Mako walked a few feet from the room. "So, what'd you find out?"

"Most of those DNA samples you sent me seem tainted, and most labs would have ruled them as inconclusive."

"That's not helpful."

"I said most labs," she reiterated. "I've seen results like this before, as you know; otherwise, you wouldn't have involved me. Two of the men at the burglary popped in the criminal database, but the sample of your third perp came up clean. However, the clean sample's DNA was also present in the seemingly tainted sample from the Broadway Mall killing."

Shifting the phone from one ear to the other, he said, "I don't get it. How are the samples similar but not?"

"I have some theories. It appears something happened to the third subject between the burglary and the murder at the mall, altering his DNA."

"Altering it to what?"

"Like I said, I have some theories. I'll tell you more when I get there."

"You're coming here?" Mako's surprise couldn't be contained.

"Is that a problem?" Jacquie's defenses kicked in.

He didn't know what to say. "It's not necessary, especially since I won't be around for a few days."

"Oh really?" Her tone was reminiscent of their dating days. "Where are you going?"

"Witness protection."

"What witness?"

"A kid named Falcone," he whispered. He figured no one in Georgia but Jacquie would have any interest in this case, so she'd be in no danger of knowing. "He may have seen a murder and was nearly kidnapped in front of the precinct today."

"Did you say Falcone? Louis Falcone?"

"How did you know?"

"The clean sample I ran came back with his name."

"He's got a rap sheet?"

"No. He was printed for a civil service job, but that's not the point."

"What is your point? I don't want to leave him alone too long."

"You're with him now?" The alarm in her voice was frighteningly clear.

"Yeah, why? What's the problem?" As Mako became more engrossed in his conversation, he failed to notice the well-dressed man sneak into his motel room.

THIRTY

Ethan Walker followed the detectives from the time they left the Second Precinct with Louis. He hid outside the motel room, waiting to make his move. His sensitive ears picked up the entire conversation as Mako forcibly extracted information from his witness. And even though there were parts that Louis greatly embellished, Ethan remained out of sight until the exchange was over and the detective had left the room to answer his cell. Then he coolly stepped out of the shadows and snuck inside. "That's not exactly the way it happened, now is it, Mr. Falcone?"

Louis didn't recognize him. "I'm sorry. Do I know you?"

"Not by name," he replied. "But we have met previously."

"I would remember if we did. Are you a detective?"

"Not remotely; however, your scent is permanently etched in my brain. I could find you anywhere you go."

Shuddering at the ominous statement, Louis inexplicably felt a connection with the stranger.

"Search your mind. You must remember me from that night when you so bravely stood guard at my employer's elevator while your friends were fleeing for their lives from the monster on the thirteenth floor."

Louis' eyes widened as Ethan's silver hair sparkled under the fluorescent lights, triggering a memory. "You were there," Louis stated, amazed at the idea that the man in front of him was not what he appeared. "You were the dog!"

"Wolf, actually," Ethan corrected. "And if I remember the events accurately, you soiled yourself as I lunged for you and sank my teeth into your fleshy forearm. Yes, you hit me with your flashlight, with all the force a small child could muster, but I only let you go when I heard your friend approaching. Unfortunately, you got away before I could find you again. But here we are, together at last."

"Wh-what do you want from me?"

"Haven't you heard a word I said?" Jacquie sounded more exasperated by the second. "Falcone's DNA has the presence of … other genetic material mixed in."

"And that means what to me exactly?"

"You can be so stubborn sometimes!"

"I have no idea what you're talking about." Mako suddenly felt like they were dating again.

"If my theory is correct—"

"Your theory," he interrupted. "You haven't said shit about your theory. Why don't you tell me what it is, and maybe I'll understand what you're trying to say."

"Johnny." She paused for a moment. "I don't know exactly *how* to say this."

"Spit it out."

"I think Falcone is a werewolf," she said, quickly before her logical mind had a chance to prevent her from voicing the words. "I know it sounds crazy, but—"

"You're the second person who's told me that, and I still don't believe it."

"What did you think I would conclude from this DNA, when you know I think my parents were killed by something …

unheard-of? I thought that was the whole reason you asked me to be a part of this."

Frustrated, he said, "I don't know what I thought. You're the only person I know who could have helped me without Grimes finding out. And you're good at what you do. I had thought you'd outgrown the fantasy and acknowledged that a man murdered your parents."

"I can't believe you just said that to me," said Jacquie. His words temporarily stunned her, but there was more at stake here than pride. This was a chance to get one step closer to finding her parents' killer. "I'm coming up. Don't try to stop me!" she maintained. "I've already cleared my schedule, and if I'm right, you're going to need more help than I can provide from here."

"I don't suppose I can convince you I'll be okay?"

"Is there some reason you don't want to see me? Or is it that I'm only good enough until you got what you needed from me?"

"It's not like that. You know—"

She cut him off, "I'm catching the first plane out. Hopefully, I'll be there prior to you getting yourself killed." She hung up before he could voice more objections. Double-checking the data as her assistant entered the room, she was taken back to her early days as a Boston police officer. She remembered all the strings she'd pulled to reopen the case involving her parents' murders, how she'd devoted all her free time to solving the homicide, against her captain's wishes. Desperate to solve the case before her C.O. closed it again, she'd stumbled onto DNA evidence that was sure to put her parents' killer away for good; but regrettably, it was found inconclusive. She'd insisted it should be studied further, but was told it was a futile effort. The case was sealed indefinitely. She kept all public records, and some classified data, secretly vowing to not stop searching until their deaths were avenged.

"Are you okay?" Hartman asked, observing a change in her mood. "Hey," he said again, trying to get her attention. "Are you all right?"

Swallowing the lump in her throat, Jacquie answered, "I'm all right, Max."

"What are the findings? Is Jarvis guilty?"

"It's not that case."

"Are you working on whatever your friend in New York sent you?"

"Yes, I am," she answered, sensing her assistant's disapproval. "Do you have a problem with that?"

"Our first priority should be Dave Jarvis."

"Priorities change," she said, retrieving her phone and jacket. "And right now, I need to get to New York right away."

"But—"

"Get me the first flight out."

"But—"

"You'll keep me updated on the Jarvis case from here."

He figured it was useless, but another try couldn't hurt: "Are you sure?"

She flipped her cell open and keyed in the number she wanted to dial, but before she hit the SEND button, she turned to him and answered his unspoken questions: "I'm sure my supervisors here will have a problem with me leaving. I'm sure you think I'm making a rash decision. But I'm also sure of one more thing. For reasons you are not privy to at this time, I'm sure I need to do this. And you will help me, not because I'm your boss, but because I'm asking. Please."

Hartman weighed his ethics against the sincerity in her voice before yielding. "What do you need me to do?"

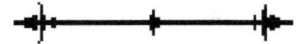

Since discovering his visitor's identity, Louis was only interested in getting away as quickly as possible. He stopped listening to the man's speech about loyalty, self-preservation, and great power within oneself; but as much as Louis wanted to run, his cuffs prevented it. Instead, he hoped the detective would come back to save him.

Ethan droned on until he realized Louis wasn't paying attention, and then he snapped his fingers in front of the young man's face. "It's rude to ignore someone who's speaking to you."

Not wanting to offend the scary individual in front of him, Louis remarked, "I heard every word." Not a convincing statement, but he'd tried.

"Do you not realize the opportunity I am giving you here?" Ethan was agitated by the lie. "Can you not imagine the power that would be at your disposal? All I am asking is a favor from you in return for the gift bestowed upon you."

Louis didn't know how to answer, which only served to fuel his visitor's rage. Ethan's breathing became heavy, and his eyes rolled to the back of his head, leaving only the whites showing. Mesmerized by the changes happening to the silver-haired man's hands—the fingers were growing larger, and the fingernails were extending like mini-daggers—Louis determined it would be a good time to yell for help, and filled his lungs with air.

Ethan's pupils snapped back into place, and he grabbed Louis by the neck with his normal hand. Lifting the overweight young man, still attached to the chair, with ease, Ethan slammed him into the mirrored closet, cracking the glass. "First you insult me," he growled. "Then you try and escape me. I don't know what's wrong with the youth of today, but when offered great things to change your otherwise dismal lives, you have the audacity to spit in the face of the one who extends a helping hand. Well, Mr. Falcone, I am not in the mood for discourtesy, so now I have another hand to extend to you."

"No, I didn't mean to—"

Louis was about to pee himself, when suddenly, he felt a sharp pain in his stomach. Hesitantly, he looked down. He screamed, seeing the blood pour out of him in bucketfuls.

Ethan loosened his grip on Louis' shirt, dropping him to the floor, and the boy fell to his knees as soon as his feet touched the ground. Ethan watched Louis attempt to cover his wound and stop the bleeding, but he knew Louis didn't have much time as his lower intestine began to creep out of his body. "Pitiful," said Ethan. It was the only word he could muster to describe the weeping mess before him.

"Oh, shit!" Mako reached for his gun upon hearing the commotion and ran to Louis. Throwing open the door, he struggled to see inside the now darkened room. He searched for a light switch while swinging his gun arm from side to side, looking for a target. "Louis! Are you okay?" He waited for an answer that did not come. "Say anything so I know you're all right." As Mako's hand grazed the wall plate that surrounded the switch, large, powerful fingers gripped Mako's forearm and flung him clear across the bed, nearly pulling his shoulder from its socket.

His back slammed into the sliding closet doors, and he protected his face as small glass shards fell around him. He heard a low, menacing growl from the other side of the room; he tried to convince himself he was imagining the sound, blaming it on all the silly stories he'd been told the past few days. The growl closed in, and Mako wasn't taking any chances. "Louis! If you can hear me, get down!" He raised his gun and fired three shots, hoping to hit whatever was in the room with him. Experience and random noises told him he killed a lamp, the television, and part of the door frame. But luck shone upon him as Ethan lifted his arm, preparing to deliver the killing strike, and the fading sunlight reflected off his razor-sharp finger-knives. Gasping in horror, Mako automatically aimed at the glimmer, yelling, "NO! YOU BASTARD!"

The gun exploded and a single bullet rocketed from the chamber; even though Ethan possessed incredible reflexes, he could not get out of the way in time. He maneuvered his body backward to evade the projectile, keeping his deformed limb above his head to remain balanced, but the bullet tore through his flesh and shattered most of the bones in his hand. The werewolf snarled, bearing his pronounced canines.

Mako pushed off the floor to get upright, but he lost his footing in a slippery substance and fell again. Although he couldn't see it, as soon as he rested his hand in the slick liquid, he knew what it was and feared the worst.

Ethan was about to lunge at the detective a second time, fully intending to rip his throat out, but fast-approaching sirens caught his attention. It was a matter of fight or flight. Holding his injured hand, he shouted, "Another time, Detective." Taking the intelligent route, he darted out of the motel room and dashed away before the police arrived, leaving Mako lying in a pool of Louis Falcone's blood.

Crawling to the opened doorway, Mako stood up; his body was badly bruised from the encounter. Flicking the lights on, he saw Louis' mangled body. He was about to check for a pulse when Bailey jumped out of his car, calling out to him, "What happened?

A call came in that shots were fired from this location. How's Falcone?"

"It's over," Mako said. "It's fuckin' over."

THIRTY-ONE

For most of the following day Lieutenant Grimes fielded phone call after phone call as he was reprimanded for losing a prisoner under his protection, and his air was one of muted rage. On a call with yet another irate superior, he said, "Yes, sir." He waited as his superior spoke. "Yes, sir. I understand. I'm not sure what happened either, but I'll find and burn whoever's responsible." He paused again. "Of course. I'll keep the media out of it for as long as possible. Thank you, sir." Feelings of relief surfaced when he placed the receiver down and it didn't ring again.

Thinking quietly for what seemed to be an eternity, Grimes kept Detective Mullins waiting for an uncomfortable amount of time. As his subordinate was about to speak, the lieutenant asked, "How could he have possibly messed this up?" Mullins knew Grimes meant Mako but he offered no response. "Can you tell me how? Because I can't come up with an answer. It's un-fucking-believable! All he had to do was babysit some asshole so some other asshole couldn't hurt him, but he royally fucked up on both counts!"

"With all due respect, sir, Mako was pretty banged up. It appeared he fought back the best he could."

"The hell?" Grimes looked around the room in frustration. "Don't try my patience by sticking up for Mako. That jerk-off is going to ruin both of us! According to Bailey, Mako might not have even been in the room when Falcone was murdered."

"Where was Bailey?"

"He went to secure dinner."

"Then it seems to me he wasn't inside the room either."

"What are you saying, Mullins?"

"He isn't completely off the hook."

Grimes slammed his fist on the desk. "You listen to me and keep that shit to yourself! I don't want you saying anything to anyone about this matter. *I'll* decide how to handle it, and *I'll* determine who goes down for it! Do you understand my meaning?"

There was no love lost between Mullins and Mako. But fairness was something Mullins believed in, and he knew fair would have nothing to do with the inevitable outcome. But he had no choice but to agree, unless he wanted his head on the chopping block too. "I do … sir."

Mako's feet dangled off the edge of his hospital bed as he waited for the nurse to return with more pain medication. He'd suffered three fractured ribs and several pulled ligaments in his nearly dislocated shoulder; it was difficult to move normally without experiencing pain. Hinges creaking behind him indicated that someone entered the room.

"How are you feeling?" a man's voice asked. "I found out you blacked out from your injuries at the motel and have been sedated since last evening."

Turning around, Mako saw a familiar face. "What are you doing here, Brody? And don't tell me you were concerned with my health."

Jason moved to his front, so the detective did not have to strain by twisting. "I told you this would happen. You should have listened."

"Everyone has an 'I told you so.'" He laughed slightly, and then grabbed his torso to quell the pain. "You were wrong. You said I'd be killed, but who's still standing? Well, I will be standing as soon as you throw me my pants."

Handing the detective the jeans that hung on one of the chair backs, Jason said, "I'm glad my prediction did not come to pass."

"I wish I could say the same for Falcone. I promised to protect him."

"I know you believe you saw a murder, but you did not."

Mako grunted as he slid his pants over his waist and fastened them. "The kid's guts were spilled all over the floor. I was soaked in his blood. Don't tell me what I saw."

"Did the beast take his heart?"

"What?" The detective struggled to get his shirt on.

"Did the," Jason paused, making sure no one was in earshot. "Did the werewolf take Falcone's heart?"

Spinning around, angry, Mako said, "Enough with this fairy tale shit! There are no such animals!" Realizing he was raising his voice, Mako quieted down. "I admit there were some … things that were strange about my attacker, but I couldn't see anything in that room that would make me believe it was a werewolf."

"How do you account for its strength? Its speed? Falcone's injuries?" Jason seized Mako's arm, jolting him a little too hard, so that his wounds made him wince. "I didn't have to be there to know that you were asking yourself the same questions, or that you were scared you wouldn't live long enough to get the answers."

Jerking away from Jason, he said, "You're right. I did want to know how whoever that was got the drop on me so fast, and how he was able to toss me—a 200-plus man—across the room like I was nothing. And when I find him, I'll be sure to ask."

"You can't be serious."

"About what?"

"Going forward with this. You've been given a second chance. Don't waste it."

"You're the one who dragged me into this."

"I, I made a mistake," Jason admitted.

"Your 'mistake' cost Falcone his life! And on my watch! I can't let that go!"

"There was nothing you could do."

"Falcone was my responsibility, and I failed him. The least I can do is even the score."

"You aren't ready for this!"

"You're wrong. After what that skel did to me and that poor kid, he's gonna find out he's not ready for me."

"You're going to pursue this regardless of what I say, and I don't want your death hanging over my head," said Jason. Prepared to allow the detective to back his statement up, he added, "If you really feel how you claim, I'd suggest you leave with me right now. I know where we can begin your redemption."

The cab ride to Mako's apartment was awkward, as was being in New York. Applying Chap Stick to her full lips, a habit of hers whenever she was anxious, Jacquie hoped her return wouldn't prove to be a bad idea. She stared out the rear passenger window and wondered what his reaction would be when he first laid eyes on her; she wished it would be the same as when they were dating. Her emotions were off the charts, but she couldn't lose sight of her goal. Two years had passed, and she'd fully gotten over the man—or so she'd believed. But her feelings for him were still intact; she'd never let go of the premise that he was the "One."

She approached the front steps and heard a loud scream emanate from inside the home. Dropping her luggage, she reached for her gun—ready to deal with any potential danger—but relaxed her grip once Rikki flung open the front door with his arms outstretched. He was squealing with delight.

He ran over to Jacquie and gave her a squeeze. "Oh my God! Look who's in town. It's been ages!" His head bobbled from side to side as if his neck couldn't fully support the weight. Stepping back, he continued to hold her hands as he eyed her up and down—from her wavy brown hair, sparkling eyes, and that surprised, wonderful smile she flashed, all the way down to those long slender legs of hers. "Oh my goodness," he said, hugging her again. "You look amazing! How do you do it? Let me help you with those." Grabbing a suitcase, he led her upstairs to the apartment, pulled out a kitchen chair, and chased the animals away, scolding, "Shoo! Get away! Don't mess up Jacquie's clothes. Which by the way, that is a beautiful top. Here. Sit. Can I get you anything?" He took the seat opposite her and took a breath.

Overwhelmed by his greeting, she said, "It's good to see you too, Rikki. I wasn't expecting a hello quite like that."

"Why not?"

"I really don't know why. I guess I didn't think you liked me that much."

Placing a hand over his heart, stunned at the accusation, he held her hands and said, "Sweetie, you were my favorite out of everyone Johnny ever brought home."

"Thank you. But truthfully, I always thought you gave me a hard time whenever he and I went out."

Embarrassed, Rikki admitted, "Can I be honest with you? The reason I might have been … moody with you is because I was a little jealous. I was having a bit of a dry spell back then, and every happy couple that crossed my path made me nauseous. But don't tell Johnny. He'll think I'm petty and possibly take my keys away." He directed his attention to the two dogs waiting patiently for attention. "And then I wouldn't get to see my babies for a while."

"I understand," she said sincerely. "I get jealous of others too at times."

Rubbing her hands, he gave a consoling smile. "I don't see why. You can have your pick of guys. Let me grab a bottle of wine from my apartment, and we can talk about it."

"I would love to, and maybe later we will," she said, not forgetting the reason for taking the trip. "But I need to speak to Johnny right away. Do you know where he is?"

"I thought you knew already." Rikki was puzzled. "Isn't that the reason you came?"

"What's wrong?" she asked, fearing the worst because he'd refused to heed her advice about Louis.

"He's in the hospital."

"That idiot," she thought out loud. "I told him this would happen. He never listens."

"I'm sure you're not the only one to feel that way." Still, Rikki was surprised by her reply. "When did you speak to him last?"

"Yesterday. And I warned him how dangerous his assignment was, but he basically called me crazy. Do you know which one he's in?"

"Yes and no."

Unwilling to be frustrated by his flakiness, she said, "Is he in the hospital or not? You sounded like you were sure."

"Yes. I mean, I think so." He turned on the television and flipped through the channels, stopping at the news. "There was a report about a cop injured in the line of duty at a motel. The names weren't released, but one person was killed, and the cop went to

South Shore hospital. I tried to call his cell, but it must be off. It went straight to voice mail."

Dialing information, Jacquie got the hospital's number and was soon on the phone with a receptionist. She claimed to be an immediate relative and was informed that without proof, the staff could not give her any information on patients or anyone potentially under the hospital's care. After contemplating her next move, she called the police precinct, asking the desk officer to speak with him. The officer transferred her, but someone other than her desired party picked up.

"Second Precinct. Detective Bailey speaking."

She didn't want to tell the same lie to someone in her line of work as she had with the hospital staff. "Hi. I'm Investigator Jacquie Dale, working out of the Georgia police department. Is Detective Mako available?"

Her name gave Bailey pause, as it sounded familiar. "No, he isn't. What is this regarding?"

"It's a personal matter. I'm an old friend." Although she didn't want to lie, she saw no reason to be entirely honest either.

"Would you care to leave a message, and I'll give it to him when he returns?" He was stalling for time.

"No, thank you," she said. She'd gotten all the information she needed. "I'll try again later. Do you know when he'll be back?"

"I'm sorry, Miss Dale, but I don't. Have a good day." And the phone disconnected.

Rikki began to worry. "Where is he, and why will no one update you on his whereabouts?"

"Stay calm." Jacquie had a trick or two up her sleeve, but they were rapidly running out of options. "I might have another way to find him."

THIRTY-TWO

Jason drove away from the hospital with Mako hidden in the back of his van. Two orderlies and a doctor darted through the front entrance, presumably looking for their escaped patient, but the three of them quickly faded out of sight in his rearview mirror. Once he felt they were safe, Jason motioned for his passenger to move up to the front.

Despite being lied to already by Jason, Mako would rather trust him than be incapacitated in a hospital room, unable to exact pay back on his motel attacker. "Where are we going?"

"There's been a sighting."

The detective had already expressed numerous times that he did not put any credence to his associate's claims of the existence of supernatural monsters, but instead of arguing the point yet again, he played along. "How do you know?"

"Hold on." Jason pulled off the road, shut the van's engine off, and hopped into the back with all of his technical gear. Switching the audio equipment on, he rewound a recording and began to play it. "This is a nine-one-one call about a 'shots fired' incident just minutes before my arrival at the hospital."

"How did you—"

Jason held up something that looked like a walkie-talkie. "Police scanner."

"Of course." Mako wasn't surprised. "No mention of a werewolf, I assume?"

"No, but I heard growling in the background." The tape continued to roll. "There." Jason pointed to an imaginary spot. "It's right there." Then the sound of gunshots was heard.

"I don't hear anything."

"Let me clean up the sound." Rewinding the tape, he made a few adjustments to filter out ambient noises and distortions. "Listen."

Mako leaned in closer, aiming his ear at the speaker. "I still don't hear anything."

"Trust me. It's there." After toggling the switches to the off position, Jason jumped back into the front seat, started the engine, and sped away. "I don't have time to fiddle with it any longer or we risk it getting away."

"Did you tell your friends?" Mako was referring to Nathan's Lunar Guardians.

"They're not my friends, and no I didn't. Nathan would have been monitoring police activity too, and he'll be looking into a 'wild dog' call put out close to the same time as the 'shots fired' call."

"What about the growling?"

"If you didn't hear it, he won't. He doesn't have the same tools I have. Besides, Nathan may be resourceful, but he's predictable. He'd rather stick to literal translations than think out of the box." Jason swerved around a slower driver. "But please, Detective, you must be prepared for what you are about to see. It can be … jarring the first time."

Mako didn't answer because he believed there would be nothing to see once they arrived at their destination. At the moment, he was more concerned about how much trouble he was going to be in once his lieutenant got word that he left the hospital without proper clearance. Mostly, he dreaded the foreseeable yelling.

"Let me out!" Jacob demanded, only to be ignored again. His fear mounted. He was trapped in the back of the armored vehicle, being transported to a place only known by his captors. "LET ME OUT!" He roared, slamming his fists into the interior wall.

The blow was so fierce it rocked the truck, and Chainz had to yank the wheel to get it back on the right side of the road. But Chainz and Mr. Ball continued to disregard their passenger's pleas. Deliberately driving to one of the more neglected areas of Nassau, they stopped next to a derelict playground. The chain-link fence surrounding it had been torn down completely in some spots, and gaping holes existed in others. The basketball court was littered with garbage, the rim hanging off the graffiti-sprayed backboard had long since been missing its net, and the dumpster off to the side was overflowing with bags upon bags of filth.

Mr. Ball was the first to exit the vehicle but was soon joined by Chainz behind the truck. Just as Jacob was in the middle of another chorus of "Let me out," complete with banging on the cargo doors, they flung the doors open without warning and he fell unceremoniously to the hard concrete. Wiping the blood from a cut on his cheek, Jacob was relieved to be free but did not like the look of his new environment.

Mr. Ball crouched next to him. "This is your last chance. You either accept what's happened to you or not. I don't get paid to care which. But we will be watching, and we were told to take you out if necessary."

"'Take me out'?" Jacob sort of understood what he meant, but wanted it clarified in case he was wrong.

Running a finger across his throat, Mr. Ball made his meaning clear. "Here's the deal, kid. This is Lakeside Kings territory," he said, gesturing to a group of men standing in the playground. "And they don't take kindly to strangers. It's either you or them, and you don't have much time to choose."

As the group drew near, one of the individuals moved a bat, hidden behind his back, into view. Another took a stiletto from his pocket and clicked the blade out of its hiding place within the handle. And yet another picked up a piece of gnarled wood with a few nails sticking out of it. The remaining two men refrained from revealing any weaponry they might be carrying, for the moment.

"Have fun," Chainz added with a sly grin. He and his partner left the scared and confused young man to fend for himself against the violent gang members, and then they drove away.

Slowly encircling Jacob, who still lay on the ground staring up at them, the group mocked him in a language he didn't understand. After they'd had their laugh, the leader set his sights on Jacob. "You don't belong around here, *cabron.*"

One of the men punched Jacob in the mouth and chuckled as the blood trickled out from between Jacob's lips. Another gang member kicked him in the ribs and knocked him over onto his back. Jacob coughed, trying to regain his breath, and the leader knelt beside him and whispered, "You're going to die tonight."

Looking past the circle of predators, he saw the waning moon hanging high in the sky, and for the first time since the night his life was drastically altered, Jacob welcomed the imminent transformation. He said in a voice almost unrecognizable as his own, "Are you sure about that?"

The leader straightened his legs until he was at his full height of five-foot-six and shouted something unrecognizable to his followers. They immediately closed in, hammering Jacob with every weapon at their disposal.

From a distance, inside their vehicle, Chainz asked, "How much longer?"

"Watch."

One of the gang members was tossed from the pile like a rag doll and flew through the air, slamming into the dumpster nearly twenty feet away. Two more were viciously forced back as a giant claw swatted them like flies, and the remaining two backed up to a safe distance, out of the reach of what they'd thought would be easy prey.

The park was close to an apartment complex, and an elderly woman watching from her third-floor apartment window quickly pulled her head inside and called the cops.

Jacob got his feet under him once more, but he was clearly not the same scared individual who'd fallen out of the truck. His body increased in size and mass, with fur protruding from random tears in his clothing. His face was partially covered with hair, his teeth had become like daggers, and his breathing was heavy, though not from fatigue. The pain he experienced as the change altered him from man to beast took a toll, but the animal inside showed no sign of weakness. He fixed his eyes on the leader; somewhere within his mind, Jacob remembered that this was the alpha male vying for dominance. He growled and took a single step forward.

The gang leader's eyes widened to almost abnormal proportions as fear gripped his heart, but he managed to reach for his pistol, make the sign of the cross, and fire. Four bullets penetrated the monster's chest, and the impact forced Jacob off his feet and onto his back again. He lay still on the pavement.

The leader looked around at his troops who were just regaining consciousness. He felt a sense of relief and pride at being the one to eliminate the target, knowing his role would be cemented once the others witnessed his success. He stared at his latest victim for several minutes before accepting his victory, finally waving his gun in the air and praising his courage.

Without warning, Jacob's head snapped forward, now more bestial than before, and his roar echoed in the streets.

The color rushed out of the gang leader's face, and he stood frozen in place. His men experienced the same sensation—except for one who had the good sense to run away.

The werewolf sprung off the floor and onto all fours. Drool fell from his mouth as hunger took over, and he was not about to leave without a meal. The remainder of the petrified gang drew previously concealed pistols, shooting wildly and repeatedly. Jacob jumped forward, easily dodging the sloppily aimed bullets. He targeted the leader yet again, reaching his goal in mere seconds. He slammed his huge hands into the little man's chest and sent the gang leader flying through the air.

The passengers of a lone vehicle driving on the street didn't even see the body until it crashed through the windshield. Panic caused the driver to careen into a parked car on the other side of the road.

The werewolf didn't give a second thought to the man who now lay on the hood of the car, his back broken. He merely lunged at another of the former leader's cohorts, looking to satisfy his appetite.

Mako and Jason hadn't spoken a word to each other since entering the disreputable neighborhood. Ejecting his gun's ammunition clip, the detective checked that it was fully loaded and then snapped it back into place. Jason noticed the slight tremors in his colleague's hands, indicating that his adrenaline was rising from anticipation.

"Take these," he said and handed Mako two gun clips filled with shining ammunition he took from his coat pocket.

Mako examined the magazines and chuckled. "What are these? Silver bullets?"

"I snuck them out of Nathan's arsenal. If you're serious about finding Falcone's killer and his kind, you're going to need them. Use them sparingly. That's all I could take without someone noticing."

The GPS instructed them to turn left at the next corner, and almost immediately after doing so, something crashed violently through the front windshield.

"What the fuck!" Mako instinctively shielded his face. A few seconds after the initial impact, Jason crashed into a parked automobile on the opposite side of the road. Mako was jolted forward but was prevented from hitting the dashboard as his seatbelt locked into place.

The shaken occupants got out, and the detective was the first to notice the person sprawled on the van's hood. The man's head was stuck halfway through the thick, shatterproof glass. Mako moved to the bloodied body and checked for a pulse; he could tell by the way the individual was lying that he must have suffered severe back or neck trauma, and that death had been instantaneous. Jason surveyed the area in order to find out what could have caused the incident.

"Glad this isn't my car."

"I didn't realize you were so compassionate." Jason's sarcastic side surfaced.

Mako looked the dead man over. "I wouldn't shed any tears over this guy, if I were you."

"And why's that?"

"See the ink on his neck?" he asked, pointing to a LK tattoo on the side closest to him. "He's part of the dominant gang in this area. I'm guessing he was either tossed from a roof by a rival crew, or by one of his own who was looking to replace him."

"I don't think so, Detective," Jason said.

"Tell me, then. How did this guy end up in your windshield?"

"That's how." Jason pointed into the distance.

Spinning around, Mako observed the other gang members on a run-down basketball court, firing their pistols at something obscured from view by a large dumpster. Abruptly, a giant wolf-like creature pounced on top of one of the men and ripped him to pieces in front of their eyes. His heart pounding faster, Mako unconsciously took a step back before his legs locked in place from sheer panic. For the first time that night, he was speechless.

"I tried to tell you they existed, but—"

"Not another I told you so!" Mako said. Jason's words had cured his muteness. The detective took another look at the werewolf and recalled the expression his associate had used to describe what it would be like to see one for the first time: "Jarring." Mako felt there was a stronger, more appropriate word, but fear stopped his higher brain functions from coming up with one. All he could think was that the two of them were going to need help taking this monster down.

THIRTY-THREE

"This is your other way?" Rikki asked skeptically as Jacquie rummaged through the bedroom closet in Mako's apartment. "I don't know what you're expecting to find in there besides jeans, jeans and more jeans." He thought out loud, "Would it kill the man to add a nice pair of slacks to his wardrobe? I mean, really."

Shifting the hung clothing from left to right and searching through numerous boxes on the closet floor, Jacquie's frustration continued to build. "Come on already. It's got to be here."

Rikki peered over her shoulder to see if he could find anything of use, but everything appeared to be of no importance. "Maybe he threw whatever it is you're looking for away."

"Not likely. I know Johnny," she said as she changed her attention from the floor to the shelf above the hanging items. "He's a bit of a pack rat. He'd never throw anything away he feels might come in handy one day."

"I wasn't aware he was a hoarder."

Sliding a stack of empty computer-accessory boxes to her left, she said, "Not one of his most redeeming qualities, but none can say he's unprepared." She thought for a moment and mumbled after realizing similar items were packed together, "And extremely organized. If I could only find the right … got it!" Jacquie shouted while pulling a milk crate down off the shelf. Darting into the kitchen with it, she placed it on the table and began sifting through its contents. It was all of Mako's things he'd been given since day one on the force: Department Manual, a beat-up holster, log book, name plates for his uniform shirt, miscellaneous junk, and a seemingly meaningless page of radio channels and frequencies that she removed from the crate.

"How is that going to help us find Johnny?" Rikki couldn't understand why she was smiling.

"By itself … it won't." Digging through her suitcase, she pulled out a radio receiver with a numeric key pad and LED display on its front. "Using it with this, will." She twisted the power knob to the ON position, and garbled police radio transmissions began to trickle through.

"If you needed a police scanner, why didn't you say so? I have one in my apartment." Rikki gestured to the door and shifted his feet as if he was going to go get it. "I used to listen in occasionally, but now I'm kind of a buff," he added, grinning.

Jacquie rolled her eyes and said, "I'm going to pretend I didn't hear that."

"What?"

"I usually find buffs to be a bit … exasperating." She tried to be polite, and then switched back to the previous subject. "And leave your scanner where it is. It's doubtful I could even tune into the necessary transmissions I'll need to narrow down a search for Johnny."

He made a face, insulted by the remark.

"You don't understand," she felt the need to explain further to save Rikki's bruised ego. "Most police scanners are analog whereas many of the departments upgraded to digital. An analog scanner will not pick up digital transmissions. How long ago did you buy yours?"

Knowing he didn't have an updated piece of equipment, he turned his head to the side, waved her off and said, "Let's just use what you brought. Time is wasting."

With the radio receiver in one hand and the list of channels in the other, Jacquie keyed in the first channel on the keypad and listened.

"HQ to 419, 405. Respond for an aided case at 346 Tulip Road. Cross Streets are West Main Street and Poughkeepsie Boulevard. Elderly male with chest pains and has a history of cardiac problems. Village Fire Department ambulance already en route."

Rikki's eyes were opened twice as wide than normal. "What was all that?"

She giggled when she saw his expression. "I'm sure most doesn't need to be clarified, but as you can probably guess from the 'ambulance already en route' an aided case is a person who is either sick or injured that usually requires medical care." She then switched to another frequency.

"616 respond to an alarm for a possible burglary in progress at 12 Crest Lane. Cross Streets are Bell Road and Palm Circle. Complainant advised she can hear someone walking outside in the backyard, attempting to open the rear sliding door."

"Burglary in progress," Jacquie whispered to Rikki, still listening to the call.

"I got that," he said sarcastically.

Becoming upset, she keyed in yet another channel.

"HQ to 181, 182, ambulance 4564 and a patrol supervisor to respond for a violent 10-62 … has a history of schizophrenia and bipolar disorder … aggressive and armed with a knife …"

"What's a 10-62?" Rikki interrupted.

"A person with mental illness," Jacquie answered.

"That could be Johnny," he said with some enthusiasm.

She gave him a look of disapproval.

"Well, it could be him," Rikki muttered. "I mean I don't know about the schizophrenia and bipolar, but Johnny can definitely be aggressive."

Jacquie ignored the comments and continued searching for something … anything … that would tell her what she wanted to know.

"HQ to 525, 530 and 531 to respond for an elopee from South Shore hospital."

This sounded promising.

"What's an elopee?" Rikki asked.

"Escaped patient. Now Shush!" she snapped. "I need to hear this."

The call continued, "Subject is a male, mid-thirties, six foot tall, dark hair, blue eyes and was admitted with severe injuries, hours ago. Last seen wearing a hospital gown and heavily bandaged, but the clothes he was brought in with are missing."

"That's definitely him," she said without a doubt in her mind. "Now if I can only figure out where he's going."

The next frequency she keyed in belonged to the adjacent precinct. The call was already in progress.

"Respond to 76 Elm Place for a loose dog, unknown breed, but complainant stated it sounded like a big animal … possibly rabid. Animal knocked over her garbage cans and is now sniffing around the side door. Complainant is afraid the animal will get inside."

Jacquie was skeptical about the call because although she warned Johnny of the danger he was in from what she believed was a werewolf, the "loose dog" in question wouldn't simply knock over garbage cans or sniff around a door. If it wanted in, there was pretty much nothing that could keep it out. She jotted down the address, but instinct told her to look for something more definitive.

Not far from the hospital but in the opposite direction of the stray dog call, a more familiar alarm was broadcast: "Shots fired on Fulton Avenue. Cross streets are Carrie Road and Park Drive. All available units start responding for shots fired near 422 Fulton Avenue. Ambulance 4527 and a supervisor respond to location as well. Complainant saw from her apartment window at 422 Fulton five male Hispanics in a physical altercation on a playground with another lone male before returning inside to phone police. She then heard four gunshots and …"

Jacquie was about to change the call but hesitated as something told her to listen through to the end.

"… a few seconds later, several more gunshots accompanied by chaotic screaming and what the complainant believed to be … growling and roaring?" The dispatcher sounded unsure if she was repeating the 911 call correctly. "Be advised … subjects are still at scene and confrontation is ongoing."

That was it. Her gut told her that was where Johnny would be, and Jacquie was not about to miss this opportunity to catch up with him before he disappeared again. "I need to borrow your car," she shouted to Rikki.

"I'm coming with you."

"Too dangerous."

"You can't come back after all this time and—"

There was no time to engage in a pointless dispute. Johnny's life was at stake. "Get your keys. You're driving." Jacquie grabbed a long cylindrical case from her belongings and darted out the door.

Rikki pulled down on his shirt collar while making his best tough-guy face, impressed he convinced her without even having to finish his speech.

"Let's go!" she yelled from downstairs.

Unwilling to press his luck, he ran after her without argument.

Jason reached for his rifle case behind the van's driver's seat and began to assemble it. He said, "I think you should let me handle this, Detective."

"Like hell!" Mako discarded his initial fear. He replaced his cartridge of ordinary bullets with the clip packed with silver bullets. "Redemption is not earned by sitting idle."

Jason attempted to stop him from making a terrible mistake, but he was too late as the stubborn detective was already out of earshot. Returning to his task, Jason attached the scope to the top of his rifle and heard a muffled noise behind him. He spun around with his gun, but there was nothing. Hearing a similar noise off to his right, he quickly adjusted to better observe the swift-moving object. He saw a small fragment of debris hit the ground next to one of the apartment buildings near his location. Looking up, he spotted a large shadowed figure running across rooftops toward the werewolf on the playground.

While his partner was busy with other things, the detective cautiously moved closer to get a better shot, raised his firearm, and took aim. His finger slowly pulled back on the trigger.

"Watch out!" Jason yelled.

An instant after the warning, a large chain smashed down onto Mako's forearms, nearly shattering them. It caused him to drop his pistol. He went for his gun, but the chain slammed the ground between it and his hand, forcing him to leave it where it lay for the moment.

"Wanna try your luck again, pig?" Chainz asked, swinging his chain above his head.

"Pig? They still use that term, or are you too stupid for polysyllabic words?"

Mako grunted in pain when an unseen blow connected with his kidneys. Then he was hoisted into the air and tossed backwards onto another parked car's hood, near Jason's damaged van. He lifted his head and saw Mr. Ball confidently walking his way.

"Remember us, Detective? You stuck a gun in my face. Twice. I don't take too kindly to that." He cracked the knuckles on both hands. "It'd be wrong to tell you the beating you're about to receive is only business, because the truth is, I'm gonna enjoy it too damn much."

Chainz arced his chain down at incredible speed, hoping to connect with the detective's head. "You and me both, dude!" he told his partner. "I hate cops! A pig like this shot my brother and put him in a wheelchair for life. Paralyzed from the waist down. He'll never ride again!" The chain caved in the metal hood, narrowly missing its intended target as the detective rolled off the car and onto the pavement.

Mako, scrambling to get to his feet, fired back, "Well, now you two have something in common seeing as you're paralyzed from the neck up."

Chainz screamed in a fit of rage and charged toward him. "I'll kill you!"

Angry spittle sprayed Mako, who was still not far enough out of reach. "Oh shit," he managed to say before Chainz tackled him, sweeping him off his feet and driving his shoulder onto the hard concrete. Mako moaned with the impact.

Jason resumed looking for the unforeseen intruder but found nothing, and his rifle's scope proved to be no help. Fearing the worst, he crouched behind cover, reached for his cellphone, and dialed the one person he detested talking to more than anyone else: the leader of the Lunar Guardians.

The phone scarcely completed its first ring when Nathan answered. "Called to gloat, have you?"

"What are you talking about? Did you find anything?"

"We found something all right. The reports of a wild dog were exactly what they sounded like: a stray, domestic canine knocking over garbage cans and digging through the trash."

"Were you able to handle it?" he asked insultingly.

"We killed it for our troubles," Nathan said, knowing his actions would disturb his sensitive colleague. "Now, what did you want? We're already on our way back to the hotel."

Jason wanted to hang up, but his troubles were more pressing at the moment. "I think you should come to Fulton Avenue in Hempstead right away. I have one confirmed sighting with a possible second lycanthrope close by."

"You had better not be mistaken."

"I'm not," he said. "I have more experience than all of you dealing with werewolves as I'm the only one of you who's been on the receiving end of one their rampages." Although he worried for Mako's well-being as the two giants continued their onslaught, this concern could not outweigh the potentially deadly circumstances for all of them should help not arrive soon.

Mr. Ball grabbed the detective by the collar, effortlessly lifting him off the ground. He ran Mako into the armored truck, slamming his back into it hard enough to slightly dent the vehicle. "You think you're funny, don't you? See if you find this funny." He punched Mako in the face; his huge fist would have broken Mako's jaw if Mako hadn't rolled with the blow. Dizzy, Mako blocked a second punch with his injured arm, and the pain on contact caused his eyes to roll to the back of his head. A following shot to

Mako's stomach forced the air out of his body. Trying to break free of Mr. Ball's grip, Mako punched him solid in the face, twice. The big man didn't loosen his grip any but was momentarily stunned. Upon recovering, the ticked-off, giant body slammed Mako onto the pavement. Too battered to stand, the detective attempted to crawl away from his attackers, but Chainz closed in to finish him off.

"You're done, pig!"

Mako decided to hold back a clever remark to conserve his strength.

Chainz swung his weapon high over his head at rapid speed and threw his arm back so that he could bring the chain crashing down with that much more force; but when the chain whipped behind him, it was unexpectedly caught on something. He pivoted to see what was preventing him from delivering his killing blow, only to find his weapon wrapped around a thin black case attached to a very delicate arm.

Jacquie stood in the middle of the street, holding the cylindrical container above her head, the chain tangled around it. She was relieved that she'd stopped the thug from finishing off the man she'd once thought was the love of her life.

"You got balls." Chainz sounded impressed. "But don't think that just 'cause you're a chick I won't rough you up same as a man if you get in my way."

"I'm in your way now," she mocked. "Rough me up."

His eyes widened as anger took over, and he whipped his weapon back toward him. She released her hold on all but the bottom portion of her case, and as the chain snapped back it exposed the majority of the case was a sheath, and she now held a shining samurai sword in hand. It took a moment for the bewildered Chainz to register what she was actually wielding.

She executed a few moves, revealing her knowledge of the weapon. She then ended her display, the equivalent of a seductive dance, by scraping the point of the sword along the ground in a semicircle around her feet and stopping when the sword was positioned behind her. She winked at Chainz, challenging his manhood.

Forgetting the fallen detective, he charged, swinging his chain overhead. Undaunted, Jacquie ran directly toward him with her sword dragging behind her, sparks licking the asphalt, destined for a head-on collision.

In the meantime, Mr. Ball picked the injured detective off the ground and went to hammer him with his fists again, but his partner's scream caused him to lose focus. He had to see what caused the agonizing cry.

Waiting until the last possible moment, Jacquie skillfully tuck-and-rolled underneath the muscular arm holding the thick chain, avoiding a strike that would have taken her head off. After regaining her footing, she kicked Chainz in the side of his knee. The impact blew his kneecap out, and he screamed; but it wasn't enough to make him fall. She remedied that with a foot sweep, knocking his good leg out from under him. Chainz, writhing in pain, was out of the fight—permanently.

"Your turn!" Mako said, kicking Mr. Ball in the groin and causing him to double over. With his feet firmly planted on the concrete, the detective mounted his last ditch effort by taking his opponent by the head and driving his knee forward while pulling Mr. Ball toward him.

Falling to his knees, the enormous man smothered his face with his large mitts, blood pouring through his fingers. "My nose! I think you fuckin' broke it!"

Running to Mako, Jacquie caught him as he fell forward, holding his bruised body. She supported his weight, aiding him to safety. "Easy. I got you," she said.

"You're an angel."

"You say the sweetest things when you're delirious. And don't forget to thank Rikki. He did get me here in time to save you, after all."

He pointed to her sword. "Adding ninja to your resume?"

Using the flat end of her blade, she flipped its case off the ground and into her hands, and then she slid the sword back inside its cover. "I needed to keep myself busy when we parted ways."

"Good thing for me that you did." He gave her a friendly smile.

"I initially imagined a very different scenario involving you and this sword."

"Ouch," he said, covering his groin with one hand. Quickly changing the subject, he asked, "How did you find me?"

"Haven't I always told you that you couldn't hide from me?" She slyly smiled. Startled by a loud roar, Jacquie flinched like a frightened moviegoer watching a horror flick. Just then, the werewolf responsible for the roar came into view. "Is that a, a—"

"I hate to say it, but yes."

Meanwhile, Jason wanted to pursue the mysterious roof-runner, but Nathan would not allow him to hang up. One werewolf was hard enough to handle, but if he was right, and the shadowed figure was a second werewolf, the two monsters could annihilate all of them without much effort. "Did you hear what I said?" he asked Nathan.

"Yes, I heard, and we are en route. ETA: seven minutes." There was silence on Nathan's end, but he had not hung up the phone. After marshaling his exasperation, he told his junior associate somewhat caustically, "Brody, try and contain the situation if that's at all possible."

"I'll do my best."

"We can only hope you'll do better than that." The call disconnected.

Mako regrouped with Jason. Police sirens sounded in the distance, but Mako knew local law enforcement's efforts would be futile against the werewolf. "Thanks for the help," he said to Jason, oozing with sarcasm.

Jason pointed to the gun, still resting on the ground from where it'd been knocked out of his hand. "I'm sorry," he said as the badly bruised detective went to retrieve it. "I had to call for backup."

"From who? The Looney Bin?" Mako asked, checking his own pistol for damage.

"As much as I hate to admit it, the Lunar Guardians are best equipped to manage the situation."

"Who's your friend, Johnny?" asked Jacquie.

"Jacquie, Jason. Jason, Jacquie." He half-ass introduced them.

"Hey, cutie," she said, shaking Jason's hand with a flirtatious grin.

Jason returned an uncomfortable smile, and shook hands. "Nice to meet you."

"If you two are done," Mako started, "I think we should get out of here before the cops show."

Jason knew he had to act before the beast escaped under the cover of night. Grabbing his sniper rifle, he jogged toward the playground. "I'll go after the creature. You two stay and talk to the police. Let them know what happened."

"Sure," Mako answered. "I'll tell them what happened—and they'll lock us up with the rest of the freaks."

Meanwhile, Chainz cursed the woman who'd incapacitated him. He clasped his knee with both hands. With blood still flowing from his nose, Mr. Ball didn't entertain his crippled partner's thoughts of revenge. Instead, he helped him inside their truck and drove away, refusing to end up behind bars again.

The werewolf was startled by the sirens too and retreated, leaving the last gang member inside the run-down playground with only a bite on his arm. As the werewolf climbed the building adjacent to the park, the gangbanger huffed and rested his head on the blacktop, thankful his life was spared. Once Jacob reached the top of the four-story building, he howled loudly at the moon before disappearing into the night.

THIRTY-FOUR

Standing at the base of the building the werewolf had scaled, Jason gazed at the roof's ledge. The claw marks left behind were deep and menacing. It was no surprise that those claws could easily slice through soft flesh, when brick posed no trouble. He peered back at his associates beside the totaled van. Jacquie had her back to him. Mako was reloading his gun with regular rounds, intending to only sparingly use the silver bullets.

Jason figured this was his best chance to pursue the lycanthrope without being noticed; he jumped for the fire escape, effortlessly reaching the second landing of the metal construction, nearly twenty-five feet off the ground. His second vertical leap, just as impressive as the first, allowed him to reach the roof's ledge—only this time his spectacular display did not go unnoticed.

Having reloaded his weapon more quickly than anticipated, Mako spotted Jason soar through the air like no human could. The part-time photographer's movements reminded the detective of … of the same creature they were hunting, and Mako would have chalked what he saw up to his imagination if he hadn't already just seen a creature that was not supposed to exist. He had to investigate further. "Jacquie, I'm going to give Brody some backup. Wait for the cops, okay?" He didn't hang around for an answer.

The detective turned his concentration upward and could see Jason already a block away. Realizing he wouldn't catch him on foot, he looked for alternative means to give chase. Luckily, a lone bicycle was propped against one section of the playground's damaged fencing. He pulled it to him, but the bicycle abruptly yanked back to the fence. Mako winced and grabbed his body as the sudden movement aggravated his injured ribcage. Then he noticed it was chained up. He aimed his gun and fired one shot into the chain, breaking it. Gingerly lifting one leg over the frame, Mako got on the bike and began pedaling down the street, trying not to lose sight of his objective.

Jason saw the werewolf only a few rooftops away, and he was determined not to let it out of his sight. He bounded from one building to the next without fear of falling through the cracks.

As a werewolf, Jacob was fast and nimble, zigzagging across the structures on all fours, his claws ripping up the ground beneath him.

Mako pumped his legs as fast as he could and still found it difficult to keep up. He couldn't see either one of them. Luckily, every so often the detective glimpsed a silhouette leaping between buildings, which made them easy enough to follow.

Jason sprang over scattered construction equipment on top of a roof that was being repaired, just after Jacob barreled through it without even slowing. He knew he had to act fast before the werewolf reached a populated area; a panicked crowd would make it impossible to get a clear shot. Intertwining his left forearm in the rifle's strap, he grabbed the trigger with his right hand. He needed a clear space to fire his weapon, a space free of obstructions or anything that could cause his balance to be off even slightly. Finally, he spied a clearing up ahead. He'd have to take aim and shoot hastily, but he was fairly confident he could take the werewolf down.

Jacob was doing all he could to evade the hunter, but the human's tenacity proved quite frustrating. Somewhere in the recesses of the lycanthrope's mind, his human consciousness exerted some control over his more animalistic urges and forced his body to pick up a loose brick while running. In one smooth action the werewolf flew through the air, twisting his body in a somersaulting motion so his hind feet were above his head, and hurled the brick at the huntsman with great strength. He landed on his back, rolled onto all fours, and continued on his way without ever decelerating.

Meanwhile, the out-of-breath detective ditched his "borrowed" bicycle and was half-way up a second fire escape on a building a few blocks away from where his chase had begun. He paused momentarily until his wheezing stopped and proceeded to the battleground above.

Attempting to identify the fast-moving object headed for his skull, Jason determined it was best to get out of the way no matter what it was. He contorted to one side. The brick whizzed by, and Jason slid into the open space he chose for his shooting area, pulling the sniper rifle into his shoulder while simultaneously taking aim in the gun's sight. The werewolf was in the crosshairs.

A voice to his right shouted, "Carl!"

The unanticipated interruption caused Jason's concentration to falter, and the silver bullet forcefully ejected from the gun missed its mark by a hair. The werewolf dropped off the rooftop and down to the street. Jason wouldn't see it anymore that night.

Mako reached for the roof's ledge as the projectile meant for Jason lost altitude and exploded against the ridge, almost taking the detective's hand off. "What the fuck?" He drew his hand back and peered over the edge before climbing the rest of the way up. No one was on the rooftop of the building that he was currently hanging onto, but Jason and one other were on the structure adjacent to his. To his disappointment, the werewolf was nowhere to be found.

Relaxing his grip on the sniper rifle, Jason rose to full height. It took a minute to register, but he knew there were only two people in the world who would call him by that name. One of them wouldn't have bothered to say anything until he was lying half-dead with his entrails spilled out; the other one would be: "Ethan. I was wondering if I would run into you."

Ethan Walker shuffled closer. The moon brought out his bestial nature: claws and fangs had grown to abnormal proportions. His bone structure transformed to the point where he seemed to be more animal than man and silver hair covered most of his face and body. But the man within tried to fight off its effects for a few minutes longer. "Good to see you again, Carl," he growled.

"What are you doing here, Ethan?" Jason pivoted his rifle in case he needed to fire it a second time.

"Spare me the pathetic threat. I could have killed you already if I wanted to. Your time among the humans has dulled your senses. I have been tracking you since you arrived with that loathsome detective."

"I thought I saw something on the rooftops above me. Why are you following me?"

A grotesque chortle escaped him. "Don't flatter yourself. I was observing how your father's latest acquisition was adjusting to his new state of affairs. Not too shabby for the boy's first outing, don't you think?"

"Still looking to recruit for your private army?"

"Why? Are you interested in joining?"

"I'll settle matters with my father on my own terms." Jason paused for a moment. "And then I'll deal with you."

Ethan's smile was distorted as his features became more wolf-like with every passing second. "Keeping me alive in case I finish the job before you do? Your senses might be dull, but you still have a bit of a nasty streak within you." He sniffed the air. "We have company." He whipped around to face the detective, standing on the neighboring building with his gun drawn.

"Somebody want to tell me what in the hell is going on here?" Mako limped closer, not entirely sure who he should be aiming at.

Now fully in wolf form, Ethan snarled at the officer while Jason did the talking. "Take it easy, both of you. You've already been told, Detective, there are a lot of things going on that you will not understand. This is one of them."

Mako fixed his gun on the sniper. "Start explaining. I have all night." He shifted his gaze to Ethan and noticed his hind paw stiffen slightly. He aimed at the werewolf. "Heel, Rover, before I get the paper."

"Aim for his head," Jason instructed.

"What was that?"

"Aim for his head," he repeated.

The beast looked at Jason as if he understood what was going on.

"Sorry, Ethan, but I need his trust if I'm to put an end to this."

More confused than ever, the detective asked, "You … know each other?"

"Yes, Ethan Walker and I have known each other for many years. We share a common goal, but that doesn't mean I approve of his methods. He was a good man once, and that's why I haven't killed him … yet."

Mako swiveled his head to Jason. "The same Ethan Walker I met the other day at Stumpp Industries?"

"Yes."

"No wonder that scrawny bastard was so strong."

Insulted at the remark, Ethan snorted at the detective.

Gripping his gun tighter, Mako aimed between Ethan's eyes. "Are you sure this will kill him if he attacks? I didn't have time to reload with the S-I-L-V—"

He had spent too much time around Matt's children, spelling out anything he didn't want them to comprehend.

"You don't have to do that," Jason cut him off. "He may not look like it, but Ethan understands everything we say, even when he's in wolf form. In its early transformation years, the lycanthrope operates on animal instinct; it isn't usually able to fully utilize its human brain. But Ethan has mastered his control over the beast and can combine the best qualities of both sides in either form. And to answer your question, no, the regular bullets in that gun won't kill him."

Mako started to lower his weapon. "So, why am I bothering with this?"

Ethan shifted his feet again, ready to pounce.

"I would keep my gun on him, if I were you," Jason warned the detective. "I said the bullets in your gun won't kill him, but they can injure him enough to make him helpless."

"I don't follow." But Mako aimed his pistol at the werewolf anyway.

"Only an object made of silver can kill a werewolf; but if the creature is wounded sufficiently, it will sink into a coma-like state until its body can heal itself, or until someone finishes the job. A head shot is guaranteed to take down the beast for a significant amount of time, no matter how strong it is. And don't worry about having enough time to take the shot. Lycanthropes are extremely fast, but they're not fast enough to dodge bullets at this range. Even at greater distances, he would have to sense the bullet being fired in order to evade it."

"Happy now, Detective?" a raspy, strained string of words came from the werewolf's mouth. "You know our weaknesses."

Mako did a double take before asking, the shock apparent in his voice, "Did that thing … speak?"

"Not all lycanthropes can verbally communicate," Jason answered. "But some, like Ethan, have through years of concentration altered themselves to make their vocal cords capable of speech. It takes a tremendous effort."

"So does listening to the two of you," Ethan spewed his sarcasm like venom. "When you're ready to talk, Carl, come and see me." With that, the silver-haired werewolf used the powerful muscles in his legs to thrust him up and away, breaking up the trio. "Another time, Detective." His last words carried on the wind.

"That voice," Mako said, recalling the last words his attacker had said to him in the motel room. "He was there! He murdered Falcone and nearly killed me!"

Jason noticed the detective tense up and realized he might shoot at Ethan, so he moved into his line of fire. "Let him go. You won't be able to do any damage now, and he isn't interested in killing innocents for the moment."

The detective hesitantly surrendered and lowered his weapon. "Did you know it was him at the motel? Don't dare lie to me either. And whose side are you really on? I saw how you got onto the roof back there."

Defeated, Jason came clean. "I had my suspicions that he was the one behind your attack, but I am not trying to defend him. We have a tenuous alliance. When the time comes, I will not stand in your way."

"Why did he call you Carl?"

"I have had many names over the years," Jason admitted. "I was hunted by my father until Nathan's ancestors found me and took me in. They treated me as family and kept me safe. But eventually they knew I would have to venture out on my own again, so they trained me to be a soldier. Using my strengths to develop any latent skills I might possess, I eventually learned to fight and shoot. My sight was so acute that I became a sniper.

"I've killed many lycanthropes over the years, but I don't want to face my father. The last time I saw him, he left me for dead. When he found out I wasn't, he began hunting me again. I'm not anxious to relive that part of my life. Ethan and I met years ago, after he came into my father's employ, and he has his own reasons for hating my father. He secretly wants to destroy him too, but like I said, I don't always agree with his methods."

"The enemy of my enemy is my friend. Is that how it is?"

"I suppose. So, you see there is a lot of history here. I'm sorry I dragged you into this."

"Why did you?"

Jason shrugged his shoulders. "I thought you would be able to use your resources to help bring this madness to a close, and then I wouldn't have to hide anymore."

"Yeah, but why me? There are hundreds of cops to choose from."

"I found your name in an old newspaper article after I recognized you at the Muttontown Preserve. You were branded a hero, and that's what I was looking for."

"You came to the wrong place." Mako holstered his gun. "I'm far from a hero."

"Your actions say otherwise."

The detective was humbled by Jason's sentiments, however misplaced he believed them to be. "Let's get down from here, and we'll see what I can do."

A short trip to the street left the pair right where they'd started, and Mako remembered an important question he wanted to ask. "You're really Stumpp's kid?"

"My name at the moment is Jason Brody. The name my birth parents gave me is," Jason took a deep breath, "Carl. Carl Stu—"

"At ease, Brody!" Mark Bronson shouted out.

Jason looked to his left to see a trio of armed Lunar Guardians approaching. "I'm not part of your group, as Nathan points out as often as he can. Go order someone else around."

Bronson stopped directly in front of Jason and blocked his way. "Negative. Williams wants you back at the command center for debriefing. Now."

"Wait one minute." Mako advanced on Nathan's second, only to have the other two shove their guns in his face. He pointed his finger at Bronson. "Listen, you prick. If one more of your goons threatens me, you're going to have more than monster troubles on your hands." Mako knew he was hardly capable to back his words up in his weakened condition, but he was hoping the threat would suffice.

"I don't have time to entertain this." Bronson circled his finger high in the air, and a black Hummer rolled up alongside. One of the armed men grabbed Jason by the arm and pushed him into the vehicle. Bronson and the other soldier followed closely behind.

"I saw what you could do, Brody," Mako shouted into the vehicle. "Why do you let these guys push you around like this?"

"I told you already. Nathan's family treated me as one of them. I won't disrespect their memories just because he doesn't share the same opinion of me." With that, the door was pulled shut and the Hummer drove away.

Soon after, Jacquie pulled up in Jason's banged-up van. It looked as bad as Mako remembered, but at least it still ran.

"Need a lift?" she joked.

He walked around to the driver's side and opened the door. "Move over," he said while pushing his way inside. Twisting his body to get behind the wheel, a sharp pain shot up Mako's side. "On second thought," he grunted. "You drive."

Already moving to the passenger's side, Jacquie reversed direction as Mako walked around the van and entered the other side.

"So, what happened with the cops?"

"I didn't wait around to find out," she said, climbing back into the driver's seat. "Once I thought about what I was going to tell them, even *I* would have thrown me in a cell. Besides, reinforcements showed up, and I was tired of getting hit on."

"What do you mean?" Mako appeared momentarily concerned.

She shot him a smile. "You jealous?"

"No. I was just wondering how far your standards fell after me." He shifted the car into drive and sped off.

"Where to?"

"A quick stop home, and then to the Marriott Hotel."

"I can be quiet, if you're concerned about Rikki hearing all the noise coming from the bedroom," she said with a wink.

"Sorry, sweetheart. That's not what I had in mind." He grunted as a large pothole bounced the van, and the impact irritated his previous injuries. "I have some files on my nightstand to review. As far as where we're going afterward, I thought you'd like to meet some of the other players in the game."

THIRTY-FIVE

Nathan told his driver to slow the Hummer to a crawl as they approached Fulton Avenue. He saw several mangled bodies lying on the ground both near and inside the abandoned park. He also noticed an attractive woman standing by another body that was sprawled out on the hood of the van he recognized to be Jason's. Hearing incoming sirens, he instructed his driver to park elsewhere.

Exiting the vehicle, he signaled for the second black Hummer, which was following them, to pull alongside. The driver of the vehicle complied, but it was Bronson who leaned out the passenger side window. Nathan dispatched the men in his own Hummer to scour the scene, and then he turned to speak with his second. "I want Brody found and taken back to the Marriott for a full debriefing ASAP."

Bronson tapped the automobile's door twice, and his Hummer pulled away and turned the corner a few blocks down. As the truck rolled out of sight, Nathan proceeded to the last known sighting of the lycanthrope that Jason phoned him about, hoping to gather any clues to facilitate his hunt.

The first thing he spotted, however, was that his troops were hovering around the beautiful woman who stood by Jason's van. He could not hear what they were saying but could only imagine. His men had very little free time to devote to personal interests, but now was neither the time nor the place for romance. He whistled loudly, and they scattered like children with their hands caught in the cookie jar. Nathan had no interest in mixing business with pleasure, but his eyes lingered for a while longer in Jacquie's direction before he returned to the task at hand.

Jacquie struggled as she removed the dead body off the hood of Jason's van, and after finding the car keys, she drove off.

Nathan didn't know why she left in such a hurry and really didn't care, but he did tense up slightly as the police arrived with sirens blaring. Two marked cars, one ambulance, and even a small fire truck took up positions on the street. He blended in with the growing crowd, but his eyes never stopped searching for anything relating to the reason Jason had summoned him here.

The gang member who was left alive drew Nathan's attention. Paramedics loaded the man onto a stretcher, but Nathan needed to get closer to see what damage was done. If the man was bitten, Nathan refused to let another fall victim to the curse and was prepared to prevent the transformation by any means necessary.

Officers worked fast to cordon off the area, and that was when Nathan made his move. His men, mixing with the crowd, were silently ordered to divert the attention of the medical personnel and local law enforcement.

One of the soldiers yelled out, "There's another wounded over here!" and pointed into the distance at a fictitious body.

After securing the live victim inside the ambulance, the medic gathered supplies and followed the soldier's lead. The remaining troops worked on the bystanders' curiosities and fears to incite a mob so that the authorities were forced to reprioritize.

Pleased by his group's performance, Nathan headed for the emergency vehicle, unnoticed by anyone of importance, and climbed in the back with the injured party. He quietly closed the doors and proceeded to check the man's body for any sign of trauma. After removing the bandages from the man's upper arm, Nathan saw the werewolf's teeth marks.

The man lying on the gurney guessed that the stranger was one of the paramedics and tried to speak to him, but it was obvious that English was not his first language. Neither could communicate with the other, and the gang member became more frantic.

Calming the victim, Nathan gently pushed him back down on the gurney. "I know you can't understand me, but maybe it is better this way. I don't know where you come from or if you have a family, but life as you know it is over. You have been bitten by a werewolf."

The man's eyes lit up as if there was some understanding there. "Werewolf?"

Uncertain of which country this individual's accent originated from, Nathan did understand the apprehension in his voice, since stories about werewolves had circulated the world over. "Yes, *un hombre-lobo*." He demonstrated his limited multilingual skills. "It is a terrible monster, and it has made you one of its kind."

The man laughed uncontrollably.

Nathan was not pleased at being mocked. This peasant's impudence made it easier for him to carry out what he'd planned on doing all along. A malicious scowl formed on his face, and he reached behind his back with one arm. "You would think that one in your position would be a bit more humble. Even after seeing the truth before your eyes, you would rather believe me to be a fool. Well, you have been bitten, my delusional friend, and I will not allow you to become a plague on mankind." His arm reappeared high over his head with a silver dagger clutched tightly in his hand.

The wounded man wanted to scream, but a pillow was shoved in his face, smothering him on the stretcher.

"You are a monster, and the only cure for your affliction," Nathan declared through gritted teeth, "is me!"

The dagger sliced through the air until the silver blade penetrated the gangbanger's chest and pierced his heart. It was the only way to be sure, so Nathan twisted the knife, preventing the wound from closing. Bloodied hands struggled to remove the object from its resting place, and Nathan did not loosen his hold until the man lost the will to fight.

Flailing arms dropped down on each side of the gurney as the man's breathing slowed and his heartbeat became almost nonexistent. Nathan let the pillow fall, and the dying man's eyes fixed on his. Nathan didn't turn away until the man's eyes glazed over and he was sure the evil passed from this world to the next. He removed the knife and wiped it clean before returning it to its sheath on his belt. Exiting the vehicle, he planned to rejoin the crowd when a voice cried out, "You! Stop!"

A patrolling fireman caught a glimpse of Nathan leaving the ambulance and knew a civilian when he saw one. Peering inside the back window, he discovered the body, which only moments ago had had life left within it. He then charged Nathan, intending to detain him for the police.

Nathan did not panic. He didn't even flinch at the sight of the stocky figure swiftly approaching. Instead, he sidestepped his attacker, tucked his thumb into the palm of his hand, and struck the man in the throat with a reverse knife-hand. The fireman clutched his neck and dropped to his knees, gasping for air. As a crowd formed around the fireman, offering assistance, Nathan slipped past them all and regrouped with his men. He calmly entered his vehicle.

"Bronson just called, sir," the driver said. "He has Brody and is on the way to the hotel. Detective Mako was with him, but it is uncertain how much more he knows."

"This situation has gotten too far out of hand, and although the detective is inconsequential, his interference is costing us precious time," Nathan said. He thought for a moment. "Let's end this."

THIRTY-SIX

The apartment door swung open, and Mako and Jacquie stumbled inside the darkened kitchen. He moved stiffly and awkwardly, having been tenderized only a short while ago, but she did all she could to steady him.

She made it to the light switch first. "What do you mean you wanted to see how far my standards fell? I only expect the best, and I won't settle for anything less."

His joke had been taken the wrong way, but he didn't bother to correct her interpretation. Instead he added fuel to the fire. "Why are you so hung up on me then? I don't regard myself as 'the best.'"

She slumped into a chair, pulled off one shoe, and pointed it at him, saying, "That should tell you what I think of you, then. How many other people can you say thought of you like that?" The shoe fell to her side, and she went to work on the other foot.

"I'm sure I don't know. Next time I'll take a survey and send you the results." He spoke from behind an open refrigerator door, removing a dish containing leftovers from a few nights ago. "Want some?"

She wrinkled her nose. "You're such an ass." Lowering her voice, she attempted to imitate him: "I'll take a survey and send you the results."

Mako's shoulders shook with silent laughter as he placed his meal in the microwave. He asked again, "You want some? You didn't answer me."

"Have you forgotten everything?" She sounded defeated. "You know I don't like leftovers, especially when you heat them up in the microwave."

"Why? What's the big deal?"

"The microwave changes the properties of the food."

He scrunched his face at her. "Get the hell out of here." Now it was his turn to impersonate Jacquie. "The microwave changes the properties of the food," he said in a high-pitched whisper.

"I don't sound like that."

"To me you do."

"Shut up." She waved a hand at him, getting more comfortable in the chair. "No, I don't."

After pushing a few buttons on the microwave, he was ready to eat his late-night meal and set the table for one. The dogs, which uncharacteristically didn't scramble to greet him when he first came through the door, now entered the room after the food's aroma awakened them. He filled two glasses with water and put them on the table. He then got his plate and sat across from Jacquie, staring into her eyes.

She looked back but didn't say anything.

"Wild night, huh?"

She sipped her drink. "I'm not sure my brain is registering what we saw. I mean, was that for real?"

"It must've been because I didn't know whether to shoot it or piss my pants," he said as politely as he could through a mouthful of food.

"You didn't look scared."

Still chewing, he muttered, "Anger had a big part in that." He swallowed and changed the subject. "I still can't get over it: you know how to use a samurai sword."

The fact that he was impressed caused Jacquie to smile. She always liked surprising him, in so many different ways. "That's not the only trick I've learned since we were together," she replied in a flirtatious tone. "And how do you do it?" she asked, maintaining her playful behavior. "How do you look so good after you've been in a fight?"

He looked at her like she was a crazy person.

She knew what he was thinking. "No, I'm serious. Look at you. You're still so handsome. There's not a scratch on you," she said, not mentioning the bruises on his cheek and forehead.

"My injuries are internal," he responded, completely serious.

She leaned over the table, holding her arms close to her body to squeeze her breasts together. The neckline of her loose-fitting blouse plunged lower. "Anything I can do to make you feel better?" she asked hopefully.

Mako took the bait, sort of. "Nice cleavage; but unless one of your new tricks is internal medicine, I don't think you can help." He rose from the table and brought the dirty dishes to the sink.

Determined to get her man, she followed and rubbed her hands along his arms as he washed the tableware. "Come on. It's been such a long time, and you know we never had any problems in the bedroom."

Shaking the excess water out of the glass and placing it in the drain, he said, "No, we didn't, but that's because you made me do all the work."

Realizing he was trying to rebuff her advances with stubbornness, she wasn't about to let him off the hook that easily. "I know you don't mean that. Come with me, and let's take our minds off everything else for a little while." She took his hand and led him into the other room. She spun around once they reached the side of the bed and threw her arms around him, lightly kissing his cheek and neck.

He allowed her to continue while he gave nothing back, but his thoughts drifted back to a time when they were close and shared moments like this frequently. He remembered how it felt to kiss and hold her close: her skin's softness, the taste of her lips, and the feel of her tongue against his. He remembered what it felt like to make love to her. Suddenly, his hands began to caress Jacquie's body and his mouth captured hers. The kiss was long, hard, and passionate, but he couldn't get into it wholeheartedly. He wanted so badly to enjoy this, but there was a disturbing feeling in the recesses of his mind that wouldn't allow it. He grabbed her upper arms and gently pushed her away from him. "I can't do this," he said, almost embarrassed to reject a beautiful woman's advances.

"What's wrong?"

"This isn't going to work. We shouldn't do this. It will only give hope where there is none." He moved back a few steps.

"What are you talking about?"

"You." He was unsure exactly how to finish but carried on anyway: "I feel like you want to rekindle the flame we once had. If we go any further tonight, you'll think we have a chance when we don't."

"You're pretty full of yourself. What makes you think I want you back?" She buttoned up the few buttons on her blouse that were undone. "I only wanted to put the remainder of my adrenaline rush to good use."

"You really have changed." He wasn't sure if she was serious. "I didn't think you were like that."

"Did you ever tell that to the girl you replaced me with?"

"Don't start this again, please." He felt bad enough for spurning her advances.

"Why not?" she spat out. "Did you ever tell her you were seeing someone and she should keep her slutty hands off? Or maybe you should have told her the same thing you just told me."

He turned away and considered walking out of the room, but he knew if this wasn't settled now, there was no telling how long it would go on. "I've already told you, I was no longer with you when I started dating someone else. Just because you couldn't let go doesn't mean we were still a couple."

Her temper flared up and was made worse by the fact that he wouldn't look at her. "I don't get you! Why did you even get me involved with this case of yours? Why couldn't you leave me in my own world away from you? You didn't have to drag me back into your life when I was doing fine without you!"

"I made a promise that I would help you find out what happened to your parents if I could. I never expected anything like this—"

He stopped himself, feeling nothing he said would help the situation.

Interpreting his silence as indifference, she added, "My feelings don't mean half as much to you as saying you kept your precious word. There was a time I would have trusted you with my life. Now, I'm not so sure anymore."

Anger overrode his hurt. "Brilliant detective work. I'm the cold-hearted scumbag you've painted me out to be. You can be mad at me all you want, but we still have work to do."

Mako's charcoal gray Mitsubishi Lancer pulled in front of a quaint house in Farmingdale. His friend's car was in the driveway, and the living room light was on.

"Where are we?" Jacquie asked.

"At Matt's." The conversation between them had been limited to only a few words at a time since the argument.

"How come?"

"He's got some research for me." He walked around to the passenger door and stuck his head inside her window. "I'll be right back." Leaving her, Mako proceeded to Matt's doorway and heard ferocious barking coming from inside. His friend came to the door, and behind him was a medium-sized brindle-colored pit bull terrier mix, with her top lip raised and teeth showing. Matt opened the door wider, and the dog charged.

Dropping to one knee and stretching out his arms, Mako caught the dog as she barreled into him. He waved his arms furiously, trying to regain his balance, as the dog excitedly attacked him with her wagging tongue. Again, she showed her teeth in the same manner as before. "Are you smiling at me?" he asked. "You're a good girl, Copper. Yes, I missed you too."

Matt rolled his eyes. "You want me to leave you two alone?"

Copper wasn't satisfied until she licked Mako as close to the mouth as possible, but he gave her his chin instead. "I hope I didn't wake the kids."

"No, they're still asleep. Diane too, in case you were wondering." He wasn't.

"Want to come in?"

"Only for a minute." Standing back up, he continued to pet the excited canine.

"A little late for a visit, isn't it?" Diane said, trudging down the stairs in her robe and slippers.

"I said it was okay, hon. I had something for him," said Matt.

Mako understood that she'd never cared for him, even while she and Matt were dating. But he made the effort to be sociable. "Hi, Diane. How are you?"

Slowly, almost painfully, she turned her head to see her rival eye-to-eye and offered an insincere smile. "Hi, Johnny. Everything's great. Would you like to sit?"

"No, thanks, I won't be long." He knew full well the only seat she would like to offer him was one with an electric current running through it.

"Aw, that's too bad." She tilted her head as if she was deeply disappointed. "We don't get to see enough of you. At least Copper is happy." She tried to sting him with the notion that no one besides the dog wanted to see him.

"Copper *is* the main reason I come by in the first place." He remembered the day they brought the dog home from the shelter. They'd just moved into their apartment, and Copper was the only way Matt could get him to stop by.

Diane shut her mouth. Even though she despised the man, she couldn't argue the fact that Copper loved him. The dog would sit by Mako's side for the duration of his visit; and for Mako's part, he would defend Copper against anyone, including Matt.

Practically sweating from the awkward conversation, Matt tried to change the subject. "Why don't you go back to bed, D? We'll keep it down."

She started back upstairs. "You come to bed soon too." It was not a question.

"Okay, give me what you got," Mako was anxious to split.

Handing his friend a small stack of papers, he said, "This Stubbe guy was a freakin' psycho. Where did you hear about him?"

"Long story. I'll tell you about it sometime."

"Not much on the Silver Heart," Matt said, shaking his head. "All Google gave me were different sites for jewelry and jewelers. Got some ideas on what to get D for her birthday though."

"Great." Mako didn't want to make his contempt for Matt's wife so apparent, but he couldn't help it. "I gotta get going. Places to be and all that."

Matt looked at the car, still running at the foot of his driveway, and saw the silhouette of a woman in the passenger seat. "Is that Jacquie with you?"

Before Mako answered, she put her head out the window and waved. "Hi, Matt."

"Hi, Jacquie. Nice to see you again."

Mako kissed Copper on top of her head, motioned for her to go inside, and hopped down the small flight of steps. He jogged to his car and waved behind him. "Thanks again, I'll call you in a couple of days. We'll grab some lunch or something. My treat."

"Later," Matt said. "Bye, Jacquie."

She waved back, shouting her farewell as the Lancer peeled away. "What did you do that for? I was only saying goodbye."

"Do you want to get going on this case or not?"

"Fine," she said, sounding disappointed. "Let's do whatever *you* want to do."

Handing her the new stack of papers, he instructed, "Here, put these with the others and start reading some of that stuff to me. Tell me about the Silver Heart, okay?"

"You broke *my* heart when you left me," she mumbled loud enough for him to hear.

He rolled his eyes and shook his head simultaneously. "This is gonna be a long night."

The pair arrived at the Marriott Hotel just before eight o'clock, and Mako escorted Jacquie to the Lunar Guardians' room, quietly reciting the information read to him on the drive over and formulating some new questions for their leader.

The suite's door cracked open ever so slightly, and an eyeball peered through the tiny fissure before the door closed again. Finally, Bronson swung open the door. "Who's this?" he asked.

Mako stared at him with a silent warning in his icy blue eyes when he noticed Bronson ogling her. "This is Jacquie. My partner." They entered the suite but went no farther than instructed.

"Wait here." Bronson disappeared into the other room.

Nathan appeared a few moments later. "To what do I owe the displeasure, Detective?"

Mako observed Nathan's troops winding down from a night on the town of hunting. He turned his attention back to the man in charge and countered with a question of his own: "What have you done with Brody?"

"He's none of your concern."

"You really want to play it this way?"

"You don't frighten me, Detective."

"I didn't come here for a pissing contest," Mako said. "But I know you've been having as much trouble as I have catching this thing."

Nathan tried to play coy. "Whatever do you mean?"

"Spare me the routine. I've been to the morgue. I saw your butchered buddies. You did a good job messing up their faces so no one would be able to identify them, but I recognized them from the other day."

Nathan clapped sarcastically. "Your powers of observation are sharp indeed, but I'm sure you're not here to offer your condolences."

"I'm here to give you some help. You're down two men, and I just happen to have brought along a friend."

"Oh, 'a friend?'" Jacquie interrupted. "Is that all you consider me?"

"Ball-breaker," Mako whispered.

Nathan looked her over. "What makes you think I would allow the two of you to join my group—even temporarily? Surely, you didn't think her beauty alone would sway my opinion from last time."

"See," she said, leaning close to Mako's face, "*he* thinks I'm pretty."

Mako gritted his teeth through a closed mouth, hoping this wouldn't become a circus. "She's worth at least three of your men, and I'll bet on that even without seeing them in action."

"So, you're a believer all of a sudden?" Nathan's snide remark hit home. "I thought you don't take any of this seriously."

"I'm sure you know what I saw tonight."

"I do."

"So, I'm a believer."

"I still don't require your help."

Mako wanted to get his attention. "Tell me about the Heart of Lycaon."

Nathan's eyes widened, and his look of surprise indicated that the question had the desired effect. "How do you know of the Heart?"

"Harris told him."

Mako spun in the direction of the voice. "You all right?"

Jason walked somewhat timidly into the room, his sniper rifle in hand. "I'm good."

"Did you think otherwise?" Nathan asked, hoping to distract the detective.

"The Heart, Williams." Mako had a one-track mind. "Tell me about it."

Nathan moved over to the couch, sat, and reached for a glass of water on the table in front of him. "Why don't you tell me what you know first?"

Not in the mood for immature games, Mako gave up the information found in Harris' file. "The Heart of Lycaon is an ancient relic—the only one of its kind. And Peter Stumpp supposedly stole it from Harris and his buddies, which led a young man named Robert Mane to attempt to steal it back. Only problem is Mane is dead, and I don't have any proof this Silver Heart exists."

"Oh, it exists, Detective." Nathan sipped his water. "Sit and I'll give you a brief history lesson about what it is we're dealing with." He waited for them get comfortable. "Legend has it that in ancient Greece, in a place called Arcadia, lived King Lycaon, who was a ruthless and wicked man. Zeus, king of the gods, paid Lycaon a visit in the appearance of a starving traveler, but the Arcadian king saw through the disguise. Meaning to humiliate Zeus, Lycaon attempted to feed him human flesh, but Zeus uncovered the deception and became outraged. He used his immense powers to transform the wicked king into a horribly disfigured creature that was part wolf and part man, and that was how Lycaon was supposed to live out the rest of his life: exiled from his kingdom and constantly hunted by his former subjects.

"Ensuring that Lycaon couldn't prematurely end his torment, Zeus made him immune to all illness or death by any means. It has been written that the former king was stabbed, hung, bludgeoned, disemboweled, skewered, and impaled. The Arcadians even threw him in a pit for months, leaving him to starve, but this did not meet with success either—and I can only imagine the bloodbath that ensued once he broke free. His once-loyal followers continued to hound him until Lycaon gave them something to fear."

Mako's right eyebrow lifted up, and he glanced at Jacquie to see if she comprehended what Nathan was saying. "This is supposed to tell me what exactly?"

"I wasn't finished," Nathan said. "Lycaon's legend becomes hazy at best. Some say he lived out the rest of his days far away from humanity. But others—and this is the tale I'm inclined to believe—tell a completely different story.

"You see, Lycaon was something of a sorcerer, and there are those who claim that before Zeus' curse took full effect on him, he manipulated the blight to suit his needs. He was only a mortal and could not undo the will of a god, so the deposed king did the unthinkable and modified the curse to include all the people of Arcadia: his infliction would be spread through his bite. Any and all who fell victim to his diseased saliva would be transformed into a hideous beast like him. Unlike Lycaon, however, the cursed only changed during certain phases of the moon, temporarily losing their humanity. Also, to Lycaon's surprise and pleasure, those who were bitten could also spread the disease through their bites."

"This is all very exciting, but can we get to the part about the Heart now?"

"Very well." Nathan felt as if he were being teased in some way. "Lycaon plagued the town for years until Zeus returned, this time disguised as a soldier. Making his way to an inn, he spun a fictional tale of a similar monster that wreaked havoc on his town. He told the Arcadians the only way to kill the beast was with an object made of pure silver. Apparently, he found it fitting for something completely untainted to be used to destroy something as vile as King Lycaon.

"A hunting party trapped Lycaon inside his own den. A silver dagger given by Zeus to the Arcadians proved to be as effective as he had said—and why wouldn't it be, since Zeus himself altered the curse to make it so—and the murderous monster lay dead at their feet. The hunter who struck the final blow cut out Lycaon's heart and encased it within a silver shell. The Heart of Lycaon was passed down from generation to generation until his legacy of evil became a mere bedtime story to warn children not to venture too far from their parents' sides. There has been no formal proof of the Heart's existence, but in recent years, we've stumbled across more than one reference that said it does." Nathan fell silent.

"That's it?" Mako asked.

"What else were you looking for?"

Jacquie swayed forward to get a closer look at Nathan. "Finish it for real. What happened to the Heart? And what makes it so special that Stumpp, or whoever the hell Harris is, or even your little group here wants it so badly?"

Realizing the two of them wouldn't let this go, Nathan debated having them expelled from his room; his troops took up positions around the loveseat, ready to move at a moment's notice.

Jason knew what Nathan was thinking, but he didn't allow him to implement his plan. Jason spoke up: "The Heart of Lycaon is said to benefit any who symbolically bears the mark of the wolf. The lycanthrope that has bonded with the Heart will heal completely from virtually any injury, even from an object made of silver, unless it was there before the individual was bitten."

Mako got up from the small sofa. "So, what are you saying? If someone had a limp before they were bitten, they would still have it afterwards?"

"Yes," Jason said. "And it also applies to scars and birth defects too."

"What other kind of benefits does the Heart provide?"

"It is unknown." Nathan rose from his seat, interrupting the conversation. "We would actually need the item in order to find out."

"Do we even know if Stumpp has it for certain?"

Nathan moved to his desk and didn't look back as he answered, "Harris may be a scoundrel, but he hates Stumpp as much as we do—maybe more. If he said Stumpp has the Heart and is willing to seek outside help to steal it, then I'm of a mind to believe him." He turned to his two guests. "We're done here. Please see yourselves out." To guarantee they did, several armed Guardians flanked and escorted them to the exit.

"Wait a minute." Mako carefully turned as to not provoke any violent outbursts from his men. "If Stumpp has the Heart, is it possible he is also hiding his ancestor, Peter Stubbe: the Werewolf of Bedburg, or is the Heart just his leverage to control Stubbe?"

"I said we're done." Nathan's tone suggested his politeness was at an end.

Concerned for her safety, Mako led Jacquie out of the hotel room without uttering another word. The two got in the elevator, and on the way down, he punched the car wall out of frustration from being rejected a second time. He rubbed his fist with his other hand to quell the stinging.

"Take it easy," she said. "You always let your temper get the best of you. Let's figure this out on our own."

"And how do you propose we apprehend a centuries-old werewolf?" he asked angrily. "It's stronger, faster, and has more experience evading capture than any living thing."

The elevator chimed once they reached the lobby, and she was stunned to see Jason standing on the other side of the doors. "How did you get down here so fast? I didn't see you leave the room," she said.

"I ran varsity track. Hurdles were my specialty," he replied. "Stairs don't pose a problem for me."

For the time being, Mako kept Jason's secret between them. "What is his malfunction?"

"Nathan has a problem with everyone. Me included."

"I noticed," Jacquie interrupted. "Why is that?"

"We have a complicated history. However, it's the present that concerns me now. We haven't much time left to catch Stubbe or any of the other cursed individuals still roaming free."

"What makes you think that?"

"It's what Nathan said about the curse and the phases of the moon. Only Stubbe, who is protected by the Heart, can resist the transformation when the moon is right. We suppose it's another benefit of the Heart, but his subordinates can't. No matter how much control they have over their affliction, they can only prolong the change; they will eventually be forced to take on their more beastly forms."

"You mean when the moon is full?" Jacquie asked.

"Not exactly," Jason answered. "I mean when the moon is right. There are many misconceptions about the mythology. The full moon is the time when a werewolf's powers are at their peak, but the full moon only lasts for a short while. There are other phases of the moon that reflect sufficient amounts of light to cause the transformation. All in all, the victim of a werewolf's bite will inevitably transform for approximately one week."

"That doesn't leave us with much time to find our killer," Mako said.

"How does one more day sound?"

"Not good." Mako said, checking his watch. "It's late. We should all get some sleep. Tomorrow is going to be a busy day."

THIRTY-SEVEN

"Good morning. Care for some breakfast?"

Light green eyes strained as a flood of sunlight struck them head-on, and Jacob held his hand up to block some of it while using the other arm to prop himself up on the queen-size poster bed in which he'd apparently spent the night. His body was sore, but his mind was cloudy about the previous night's events. Looking around the extremely large bedroom with its fancy decorations, he instantly knew he'd somehow ended up back in Peter Stumpp's home.

"Would you care for something to eat, sir?" Charles got the young man's attention.

"How did I get here?" He rubbed his aching jaw. "And why does my entire body hurt?"

The manservant wheeled a cart next to the bed and placed a cloth napkin across Jacob's lap. "There will be plenty of time for questions later. Right now you need to regain your strength." He moved to a large dresser and tapped the doors. "You will find a clean change of clothes in here, and you can join us downstairs in the courtyard whenever you're ready. Is there anything else I can do for you?"

Jacob's head was still spinning. But he was famished, and the food looked delicious. There didn't seem to be anything for him to worry about at the moment. "No, thanks. Charles, right?"

As the butler made for the exit, he turned back with a smile. "Yes, it is." He paused for a moment. "Are you sure you're all right?"

"I'm not sure of anything at the moment," he said, swinging his legs off the bed to face the food cart. "How do I find the courtyard?"

"Just follow your nose." Charles closed the door, leaving Jacob to look over the tray of food and decide what to devour first.

The smell of fresh brewing coffee helped Mako awaken from his sleep. He opened one eye and rolled it around until it focused on the doorway of his kitchen. Jacquie sat at the table with her legs crossed, in her long pink robe, as the dogs circled like sharks in search of food. He opened his other eye and waited for it to adjust to the light before scoping out the neatly set kitchen table.

Sitting up and stretching the muscles in his back and arms, he let out a subtle groan before leaving the sofa. Not that she hadn't seen him in boxer briefs before, but he decided to slide into a pair of sweat pants and a t-shirt before going to the other room. "Want me to make you something?"

She didn't answer.

Mako grabbed the frying pan out of the cabinet and placed it on the stove. "I still make a good omelet." Opening the refrigerator, he collected everything he needed and set it all on the countertop.

"I do miss it," she said.

"What's that?"

"This." She sounded sad. "Waking up with you. Watching you cook. Spending time with you." Taking another sip from her coffee, she looked away.

Unwilling to harbor resentful feelings, he sat next to her at the kitchen table. "Listen, about last night—"

"Don't worry about it," she cut him short, shifting to face him. "You were right. I shouldn't have said what I said." Taking his hand, she said, "I understand you never purposely meant to hurt me. If I really thought that, I would not have come to help you."

"I appreciate it. If not for you—"

She stopped him: "Oh my goodness. Rikki."

"What'd he do now?" Mako wasn't sure where she was going with this.

"He dropped me off last night. And I told him I would wake him as soon as we got back, so he'd know we were all right. He must be worried sick. I should wake him now."

Enjoying the morning calm, Mako said, "He's not going anywhere. Let him sleep." He went back to the stove. "As long as we're okay, I'm good." Checking the food, he threw a few bacon scraps to Chip and Bruno, who happily gobbled up the rare treat.

Jacob admired the expensive button-down dress shirt and thought how it would set him back a month's pay if he were to buy it for himself. He descended the stairs to the first floor of the mansion and stood in the empty foyer, searching for any signs of life. No one seemed to be home. Strolling around, he hoped to run into somebody, anybody, but it appeared they had left him alone. "Follow my nose," he whispered. Closing his eyes and trying to use his new abilities the way his tutor showed him, he strained to detect a scent of anything that would lead him to the courtyard within the massive house. Finally, he found one.

He opened his eyes. He noticed a new fluidity to his movements but was unsure if it was due to his new constitution. His body didn't feel as sore as it had when he first awoke, but his memory continued to be fuzzy about the events that had transpired the night before. He remembered his training lesson followed by the horrible screams, and he recalled being attacked and locked inside the armored truck. Although he wanted to remember what happened after he was freed from the vehicle and assaulted by that group of men, the images wouldn't come. Jacob put his memories on hold once he reached the courtyard.

"I was beginning to think this was a wasted exercise," Stumpp said.

"Not with that cologne it wasn't. I might have been able to smell that even without heightened senses." His attempt at a joke wasn't appreciated, so he tried gratitude instead. "Thanks for the change of clothes. I'll have them washed and returned to you as soon as possible."

"Nonsense," he scoffed. "They're yours. They suit you better than the outfit you were wearing when I saw you last." He gestured to a trash can that held Jacob's bloodied outfit.

The sticky red substance covering his ripped shirt sparked a memory, and suddenly the previous night's incident came rushing back. The gunshots sounded loudly in his mind as the image of the gang member, hand outstretched, put four bullets into his chest. He remembered the pain right before he blacked out. He ripped open his designer shirt to inspect his chest, but there wasn't a single wound—not a scar, a scratch, or a scrape anywhere on his body. He didn't know how that was possible.

Before Jacob could even ask the question, Stumpp held out a newspaper with the headline, "Gang Members Mutilated by Unknown Assailant," and said, "This is your handiwork, my boy."

Jacob grabbed the paper and briefly read the front page. "How can that be? I was shot point-blank. I should be dead."

"If you were normal, you would be. But you are much more than you were, as I told you already, and because of the new identity that has been bestowed upon you, you never have to be afraid again. You can always find some way to restrain your animalistic side from harming anyone during the times of transformation, but from my viewpoint, you did the community a great service last night." He tapped his finger on the newspaper headline.

"They wanted to kill me, but I turned out to be the murderer. I'm no better than them!"

Stumpp moved over to the boy and placed his arm around him "I disagree. You weren't out for murder. You were fighting for survival. Your survival. These others who call themselves men were the ones out for blood, for no other purpose than to satisfy their own egos. Your kills were righteous. Their deaths allow others in their community to breathe a little easier this morning." Lighting a match, Stumpp threw it into the steel drum, igniting the old garments as a visual symbol that Jacob should put the past behind him—whether he wanted to or not. "Come with me back to the place where your new life began. I have to meet with a detective, and I want you to witness the perks that come with power."

Jacquie sat on the couch, looking at a boatload of papers spread over the coffee table. "Here," she called out, "look at this."

Emerging from the bedroom, buttoning his shirt, Mako took the page she held out to him. It was a forensics report detailing materials like blood, semen, or any other physical matter that determined DNA; but since he wasn't a forensic scientist, he had no idea what he was looking at. "Mind explaining this to me?"

"Sure." She enjoyed moments when she knew more than him. "The sample I just gave you shows the genetic code belonging to Jacob Connors, as collected the morning after the attempted burglary at Stumpp Industries." She handed him another sheet.

"This is a sample of Jacob's DNA already on file for an attempted felony when he was in college."

Scrutinizing both patterns, Mako discovered something. "These don't seem to be the same."

"You're correct," she said. "In college, our perp was completely human. After the break-in, however, tells a completely different story. There are traces of canine DNA mixed with his." She paused. "Johnny, I think whatever happened that night turned him into one of those things."

"Can't be. That would mean the curse, or virus, whatever you want to call it, would have to take effect as soon as it entered the bloodstream." He thought for a minute. "Can it do that?"

"I guess it's as plausible as werewolves living in the modern world, but I know who we could call to find out." She handed him his cell.

"Don't answer that!" Nathan yelled, spotting Jason about to retrieve his phone.

"Why not?"

Nathan, packing up the information temporarily stored in the hotel room's desk, responded in his usual condescending tone: "We are done here. We came here to kill a beast, perhaps the worst one of them all, because you believed he personally committed murder nearly a week ago. Before we arrived there was a second murder involving a different lycanthrope, and now we have an interfering cop, who you mixed up in our affairs. Two of my men have been killed. Harris showed up to complicate things further. And there's only one night left to find any number of beasts that may or may not be stalking the streets of Long Island. If this doesn't sound like a complete fiasco to you, then I don't know what would."

"And what should we tell all the potential victims and their families about your excuse for shirking your responsibility?"

Nathan smiled smugly. "I wouldn't tell them anything. But I would enlist them to our cause, if they were willing to join."

"You're such an asshole."

"I make the calls no one else wants to. I thought you'd understand that by now." He put the last of his files in a briefcase and slid past Jason to a bookcase on the back wall, browsing through the books. "Are you sure there isn't anything else you didn't tell me last night during your debriefing?"

Knowing full well that he'd left out the part where a monstrous Ethan met with him on the rooftops—the part where he allowed the lycanthrope to leave unharmed and prohibited Mako from shooting him—Jason lied through his teeth. "No, I told you everything."

Nathan returned to his business, repossessing personal belongings and paying no attention to his company.

Jason imagined that the other Guardians were doing the same in the adjoining rooms, but he didn't want it to end this way—not when he was so close to being rid of the monster that plagued his memory for years. He needed to find a way to prolong their stay, even if it was only for one more night. "Nathan," he said.

"You're still here?"

Expecting nothing less from the man, he continued, "Are you going to leave your fallen comrades? In a strange place? With no hope of a soldier's burial?"

"Trying to goad me into staying? Do you think I don't care for the welfare of my men, breathing or not? It would be disrespectful to abandon their bodies. After we pack, we will liberate them from the morgue and head home. Nice try though."

"You'll have a problem getting two corpses past security."

Nathan closed a third box filled with files, went over to the desk once more, and opened the center top drawer. He pulled out the pistols with his family's crest engraved on the handles, and he stuck them into holsters hanging off his belt behind his back. Despite realizing what his colleague was getting at, he voiced the question anyway. "You want me to ask Detective Mako for help, don't you?"

"It would be the easiest way."

"What if he refuses?"

"He won't," he said confidently. "Not if he doesn't know why you'd really be there."

"Jason," Nathan said, shocked. "Are you suggesting I lie to the man? That's despicable." His expression of surprise turned to one of amusement. "I love it," he laughed. "When we're ready, you'll make the call."

"Me?"

"Of course. It was your suggestion. And if it's so important to you that I linger here a while longer, then you shouldn't have a problem with it."

Jason hated to withhold information from Mako yet again. "I'll do it."

"He's not picking up."

Jacquie shrugged. "It was worth a shot." She thumbed through the newspaper, stopping at the article referring to last night's gang assault. "I wonder …," she thought out loud.

"What's that?"

"I wonder if the werewolf we saw last night was Jacob?"

"Connors hasn't been seen since the night of the break-in. And don't forget how you jumped to conclusions about Falcone and were mistaken."

"I'm not so sure I was completely wrong about Falcone, and if it wasn't Jacob last night, who could it have been?"

Mako already knew it wasn't Ethan Walker. He was still having trouble with the fact that it was Ethan who'd nearly killed him at the motel. And he knew it couldn't be Louis Falcone, who Jason claimed was a werewolf too, considering Louis had been gutted by Ethan. Robert Mane was dead, as confirmed by the medical examiner. So it could only be Jacob, or Stumpp's ancestor. There was only one person who might be able to shed some light on the subject. "I'll call Mullins," he said, dialing.

"What for?"

But Mullins answered before Mako could respond to Jacquie. "Jimmy, it's Mako."

"I got nothing to say to you."

"Don't hang up. I have an important question."

"Every time you have a question, you get me into deeper shit." Mullins was aggravated. "Do you realize Grimes is speaking to the Review Board after you disappeared from the hospital? He thinks I'm allowing you to go rogue!"

Mako hadn't comprehended all the problems he would create for others around him by trying to bolster his own career, but he'd come too far to stop now. It was going to be all or nothing. "Your meeting with Stumpp yesterday. How did it go? Was Jacob Connors with him?"

"Go fuck yourself. How dare you disregard everything I just said to you?"

"Jimmy, relax. I can help you this time."

"Because your incompetence led to Falcone being murdered, and then because you escaped the medical center without authorization, I haven't been able to see him yet. I've been up to my asshole in paperwork over shit I had no part of." It sounded as if Mullins hit something. "Leave me alone, and don't call me again."

The phone clicked off, and Mako mimicked throwing his cell across the room but did not let go of it. Instead, he made a call to the Second Precinct. "Hi. Can I speak to Detective Mullins?" He knew giving his real name would instigate a police car being dispatched to his home, and he had to stay hidden a few hours more. "Do you know where I could find him? It's about … his dad." Because Mullins' father was well-respected throughout the department, he figured that would get him what he wanted to know. It did. He thanked the desk officer and closed his phone, turning to Jacquie. "Come on, we're going to Stumpp Industries."

"I don't think that's a good idea. I heard some of what he said to you."

"We don't have a choice. But you can stay here, if you're not comfortable."

"Let me get my coat." After all that she'd experienced, she wanted to see this through to the end.

"And grab the file on Peter Stumpp. I want to know more about him before we meet."

THIRTY-EIGHT

Strolling through the front doors of Stumpp Industries, Mako was relieved that the only cop car he'd seen in the lot was Mullins'. He knew he wouldn't be welcomed, so he brought a peace offering to hopefully quell any hostilities: copies of every file pertaining to the murder investigation, minus the proof that werewolves existed. Jacquie's presence would also probably cause friction once they reached the makeshift interrogation room, but he guessed her feminine charms could wear Mullins down.

He took an extra couple of minutes to examine the lobby area. This was the third time he'd entered this building, and each time was special, but now anyone would be hard-pressed to determine that a crime had been committed. The caution tape was discarded, the glass was swept away, and all surfaces were cleaned and made to look good as new. Even the damaged elevator had been removed, with the outer doors freshly replaced. The only sign of something amiss was the placard posted in front of the elevators, stating that one of the cars was out of order.

Mako surmised that Mullins was interviewing Stumpp in his office, and he tried to find it on the company directory, running his finger down the column of names until it jumped out at him. It was on the thirteenth floor, which confirmed that what Louis had told him about that night was at least partially true. Mako hadn't gone to the upper floors on any of his other trips, but he had not forgotten the sound of Officer Sanchez vomiting because of all the blood he'd found. Searching for Jacquie, he found her admiring the wall-sized portrait of a man and his dog. "Coming?"

"Is Peter Stumpp full of himself, or what?" she said, sidestepping Mako's question.

"What makes you think that's him? I made the same mistake too," he said, motioning to the small sign next to the portrait. "Read the name."

She did as instructed. "Uncanny family resemblance."

"You've met him before?"

"We weren't formally introduced," she said. "But I've seen him from afar. He was smug then too. He came under investigation a few times, mostly when my father was still ali—, uh, on the force. But he moved his headquarters here shortly after I took over the case. He thought he could buy his way out of any situation. I don't recall any portraits like this in any building of his I ever visited, but his face practically rented space on the front page of virtually every newspaper the town published."

"Why didn't you tell me this before?"

Shrugging her shoulders, she said, "I didn't think you would let me come."

"You're absolutely right. I don't need your emotions getting in the way and making this personal."

"It happens to you all the time."

"That's why one of us has to have a clear head. I was hoping it'd be you."

"Right now it's your turn." She stormed away from the painting. "I happen to believe he knows how my parents died."

"And if he does," he said, darting after her, "we'll get it out of him." Rubbing her shoulders in a calming manner while she impatiently hit the call button for the elevator, he said, "Remember, we aren't supposed to be here. Let Mullins handle the questioning.

If he doesn't arrest me on sight, we'll check for any inconsistencies in Stumpp's story. Think you can do that?"

"Can you?" she remarked as the working elevator arrived. "Which floor?"

"Thirteen."

"Unlucky for some," she said ominously.

"Yeah, let's hope not for us."

Mullins, already speaking with Stumpp, cycled through the basic questions and referred to his notes. He was about to get to the heart of the matter when Stumpp had an inquiry of his own. "Are you expecting someone, Detective?"

Mullins lifted his eyes off of the small pad he was looking over. "Excuse me?"

"Well, they're not my people," he said, persuading the detective to step into the hallway.

Figuring this might be a stalling tactic, he decided to humor the man by investigating. "How the hell?" the detective thought out loud, spotting Mako and company walking from the elevator, past the cleaning crew, in the direction of Stumpp's office. "I can't believe this," he stated, walking toward them.

"Don't fly off the handle," Mako started.

"I should have you arrested you son of a—" Mullins stopped himself, practically slapping his own forehead in frustration. "Give me one good reason I shouldn't." Then, upon realizing who was with Mako, he asked, "Why is Dale here?"

"Nice to see you too, James," she said. A while back Jacquie had helped the NCPD solve a case Mullins headed, which was how they knew each other. He'd developed a small crush on her, and she contemplated using it to her advantage.

He gave her the once-over. "Still looking good. You want to see how a real man operates now that you're not with this loser anymore?"

"Sure," she said, lightly running a hand up the detective's protruding belly and onto his man-breasts. "You know where I can find one?"

Mullins' face went from flirtatious to offended, and he swatted her hand away. "Funny, Dale. Too bad your sense of humor isn't as nice as your ass." He stuck his index finger in Mako's face. "All right, dickhead. This is the deal. I'm not postponing this interview again, so you come in and keep your mouth shut. If you can't act like a professional, I'll treat you like a criminal."

"What about Jacquie?"

"What about her?" Mullins returned, as if Mako should know the answer already. "She stays here."

"No way, Jimmy," she came to her own defense.

Mullins didn't have time for a lengthy argument, so he submitted. "You're in, but you better abide by the same rules. Don't say a word." The couple followed Mullins to the office, but before they entered, he spun around and reminded them, "Not a word. Understand?"

Jacquie nodded innocently in agreement as Mako pulled an imaginary zipper across his lips. When Mullins looked away, both of them extended a middle finger to his back, and after a hushed giggle, the two of them went in behind him.

Upon entering, Mako immediately scanned the room for anything suspicious. He found Stumpp sitting patiently behind his desk with his two bodyguards standing to one side. Mako recognized them. Mr. Ball's broken nose was bandaged, and even dark sunglasses couldn't hide the black-and-blue bruises beneath his eyes. Chainz balanced on crutches, thanks to the blown kneecap Jacquie had given him. Neither giant looked too pleased to see the officers again. The last person standing in the room with them elicited a response from Jacquie, who recalled his mug shot.

"That's him," she whispered to Mako. "Connors."

Jacob rested beside Stumpp's desk like a puppy lying at its master's feet.

"You sure?"

"He looks a little different than his college days, but judging by the bone structure and physical description, I'm positive."

"Hey!" Mako pointed an accusing finger at him. "Why have you been hiding all this time? We thought you were dead." The outburst provoked a negative reaction from Mullins.

Afraid to answer, Jacob wished he could become invisible until Stumpp rose from his chair and placed a calming hand on his shoulder. "Can I help you?" Stumpp said to Mako. "I thought Detective Mullins was conducting this interview."

"I am," Mullins reinforced. "Stand down, Mako."

"Ah. The infamous Johnny Mako; the detective with a thug's name," Stumpp said.

The revelation shocked Mako. "Have we met?"

"No. But I do keep myself in the know, especially when it comes to anyone harassing my employees."

"Your employees should be behind bars, not collecting hefty paychecks."

Stumpp inhaled deeply. "That's a contemptible accusation, Detective. You had better have some hard evidence to support your claims, or I will sue both you and the Nassau County Police Department for slander or anything else my lawyers see fit."

"There won't be a need for that, Mr. Stumpp," Mullins attempted to keep the peace.

"Don't threaten me with lawyers." Spittle flew from between Mako's gritted teeth. "Did you know your goons physically assaulted an officer of the law? Not to mention that animal, Ethan Walker, murdered Louis Falcone while he was under my protection."

"Burden of proof, Detective."

"I bet you ordered the hit, you piece of—"

"NOW WAIT A DAMN MINUTE!" Mullins stepped between them, seizing Mako by the upper arm and pulling him off to the side. "I am the officer in charge of this case, Mr. Stumpp. If you'll kindly take your seat and cease this talk about lawyers and suing, we can get back to the matter at hand. My associate will not be a part of the remainder of this interview." Then he whispered in Mako's ear, "Listen to me. I will not have a repeat of the disaster you started with the Walker interrogation. Now, shut the fuck up, or get the fuck out."

Stumpp politely moved to the back of his desk, but he did not sit down. He eyed Mullins with disapproval. "This meeting is over, gentlemen. I think Walter Sickert put it best when he said, 'Come again when you can't stay so long.'"

"I'm sorry, Mr. Stumpp, but that isn't going to happen," Mullins said.

"Why? Was I not clear?"

"Just arrest this guy already, Jimmy," Mako said quietly, tapping Mullins on the arm.

Stumpp tilted his head sideways a bit. "You are an annoying little man, Detective Mako. Don't you realize I'm not someone to be trifled with?"

"Is that a threat?" he asked, surprised Stumpp had even heard his remark. "I think he just threatened me," he said to Mullins.

"Everyone, take it easy." Mullins nodded his head with a frown on his face, but he was not ready to be dismissed so easily. "We could do this your way, Mr. Stumpp. But remember one thing: I can be back in as little as an hour with a warrant to tear this office building apart. So, you can either answer my questions now, or you can answer them later when I have a squad of uniformed officers crawling so far up your ass, you'll wish you'd have cooperated with me. Your choice."

It was not a difficult decision, as he was not going to take on the whole police department—at least not yet anyway. "Proceed."

Mako wanted to speak, but a stern look from Mullins shut him down.

Through the entire dispute, Jacquie had been studying Stumpp's face, and something about it struck her as peculiar.

"So, tell me," Mullins said to Stumpp, "where were you the night of the break-in?"

"I believe my assistant, Ethan Walker, the 'animal' Detective Mako was referring to earlier, already told you. I was on a plane headed to my hometown of Bedburg, Germany."

"Why no night watchmen or security guards? And how come there aren't any cameras past the lobby area?"

Stumpp sighed out of sheer boredom. "I only keep security personnel during normal business hours. It keeps my staff satisfied. Security occupies the front booth when you first enter the building, and they go on routine walk-throughs twice a day. I trust them only so far. They are only human, after all. When they leave for the day, I lock the doors from the inside, and I allow my pets to roam free inside the building. It keeps *me* satisfied that my belongings are safe."

Stumpp continued, "As far as cameras go, it is my prerogative where and how many I wish to have in my building. I only need to see who walks through the front doors. If there is a dilemma, I can sniff out who the troublemaker is."

What is it about his face? Jacquie mused.

"How do you get out of the building if you lock up from the inside?" Mullins asked.

Removing a key from his inside jacket pocket, Stumpp showed it to the detective. "This permits me to access a lower level in this building with its own private exit. Only I and Mr. Walker possess identical keys. Again, another security measure I have in place."

Mullins chose his next question carefully. "These so-called security measures of yours aren't really foolproof, are they?" Stumpp was about to return with a response, but Mullins raised a hand in order to stop him. "Let me finish, please. What I mean is you trust your pets more than you rely on human beings. But would human beings have so brutally attacked a young man just a few feet from your office, or would human beings have merely detained the intruder until the proper authorities could come by and deal with him accordingly?"

Stumpp smirked, knowing what the officer was getting at. "First of all, Detective, let's not pretend criminals are anything more than what they are. Being human does not mean they are entitled to humane treatment. Let me put it in terms you can relate to. If someone entered your home uninvited, and placed your family members in danger, would you not defend them to the fullest of your extent, even if it meant killing said intruder?"

He hesitated to answer.

Stumpp didn't need an answer. "A hard question, I know, especially because you feel the need to operate within the law. Now, I suppose you could say this is not my home, that I have no family here to protect; but you'd be wrong. I have put in many long hours here, and sometimes I do spend the night. My pets are my family, and just because they are covered with fur, it does not make them any less important than a human family." Now Mullins wanted to speak but he wasn't allowed. "Before you ask, Detective, they aren't here, and I will not be showing them to you or anyone else. Ever. I will not put my family through any unnecessary trials to satisfy a court, only for the court to determine that they need to be put down. It will not happen, and I will fight to keep it that way."

Stumpp continued, "Besides, the person you say was so brutally attacked is standing right beside me. Young Jacob here is a bleeder. His blood simply does not clot as fast as the rest of us, I'm afraid. We've worked things out amongst ourselves, and he doesn't wish to press charges."

Mullins glared at the unusually shy young man. "Is this true? I need to hear the words from your mouth."

"Yes," said Jacob, offering only the one-word reply.

"You see," Stumpp cut in, "I am not a bad man."

At that statement, Mako could not maintain his silence. "Tell it to Louis Falcone who's lying in the morgue."

"Johnny!" Mullins shouted.

Stumpp was out of his chair. "Let him speak. I'm interested to hear what he has to say."

Mako reached out to Jacquie, and she instinctively handed him the file on Peter Stubbe. Moving past a stunned Mullins, he headed to the forefront and stopped inches away from Stumpp's desk. "You're a liar. Evil is in your blood. Your ancestor had it, and it was apparently passed on to you." He placed the file inches away from Stumpp's nose. "Are you going to tell me you didn't know your assistant murdered Louis Falcone?"

"I was not aware of that."

"Or that he sent me to the hospital when I tried to stop him?"

"I do not monitor his every movement, Detective."

Mako was perceptive enough to realize that Stumpp wouldn't acknowledge any unlawful activities perpetrated by any one of his employees, but he figured he could at least give him a shock by mentioning something no one was supposed to know about. "What about the Heart of Lycaon?"

Stumpp's features froze in amazement. "What was that?" he mustered, once control of his facial muscles returned to him.

Satisfied that he had Stumpp's full attention, Mako proceeded further. "The Heart of Lycaon. The Silver Heart. Don't pretend you don't know what I'm talking about. That's what these guys came here to take from you that night. It's supposed to be in your office."

Jacob cleared his throat but looked at the floor once the detective's eyes shifted in his direction.

"You have something you want to say?" Mako asked him.

"Hold on a second," Mullins interrupted. "What the hell are you talking about? Silver hearts and, what was that other thing you said?"

Mako handed Mullins a page of hastily scribbled notes. "This is what Louis Falcone told me before he was murdered. Read it yourself. It's a one-of-a-kind item that Stumpp has in his possession. It's what they were after."

Carefully contemplating his response while the officers were chatting with one another, Stumpp gave Jacob a stern gaze to tell him to control himself for the duration of the meeting. Then he decided to do what he so rarely did in life: tell the truth. "Go ahead, Detectives, snoop around. I have nothing to hide."

"No, thanks," Mullins said. "We'll take your word for it."

"Very well," Stumpp said with a grin. "Besides, if such an item did exist, do you think I would keep it here instead of in my home, where I could safeguard it personally?"

"I can't say what you'd do," Mako answered. "I don't have the mind of a madman."

"That's unkind, Detective. You don't know me well enough to make harsh judgments."

"Proclaim your innocence all you want. We both know you're not above suspicion. Walker practically admitted to me that he killed Falcone. Come clean and save the performance for court!" Frustrated, Mako slammed his empty hand on Stumpp's desk.

The hostile action by the detective cued a response from Ball and Chainz. They shifted positions in case they were given orders to subdue the officer.

Noticing their actions, Mako gazed at them. "Settle down, boys. We don't want to take this somewhere you don't want it to go." He slid a hand into his jacket as a warning to the bodyguards.

Stumpp addressed his men. "Relax, Mr. Ball. You too, Mr. Chainz." In an eerily calm voice, he spoke to Mako. "You have overstayed your welcome, Detective. Leave now, or else."

"Nobody's going anywhere yet." Mullins tapped his colleague on the shoulder. "Is what you're saying a hundred percent accurate about that night at the motel?"

"Have you checked the body?" Mako locked eyes with Stumpp. "Cause of death will read a stab wound to the abdomen, causing the victim to bleed out. At least that's how the medical examiner will see it. But we know different, don't we?" The detective insinuated that he'd uncovered the truth behind the man's "pets."

Mullins wrote down every word as it was spoken and pointed his pen at Stumpp. "If this checks out, I'll be back, and you'd better be ready to hand over your assistant. Let's go, Mako." Mullins walked past Jacquie. "You too, Dale."

Hearing her name struck a chord within Stumpp. He knew her, or at least, of her, and he felt compelled to share. "Dale? Not Jacquie Dale of the Boston Police Department?"

The query caused her heart to skip a beat. She didn't want to let on how rattled she was, but the more she told herself to remain calm, the more she felt she was showing her nervousness. "No, not anymore," she answered. "I remember you too. Even though we've never actually met, I feel like we're old acquaintances."

"What's going on?" Mullins whispered.

"You'll see," Mako whispered back.

Stumpp approached Jacquie, and with every step he took, her skin crawled a little more. She didn't like being this close to the man. She hadn't understood a lot surrounding her parents' deaths when she was a rookie in Boston, but now the picture was becoming clearer with every new piece of the puzzle that revealed itself.

"You are even more beautiful than the photos in the newspaper would have one believe." He went to take her hand, but she pulled away. Her rudeness had consequences. "It's a pity about your parents though. Cut down in their prime."

"Don't talk about my parents, you lowlife scum!" she spat out viciously. "My father was investigating you when you lived in Boston, but you moved shortly after his murder."

Turning his back on her, Stumpp extended his arms outward to his sides and said in an almost cheerful voice, "Don't you mean accident? The way I heard it, he was camping in the woods when a pack of wild dogs mistook him for a T-bone."

Jacquie lunged forward, but Mullins grabbed her before she could reach him.

"Your mother," Stumpp continued, "was found several yards away, apparently running for her life. But she couldn't run quite fast enough, could she? Imagine that. Two people supposedly so devoted to each other, and she still didn't make an effort to help her precious husband." He spun back around to look at Mullins. "Now, maybe you'll understand why I don't trust humans, Detective."

Jacquie's tears fueled Mako's rage, and as Mullins struggled to remove her from the office, Mako stormed up to Stumpp. He needed to peer upward to meet the other man's stare. "You're a piece of garbage. Don't think about taking any more trips out of town either, because I'm not done with you."

"I doubt we'll be seeing each other again," said Stumpp, snapping his fingers. His bodyguards made a move toward the lone detective.

Mako exited, unwilling to continue an argument with the odds greatly stacked against him, and joined his associates who were already at the elevator. Once the three of them were out of sight, Stumpp whipped around with a roar, causing Jacob to nearly jump out of his skin. Ball and Chainz would have laughed, if they weren't just as frightened. "Imbeciles!" He pointed at the hired help. "Use your resources and get me an address for Detective Mako. And I want it yesterday!"

Vacating the office, Mr. Ball whispered to his hobbling partner, "Good thing Walker has it stashed in his office already. He figured we might need it after the first time he met him."

"Jacob," Stumpp said, putting his arm around the terrified boy, "I have a special task for you."

"Are you sure? It's almost dark, and I can feel the change taking hold of me again."

Ignoring the question, Stumpp said, "A good friend of mine, Al Ries, once told me, 'Strategy and timing are the Himalayas of marketing. Everything else is the Catskills.' He, of course, was applying it to practical business purposes, but I do believe it can be utilized in all aspects of life. Come along." He led him into the hallway. "We're off to the Himalayas."

THIRTY-NINE

Mullins angrily shoved his way out of the elevator and into the lobby, even before the doors fully opened, pissed that he'd once again lost control of a situation and been blindsided with information he should've been told before questioning Stumpp.

Jacquie was the next to exit, still reeling from the comments made about her parents. She knew what was said wasn't true, but it didn't make it hurt any less. She held back the tears as the resolve to find her parents' killer strengthened, and she knew it was only a matter of time before the evidence presented itself.

Mako was the last to emerge. He didn't regret what had happened in Stumpp's office, nor did he intend to break his word. Never one to reward bad behavior, he was prepared to do what it took to see any and all who were responsible for these crimes finally suffer the consequences of their actions. The only curiosity on his mind, as he exited the building and the cool air hit his face, was why Mullins hadn't turned him over to Grimes yet.

"Does somebody want to tell me what the hell happened back there?" Mullins yelled.

"Which part?" Mako asked.

"Now is not the time to be a smart-ass. I want an explanation."

"Here." Mako offered him a folder.

Mullins immediately flipped through the pages. "What is this? This is a file on a guy named Stubbe. I thought you had information about the item those kids tried to steal."

"One thing at a time." Receiving the other files from Jacquie, Mako picked three out of four and surrendered them to his colleague. "Here's the rest, but as for what went on in there, it's in the Stubbe file."

"What does one have to do with the other? This Stubbe guy lived in the fifteen hundreds."

"Stubbe is the ancestor of Stumpp. The surname changed in the late seventeen hundreds to escape the family legacy."

"Get to the point."

"Peter Stubbe was better known for his title," Mako said, pausing dramatically, "the Werewolf of Bedburg."

"You're shittin' me."

"Wish I could say I was. The guy was sick. This is the kind of stuff you don't want to remember, but it ingrains itself into your head."

"Are you going to elaborate, or would it be quicker for me to read it?"

"Don't strain yourself. The big words might give you a headache."

"What'd I say, Mako?"

"Relax," he said, bouncing his hands in a downward motion, signaling Mullins to keep his blood pressure low. "Stubbe was accused of killing sixteen people, including two pregnant women and thirteen children, but his M.O. earned him the werewolf title. Either ripping their throats out or tearing them to pieces, he ate pieces of their flesh and drank their blood. One of the slain women was never found because it was thought that he ate her completely.

"If that wasn't bad enough, he had an incestuous relationship which produced a baby boy. Jimmy, the guy killed and cannibalized his only son, reportedly eating his brain. He was tried, and the judge ordered Stubbe to be tortured before being put to death. He was tied to an iron wheel where his flesh was pulled off his body with hot pokers, his limbs were broken, and his head was cut off. His lifeless body was then supposedly burnt to ashes."

"I'm bored. What does this have to do with Stumpp?"

Mako thought it would be obvious. "He's been lying to everyone his entire life. You think if people knew this, he'd be as successful as he is today?" Defeated, he turned to Jacquie. "You want to take it from here?"

"Most of what I know is a matter of public record," she said. "The Stubbes left Germany over a century after the execution in order to escape their failing financial status. They settled in Philadelphia. They continued to run their business under the family name, amassing even more wealth here than in their native home. But when they moved to New Hampshire in 1871, they changed the name to Stumpp Industries. Their family's legacy had caught up with them. Even so, during that stretch, many unexplained disappearances had witnesses pointing fingers at them. Initially, the homeless population declined, but once a prominent citizen vanished without a trace, people started to care. When the witnesses disappeared too, that's when panic set in.

"A formal investigation was conducted, which was when Stumpp decided to move his headquarters to Boston. He remained there for quite some time before another examination of his business practices was headed up by my father. I was sixteen when my parents were murdered in our backyard; they were mauled to death, and their throats were torn out. My father had defensive wounds on his hands and arms. He was trying to give my mother time to get away while he struggled with their killer. She didn't leave him to die." Her emotions seeped out.

"Dale," Mullins interjected politely, "no one ever questioned the love your parents had for one another. But I thought he said they were on a camping trip?"

She fought back another bout of tears. "Any time he was asked about it, Stumpp made light of it, concocting random scenarios, and soon the press began questioning my story, even though there was actual evidence to back it up. He and his money had the public brainwashed. Anyway, after my father died, no one wanted to take up the investigation. So it was ruled a wild dog attack, not that any wild dogs were ever found, and the case was closed. When I was able to, I joined the force and reopened the case, unofficially, of course. I didn't have the authority to legally snoop around his business to catch him with his hands dirty, but I wasn't about to let my parents die in vain. I was onto something, and Stumpp knew it. He reported me, which almost got me fired, and he moved his business here. That arrogant ass knows who killed my parents, and I can't rest until he tells me."

Running his fingers through his comb-over, Mullins said, "That's some story, Dale." He spoke as delicately as possible. "But you don't have any data to support your premise, and you're way out of your jurisdiction here. You can't touch him. I can't even touch him on those allegations. You should let it go and move on."

"Thanks for the advice." The sarcasm in her voice was evident. "But you'll have to excuse me if I don't follow it. When I got wind of what was going on up here, I had to come and check it out for myself."

Mako uttered a quiet "thank you" that she didn't slip and tell Mullins where she'd gotten the evidence to pique her curiosity.

Mullins wanted to make an argument. "The point is—"

"The point is," Mako said, making a habit out of interrupting his colleague, "Stumpp is evil. It's in his blood. It's only a matter of time before it comes out, and when it does, it's not going to be pretty."

"You can't condemn a man because of the sins of his father, or his father before him." Mullins shrugged. "Besides, none of this would hold up in court." Noticing that his associate's attention was elsewhere, he asked, "You listening to me?"

"Isn't that the car we saw at the morgue?" Mako pointed to the street.

Mullins spotted the light blue Chevy Camaro parked across the street from Stumpp Industries. The windows were tinted, and even if they weren't, it would be difficult to identify an individual sitting inside from this distance. "How the hell should I know? That's an even bigger piece of shit than your car. Why?"

"Call me a paranoid idiot, but I think that car's been following me for days now."

Mullins didn't hesitate to respond. "You're an idiot."

"What about the paranoid part?"

"It doesn't matter," Mullins said. "You're an idiot either way."

"Fat fuck," Mako whispered.

As the boys bickered between themselves, Jacquie investigated the Camaro. When she was close enough to make out the silhouette of a man sitting behind the wheel, the engine roared, and the vehicle drove off, leaving her in a cloud of exhaust. Fanning the smog away, she hoped to get a glimpse of a license plate number, but she returned empty-handed. Unluckily, the car either didn't have one, or the smoke was too thick to see through. Nevertheless, she did have one piece of information to offer. "Well, you are neither paranoid nor an idiot. I think whoever that was has definitely been following you."

"That's her opinion. I still think you're an idiot."

Raising her voice so the name-calling would cease, Jacquie asked, "Any idea who it could be?"

Mako shook his head, thinking of possible suspects. "I've met so many weird characters since this investigation began, it would be easy to accuse any of them."

"Wouldn't be that way if you stayed out of my business," Mullins said matter-of-factly.

"Maybe if I was shown a little respect, I wouldn't feel the need to prove myself."

Mullins felt slighted by that remark. "What do you think? You get a shiny new shield and a promotion, and people are supposed to worship you? You have to earn it, Mako! You think people respect me? Really respect me, and not flash fake smiles because of who my father was in the department? They think I don't know what they say behind my back, but I do. I just don't give a shit anymore."

There it was: the reason why Detective James Mullins was such an unlikable person. He was angry because he realized he didn't have any true friends.

Mako offered a suggestion. "Then why don't you try not being such a, such a," he struggled for the right word, but all that came out was, "prick?"

"Nice." Disappointed at the reaction, Mullins had enough and headed for his car. "I'll be at the morgue reviewing these files and looking into your claims." Sliding into the driver's seat, he held the manila folder over his head and warned, "Everything better be here, Mako." With that, he left.

"That wasn't very kind," Jacquie said, now that they were alone. She wouldn't want to show disloyalty by challenging him in front of others, but in private, she could speak freely.

"It's not like we're friends." Despite not wanting to appear soft, deep down, he agreed with her.

"But maybe he was trying to extend you some professional courtesy by letting you sit in with him today. You, of all people, should have been more understanding." She knew he could relate to everything Mullins said.

"Whatever. Let's get the hell out of here. Moon's out already, and we've only got tonight to catch a monster." Realizing he was walking by himself, he swiveled his head and gazed upon Jacquie's saddened face. "All right. I'll apologize the next time I see him, okay? Can we go?"

Her mission accomplished, she hugged him. "Do you think Stumpp is hiding Stubbe? Nathan never did give you an answer when you asked him at the hotel," she said, getting back to the case.

"I know we couldn't explain that to Mullins, but what else can it be? If that psycho Williams is right, and this Werewolf of Bedburg *is* running around, I don't know any other way he could stay hidden for so long without help."

"What are we going to do, Johnny?"

"Pray for a miracle."

From his office window, Stumpp watched them depart as he answered an incoming call. "Hello. Very good, Mr. Ball. Even quicker than I'd hoped. Send the information to Jacob's phone." He disconnected the call, smiling, knowing his enemies would soon be a memory.

FORTY

Memorizing the address in the text message he received, Jacob closed the flip phone with a snap and returned it to his jeans pocket. He dragged his feet down the nearly deserted street, trying to hide his appearance by pulling his coat tighter around his body, hunching forward, and adjusting his collar to partially cover his face. He couldn't believe Stumpp would throw him out on the street at such a crucial time, for soon he would be a danger to every living thing around him. Understanding what was expected of him, and realizing what would happen if he didn't follow Stumpp's orders, he continued to rationalize the situation. *So what?* he thought. *It's only one cop. No one's going to miss him. They'll probably give him a hero's funeral. Besides, it's him or me.*

The moon sat high in the night sky, and Jacob didn't look the same as he had when he woke that morning. His dark brown hair, now much shaggier, had expanded its territory as it moved around his jaw and brow line. The facial hair, however, wasn't his only concern, for his hands, his body all the way down to his feet, and almost every inch of his flesh was covered in fur. Whether his clothes hid it from view or not, he knew it was there; he felt it sprouting, and it was quite uncomfortable. But the process couldn't be stopped. His fingernails became finger-knives, and the larger they grew, the more pain that came with them. His toenails tore through his sneakers. His upper lip looked swollen, as he tried to conceal the razor-sharp fangs sitting behind it. His skin felt tight as it was stretched to its limits and beyond because the muscles resting under the surface were developing to bestial proportions. The agony increased as the transformation neared completion.

His skeletal system began restructuring. The breaking and reforming of bone was excruciating, and it took all of his will not to fall down crying on the spot when his arm involuntarily snapped. Continuing to focus on the mission at hand, he did his best to ignore the agony wracking his body. Appendages elongated to accommodate his wolf-like frame, and Jacob screamed as his snout pulled farther from his face until it completed its monstrous visage. Unable to support his own weight, he fell on the concrete when the alterations forced his legs to shatter in several places simultaneously. The bones took new shape and healed almost immediately—as did the muscles, ligaments, and tendons—but the pain involved was pure torture. Jacob stumbled and fell into the thick bushes next to one of the homes on the block.

The change only lasted a few moments, and then, it was over.

Jacob's breathing was labored as his body recuperated from the ordeal, but he recovered quickly and stood upright again. His clothes, or what was left of them, lay in tatters at his feet, and in front of him was the home of Detective Johnny Mako. Appearing to have lost everything that was human inside of him, he sniffed the air and snarled at an unsuspecting couple passing by. Even though his humanity was absent, somewhere in the recesses of his mind he remembered why he was here; although the wolf persona wanted to follow its instincts and make a meal of the couple, the man understood there would be consequences for ignoring his master. Jacob's human element won, and the couple lived to see another day.

Moving cautiously toward the house, he came out of hiding and crept silently up the porch steps to the front door. He scratched gently at the front door lock but couldn't quite fathom how it worked. Lacking the comprehension skills he would otherwise have in human form, he still knew the physical benefits his new form possessed. He dug his claws into the doorjamb beside the lock, and using the tremendous strength at his disposal, he slowly curled his fingers into a fist, damaging the frame and making the lock ineffective. The front door swung open without any resistance, and the creature slipped inside.

The microwave alarm beeped throughout Rikki's apartment, and he hopped out of his favorite rocking recliner. He wore his purple robe with matching slippers and loose-fitting pajama pants. Snatching the tray of food, utensils, and a drink, he hurried back into the living room as a rerun of *Ellen* resumed after a lengthy commercial break.

The dance music blared loudly from the television's speakers, and Rikki came to rest in his cushy chair. He stuck a forkful of food into his mouth and flinched when the dogs in the apartment above him unexpectedly barked aggressively. He stared at the ceiling, wishing a glare through sheetrock and plaster could have the desired effect. Increasing the volume, he tried to ignore the racket. The audience was amused at the witty banter between host and guest, and laughter broke out at least three times; but Rikki didn't join in on the hilarity. Apparently, he wouldn't be able to ignore the howls and cries of his two favorite pets, the ones he referred to as his babies. Disgustedly pulling himself off his recliner, he went to the kitchen and took a broom from the closet, thumping the ceiling a few times and hoping it would bring about some end to the noise. He steadily became more agitated when it didn't, so he yelled through the floor, "Cut it out, you guys. Some of us are trying to watch television!" Hoping that would silence the dogs, Rikki returned the broom to its resting place.

In the second floor apartment the dogs went wild, sensing the uninvited intruder. Jacob paid them no mind and continued to inspect his surroundings within the small foyer at the bottom of the stairs, listening to the commotion behind the door to his left, belonging to the downstairs apartment.

Placing his nose to the tiny gap between Rikki's door and door frame, Jacob inhaled deeply. Not recognizing the scent, he advanced to the second floor. Each step caused the loose floorboards to creak slightly, but it was remarkably unnoticeable for a beast as large as the lycanthrope. Once he stood beside the upstairs apartment door, he was again presented with the insignificant problem of a lock. Repeating the process he'd used to defeat the front door; he found that this less sturdy frame splintered more easily.

Barking turned into vicious growling from the dogs inside.

An animal usually knows when a fight is looming, and Jacob was now no different than a subordinate male in a wolf pack, contending for dominance. Using his incredible hearing, he determined that the animals had backed away. He launched himself through the threshold with a roar, intending to take his opponents off-guard, killing them before they wounded him; but his combat inexperience led to a grave miscalculation.

His lightning-quick reflexes were ill-prepared for the vicious assault from his canine cousins. The 110-pound pit bull lunged at Jacob's upper body and sank his teeth into his right bicep while Chipdug his fangs into Jacob's left forearm. The sheer force of the attack knocked the werewolf off his feet, and all three crashed down on the kitchen table, completely destroying it.

In his human form, Jacob would have been down for the count, but his bestial alter ego was only getting started. Pain was experienced in a whole new way. Things that would have been agony were now sheer annoyance. Cuts and scrapes mended instantly, and the gaping wounds on his body started to close almost as soon as the dogs retracted their teeth.

Thrashing wildly about, Jacob tossed both animals aside with a single wave of his arm. The dogs slid across the kitchen floor but did not topple over. However, the wall didn't fare very well when their hindquarters banged into it: a portion of the sheetrock broke off, leaving two nice sized holes behind. Jacob hurried to his feet, but he was clumsy in his new skin and slammed his back against the countertop, swinging his arm and knocking most everything over while spinning around to see what was there.

Chip didn't waste a moment to renew his attack and grabbed Jacob's calf, shaking his head vigorously from side to side in an attempt to bring the intruder down. The werewolf howled but was prevented from grabbing the shepherd as Bruno charged, jumped up, and hit him in the chest with two large front paws. Although his balance was compromised, Jacob refused to fall and grabbed the pit bull around his barrel chest, heaving him into the living room. Bruno yelped when he hit the floor hard, and Chip soon flew past him into the couch.

Limping slightly, Jacob pursued his opponents to finish them off, but there was still plenty of fight left in them. The trio circled each other, looking for an opening to strike, and because Jacob was outnumbered, he needed to be extra-observant. They postured with growls in the hope that someone would back down. For the dogs, this confrontation was in defense of their home and the protection of all they knew. For Jacob, winning this match could mean his very survival. All had something precious to lose, and none would submit easily.

The creatures lunged for each other, and the resulting melee was a frenzied attack. Fur flew as it was ripped from their bodies, and the yelps and cries followed by snarls and howls were heard down on the street, causing neighbors to wonder what was happening. Furniture broke, knick-knacks shattered, walls crumbled, but the beasts were unrelenting. Someone would die this day as teeth and claws hit their marks over and over again, spilling blood and steadily weakening their bodies. Jacob's healing factor was a distinct advantage. He didn't appear to tire, but the dogs were showing signs of slowing.

An animal would usually sense when it was bested, and one could only wonder if Mako's dogs were feeling that now. Most would seek a way out when the battle was not going their way, but retreat was not an option. Not only was Jacob's massive body blocking their escape route, but he wasn't about to let them leave alive.

Jacob slashed at the pit bull with his razor-sharp talons and ripped open his side. Bruno cried out and was sent flying across the room into the far wall. The dog flew into the sofa, flipped over it, and landed on the floor behind it with a thud. The tremendous impact forced the couched to slide backward into the wall, cracking it.

Chip bit into Jacob's neck, and the mighty lycanthrope screamed. He slammed his fist down onto the end table beside the toppled couch, and smashed it to pieces. With the same hand, Jacob seized Chip by the scruff of the neck and pulled him off, tearing some of his own flesh in the process. He maneuvered the shepherd in front of him until they locked eyes, still snarling at each other. Finally, he hurled the dog into the bedroom. Chip landed with a crash.

Silence.

Jacob wanted to strike the killing blow, but a creak outside the apartment alerted him to another's presence. Diving into the bathroom to hide in darkness, he remained motionless and listened as the individual moved about.

Sinking back into the comfy chair, he lifted his glass. The commotion hadn't stopped, but it seemed to have let up a bit, and Rikki believed he'd put enough of a scare into his babies to quiet them down. He leaned his head back and placed the drink to his lips. The cool liquid trickled over his tongue and brushed the back of his throat, making its way down to Rikki's stomach. Abruptly, a loud crash forced all the fluid back up and out of his startled body, spilling onto his clothes. He slammed the glass down on the table beside him, and then he picked it up again to make sure he hadn't scratched the furniture. He wiped the area clean with his fingers to check for scuff marks, and gently set it down again before making his way up to Mako's apartment.

Storming up the stairs, amid the ensuing chaos, he reached for the doorknob but stopped short of grabbing it. The noises ceased once he reached the top step, but the damaged door frame disturbed him. Could that have been the crash he heard?

No.

He was sure the banging came from inside, but what did this to the door frame? *Is Mako home? Are my babies okay?* Other questions flashed through Rikki's mind, but he knew he'd only get answers if he stepped through the doorway. Holding his breath, he carefully situated his fingertips on the door beside the knob and gingerly pushed it open. The door creaked as it swung around. His jaw hit the ground—the view inside the dwelling was almost indescribable. "Oh my goodness. I don't think the security deposit is going to cover this."

The apartment was in shambles. The furniture that wasn't broken was overturned. There was stuffing from pillow cushions floating around and gaping holes in the walls that hadn't been there before. He clearly saw the demolished kitchen and the partially disheveled living room, and got a shiver up his spine when he tried to visualize what could have caused all this destruction. There was no sign of the dogs, or their owner, and Rikki silently cursed himself for entering instead of phoning the police.

"Johnny? Are you in here?"

Stepping over debris that used to be the kitchen table, he moved into the next room and stood beside the wall unit that miraculously hadn't been touched. "Johnny, this isn't funny." His fear was obvious.

From across the room, something stirred.

Rikki froze, hoping whatever it was would go away. The couch had tipped backwards with the back resting against the now cracked wall behind it. The smashed remains of the end table to its right started to shift. Something was beginning to crawl out from under the furniture. He swallowed hard in an attempt to get rid of the lump developing in his throat. The bloodied snout of an animal poked through the rubble, and Rikki shut his eyes tight. If this was the end, he didn't want to see it coming.

Perceiving a whimper, he instantly knew it was one of his babies and ran over to the dog, which hadn't made any real forward progress. He moved the damaged furniture and helped Bruno out. The grateful pit bull licked his savior's face and the extent of Bruno's injuries was now visible. Other than the minor lacerations on his snout, there was a large cut in the dog's side slowly leaking blood. Rikki used some of the ripped couch cushions to tie a tourniquet around Bruno' body. Another cry for help came from the bedroom, and the shepherd limped out of the room. Both dogs looked like they'd been fighting, but Rikki didn't understand why. "What's wrong with the two of you? Why would you do this?

You've never fought before." He left Bruno for a moment to tend to Chip.

As he stepped carefully over the couch, Rikki heard a low rumble. Not looking behind him, he said in as commanding a voice as he could produce, "Watch yourself, Bruno. You two are in enough trouble as it is without growling at me." Chip snarled in Rikki's direction too, and Rikki became petrified all over again because of their unusual behavior. "What's going on, fellas? It's your Auntie Rikki. Why are you so angry?" Realizing Chip was looking past him, his body tensed up. "M-Mako," he stammered, "that better be you behind m—"

Another growl cut his sentence short, and Rikki answered with a back spinning kick, only to have his ankle caught midair in a vice-like grip. He shrieked as the pain shot up his leg.

A giant, clawed hand slammed him, tossing him backward at full force until the wall stopped his motion. He left another hole in the wall in the process. Dazed, Rikki touched the back of his head and saw blood on his fingertips. His vision was blurred, but he discerned that the feet positioned only a short distance from him were not human. Reluctantly, he craned his neck to view the entire shape of his attacker. All he could do was sit in the spot where he'd landed, immobile from shock, while tears rolled down his cheeks. "Oh shit," was the only phrase that escaped.

Rikki's screams soon echoed through the house.

FORTY-ONE

After stopping for a quick bite, Mako and Jacquie were on the move again. Mentally reviewing all the details of each crime, including the names and faces of all those implicated, more than one possible suspect for the killings at the Muttontown Preserve and the Broadway Mall stuck out in Jacquie's mind. Yet, no matter how hard she tried, she couldn't get the meeting with Stumpp out of her head. The things he said about her folks. The disrespectful tone he took about their deaths. She forced her thoughts on other parts of the conversation, and then it hit her. "I think we should look closer at Jacob Connors."

"Why him?"

"Because of what Stumpp said about Jacob being a bleeder."

"What does that have to do with anything?"

"Stumpp admitted one of his pets bit Jacob, and we both know we're not dealing with your average cocker spaniel. Chances are it was a werewolf, and now I'm thinking Jacob was the one we saw last night. Besides, both Stumpp and Stubbe are dead ends for now. That Falcone kid is on a slab. And Ethan Walker hasn't been seen since that night on the rooftops. Where would you like to start?"

"I have to stop home first. After that, we'll head over to Connors' address and see what we can find."

Spying the moon, she said, "By the time we get there, if he *is* one of them, won't he already *be* one of them?"

"Probably. But what other choice do we have? At least we know what we're in for, right? No surprises."

"I wish I could believe that."

Turning onto his block, Mako saw a mob gathering in front of his home. "What the hell is going on?" Mako asked, making sure not to hit any of his immobile neighbors as he pulled to the curb. "Hey, Joe," he called to the guy across the street. "You know everything that goes on around here. What's with the crowd?"

Cautiously approaching, Joe said, "There's been a lot of banging inside your apartment, and it sounds like your dogs are going wild."

"Is Rikki's tribute band rehearsing 'YMCA' again?" Mako shook his head. "The dogs hate it when they sing."

A loud crash was heard inside the upstairs apartment, and as Joe backed away, back to his side of the street, Mako drew his pistol.

"That doesn't sound like the Village People," Jacquie whispered to him.

"Stay here," he ordered and crept toward his porch stairs. "I'm going to check it out." Halfway up the steps, Mako saw shredded clothing near the bushes on his front lawn. "Jacquie," he said, waving her over. "Take a look at those. That better not be what I think it is."

Rummaging through the pockets, she found a wallet. Her expression darkened upon flipping it open, and she turned the wallet around to display identification belonging to Jacob Connors. "So much for no surprises."

He noticed the damaged door frame and used the toes on his right foot to gradually swing the door back, keeping his gun aimed in front of him. With nothing in his direct line of sight, he carefully entered the premises. To the left of him, Rikki's door was wide open. Mako gave a hurried look inside, but he was relatively sure no one was home. Gazing up the stairs leading to his home, he pointed his firearm upward and slowly made his way to the top.

A bloodcurdling scream rang through the house, sending a chill down his spine, and he darted up the stairs, two at a time. As his foot landed on the last one, he heard a snap.

Was that the step or something else? Mako thought. *Please let it have been the step.*

Rikki sat stationary, staring at the seven-foot-tall creature coming toward him. He hoped someone had heard the commotion and come to investigate, but so far there wasn't even a hint of salvation.

Saliva dripping from his enormous fangs, Jacob ogled his prey like a starving man about to finally eat a meal. The sound of the werewolf's toenails scraping into the hardwood floors with every step was maddening to his terrified prey.

Thrashing his legs about, trying to scurry away from the werewolf, Rikki was out of room as his back was literally against a wall. He realized the dogs were in no shape to tackle the intruder, despite their fierce front. But over the shoulder of the ravenous animal, Rikki detected a small white shape moving on top of the wall unit.

Booger, the "devil" cat, had escaped the werewolf's notice and somehow managed to reach the top of the large piece of furniture. Watching the intruder through his differently colored eyes, he lowered his body as close to the wall unit as possible and stalked the werewolf.

Nearly on top of the petrified man, Jacob raised an arm high above him; moonlight reflected off his finger-knives.

Left with no other recourse, Rikki screamed for his life, but the sound didn't even startle the werewolf.

From the wall unit, just above Jacob's massive bicep, Booger found his opportunity and launched himself through the air. Claws extended, the cat slashed the lycanthrope under his eyelid, right in the soft flesh of the cheek.

More surprised than hurt, Jacob recoiled from the attack but used his amazing reflexes to catch Booger in midair. The cut on Jacob's face was already healed, but given the chance, Booger would inflict more punishment. Too bad for the little white cat, he was grasped firmly in massive fingers, held far enough away that his claws couldn't reach no matter how hard he tried. Jacob sniffed the cat and then growled at him angrily. Booger flattened his ears against his head and returned with a hiss and growl of his own. The larger monster was definitely more intimidating, but the tiny terror showed no sign of submitting.

Rikki watched the werewolf tighten his fist. He heard a snap at the same moment that someone landed hard on the top step outside the door. *Was that the step or Booger's back?* he thought. *Oh, please, let it have been the step.*

Jacob brought the limp cat closer to his mouth, opened wide, and was about to chomp Booger's head off, when suddenly, a small projectile tore through his wrist.

"Let's see you try that shit with me!" Mako stood in the doorway of his apartment, his smoking gun aimed at the intruder.

Pain registered differently in his lycanthrope form, but a bullet still hurt like hell if it hit the right spot. Howling, Jacob dropped Booger and focused his attention on Mako. The cat landed on his feet and ran for cover in the bathroom. Bleeding profusely, Jacob whipped around, ready to return the agonizing gesture.

Mako took a half a second to survey the room. Seeing his home destroyed and his pets injured caused a rage to well up inside him that clamored to be released. No words came to mind. No witticisms to waste on this unthinking beast. The creature had invaded his home and threatened the lives of all he held dear.

Nothing less than death would suffice.

Jacob heard the gun's hammer click into place as another bullet was about to be fired. He roared at Mako, spun his gigantic body toward the window at the far side of the room, and sprinted for it.

As Rikki's unbelieving eyes took in the events unraveling before him, the next few seconds passed as if time slowed to a crawl.

Bullets exploded from the pistol, as Jacob fled. Most missed their mark; some penetrated his back. But Jacob smashed through the window and fell to the ground below.

The sudden boom of gunfire finally reached Rikki's ears, startling his senses, and time resumed its normal pace.

Running to the window, Mako couldn't find any sign of Jacob. He saw only very confused and frightened neighbors. Chip was closest to him, so he knelt down to see the extent of his injuries. The dog's front leg was either sprained or broken, but either way, he needed to get to a vet. Minor cuts were also apparent on the snout and side of the body where patches of fur had been torn away. Mako patted the dog's head, reassuring him that everything would be all right, and Chip managed a friendly tail wag. "You're a good boy. Don't move," he said.

Rushing past Rikki, who was starting to stir as the shock left his body, Mako tended to Bruno, who was still standing next to the overturned couch. The pit bull lovingly licked his owner's cheek. "Hey, tough guy, we'll get you fixed up too." Checking the makeshift bandage tied around the pit bull's body, Mako tried to think of their veterinarian's phone number. But his thoughts were interrupted by a somber voice.

"Oh no," Rikki said, staring into the bathroom.

Leaving Bruno alone for the moment, Mako stood next to his neighbor, looking in the room to view the sad sight of his nearly lifeless cat lying on the cold tile floor. He took his jacket off, placing it on the ground beside him, and picked the cat up to lay him on top of it. A barely audible whimper escaped Booger's mouth, and a tear rolled down Mako's cheek. The cat's chest expanded slower with each breath, his eyes glazed over, and he made no attempt to move.

Jacquie ran into the apartment and stopped next to Rikki, watching as Mako stroked the soft fur of his beloved pet and wiped away another tear. Her heart went out to him, knowing how he felt about his animals. She moved inside and touched his shoulder.

"My cat's dying," he said, trying to hide the lump in his throat. "I don't know what to do."

Rikki offered a contemptible suggestion. "Why don't you try mouth-to-mouth?"

Jacquie was mortified at the implication.

Mako's rage resurfaced at the thought of someone poking fun of something he placed above all others, especially at a time like this. Moving away, he made a bee-line straight for Rikki, who backed away in fright now that Mako was looking at him the same way he'd glared at the monstrous intruder only moments ago. Soon Rikki was forced against the wall by two freakishly strong hands.

"Come on, Johnny, I didn't mean anything by it." He fumbled for the right words. "I don't even know what's going on here! I mean, what was that, that … thing?"

Mako's fingers fought against themselves while curling into a ball of fury. Mako's vision was blurred from tears and rage, but his fist seemed to have a mind of its own. It was ready to take out its aggression on anything—even his neighbor.

"Hey! Stop it!" Jacquie shouted at them, narrowly saving Rikki's delicate face. "He's not dead yet. If we can get him to a vet, he can still make it."

"What if we can't?" Mako released his hold on Rikki, focusing on his priorities.

She remembered how easy it could be for Johnny to become pessimistic in times of great stress, so she had to act fast. Looking around the bathroom, she set her eyes on the white vanity behind her. "How attached are you to this?"

Mako was unsure how to answer such a random question.

The inquiry was purely rhetorical as she knew time was not on their side. In one fluid motion, she spun around, grabbed the handle of the cabinet door that swung out to her, opened it and slammed the palm of her other hand into it, next to the hinges. The cheap particle board splintered as the screws tore out of the side wall of the cabinet.

"The hell are you doing?" Mako sounded just as confused as he was angry.

Jacquie set the door face-down next to Booger with the handle near her so it would slant down toward the cat. "There's no way we can transport him this way without causing more damage. He needs to be boarded," she said, gently sliding Booger on Mako's coat to the edge of the vanity door.

Mako knelt beside her to help with the cat. "I...I don't know where there is an emergency vet," he was ashamed to say.

"But I do," Rikki said. "I worry what I'd do if something happens when you're not around, so I memorized one. I'll grab my keys."

"Make it fast," Mako barked after him.

"You know," Rikki said, hoping his next comments would smooth things over, "I wasn't making fun. He saved me. Funny as that sounds, he really did. I don't want him to die."

"Then why are you still talking to me?"

Rikki took off.

Mako turned his attention back to Jacquie as she carefully stroked Booger's soft white fur, trying to comfort him. Pausing, she said, "Don't worry. I've got this under control. Go do what you have to."

"And what's that?"

"I know you want to stay and help, but there's nothing you can do here. I also know there's one thought running through your head right now, and you won't rest until it's done."

"Take care of them." He kissed her on the cheek and then bolted for the door, reloading his firearm with the magazine of silver bullets.

"He went west!" she shouted after him, positive he heard her.

FORTY-TWO

Sitting in his car at a red light down the street from his home, Mako hadn't stopped thinking about what he was going to do to the werewolf once he found it. An unidentified caller rang his phone, and although he'd normally let it go to voice mail, something told him he should answer.

"Detective Mako?"

"Who wants to know?"

"It's Jason. Jason Brody."

"You sure it's not Carl?" Mako recalled the startling development that Jason was merely an alias.

"Please, I've gotten used to Jason, so could we keep it at that for the time being?"

It was not an unreasonable request, so Mako acceded. "What do you need, Brody?"

"Right to the heart of the matter, I see."

"I'm a little busy at the moment."

"I'll get to it, then." He prepared himself for the lie he was about to tell. "Would you mind meeting Nathan and me at the morgue? He would like to retrieve the belongings of his fallen comrades."

"There really wasn't much brought in with them other than what they were wearing, and those outfits are pretty ruined, if you ask me."

"It … it's not my call, Detective. Nathan would like them returned to him."

"What's wrong?" Mako detected a slight quiver in Jason's voice.

Trying to hide his nervousness, Jason said, "Nothing, why?"

"There's something you're not telling me."

"I don't know what you mean."

"I've been a cop for quite a while. I know when someone's holding out on me."

Jason didn't know how to answer since the detective was correct. The Lunar Guardians didn't merely intend to collect the tattered remains of clothing found on their fallen comrades. They were planning to retrieve the bodies because Nathan refused to leave his men in enemy hands. Even though he had a problem implicating the detective as an accomplice, Jason had to stall for more time, keep Nathan around, and find a way to end this madness that night.

Mako ran short on patience. "Meet me there in a half-hour. We can finish this discussion then." He surmised that if they were up to something they'd do it with or without his permission, and he would rather be there in case they needed to be stopped.

"Uh, ok. We'll see you there."

Mako wanted to figure out what it was that he specifically heard in Jason's voice, but he already had too much on his mind. A half-hour should be enough time for him to take care of business; if he couldn't find the werewolf by then, he imagined it'd be long gone. Before continuing his search, he dialed Mullins' phone number.

"Yeah, Mako. What's up?" Mullins wasn't one for polite greetings.

"You still at the morgue?"

" Just waiting for the M.E.'s report on Falcone."

Curiosity got the better of him, and he wanted to verify something Jason had mentioned after the attack at the motel. "I know this is going to sound odd—"

"I'm used to that with you lately."

"Is Falcone missing his heart?"

Mullins didn't answer right away, wondering why Mako would ask such a question, but he truthfully didn't know the answer anyway. "All I know is the kid was a mess when they brought him in, and he's been on ice since. Once the M.E. gives me the report, I'll know what condition his killer left him in."

Satisfied for the moment, Mako revisited his initial reason for calling. "Listen, Jimmy, if anyone comes down there looking to see the bodies of the two stiffs they brought in the other night, don't let them until I get there."

"What's going on?"

"I'm not sure but I'll be there in a half-hour, give or take, so wait for me. Okay?"

"What was that?"

"Clear the fat out of your ears, chunky, and pay attention."

"I'm not talking to you, moron," Mullins snapped. "Hold on." Pulling the phone away from his mouth, he spoke to someone close by. "What the fuck are you looking at me for? Go check it out." Mullins' voice came in louder again: "I'll wait for you, but there better not be any trouble."

"I make no guarantees. See you in thirty." Mako hung up. Spying the CDs in the case attached to the sun visor, he decided a little traveling music was in order. He pulled out a mix CD, slid the disc into the player, and hit the RANDOM button. One of his favorites, "Let It All Bleed Out" by Rob Zombie, started to play.

Without warning, a large object landed on top of the detective's car, and the force of the impact left a large dimple in the roof.

"Are you serious?" he yelled, annoyed at the damage to his vehicle. Leaning forward to see what was responsible, he recoiled when the startling visage of a snarling werewolf appeared, upside down on his windshield as it held onto the car's roof.

Mako stepped on the clutch, threw the shifter into first gear, and slammed down on the gas pedal. The tires screeched on the pavement, the burning rubber turned out a thick veil of smoke, and the Lancer shot forward when the tires finally gripped the road. The werewolf's head snapped back out of view, and Mako shifted the car into second gear and then quickly into third, confident the monster would be unable to hold on. Hearing the sound of tearing metal, he looked up to see the werewolf's claws pierce the roof to get a better grasp of the fast-moving automobile.

"Oh, fuck you!" He was disgusted that the lycanthrope was smart enough to adapt to the situation, but he refused to let this animal get the best of him. He reached for his gun and aimed it at the creature's left paw. He squeezed the trigger twice for good measure, and the silver bullets easily drove through the already damaged metal and into the softer flesh on the other side.

Almost immediately, he heard a howl of pain, and the claws were withdrawn. The werewolf rolled off the vehicle; its ribs made a crunching sound when it slammed into a nearby tree. Mako glanced out the rearview mirror only to find that the infuriated werewolf had recovered and was giving chase. Shifting into fifth gear, he hoped the car would accelerate faster than his pursuer, but discovered seventy-five miles per hour was not fast enough. Jacob was closing the gap between them. Pressing down harder on the accelerator, Mako watched the speedometer dial pass eighty, and then ninety.

Jacob didn't know how fast he was going. He had no dials or knobs. There was no artificial force that propelled him. He only had his muscles, determination, and rage to drive him forward. The street became harder to hold onto at this speed, so he instinctively dug his claws into the roadway to get better traction. Seeing the car pull away from him, his anxiety increased because the detective's escape meant facing punishment the likes of which he had never known.

Rob Zombie played loudly on the car stereo, and Mako mouthed some of the lyrics as he steered through the minimal traffic on the road. His dashboard strobe lights warned pedestrians and other drivers to clear out of his way. Coming to a sharp turn, where the road ended, he shifted into neutral while simultaneously pulling up on his emergency brake and spinning the wheel. His vehicle fishtailed to a ninety-degree turn and barely missed a parked car. Mako dropped the brake, shifted to a higher gear, and slammed on the gas until the car shot down the roadway.

Jacob had to make the turn too, but he was awkward in his new body and lost his footing. Soon he was stumbling out of control and rolling repeatedly on his side until he crashed into the same parked car the detective had scarcely avoided. Shaking off the hit, Jacob growled at a woman who, thinking he was merely a large dog, came to see if he was okay. With an angry huff, he lunged forward, leaving the badly damaged automobile behind.

Desperately wanting to lure the werewolf away from any live targets, Mako got an idea. He slowed down the car to ensure that Jacob wasn't discouraged from following, and then he stepped down hard on the gas pedal once he observed the werewolf bounding over other vehicles on the road. The Lancer entered the parkway, with Jacob close behind.

Mako knew the perfect place to end this game of cat and mouse.

FORTY-THREE

The Nassau County Medical Center, specifically, the morgue, was routinely desolate at night, thanks to the politicians cutting down on overtime; but for Mullins, it presented a welcome calm. He had been here since shortly after his meeting with Stumpp, working to confirm the details of Louis Falcone's murder by Ethan Walker. He debated whether to contact the deceased's family now or whether to wait until the medical examiner finished his report.

Having a victim's loved ones identify the body was his least favorite part of the job. Even though he put on a macho facade, he hated when they broke down in front of him. It was usually the women; the men tried to be tough, unless a child was involved— no one was that strong.

For right now, Detective Mullins would simply like to be James Mullins, an off-duty cop with not a care in the world. He decided to wait until morning to make the call. Taking a seat in the empty hallway near the medical examiner's office, he rested his head against the wall behind him. Off-duty or not, he was here for the duration; he wasn't going anywhere until the autopsy was done and the paperwork was in his hands. Intertwining his fingers and placing them on his bulbous stomach, stretching out his legs and crossing them at the ankles, he sighed, allowing his muscles to relax. Just as he closed his eyes, hoping to get maybe an hour's nap, his cellphone rang. He wanted to ignore it, but he didn't let it ring more than three times before answering. Disenchanted by the name on the display, he impolitely said, "Yeah, Mako. What's up?"

Louis stood guard by the elevator on the thirteenth floor of Stumpp Industries while his associates, Robert "Bobby" Mane and Jacob Connors, searched for a rare relic known as the Silver Heart. Bobby was employed at the company but had an early retirement planned at the expense of his employer, so the trio broke in to steal the unique item and sell it to the highest bidder. Louis had known Bobby since they were children, but to this day he was not sure how Bobby always talked him into things he knew he shouldn't be doing.

Louis never was particularly brave, and he'd never tried to convince anyone otherwise. He was very aware of his strengths and weaknesses, and if there was any indication he was afraid, it would be the large lump in his throat. The air was cool inside the building, but the sweat poured down his forehead. His flashlight barely shone ten feet in front of him while the rest of the corridor was black. The onset of an anxiety attack caused him to breathe heavily, but he couldn't lose his cool now. Bobby was depending on him. Jacob, he could do without, but Louis could never abandon Bobby.

On the other hand, the horrible screaming followed by gunfire might have changed Louis' mind. Easing back into the elevator, he moved his violently shaking hand only inches from the numbered buttons, but he couldn't bring himself to press the one marked for the lobby. He had to give Bobby more time. Louis mumbled a prayer, hoping his buddy would move a little faster, but the more he prayed, the longer it took Bobby to get to him.

Then he heard it.

Another scream.

Was that Bobby or Jacob? he wondered. He decided it was Bobby and wanted to run to his friend, but the fear inside him had grown to such great proportions that his legs wouldn't budge. *Please, Bobby, be all right and move your ass!* A slight trickle of pee escaped him and ran down his leg, and then a little more trickled out when he heard approaching footsteps.

There's something wrong!

The footfall was heavy, much heavier than a human's—but if it was not his companion's, then who, or what, was there with him? He remembered what he was told after entering the premises. *Peter Stumpp doesn't trust humans, but he does rely on his animals, dogs specifically, to safeguard his offices.* To Louis, the animal up here on the thirteenth floor, in the dark, sounded as big as a horse. He'd never heard a thump that loud from a single step, and his sister had a bull mastiff!

Where the hell is Bobby?

Something rustled to his left, and he had a glimmer of hope that his friend had made it back. He whispered Bobby's name, but no one answered. Speaking a little louder, he had a sick feeling came over him when there was only more silence, but he had to know for sure. Perhaps Bobby was hurt and unable to talk, or maybe he'd passed out only a few feet away from freedom. Louis would hate himself if he didn't check. Shining his flashlight down one corridor, he moved it back and forth across the floor but didn't see anything. He was about to give up when, behind a large potted plant, something shimmered as the light hit it. He focused the beam on the object, but he couldn't tell what he was looking at—until it moved.

The Heart of Lycaon 325

The object flinched but didn't change position. Studying it closely and discovering that it was a mass of silver fur, Louis felt a chill run down his spine, and he swallowed hard. Once the beast crept out from behind his hiding place, Louis nearly had a heart attack. The gigantic animal, the likes of which he had never seen before, sat hunched over. It stared at him. "Nice doggie," Louis stuttered.

The "doggie" snarled as it uncoiled its body. It looked even bigger once all of its limbs were exposed and its head was out in the open, saliva dripping from its fangs. Without wasting another moment, the monster lunged!

Louis jumped up, screaming, clutching at his chest with one hand; his eyes, opened wide, saw no sign of the tremendous creature. Instead, he glimpsed an empty room filled with medical equipment and cadavers on slabs under white sheets. Confused, he surveyed his own situation only to find that he'd propped himself up on a metal stretcher, naked and partially covered by a white sheet. Struggling to remember how he got here, especially since he was very much alive, Louis felt his nerves kick into high gear because the tag attached to his toe said otherwise.

It eventually came back to him: arrested after the cops found him naked in a run-down building, almost kidnapped outside the police station, placed into protective custody, confronted at the motel by the creepy silver-haired guy while the detective guarding him was distracted, and then the sharp pain in his stomach as his insides spilled onto the floor.

Why am I not dead? I should be dead!

Throwing the sheet back to reveal his mid-section, Louis saw that his stomach was intact with no wound to be found. The blood had been washed away. The stitches that had closed the gaping hole in his torso had been expelled from his body. And his insides didn't feel empty or as if his intestines no longer occupied the area. Sliding his fingers across his skin, he pushed down on his belly to make sure he was not dreaming, and he came up with only one possible explanation. It was something he'd wanted to deny for days now, but all the evidence pointed to one obvious fact. It was the same reason he'd started to feel that awful pain again—the same discomfort that had led up to his recent blackouts with hardly any recollection of the previous night's activities. It was what Louis feared the most. The night he chose to attempt to take something that wasn't rightfully his, karma had stepped in and made him pay for his stupidity. There was something in the creature's bite that had turned Louis into a killer!

A stabbing pain in his spine caused him to jerk backwards and fall off the table. The cold tile floor rushed to meet him, but the agony he was experiencing was far worse than a four-foot drop to the ground. The pain subsided enough for him to get to his feet, but when the sting returned in his mid-section, he lurched forward while wrapping his arms around his abdomen. Because he wasn't concentrating on his surroundings, his forehead banged into a metal tray that was suspended on a chain and attached to a scale. The blow caused more of a fright than actual pain, but it was enough to make him jump back into a small rolling table that held several shiny tools that only a doctor could identify. The tools hit the floor in unison, followed by the tray and the table itself. The racket was sufficient to cause a loud echo in the hallway outside the room in which he'd awoken. Looking through the doorway, his arms still wrapped around his body to gird himself against the hurt, he spied two men: one on the phone and one in a white lab coat.

"What was that?" he heard the man on his cell say. "I'm not talking to you, moron. Hold on," he said into the phone. Pressing the speaker to his chest, he turned to the man in the lab coat. "What the fuck are you looking at me for? Go check it out."

Louis searched for a place to hide.

Mako weaved through what little traffic there was on the parkway, with Jacob right on his tail. He steered clear of the other cars on the highway. His bestial pursuer had no such qualms about the occasional hit-and-run, and while some of the startled drivers veered out of control onto the shoulder, others couldn't get their bearings fast enough to avoid a collision. The damage was minimal, which Mako was happy about, because at the speed he was driving, he couldn't call it in anyway. Nearly missing the exit, he cut the steering wheel hard. The metal frame of the Lancer screeched under the stress of the turn, and it rose up on the two driver's side tires for a split second. As soon as the car was firmly on the ground again, it tore down the off-ramp.

Twisting his neck after overshooting Mako's car, Jacob shifted his weight to his hindquarters, effectively putting on the brakes. Massive feet slid across the ground, and claws ripped up the pavement. His back end moved past the front, but it was just enough to angle him in the right direction. And as soon as he regained his footing, Jacob vaulted himself over the concrete guardrail to get back on the detective's trail.

Swerving around another car and keeping the gas pedal flat on the floor, Mako hoped to make it to the morgue before the werewolf overtook him. A peek in the rearview mirror confirmed that Jacob was gaining on him. He needed to widen the gap. The car was giving everything it had, but it was not good enough. "I'm sorry," he said, rubbing the dashboard, and slammed on the brakes!

Jacob's eyes widened in disbelief right before he smashed face-first into the Lancer's trunk. The metal folded like an accordion, and the monster slumped to the ground, momentarily stunned, bleeding from the bridge of his muzzle.

Not waiting for him to recover, Mako stepped on the gas again; the tires squealed, thrusting the car away from the scene. Proud of his maneuver, he wasn't bothered that the rear of his vehicle was destroyed. Jacob was becoming a speck in the detective's rearview mirror, but Mako uttered an, "Oh, shit" when he heard a furious roar. He decided he'd better get where he was going without further delay.

The medical examiner walked down the long dark corridor with offices on each side. He reached the autopsy room but gave a look back at Mullins, who was still standing by the front desk, before entering. Inside, he didn't notice anything amiss until spotting the spilled tray and table next to an empty gurney that was supposed to be occupied. The examiner guessed that maybe he'd put the body away already and just didn't remember doing it. It had happened before. After doing this job for so many years, the process was so routine he sometimes did things without thinking. Going over to his logbook, he checked for the name of the latest addition, Louis Falcone, and found the drawer number. He pulled on the heavy latch, the lock release clicked, and he swung the door open. But when he looked in, he saw nothing. He hadn't even had time to wonder how he'd misplaced the body when a low, guttural growl sounded from behind; the fear welling up caused the hairs on the back of his neck to stand on end. Slowly turning, he was about to scream upon gazing into the werewolf's eyes, but the werewolf clamped onto the examiner's throat and crushed his windpipe in its jaws.

Mullins reviewed the video from Stumpp Industries on his laptop while waiting for the medical examiner to return. It was late, and he wanted to go home to get some sleep. This case was taking more out of him than he'd thought. Normally, he'd investigate leads at his own pace, but now he felt like he was in a race with Mako to get this one solved. It aggravated him, considering Mako wasn't a homicide detective and shouldn't even be working this assignment. Mullins had a mind to tell Lieutenant Grimes, but the truth of the matter was that he believed he needed all the help he could get with this one—not that he would ever admit it to anyone.

On screen, he watched three masked men enter the building's lobby and fast-forwarded to the point where one of the trio rushed out the front door. Freezing the frame, Mullins discerned that the perp was Falcone, judging by his size. Resuming the video, he forwarded a little more until Mane sprinted out the front door too. Mullins wished there was sound to accompany the movement to give a better idea of what had happened that night. Letting the video play out, he observed a large shadow overtaking most of the screen until a fast-moving blur knocked out the video feed. Clicking back a few seconds and replaying the last part, he froze the appropriate frame on what appeared to be a large, clawed hand attacking the camera.

Leaving the laptop where it was, the detective walked to end of the hallway where he last saw the medical examiner enter a room. "Lenny!" he shouted. "Lenny, let's get a move on. I want to get out of here sometime tonight." He waited for a response and became alarmed when detecting the faint sound of a struggle. Drawing his weapon and keeping it close to his body, Mullins crept toward the dimly lit passage that led to where the deceased were stored. He swore the darkness was playing tricks on him because he thought he saw something move.

With his free hand, Mullins reached for the mini-Maglite hanging off his belt in its protective case. Although struggling to hold both the gun and the flashlight in one hand, he eventually twisted the reflector to turn it on, but the bulb stayed unlit. He smacked it against the top of his wrist a couple of times until it lit up. But outside the building, a car horn frantically sounded off, and Mullins decided he should check it out before proceeding. As he moved toward the entrance, he beamed his flashlight down the corridor, and if he was paying attention, he would have seen the large, snarling beast stealthily approaching his position.

Exiting the building, he was almost run over. "Hey, watch where you're going!"

"Get inside! Get inside now!" Mako sprinted past his colleague and into the structure.

Mullins swept his eyes around the parking lot and stopped when he got a glimpse of the wreck his colleague once called a car, neatly parked in a designated area. "I guess all those times I told you your car was a piece of shit, I finally turned out to be right," he joked, but was disappointed when he didn't get a comeback of any kind.

Searching for something to keep the doors sealed shut, Mako overturned any, and every, piece of furniture not nailed down. Chairs, small tables, even drawers flew out of cabinets and hit the ground, spilling their contents onto the floor. Finding a small length of chain with an open combination lock in one of the bins, he darted to the solid double doors and looped the chain through the large handles.

"What is going on, Mako?"

"Give me a hand. We have to barricade this door!"

"What the fuck for?"

Mako didn't bother to answer. Once he was satisfied the chain was tight enough, he snapped the lock shut and then grabbed chairs, boxes, and anything else he could find to fortify the door. He got into a good rhythm and was making some real progress when Mullins tapped him on the shoulder. "What? What do you want?"

"You know that door opens out, right?"

"Go to hell," he said, slightly embarrassed for not realizing it, even if he was in a state of panic. He looked down in humiliation, and he took note that his associate had his gun drawn. "Mullins," he said, treading lightly, "you mind telling me why your weapon isn't holstered?"

The detective remembered he'd been in the middle of something before Mako showed up, and shone his flashlight down the hall to the left of him. But whatever he thought he saw earlier, it wasn't there now.

"What's wrong?" Mako thought this was strange behavior for Mullins.

"Before you got here, I heard a—"

The doors to the building were slammed into with such force that the walls holding them in place began to crack! Both detectives were startled.

"What the hell was that?" said Mullins.

"That's why I was trying to barricade us in." Mako backed farther away from the door. "Those chains won't hold it for long, but we should get some help in …," he said, checking his wristwatch, "about ten minutes."

The two detectives faced the door and flinched as it took a second hit. Mako pulled his pistol, guessing he might be able to kill it solo, but hoping he wouldn't anger it further. A third strike warped one of the doors, bending a corner outward and permitting moonlight to enter the room. The assault stopped, and the light was blocked by a round, moist, black object that sniffed the air.

"Mako," Mullins whispered, "did a bear follow you here?"

"Not exactly," he quietly answered, not taking his eyes off the door.

A hushed growl was heard.

"Well, whatever it is, it sounds pissed."

Mako continued to listen intently.

The grumbling became louder and more ferocious.

"Mullins?"

"Yeah?"

"You never told me why your gun was drawn."

"Why does it matter?"

Shifting his eyes from side to side, he said, "I don't think the growling is coming from outside."

Mullins gave him a funny look. "If there was an animal in here I think I would—"

But Mullins shut up when an extremely large figure rose in the shadows behind Mako. Its face pierced the light, and all Mullins saw were enraged eyes and razor-sharp teeth.

The massive beast roared and darted forward!

"What the … move it!" Mullins shoved his associate in one direction while backpedaling in the opposite. Mako landed on his side and glided across the slick laminate flooring. Mullins, unable to get his girth out of the way, appeared to catch a lucky break as the uninterested werewolf knocked the detective out of its path and slammed into the door; a painful whine was heard from the other side.

Jacob, the lycanthrope outside, renewed his attack, but the werewolf inside struck the doors at the same time, balancing out the blow so that neither got any closer to the other. The doors thinned slightly under all the pressure, and the walls kept on crumbling; but the monsters were concerned only with each other for now.

Hoping to remain unseen, the detectives scurried behind the front desk and sat next to each other, baffled as to what their next move should be. Mullins clicked the hammer of his gun back, but Mako gently grabbed his forearm to stay his hand.

"We can't sit here and do nothing!"

"Your gun won't do a thing to that monster except annoy it, but I can hurt it with mine."

"What are you, a magician?" Mullins didn't believe him. "I can't wait 'til I can tell everyone how I was saved by Mr. Fuckin' Wizard!"

"No, you stupid ass." He pulled out the weapon's magazine and showed his partner the shiny bullets inside. "This is why I can hurt it. You wanna tell me you have rounds like these?"

Mullins attempted to touch the clip, but Mako pulled it away and reloaded it. "Don't tell me. Silver bullets." Mullins laughed at the notion.

Mako shot him a look, conveying this was not a joke.

"Get outta here!" Mullins didn't want to believe what his colleague was insinuating. "You're gonna tell me that thing behind us is a, a ..." The word was on the tip of his tongue, but he couldn't bring himself to say it.

"Go ahead. Say it."

"No way, Mako! You're an asshole."

"Doesn't change the fact that a werewolf is locked in here with us."

The beasts hadn't stopped snarling or clawing at the door, and the metal entrance was, bit by bit, being ripped to shreds by their talons. It wouldn't be long before there were two raging werewolves inside with the police officers.

"Sure," Mullins huffed. "Next you'll tell me I gotta phone in an A.P.B. on Lon Chaney Jr."

"Jimmy, this isn't *Abbott and Costello Meet Frankenstein*," Mako replied. "Although if it was," he suggested, "you'd be Costello."

"Is that a fat joke?"

"No," he said sarcastically, pointing with his chin to Mullins' stomach. "Why would you think that?"

"Like you're a fuckin' twig."

Normally Mako couldn't resist an opportunity to score on the guy, but he knew they had to focus on the matter at hand if they wanted to stay alive. "All right. All right. We're both fat asses. Now, let's get the hell out of here before these things take a chunk out of them."

"Got any suggestions?"

"I'm guessing if we get these two together, they'll do the work for us."

"There's an exit down the hall, but how do you propose we lure it there?"

"Leave that to me."

"That thing will run you down before you even get close." Mullins showed a hint of genuine concern.

Mako didn't want to let on that he noticed. Instead, he peeked over the counter at the werewolf. Both seemed to be taking a break from their rampage, and surprisingly, the doors were still on their hinges. Jacob had vanished, which Mako surmised was why the other creature calmed down.

Trying to be as quiet as possible, he put pressure on the floor to lift himself up, and it creaked under his knee. Being no match for a beast who could perceive the slightest noise, Mako ducked back down. But it was too late. The monster's head whipped around, and the werewolf charged the desk.

FORTY-FOUR

Three black Hummers veered off the parkway headed for the Nassau County Medical Center. Nathan Henry Williams, leader of this operation, sat in the passenger seat of the second vehicle, wheels spinning in his mind. He needed an effective diversion in order to complete his assignment for the evening before heading back home to West Virginia, and Mako wouldn't be easy to sidetrack. The sheer stubbornness of the man was infuriating, but Nathan wouldn't be deterred. He would liberate his fallen comrades and give them a proper funeral in the designated resting place for all those who served with the Lunar Guardians.

Jason traveled in the same car, but his views on the evening's events didn't sit as well with him as they did with his colleague. He was the one who had brought Mako into this, against Nathan's wishes. Knowing the detective was a good man, he didn't want to make him an accessory to body snatching, if there was such a charge. His troubled conscience forced him to state his opinion once again: "Nathan, this isn't right."

Nathan was tired of this conversation already. And if it wasn't for how Nathan's great-great-grandfather had symbolically adopted Jason at a young age and treated him as family, Nathan would have disposed of Jason years ago. He felt that even though Jason's appearance didn't change, his extraordinary abilities made him every bit an animal as the monsters they hunted.

"I know you heard me," Jason said, a little louder this time. "If you insist on ignoring me, I'll tell Mako your intentions as soon as we arrive."

"You will do nothing of the sort. You know as well as I do this is standard procedure. If one of us is captured or killed, we will do what is necessary to retrieve that individual. This isn't the first time we've done this."

"No, but this time is … different."

"Why?" Nathan put a sarcastic tone on his question. "Because you feel a certain kinship with this detective? Make friends on your own time. My men will not be deprived a proper burial so you can experience male bonding." The comment stung more than Nathan realized.

Jason had never had a real friend. He changed identities the way most changed clothes. Always running, always afraid his past would catch up to him and finish him off for good, he'd never been able to relax around anyone, not even Nathan or his men—*especially* not Nathan and his men. He understood the animosity they felt toward him, and he didn't have a great deal of respect for Nathan either. But the Guardians had numbers on their side. Jason feared there would come a day when Nathan decided to sic his men on him, and he'd either have to run or meet his end in battle. He desired, just once, to have a friend, someone who would watch his back, someone who would be on his side. Just once, it would be nice.

Nathan grabbed the Hummer's CB radio. "Guardians! Our ETA is approximately three minutes. We need to be swift and extract the bodies without being noticed. Teams One and Three will make their way to the rear, opposite ends, of the building. Stay out of sight and move on my signal. My team will meet Detective Mako at the main entrance and entertain him while you complete your designated task. Is that understood?" Not expecting a response, he went on. "Remember: in and out. Nobody gets hurt."

As the convoy neared the morgue's parking lot, a faint crackle came over the airwaves, followed by the voice of the Guardians' second-in-command, Mark Bronson. "Sir, there appears to be something wrong."

"What is it?"

"Well, sir … umm … you might want to have a look for yourself." Bronson wasn't sure how to describe the situation. "Check the main entrance."

Nathan snapped his fingers twice, and the soldier sitting in the back seat next to Jason handed his superior a pair of binoculars. Viewing the selected area, Nathan initially saw the detective's wrecked car. Scanning the area around it, he spotted the horrifically clawed entryway of the building. "We have a slight change in plans, gentlemen."

"We're not securing the bodies?" Bronson asked.

"We are, but it would seem a lycanthrope is on the premises, and it must be dealt with."

"You want my team to handle it, sir?" Bronson pulled the slide back on his gun after loading a fresh clip into it, forcing a bullet into the chamber.

"We'll all handle it," Nathan replied. "First, we'll form a perimeter around the building in case it's already inside. Then we'll proceed by two's into the building and hunt the beast down. First team to discover our brethren will prepare them for transport home. Go to radio silence and only report back when you are in position."

Jason assembled his sniper rifle, wondering if Mako was okay. He reasoned that if he could earn the detective's respect, he could possibly gain a friend in the process. All he could do now was hope Mako survived the night.

FORTY - FIVE

Transforming itself into a battering ram, the werewolf lowered its head and ran through the large desk. Wood exploded and splintered into hundreds of spraying fragments. The detectives barely dodged the attack, both leaping to opposite sides of the room. Mako hit his head against the wall and was slow to recover.

Mullins looked to his left at an empty office, the door was wide open and nothing was stopping him from barricading himself inside; but watching Mako try to clear the cobwebs while cornered by the massive beast made the decision for Mullins. No matter what transpired between them, Mullins would not allow another cop to die if he could prevent it. Gritting his teeth, raising his gun, and taking aim, he fired three shots, which grouped themselves nicely in the monster's back, near its right shoulder blade.

The werewolf lurched forward, yelped in pain, but shrugged it off, turning its focus from Mako to its attacker. Like a dog that's been recently washed, the lycanthrope shook its body from head to rump, and the slugs that had penetrated its skin dropped to the floor one after the other.

Each bullet's clink gave Mullins chills, and his skin paled; his life flashed in front of his eyes. With every step the beast took he thought, *Why didn't I just go through the damn door?*

The werewolf rose onto its hind legs, and a pair of superhumanly strong front arms bent upward and tensed up, displaying powerful biceps capable of ripping a man in half. It pushed off the faux tile and started to take flight, extending its fingers outward, claws eager to rip the chubby officer to shreds; but its roar turned into an agonizing bark as silver bullets embedded themselves in each of its ankles, allowing gravity to slam the creature back to earth. The werewolf's jaw hit first, sending a shock wave through its entire body, and its legs were bleeding badly, unable to heal as quickly as its back had moments ago.

Mullins opened one eye to find the werewolf whimpering in pain only a few feet from him, while Mako was half lying on the floor, aiming a gun in his direction.

"Nice shooting."

"It's not dead yet," he said, his gun still trained on the creature as he stood up. "Find some cover. I'll handle it from here."

"Let me help."

"Get in that office and secure the door."

"Mako," Mullins paused. "Johnny ..."

The werewolf stirred. It wouldn't be long before it renewed its attack on one or both men, who were well within its reach.

"We don't have time to debate. You stay in there until help arrives. If this thing kills me, at least you'll know what you're after." Mako inched toward the long corridor and the alternate exit outside. "You saved me twice. I'm returning the favor."

"That means you still owe me one." Mullins slid closer to the empty office.

"Jimmy. Sorry about all the bullshit between us. No matter what anyone else says, you're all right with me."

Mullins' crooked teeth showed through a partially open-lipped smile, a rare thing to witness, but his inner macho man had to stay true. "Yeah, you too, but ... let's keep this between us."

A motivational roar permitted the werewolf to push beyond the pain and rise onto all fours, and it couldn't have cared less

about the portly detective sprinting into the adjacent room. It
wanted to eliminate the one who truly threatened its survival. It
limped in Mako's direction but increased speed as the detective
ran down the hallway.

Although the creature was wounded, Mako wasn't certain he'd
be able to outrun it. He ducked into one of the rooms, instinctively
fastening the deadbolt but realizing a locked door was as futile
as barricading a door that swung outward. Shoving two metal
tables behind the entry for extra measure, he listened closely to
the sounds in the hallway to determine the werewolf's position.
He became nervous when the only noise he detected was the clink
of two silver slugs hitting the floor as the werewolf's regenerative
powers successfully overcame the injury.

Moving to the back of the room and scoping his surroundings
to ensure there wasn't another way inside, the detective recognized
he was in the autopsy room. Being around all these corpses didn't
create comfortable feelings. He decided to make his stand directly
opposite the doorway, and he found another empty metal table to
use as cover. Heaving the furniture on its side, he lost his footing
when he stepped in something slick. The red, sticky liquid under
his shoe was thick, and Mako had seen enough of this substance to
know exactly what it was. The only question remaining was whom
it belonged to, and the trail wasn't hard to follow. Messy spatters
and drag marks led back to the slabs where the bodies were stored.

Then he saw it and had to momentarily turn away, disgusted.

Torn to pieces, slumped next to the drawers, was the medical
examiner's body: his face had four deep slash marks across it, his
throat was ripped away, and part of his torso was heavily gnawed
on. Mako was only able to identify the victim by the bloodied
photo identification clipped to his coat. He was plagued by the

question that had nagged him since the other beast made its appearance: *Who is the other werewolf?*

Unable to produce a suspect, he returned to his post and slid the table away from the pool of blood. Mako knelt down behind it, aimed his pistol at the door, and waited. His eyes shifted to the left and he noticed a white sheet poking out from behind a cabinet.

Creeping over to it, he squatted down and tugged on the material. The cloth was snagged on the cabinet's back foot, but a fierce yank freed it, and he heard something fall to the floor. Searching the area, he found a bent tag facedown, and even though he wasn't a homicide detective, Mako knew a toe tag when he saw one. Picking it up and flipping it over, he was shocked after reading the name: Louis Falcone.

The vehicle Nathan rode in pulled up near the main entrance of the building. "Is everyone in position?"

"Team One, ready," a voice crackled over the radio.

"Team Three, all set," another voice followed.

Nathan exited his vehicle, and the others with him took point on each side of the SUV. "Proceed in two by two formation, and let's get this done quickly."

Around the side of the structure, Team One's members stepped from their Hummer and formed up into two groups. The men in the first group sprinted to the building and flattened themselves against the wall, checking the perimeter before signaling to the second group to follow.

The other two men hurried to get into position. One spotted a security panel on the wall. "Should we disable cameras and alarms?"

"Negative," the group leader answered. "If Williams wanted it disabled, he would have said so. He wants us out of here ASAP, so let's move!"

The others didn't utter another word and went straight to work, disabling the door locks with miniature cutting torches. Then the two groups slipped inside.

Team Three had two heavily armed members, one of whom was Mark Bronson. There was no door to afford them entry; but a short climb through a broken window didn't pose any challenge, and both entered before Team One.

In the meantime, Nathan walked casually toward the front entrance, with his three associates flanking him, searching the area to prevent an ambush. Jason was truly the best man to have along because of his heightened senses. He'd notice any kind of movement long before whatever caused it had a chance to reach them. This was one of those times Jason knew Nathan was grateful to have him around, not that he would ever acknowledge it.

Examining the partially destroyed front double doors, Nathan was amazed they were intact. He pulled on the handles but both budged only slightly. Peering through a gash, he spotted the thick chain wrapped around the inside grips, and he tapped the shoulder of one of the men to his side. The soldier took out his mini-torch, but Nathan stopped him, grabbing the soldier's shotgun instead. He took aim and fired. The shot echoed loudly, but it did the job. The outer handle of one of the doors was completely obliterated, leaving the inner one dangling from the other by the still secured chain.

Jason was staggered by the shotgun blast. For everyone else, a point-blank shot produced a buzz in their ears that subsided in minutes. But with Jason's keen hearing, the sound of the shotgun was amplified by ten, at least, and the ringing he heard was more of a pounding reverberation that repeated continuously for significantly longer. Nathan didn't seem to care that he'd rendered his group's greatest asset useless by essentially causing Jason to become temporarily deaf. Holding his lightly bloodied ears, Jason stumbled inside, and Nathan grabbed him by the shoulders to steady him before he fell completely to the floor.

The remaining troops stood guard by the entrance, mocking Jason's misfortune, and they were lucky he couldn't hear them. If push came to shove, he could immobilize them before they knew what happened. An opening office door opposite their location regained their focus, and they aimed at a shaky Detective Mullins.

Raising his arms high in the air, police shield out, he shouted, "Hold on a minute! I'm Nassau County Detective James Mullins. Lower your weapons."

The two men complied only when Nathan nodded his approval. "Where is Detective Mako?"

"You must be the help he was talking about." Mullins brushed himself off and glanced at Jason, who was kneeling on one knee and holding his head in his hands. "What's his problem?"

Ignoring the detective, Nathan asked again, "Where is Mako? We were supposed to meet here. I think we might be able to identify the two fatalities you brought in a few nights ago."

"Yeah, he told me, but nobody sees the stiffs until he gets back."

"So, he's not here then?"

"He's around," Mullins answered firmly. "He's … dealing with another issue at the moment."

As if on cue, a giant blur raced past the front door and snatched one of the guards. The man, easily weighing 220, most of it muscle, along with an extra fifty pounds of gear strapped to him, was swiped off the ground without his abductor breaking stride. Only a murmured sound at the initial point of contact was heard, and if the soldier hadn't screamed, the others might have missed the event entirely.

Nathan reached for his signature pistols and ran outside, followed by the only other remaining Guardian in his group. Mullins intended to lend his visitors a hand.

Jason grabbed the detective's shirt. "Wait!"

Mullins didn't even see Jason move until his hand was already on him. "Get off me."

"You should stay with me, Detective," he said, getting to his feet. "You don't know what you're dealing with."

"I know plenty."

"Can you hear a pin drop from ten blocks away?" Jason asked, even though he couldn't either at the moment.

Mullins wasn't sure what was being implied, but after what he'd learned that night, the exhausted detective wasn't about to discount the claim so quickly. "No, but I'm sure you're going to tell me *you* can." Jason started to comment, but Mullins raised his hand to prevent it. "Don't say a word. Let's just go."

The Guardians swept the area for any sign of their kidnapped comrade, but there was no indication of where the lycanthrope had taken him—even when the missing soldier's final, agonizing shriek echoed through the night. Now there were three bodies to reclaim. Detecting Jason in his peripheral vision, Nathan spun angrily to face him. "You! How come you didn't warn us of the creature's approach? That soldier would be alive if not for your incompetence!"

Tired of the constant berating and ridicule, Jason lashed out, "You should have thought of that before you fired a shotgun only inches from me! You are the one responsible for that man's death! I have never let one of your men die, even if they do look down on me as you do! You want someone to blame? Look in a mirror, you self-righteous bastard!"

The resulting hush lasted a few seconds before Nathan returned fire. "I should have known you'd be of no significance on this mission." Motioning for his loyal guard to walk with him back to the Hummer, he left Jason.

Jason could easily tear them apart, but he hung his head, defeated.

Mullins attempted to alleviate the embarrassment. "Man, is that guy a dick or what?"

Turning to look at the chunky detective, he chuckled and answered, "Yes. Yes, he is."

Mako couldn't believe that Louis was the werewolf looking to make a meal of him. He'd been so sure the boy was dead, lying there with his insides spilled onto the floor, courtesy of Stumpp's assistant; but apparently, he'd stopped Ethan Walker before he could finish the job. He resumed the more pressing issue of his own continued existence and hurried back to the cover of the overturned table. But then he remembered his final words to Louis, right before Louis was gutted. Mako had asked for Louis' trust, and said that if he agreed, Mako wouldn't let anything happen to him. Well, he'd given his word and wasn't about to go back on it now.

Leaving his safe place, the detective snuck to the locked, semi-barricaded door, keeping his body below the glass window to prevent Louis from visually confirming that he was inside. Careful not to give his position away, he strained to hear a faint sniffing and understood that Louis was right on top of him. He remained perfectly calm in hopes the werewolf would move on.

But shattering glass grabbed his attention, and he was relieved it wasn't the window above him.

Louis lifted his head in response to the disturbance, and if Mako were to stand, they would be eye-to-eye. Dashing away, Louis planned to ambush the intruders.

Once the danger passed, Mako shoved the tables out of his way, unlocked the door, and carefully entered the hallway. The click of a gun's hammer caused his stomach to flinch, but fear was replaced by irritation when the weapon's muzzle was placed against the back of his head.

"Turn around slowly," said the man attached to the pistol.

Mako obeyed and instantly recognized him. "I told you what would happen if one of you idiots pointed another gun at me, didn't I?"

"Take it easy, Detective. I'm not here to fight." He lowered his weapon.

"What are you here for then ...," Mako wasn't sure what to call him.

"Bronson," he said. "Mark Bronson."

"Where's the rest of your squad?"

"Around."

"They'd better be because we have two werewolves on the loose."

"Two?" there was apprehension in his tone.

"What's wrong?" Mako was concerned now too. "I thought you guys were used to this."

Bronson didn't want to cause a panic. "Nothing, but I'd better update Nathan."

A cry for help rang through the corridor.

"I think he already knows." Mako headed back to the main entrance. "You coming, or what?" he asked the motionless soldiers.

"We're right behind you, Detective."

Mako didn't have time to wait around, so he kept moving. The other man with Bronson began to follow, but an arm placed across his chest halted his progress.

"Sir?"

"Let him go. We have another job to do," Bronson said, showing the soldier where they were. It didn't take a big brain to figure out what was lying under all the white sheets in the room beside them. "The primary mission comes first."

Peering over his shoulder, Mako dismissed Bronson's vanishing to indifference and pressed on until he reached the reception area where the front desk once stood. Surveying the area, he noted that the office where Mullins had hid was empty and wondered if the scream had come from him. He sincerely hoped not.

He heard voices coming from outside the facility and was relieved to see Mullins sharing a laugh with Jason. As he moved toward the exit, small fragments of debris crackled under his feet. He paused to holster his weapon. But another heavy footfall crushed several small particles, and an alarm went off in his mind. If he wasn't responsible for it, he could think of only one living thing that was.

A vicious snarl confirmed it. Louis had returned!

Jacob saw his prey clearly from more than thirty yards away. He was sitting high in a tree with the partial remains of the dismembered soldier he'd snatched from the morgue's doorway minutes earlier, and he waited for his opening. Observing that two armed men clad in fatigues distanced themselves from two seemingly unarmed and potentially tasty victims, Jacob leapt off his perch, swung from one nearby tree to another, and landed with a thump on the moist ground. Light green eyes narrowed, searching for the least obstructed path. Satisfied he'd found it, Jacob took off, running on two legs and reaching close to top speed within seconds.

He barely noticed the low branches whipping his skin and swiped them aside with ease, never slowing down for a moment. The environment blurred in his peripherals, creating tunnel-vision of what was directly in front of him. He transitioned from two legs to four for extra momentum and furrowed his brow, judging distance. Once he could do so comfortably, he pounced!

At that instant, Mako made a mad dash out of the morgue, yelling, "GET DOWN!" and tackling Mullins and Jason to the floor.

Jacob emerged from the trees, pleasantly surprised that his initial target resurfaced. His claws and teeth shimmered in the moonlight, but as he was about to land on his quarry, he was hit by another bulky, fast-moving object.

Sprinting after Mako, Louis overshot his kill, landing in Jacob's arms, and the impact knocked both werewolves away from the trio. After rolling to a stop, they showed more aggression than before, except they were not interested in the humans any longer. Maybe it was an instinctive animal contest for dominance, or a sense that their human forms detested one another, but the animosity between them was evident.

Similar to animals in the wild, Jacob and Louis circled each other, sizing the other up. But being nearly the same height and weight, there was no chance either would retreat; they did the inevitable and attacked.

Mako was mesmerized by the sheer savagery of the werewolf assault. These gigantic beasts moved with the ease and grace of trained fighters, their muscles rippling with every collision and strike. He imagined their speed and agility made them the most efficient killing machines alive. Blood spilled with every swipe and bite, but neither showed any hint of injury.

Jason had witnessed this before, so he understood how unpredictable lycanthropes could be—that at any moment they could redirect their fury toward weaker targets. "Detectives. We should go," he said, lightly tugging at their shirts. When his comments fell on deaf ears, Jason used a portion of his formidable strength to pull the officers in the direction he wanted to lead them. "I said we should go. It's not safe here."

"Take it easy," Mullins said. "I need that arm." He wrenched it back, rubbed his tricep, and elbowed Mako in the ribs, whispering, "What's up with this kid? He's stronger than he looks."

"You don't know the half of it," Mako replied.

His hearing fully restored, Jason made no indication that he was eavesdropping, except for a slight smirk on his face.

Nathan had just finished using the radio in his Hummer as the three men approached, and he didn't look pleased. Grabbing a rifle, he checked the magazine and snapped the clip back into place. A second vehicle pulled up nearby, and four men jumped out, ready for battle.

The werewolves either didn't realize the danger or simply didn't care, because the soldiers' arrival didn't give them pause. They ravaged each other's bodies in the hopes that one would soon be dead.

Using hand signals to communicate with the Guardians, Nathan had them surround the creatures.

Mako briskly jogged to his side. "Hold on, Williams. We have a small problem here."

"One that will be rectified shortly," he said, commanding his soldiers to take aim.

"No. Wait a minute," the detective protested. "You can't kill both of them."

"And why not?"

"Yeah, why not?" Mullins reiterated Nathan's sentiments.

"You're not helping," Mako told Mullins. "Listen, Williams, one of those monsters is a material witness in our murder investigation."

"Don't you mean *my* murder investigation?" Mullins corrected his colleague.

Mako made a face at the other detective. "You're really not helping."

"I don't care if it's a family member of yours," Nathan said coldly. "Both die tonight."

As Nathan was about to give the order to fire, Mako offered another solution. "What about tranquilizers?" he yelled. "You have to have tranqs mixed in with all that other ammo," he said, motioning to the back of the truck. "Brody, please tell me they're back there. Go on, take a look." He nudged Jason.

"I don't have to look," Jason said confidently. "They're there. Nathan always brings them along in case he wants a live capture for his scientists to study."

"Grab a couple and load 'em up," Mako encouraged.

Nathan waved the detective off. "This is my hunt, and I say they die!"

"I gave the kid my word that nothing would happen to him." Mako's frustration was starting to manifest.

"I don't care what deal you made. I have no more time for you. We'll kill them now while they're occupied with each other." He raised an arm to signal his men to shoot.

Out of options, Mako realized he couldn't reach a verbal resolution, so he aimed his firearm at Nathan's head. "Tell your men to stand down! You may not give a damn about what deal I made, but when I give my word to someone, it sure as shit means something to me!"

Nathan froze in place, not because he was particularly worried the detective would shoot him, but more so to give his men a clear shot at Mako.

Mullins pulled his weapon and waved it around, not sure who to aim at. "Everyone, calm down! No one's shooting anyone here! We're all on the same side." He looked at Mako and shrugged. "Right?"

Rather than answering Mullins, Mako addressed his only other ally: "Jason. You understand my point. It's no different than the other night when you stood up for Walker."

"What was that?" Nathan angrily chimed in. "Did I hear correctly? Are you consorting with that animal again? I thought I told you to stay away from him."

"Thanks," Jason whispered to the detective, dreading this conversation, but he knew the time had come to stand up to Nathan. "He's right. If we don't remain true to our word, then what kind of men are we really?" he said, proud that he was able to avoid, yet address, the situation all at once.

Nathan didn't have the time or the patience to deal with a long-winded debate and lowered his arm. "Can you identify the beast you wish to save?"

"Louis Falcone," Mako answered sharply.

"Falcone?" Mullins was confused. "Isn't he dead?"

"Not now, Jimmy," he said through gritted teeth.

"Son of a bitch," Mullins muttered. "That's why he was able to bat me across the room."

Nathan gestured at the brawling beasts. "Which one is he? Can you tell the difference, or should we wait until morning when they change back?"

Glancing at the werewolves, Mullins admitted Nathan had a point. They looked the same; the only thing differentiating them was that one's fur seemed darker.

"There is a way to tell one lycanthrope from another," Jason cut in.

The Guardians' leader glared at him out of the corner of his eye. "Keep quiet, Brody."

"Two ways actually," Jason continued. "Hair and eye color don't change during the transformation. Hair color is what we try to distinguish first, because if you're close enough to gaze into a werewolf's eyes, you'll probably be dead in the next second."

Although Nathan had been bettered, he had not been bested. "Well, Detective, what color is Mr. Falcone's hair?"

Mako remembered it was brown, but so was Jacob's. He couldn't recall whose was darker. He also knew his charade would only last for so much longer: sooner or later, Nathan would figure out Mako was not going to kill him, no matter how much of an asshole he might be. "There may be another way."

"Don't keep us in suspense, Detective. What do you have in mind?"

The third black Hummer pulled up alongside the group, and Bronson hopped out, pistol aimed at Mako. "Orders, sir?"

Nathan looked at Mako. "Are you planning on telling us sometime tonight, or should we wait until the animals catch on and run away?"

Mako updated everyone of his plan, and Nathan decided to cooperate, if only for his own amusement. Signaling his men to resume their positions around the werewolves, he and the detectives inched closer to their battleground as Jason disappeared into the woods.

The monsters' movements had slowed, and their breathing was noticeably heavier, but they were oblivious to the situation until the sound of a snapping twig reached their ears.

Mullins looked under his foot at the unlucky stick, then at his associates. "Sorry."

"Nice going, Costello," Mako said.

The werewolves realized they were being flanked on all sides, and natural survival instinct took over. Setting aside their differences, and sizing up the newcomers, their threatening roars overlapped.

"NOW!" Mako yelled, taking aim with his weapon.

Everyone else followed suit. Shotguns, rifles, and handguns clicked in succession when pointed at the targets. The tension was so thick, it was enough to unnerve even those with steely dispositions.

First they heard it.

It started as a dull rumbling and built louder until it sounded like the beginnings of thunder in a bad rainstorm. The noise was coming from a werewolf, but which one was unclear. The reverberation was deep and menacing as it swelled up into the makings of a terrible bellow.

Then it happened.

One of the werewolves wrinkled its nose and squinted its eyes, and from the bowels of the beast, this frightening growl was expelled. It started as a hum, soon escalating into a blare that could only be compared to an orchestra composed entirely of tubas blowing all at once. Next came a blast of rancid air so foul one soldier nearly vomited, and after a few nauseating minutes, the clamor slowly died out as the last few sounds sputtered free.

An awkward silence overtook the combat zone.

"Did that thing just … fart?" Mullins asked, feeling that this was on everyone's mind. "Oh, shit! That's horrible," he added, covering his nose with one hand when the toxic odor reached him.

Nathan looked at the werewolf responsible and noted something he'd never seen before. He was not sure if it was possible, but the flatulent lycanthrope, now with one paw on its belly, actually appeared embarrassed.

"SHOOT THE OTHER ONE!" Mako shouted loud enough for everyone to hear.

Triggers were squeezed and a hail of tiny projectiles was discharged from metal chambers. Mini-explosions caused by the repeated firing bore a similarity to a large fireworks display—only these pyrotechnics killed. Bullets closed in from all sides, and Jacob didn't have anywhere to run. Not every shot hit its mark, but most did. Jacob's body thrashed about involuntarily as the bullets penetrated his flesh, and he finally fell onto his back.

Louis, temporarily resembling a deer in headlights, decided to flee before the soldiers targeted him next.

"BRODY!" Mako shouted.

Jason dived out from behind a nearby tree, and in midair, he aimed and fired twice at the werewolf's hindquarters. The tranquilizer darts sank into the side of Louis' thigh, but he managed to take a few steps before passing out.

The soldiers kept their weapons trained on the downed monsters. Back in his human form, Jacob lay in a pool of blood; but Louis remained in his bestial alter ego.

"Oh, man," Mullins said, holding a handkerchief over his nose. "He should have that checked."

"That's what I told him," Mako commented.

Curious, Nathan asked, "Why save one and not the other?"

"I gave both of them the same option, but this one," Mako said, nodding to the lifeless body, "decided to stand at the side of a madman."

"Dumb question, guys," Mullins said, raising his hand, "but why didn't they both change back?"

Jason explained, "The lycanthrope's mystical connection with the moon was severed when it died, but this one is merely sleeping and won't change back until the sun rises."

"So, what do we do with him?"

Guessing what Nathan was thinking, Mako spoke first: "Get him locked up and keep him safe. He's still a material witness."

"You don't know how to keep this beast caged," Nathan interjected.

Mako insisted, "Keep him sedated until morning, and don't let him out of your sight."

"What are you going to do?" Mullins asked.

"I've got another score to settle." Mako turned his attention to Nathan. "You guys want to help, or do I go at this alone?"

Nathan conversed privately with Bronson before asking, "Is this going to be another live capture, or do we do things my way?"

Knowing he was going to need the help, Mako didn't argue. "You call the shots, but keep me in the loop."

"Excellent," Nathan said with a devious grin. "What did you have in mind, Detective?"

"I want to hit Stumpp where it hurts. I say we relieve him of his most prized possession, the Heart of Lycaon."

"There's only one problem. No one knows its location."

Mako smacked Mullins in the chest to get his attention. "Remember when we were in Stumpp's office and I questioned him about it? Where did he say he would keep an item like that?"

"Ow. Hands off the merchandise." Mullins rubbed his chest. "He said he would keep it in his home where he could personally protect it."

"That's right, Mary," Mako said, challenging Mullins' manhood. "Can you get one of your cronies at the station to run his name and get an address?"

"That won't be necessary," Jason spoke up. "I know where he lives."

FORTY-SIX

Rikki trembled in his seat within the animal hospital's waiting room while Jacquie paced back and forth in front of him. His close encounter with death remained fresh in his mind, and the anxiety that came along with it wouldn't go away. But then, neither would the image of the monster that common sense said shouldn't exist.

Jacquie didn't speak except for an occasional incoherent mumble. Although she was concerned about Rikki and the lives of Mako's pets, she was preoccupied with piecing the puzzle together. The meeting at Stumpp Industries gnawed at her, as did the comments about her parents made by the despicable Peter Stumpp.

"Jacquie," Rikki said shakily, "what the hell was that thing?"

Conversation diverted her attention, but she wouldn't ignore Rikki when he required answers to help him through his tough time.

"A nightmare."

"That was no dream." Rikki took a couple of short, deep breaths. "That, that thing almost killed me, and it wasn't a dream." Tears poured down his face.

"Oh, honey." She understood just how traumatic his experience was, and she hugged him. "It's okay," she said, rubbing his arm. "You're all right. Everything's fine now."

Rikki wanted to stop crying, but he couldn't control it. "I, I've never been so scared in m-my life."

"Everyone is scared of dying."

"I can't even imagine." He began to calm down. "I mean, think of it. All those men deprived of having a chance with yours truly." Levity was a way for him to cope with stress.

She smiled, though she was uncertain if he was truly joking. "I shudder at the notion."

Taking his morbid fantasy a step further, Rikki continued, "I bet my funeral would've been beautiful. There would've been vibrant party decorations and flowers everywhere. Fuchsia, peach, and lilac—the color as well as the flower." He became more animated. "All the queens would've been out in full regalia, and the memorial service would've been held at my favorite club. My mother would have loved it to be in a church, but the Catholics don't approve the lifestyle, you know." Rikki floated around the room, acting like he was actually in the daydream. "There would've been dance music, and those in attendance would've been entertained by strapping, male exotic dancers surrounding my casket." He swirled around, ending his tale as he sat next to Jacquie once more. "And after the music stopped and the guests found their way back home, everyone would've said, 'Even in death, Rikki Anderson was still the life of the party.'" He sighed and stared off into the distance.

She gave him a moment to recover. "You done?"

He affectionately turned his head until his eyes, with batting eyelashes and all, met hers. "Yeah. I'm good." Rikki caught one of the vet techs gawking and giggling, but instead of feeling embarrassed, he simply stood up and bowed. "Thank you. I hope you enjoyed that." The vet tech became self-conscious and retreated into an adjoining room.

"Glad to see you're back to normal," Jacquie cut in.

"It's hard to keep a gay man down."

They heard the tech giggle from the back room.

"I hope she's working on healing my babies in between all the laughing," he said, his concern for the animals never wavering. "They've been in there a while now. Should I be nervous?"

"Relax. I need you calm, so I can think."

"Can I help?"

"I don't think so. There's something I'm not seeing plainly, but I feel like I should know the answer. If only I could get that scoundrel's words out of my head long enough to focus."

Hoping she was not talking about their mutual friend, he asked to be sure, "Johnny?"

"No, of course not," she replied in a manner which told him that the thought shouldn't have crossed his mind. "I'm talking about Peter Stumpp."

"Of Stumpp Industries?" He trusted he had it correct this time.

"The one and only. He made a few nasty comments about my parents' deaths, and I can't get them to stop repeating over and over in my brain."

"Why would he do that? He doesn't seem the type."

"There's a lot about him the public doesn't know," she huffed. "I don't have time to get into it, but believe me when I tell you he's not what he seems."

"What a shame." The disappointment was evident in Rikki's voice. "He looks so yummy in all the photographs I've seen of him. Does he look the same close up?"

Do men ever think with the head above their shoulders? Jacquie thought, rolling her eyes. Then the answer she'd been on the verge of discovering became a little clearer. "Thanks, Rikki. Maybe you helped me after all."

"What'd I say?"

Running over to the counter, she shouted into the back room, "Excuse me! Is someone there? Hello?"

The vet tech peeked her head out the doorway and asked in an unfriendly manner, "Can I help you?"

There was no time for the attitude, which would almost certainly be followed by an argument, so Jacquie whipped out her police identification. "Jacquie Dale, Crime Scene Investigator. Do you have a computer here with internet access?"

The young woman pointed to a terminal behind the desk at the far corner, close to the exit. "You can come around—"

Plopping her backside onto the counter and spinning her legs up and over, Jacquie moved to the computer keyboard and began typing as fast as she could.

Rikki stood on the opposite side of the counter, wanting to see what was going on, but all he could make out was a search for photos of Peter Stumpp. "You don't need to find me a picture. I have enough magazines at home that show his chiseled features."

"They're not for you," she said with annoyance. "You simply showed me what I was missing. Stumpp *doesn't* look the same in person as he does in pictures."

"So, no chiseled features?"

"Stop."

"What'd I do?"

"You're about to turn your brilliant moment into a travesty."

Insulted, he said, "You've been hanging around with Johnny too much. That's something he would say—only he'd probably have added a 'fuck' somewhere in there, and I'm not sure he even knows what 'travesty' means."

Her fingers danced across the keyboard almost as quickly as she could point and click with the mouse. She opened several computer windows and glanced at the displayed images.

Rikki was having a hard time keeping up. "What are you looking for?"

"I'm trying to find the angle I need." She clicked on a few more links before hitting pay dirt. "And there it is." Pointing to Stumpp's left eyebrow, she explained, "Here. This is what's different."

"What? He doesn't have eyebrows in real life?"

"I'm beginning to see how Johnny sees you."

He gasped. "Hey, that's not nice."

"Listen," she said sternly. "In these photographs, Stumpp's eyebrows are perfect. In real life there is a scar over his eye, intersecting his left eyebrow. Hair doesn't grow in that spot."

"So? Plenty of wealthy people have their pictures retouched before print. It's not unusual."

"No, but it supports my theory that Stumpp has an image he'll do anything to protect," she said. "Still, there's something else this picture should be telling me."

"Does it tell you he'd be interested in dating a younger man?" Rikki again batted his eyelashes at her. "I wouldn't a mind a sugar daddy. How old do you think he is anyway?"

She couldn't believe he was even asking a question like that, but then she was struck by a surge of inspiration. Suddenly, she embraced him over the countertop. "Rikki, I'd kiss you if it wouldn't be like kissing my sister!"

"Really," he said, putting his hands on his hips, "stop hanging out with Johnny."

"Hold on." She typed furiously and numerous image windows opened on the monitor. There were ones in color and in black and white. There were paintings and portraits from different time periods, done in every medium available to view. But the subject matter remained the same: Peter Stumpp's family tree. Studying the faces intently, Jacquie uncovered a bizarre resemblance between the patriarchs throughout the generations. It was something her logical mind wanted to deny, but the proof was staring her in the face. She entered a few more keywords into the search field, and the resulting answer chilled her to the bone.

"Oh no," she whispered, slapping one hand over her mouth. "Johnny."

FORTY-SEVEN

"Tell me again why you didn't bring everyone," Mako shouted over the Hummer's engine noise. "If Stumpp surrounds himself with these creatures, don't you think we're going to need every available man?"

"I don't plan on lingering. If you venture into the wolf's den with the intention of staying more than a few minutes, then consider yourself dinner." Nathan shifted in the front seat to face the detective who was sitting behind him. "Besides, I've explained already. My Guardians need to be recovered from the medical center, and there is a sleeping lycanthrope that will need to be controlled should it awaken. Bronson and Winters will take care of both my concerns. Besides, your fellow officer, Mullins, didn't mind their staying behind."

"What do you mean by recovering your men? There is only one body unaccounted for, and the Nassau PD will find him."

"I won't require their help."

"What are you up to, Williams?"

"Nothing you need to concern yourself with, Detective."

"Don't make me an enemy."

Jason, also in the back seat, grew uneasy with the conversation, knowing full well what Nathan was up to. He interrupted, "Detective? How are you holding up? Your injuries—"

" I'll manage," Mako said. "More importantly, if you knew where Stumpp lived, why'd you wait so long to tell us? This could have been finished a long time ago."

"I did it to save lives. If my father is home when we arrive, my suggestion is to leave immediately! Otherwise, this is a suicide mission."

"Why are you so afraid of him?"

"You've seen the company he keeps, but he can be more of an animal than any of his beasts."

"That he controls with the power of the Heart, I'm sure. But I'm not worried about Stumpp. He's just a man," Mako said confidently. "How many creatures do you suppose we'll come across?"

Jason shrugged. "I really don't know what to expect when we arrive, and that's what scares me most."

"Then why come with us at all?"

"To keep you safe."

"I don't get it."

"It's no secret that Nathan and his men hate me." Jason spoke softly, positive he wouldn't be heard over the Hummer's engine. "Whether it's from fear or misunderstanding is immaterial. You have treated me as an equal, even after you found out I was … different. It's been a long time since anyone's shown me any respect."

"Everyone has issues, Brody. Not everyone is as perfect as him." He motioned to Nathan. "I won't condemn you for being different. Hell, I'm even a little jealous. What does it feel like, having that power?"

Jason was not used to being on the receiving end of praise and admiration. "I've been this way for so long that it doesn't feel like anything, except maybe the occasional adrenaline rush. I guess I feel the same in my skin as you do in yours."

"What about the strength? How strong are you?"

"I'm not really sure. My strength has increased as I've gotten older. But it's not like I can go to a gym and test it, so I work out using whatever I can find in secluded places. You know, abandoned lots, junkyards, anywhere people don't frequent. Cars give the most resistance."

"Be serious." Mako believed Jason was pulling his leg. "You can lift cars?"

Playfully flexing his muscles, Jason said, "Not the whole thing, but I can lift the front end even with the engine still under the hood. It's the reason I have to keep it in check so someone doesn't get seriously hurt."

"There are a few people I don't think I could hold back on."

"I'm sure you would."

"You don't know my temper."

"I've met a lot of people in my time, Detective, and I know a little bit about human nature."

"In your time?" Mako cut in. "What are you, twenty-something? You make it sound like you're a hundred years old."

"As I was saying," he continued, "you wouldn't let Nathan take the life of that young man, even though he's now a cold-blooded killer. You can say he's a material witness or whatever, but you stuck by your word—even though it was given before you knew his dark secret. I can't think of one person who would do that. And if you would do that for a monster, you would hold back against lesser fiends."

"I think I liked it better when you didn't talk so much, Brody."

Smirking, Jason sat back in his chair. He peered out the window at the eerie ambiance of Sands Point, made more ghostly by the lack of street lights. If the driver were to shut the Hummer's headlights off, the normal humans would barely be able to see their hands in front of their faces.

A ringing cellphone disturbed the silence.

"It's mine," the detective said, sliding it open. "Hey, Jacquie. What's up?" He strained to hear through the static. "What was that? The reception around here is bad." He was unsure if she heard him clearly over the background noise, so he raised his voice. "Please tell me the animals are okay."

"Ch … nd … uno … fine," were the only sounds that broke the static barrier, followed by, "Boo … er … in … ad … sh … pe."

Mako was frustrated, mostly because he made out what she was telling him. "At least we got Jacob," he said with some satisfaction. But then he acknowledged that further attempts to continue this conversation were useless. "Listen, let's talk later. This isn't working." She tried to yell something else through the phone, but he couldn't make it out. "Talk to you later. Bye."

Jason asked, "What animals were you talking about?"

"My pets."

"What happened to them?"

"Jacob happened."

Nathan angled his head to hear what was being said.

"Stumpp sent him to my home to kill me, but I wasn't there." Mako blamed himself for his loved ones' injuries. "Already in wolf form, he broke in and almost killed them—and my downstairs neighbor."

"Interesting," Nathan interrupted, beginning to understand the detective better. "If something you care for is threatened, you feel warranted in taking revenge?"

"Call it what you want. I say it's justice. And I'm not in the practice of rewarding bad behavior."

"Oh, I wasn't criticizing your motives," Nathan said. "I'm applauding them."

Mako didn't know exactly how that should make him feel.

"Quiet everyone," Jason barked. "We're here."

"Shit," Jacquie said, dialing Mako's number again. "Come on. Pick up!" Her irritation mounted as the call went straight to voice mail.

Rikki stood nearby, anxious to find out what was going on. "Did you get through? Did you tell him about Booger?"

"I tried, but he couldn't hear me, so he hung up."

"So, he doesn't know?"

"The cat is the least of his concerns right now." She struggled to contact Mako again and again, but the call wouldn't connect. "Piece of shit cellphones!"

"Relax." Rikki tried to sound soothing. "There has to be another way to get in touch with him."

Racking her brain for an alternative solution, she did the only logical thing she could and called the police. Not the emergency hotline, but the Second Precinct directly.

The desk officer answered, "Nassau County, Second Precinct. This is Officer Roland. How can I help you?"

"May I speak to Detective James Mullins?"

"Let me see if he's available. Who can I say is calling?"

"Dale. Jacquie Dale. Please hurry."

The officer placed her on hold.

She fidgeted uncontrollably while waiting. Time was running out for her former lover.

Finally, the officer came back on the line. "He's not at his desk. Can I take a message?"

"No, this is an emergency! Can you patch me through to his—"

"Ma'am, if this is an emergency, you have to dial nine-one-one."

She understood the officer was doing his job, but she could not be delayed any longer. "Listen, you little shit! You have to put me through to Detective Mullins' cellphone right now! If you don't, I will make sure your superiors know how you impeded an important investigation, and the deaths resulting from it will be on your head! How does that sound to you?"

Officer Roland didn't need much time to weigh his options. "Hold on, Ms. Dale. I'll try to reach the detective."

"So," Mullins said, looking at the downed werewolf, "you guys been at this a long time?"

Bronson, standing nearby with a radio in hand, answered, "If you're referring to hunting lycanthropes, then, yes, we have. And there were those who came before us as well as others before them."

"How do you get into something like this? You ex-military?" The detective was so used to acquiring information from others that he unconsciously asked personal questions.

Bronson wasn't comfortable divulging too much to a law enforcement official, so he kept his replies general. "Some of us are. Some of us have sustained great personal loss and are looking for a little retaliation."

"How many are you?"

"Enough."

At that moment, Mullins was aware his questions were deliberately being avoided, which served to further pique his interest. "You're obviously trained. Who's responsible for that?"

"Nathan. Would you like me to interrupt him, so he can explain it to you in further detail?"

"Take it easy, pal." He sent a bit of attitude in his companion's direction. "I'm only trying to pass the time until the cavalry arrives."

"What do you mean?" Bronson suddenly felt the need to rush away.

"I put a call into the station to get some more officers on the scene."

"Why would you do that? We have everything under control."

Mullins slid his hand to his hip holster. "For one, a man was mauled to death here—you might remember the guy your partner is out looking for. And there are certain procedures I have to follow. Secondly, if this thing wakes up," he said, gesturing to the werewolf, "I'll feel comfortable with more guns aimed at it."

"How long do you suppose until they arrive?" Bronson clicked his weapon's safety off.

"Five minutes, give or take."

The two men eyed one another until a phone rang, and although the tension levels were high, Bronson allowed the detective to take the call.

"Mullins," he gave his standard greeting.

"Detective Mullins, this is Officer Roland at the Second Precinct. I have a call for you from a Ms. Jacquie Dale. Should I patch her through?"

"Go ahead." He waited for the call to click over. "Dale? You there?"

"Oh, thank God." She was relieved to be speaking to a familiar voice. "I have a bit of an emergency here."

"Finally decided to take me up on that date, huh?"

"Please, Jimmy, I got enough problems without having to think about that."

"See ya, Dale." Mullins wasn't in the mood to be insulted.

"No, wait!" she yelled. "I really need your help!"

"Say it quick. I got other things to tend to."

"Do you have any idea where Johnny is right now?"

"Mako?" The detective was surprised. "I thought you two knew everything the other one did."

"Come on. I don't have time to waste. Do you know where he is or not?"

Sensing panic in her voice, he decided not to beat around the bush. "Yeah, I saw him tonight. Right now he's headed to Stumpp's mansion to get that Heart thing you guys were telling me about."

"Oh no."

"What? Think there'll be more werewolves running around up there?"

"You know?" Jacquie's tone suggested astonishment.

Taking another look at the beast near his feet, he said, "Oh yeah. I know firsthand. Scary fuckers, aren't they?"

She didn't have time for small talk. "Do you know where Stumpp lives? I have to get to him now!"

"What's wrong, Dale? I can have units up there in no time, but you have to let me know what they'd be walking into."

Feeling that Mullins legitimately wanted to help, she chose to fill him in on her discovery. "Stumpp is not what he seems! Johnny, and whoever's with him, is in grave danger!"

"What? Mako is in troub—"

A solid shot to the back of Mullins' head with the butt end of a rifle ended his conversation. He fell face-first to the ground, with his cell landing a few inches from his hand.

Bronson gave Leslie Winters, the soldier with him, a nod of approval.

Jacquie remained on the line, but when she didn't receive a response, she feared the worst. "Hello? Hello? Jimmy, are you there? Piece of shit cellphones!"

Bronson stomped on the phone, shattering it beyond repair, then turned to Winters. "I assume you found our fallen brother-in-arms?"

"What was left of him."

An expression of anger briefly crossed Bronson's face. "Let's load him up with the others and proceed to the rendezvous point."

"What do we do with that?" Winters referred to the caged werewolf.

"Give it another dose of tranquilizer and bring it along. Nathan wouldn't want it left behind."

"And him?" motioning to the unconscious detective.

"Leave him. Officers are approaching as we speak. We have approximately two minutes to make ourselves scarce. Let's move out." They hastily loaded up and headed out of the area.

Three patrol cars pulled up a few minutes after the Hummer was completely out of sight. The officers secured the perimeter while one rushed to the detective lying on the ground and checked his vitals. After confirming that his colleague was alive, the officer grabbed a first-aid kit and administered smelling salts to rouse Mullins.

As the detective came to, he groaned and reached for the injured part of his head.

"Are you all right, sir?" the officer asked. "What happened here? It looks like a war zone. Can you tell me who did this?"

"Mako … trouble," Mullins moaned. "Must get Mako," he mumbled before passing out again.

FORTY-EIGHT

The Lunar Guardians' leader stood alone in the foyer of the palatial dwelling. He patiently watched the seconds tick by on his wristwatch, constantly shifting his focus from it to his troops as they searched Peter Stumpp's seemingly deserted home for the Heart of Lycaon. Detective Mako wandered solo through the house. Jason hadn't been seen since their arrival.

"Two minutes!" Nathan shouted. The mission time was winding down, and he refused to come up empty-handed—not when he was so close to delivering his enemy a serious blow.

All knew the significance of what this confiscation would mean, so they hastened their hunt, overturning furniture and ignoring the fragile nature of many of the objects they came into contact with. The sounds of smashing and shattering rang loudly through the hallways.

Mako didn't share in the festivities, believing that what you do to others would be done to you. Besides, he held no grudges against the furnishings. He meticulously explored the contents of the enormous dining room.

Observing the elegantly decorated table in the middle of the room, he marveled at the sheer size of it. It stretched nearly the entirety of the room, from just inside the double-door entranceway to the back wall. A long rectangular doily protected the polished wood beneath from the various candelabras, china, and silverware resting on it. He walked from end to end, sweeping the vicinity for anything resembling the target. He gently opened the drawers of the china cabinet, looked through the decorative sideboards along the perimeter, and lightly tilted paintings away from the wall to investigate any imperfections that would indicate a hidden panel for a safe of some kind. Positive that the Silver Heart was nowhere to be found within this room, Mako was ready to proceed to the next area when he heard Nathan yell, "TIME!"

Nathan reset his stopwatch and commanded, "Move to the second floor! Three minutes to departure!" The soldiers acted without question, dropping everything and filing up the spiral staircase.

Although he never condoned the mentality of people who blindly followed orders, Mako admired their level of discipline. He was about to head upstairs too when his phone rang. He could tell Nathan was annoyed at the disturbance, so he shut the dining room doors, limiting the noise that exited or entered the room. "Hello."

"Finally!" Jacquie shouted in his ear. "I've been trying to reach you since you hung up on me!"

"I apologize. The reception on the drive up here was horrible." Mako tried to muffle his call by placing a hand over the mouthpiece of the receiver.

Nathan relentlessly inspected his watch, calling out random intervals to his men. A crackle came through his earbud, and he pushed a finger into it in order to hear what was coming over the airwaves.

"Nathan," Jason said in a hushed voice. "Get out of there now! He's coming up the driveway! I repeat. Stumpp is home!"

His heart racing, Nathan remained calm for the sake of his men, but he knew the situation was about to go from bad to worse—much worse. "Guardians," he yelled in an uncompromising voice, "our intrusion is about to be noticed! Find cover, be silent, and move on my signal! Our priorities have changed! The Heart can wait for another day!" He moved to a room on the ground floor and remembered someone was in the dining room. "Detective!" He listened. "Mako, get off the damn phone and take cover!" Car tires crunched down on the gravel driveway, and he left the detective to fend for himself, disappearing without another word.

"Jacquie, I gotta go." Mako said quietly. "I have to help find the Silver Heart so we can get the hell out of here."

Realizing if she didn't say what she had to now, she may not get another chance. "Wait! I have something to tell you about Stumpp!"

The heavy, oversized doors comprising the main entrance of the mansion were swung open by two powerful arms attached to an irate Peter Stumpp. He searched for trespassers but spotted massive amounts of debris instead. His personal belongings, some which were priceless antiques, were forever damaged. Gliding across the floor, he knelt down where a beautiful, six-foot-high oriental vase once stood, holding the last few shards of porcelain in his palm. An air overtook him, and the fact that someone violated the sanctity of his home was unforgivable. Gritting his teeth and curling his fingers into a fist, he crushed the shards into powder. "Where are you?" he cried out. "I know you are in here, and I will find you!"

He received an answer in the form of a yelp. He turned to his left and eyed the culprit responsible. A man dressed in camouflage clothing was held high by a powerful hand wrapped around the back of his neck. The hand, complete with a set of fingernails equipped to rip through flesh, ran down the muscular arm of Stumpp's manservant.

At the moment, Charles didn't retain the appearance of a typical butler. He was struggling to maintain his human guise, even though the moonlight made it impossible to resist the change. Muscles and fur bulged through his formalwear, his shoes were almost completely torn away from his feet, and his bowtie— once snug around his throat—hung off to the side, still under the collar of a partially shredded button-down shirt. His eyes, under an overhanging brow line, expressed disgust and anger. And the teeth protruding from his bottom lip made him look like a troll as he trudged closer to his master.

The soldier in his hand was alive but partially paralyzed from the force exerted against his neck and spine. His painful facial expression was frozen in place, as were his arms—not that he could have freed himself from the powerful grip if they weren't. Every so often, one of the soldier's legs jerked outward.

Stumpp faced the approaching man-wolf. "Ah, a gift for me? How thoughtful of you, Charles." At that moment he saw the gun in his servant's other hand.

Unaware of what was happening outside the room he was hiding in, Mako remained silent until Jacquie unveiled her discovery. "So what if he has a scar over his eyebrow? Is that a case-cracker?"

"Don't be such an ass, and listen for once instead of talking."

"I'm all ears."

"While we were in his office, I thought there was something off about Stumpp's face. I had never met the man, but I had seen pictures of him in magazines. Probably obeying contractual obligations, not one of the photos showed the scar over his left eye that cuts into his eyebrow. I did some checking, and there aren't any recent pictures, photos, or portraits that illustrate the small imperfection. Then I remembered the painting of Stumpp in the lobby of his building."

"It wasn't Stumpp. It was a portrait of someone else: his father, maybe," said Mako, remembering the name on the small plaque next to it. "Besides, it was painted at least fifty years ago."

"I know you're convinced of what you saw, but it wasn't an image of Stumpp's father, or anyone else for that matter."

Her staged pause insinuated that Jacquie wanted him to ask. "Then who is it?"

"First of all, it's a painting, so anything can be portrayed," she argued. "You can request an artist to depict you as the Queen of England, and they'll do it as long as you pay them. Hell, even Thomas Hill's rendition of the golden spike ceremony to celebrate the Transcontinental Railroad was only commissioned to create a cleaned-up version; the actual photograph contained champagne bottles and sleazy-looking camp prostitutes. And the painting even portrayed some people who weren't at the event, including Theodore Judah, the mind behind the project, who had died six years earlier."

"You're losing me. Get back on track."

"Sorry," she huffed. "Now, what I'm about to tell you is going to sound really wild. But with everything we've learned the past few days, crazy isn't so crazy anymore."

The butler stopped in close proximity to his master, holding the soldier firm without displaying any sign of exertion.

"Is that meant for me?" Stumpp glanced at the weapon.

"It has to end, Peter," Charles grunted.

"Peter? Since when did we dispense with the formalities?"

"This cannot go on." The struggle to speak was obvious, but Charles forced out every syllable.

"Are you handing me your resignation, then?"

Charles continued, "What you did to that poor family, that innocent child, is reprehensible. I will not stand idly by and be a part of your contemptible actions any longer."

"What are you saying?"

Pointing the gun at Stumpp's chest, he said, "You murdered my family, *my* little girl, so many years ago. And even though you cursed me to live out the rest of my days as a monster, I was and always have been powerless to take my revenge on you." The tears streamed down his distorted features as frustration and sadness overcame him.

"This is all so touching, but now's your chance. Avenge your family...if you can." Opening his arms to his sides, he gave Charles an irresistible shot at a wide target.

His gun hand trembled as he wept. "I, I can't."

"Pathetic."

Shifting his aim from his current mark, Charles pressed the pistol's muzzle against his temple.

"NO!" a voice shouted from the second floor of the mansion.

Charles closed his watery eyes and squeezed the trigger. The silver bullet rocketed from the chamber, through his brain, and he slumped to the floor in a heap of dead flesh.

The soldier, released from his temporary paralysis, fell to the ground and scrambled into a corner, eyeing the dead butler.

Looking up to the balcony, Stumpp saw his deformed assistant, his arm outstretched as if trying to seize the weapon from Charles' hand before he could fire. "Ethan," he began, "what's going on here?"

Mako heard the gunshot, and adrenaline filled his veins. Grabbing his weapon, he said, "I'm sorry, Jacquie, but you really need to hurry this along." Peeking out the doorway, he saw the manservant's lifeless body lying in the foyer.

"First, let me start with facts. You brought me in on this because of my expertise with forensics, and I've done extensive studies on the subject, including anatomy. The bone structure of an adult generally remains the same until old age, barring any unforeseen events like disease or accidents. Now, I wouldn't consider Stumpp a senior, would you?"

"Not at all," he answered, though he was not sure she wanted him to.

"Keep in mind that an artist, even though they'll paint whatever you like, will generally want to retain the actual image of the person they are painting as a testament to their superior skills. Again, this is assuming you don't commission a painting from someone like Picasso. So, working on those two pieces of information, I can tell you without a shadow of doubt, the facial structure of the man we met in the office of Stumpp Industries today is the same man in the artwork hanging in the lobby."

"So, why is that so alarming? And why should I care if Stumpp likes to play dress up?"

She was a little disappointed he hadn't put two and two together yet. "C'mon, think! I'm not saying Stumpp wants to pretend he was around years ago. I'm telling you he's lived much longer than any man on the planet!"

The man on the balcony withdrew his misshapen hand, also stuck in mid-transformation, and placed it gently on the railing. He showed genuine compassion for Charles, who was now fully human again and in an unresponsive state.

"Well, Ethan," Stumpp said, disrupting his assistant's thoughts, "I'm waiting."

"It's over, Peter."

Afraid the two individuals were headed to a confrontation while his soldier was stuck in the middle, Nathan emerged from his hiding place with both signature handguns aimed at Stumpp. "Guardians," he ordered, "take aim!"

The majority of the soldiers pointed their weapons at the same target. But two targeted Ethan, perceiving him a considerable threat even in his partially transformed state.

Stumpp's gaze passed over the intruders until he locked eyes with their leader. "At last, I get to meet humanity's savior, Nathan Williams, face to face," he declared with a sneer. "The spitting image of your father, I see."

Nathan was careful not to let his emotions get the better of him. "Don't worry, Stumpp. There are many others like me out there looking to exterminate the lycanthrope plague. I'm merely the one who has the privilege to dispose of you."

"That's a big undertaking," Stumpp said with conviction. "You sure you can live up to that claim?"

"Yes."

"Then why haven't you fired yet?"

Nathan was at a loss for words.

"Ethan," Stumpp said calmly, without turning to look at him. "Are you with me?" The ensuing silence gave ample reason for him to doubt his assistant's support.

Responding in a voice raspier than before, Ethan said, "You know I have been loyal to you throughout the years, but this is one battle you'll have to fight alone."

Stumpp twisted his head to the side to catch a glimpse of his associate in his peripheral vision. His look of disapproval made Ethan squirm, even in his werewolf form.

"I don't benefit from the protection of the Heart as you do," Ethan explained. "For me to stay and fight would be suicide."

The soldiers prepared to fire.

Ethan had to act or he'd never leave the place alive. Vaulting over the banister down to the first floor, he pushed off his hind legs and lunged into a room under the overhang of the second floor landing. It gave him sufficient cover, should any shoot at him. He disappeared from sight, but a breaking window told everyone in earshot that Ethan had escaped—at least for now.

"Running out of allies, are you?" Nathan asked sarcastically.

"Where's my son?" Stumpp drastically changed gears. "I know he's here somewhere. He would want to personally witness my end."

"I don't think he'll be making an appearance. Right now, it's just us. Make your peace," Nathan said, pulling the hammers back on both pistols. "It's time to pay for your crimes."

"Go ahead." Stumpp's breathing became heavier. "Do. Your. Worst."

Despite all the surprising facts uncovered in the course of his investigation of this case, Mako was having a hard time digesting what Jacquie was telling him.

"I did some photographic research on Stumpp's family tree as far back as I could go, even when the family name was still Stubbe, and I found some disturbing information. In all recorded images of the Stumpp—or Stubbe—family, the patriarch, no matter what his first name, bears a similar resemblance to our Peter Stumpp. And in the earlier photos that couldn't be retouched by modern technology, the scar is prominent. He's been around for centuries!"

"Are you telling me Stumpp's a werewolf?"

"That's not all," she went on. "I went back to the earliest drawings on record in the town of Bedburg, Germany. I could only find some sketches, but the scar is clearly pronounced over his eye. It was a wanted poster of the vilest serial killer of their time—perhaps of all time!"

The detective's mind fit all the pieces of evidence together until he reached the only possible conclusion. "So, you're saying—"

"Yes," she said, relieved that the two of them were finally on the same page. "Stumpp isn't hiding Stubbe. Peter Stumpp *is* Peter Stubbe, the Werewolf of Bedburg!"

At that moment, a horrifying howl echoed throughout the residence.

"What's going on over there?" she asked.

Sneaking another look through the crack in the double doors, Mako viewed an exceptionally worrisome sight: Stumpp stood in the mansion's vestibule, much larger and hairier than he remembered, yelling at Nathan.

"You have invaded my home!" His voice was deep with a raspy tone. "You have ravaged my possessions! You have threatened me with physical harm! These transgressions cannot go unpunished! You will now deal with the hell you've unleashed upon yourselves!"

Stumpp transformed rapidly from man to monster while delivering his speech. Chiseled features were wiped away and replaced by a long snout, jagged teeth, and bestial, rage-filled eyes. Neatly manicured hands became brutish mitts with gnarled claws at the ends of each digit. The designer shirt he wore became stretched as his chest expanded to enormous proportions, and he used his newly formed claws to shred it to ribbons. Expertly tailored pants didn't stand a chance against the onslaught of muscles pushing against seamless stitching, and soon they were reconfigured into rags lying at his feet. Salt-and-pepper-colored fur covered the werewolf's entire body, and Mako noted that this was the color of Stumpp's hair. Shoes exploded as giant padded feet—complete with their own set of razor-sharp nails—jutted outward from their former leather prison. Out of all the lycanthropes Mako had seen during this almost unbelievable investigation, the Werewolf of Bedburg dwarfed them all in both size and ferocity.

The newly reborn Peter Stumpp howled.

Nathan didn't give the beast time to mount an attack. "Now, Guardians!"

They opened fire on the massive man-wolf. The soldiers' assault forced the werewolf's body to gyrate and spasm as each bullet pierced his flesh. Stumpp wailed and snarled, and then, remarkably, fell onto his back and lay motionless.

The one soldier on the main floor, cowering by the front entrance, got to his feet, all the while keeping his gun fixed on the creature. He wanted to move around the lycanthrope into a safer position, but his commander gestured for him to stay in his current location.

An unidentifiable sound was heard by all.

The soldier closest to the werewolf was petrified, and his palms became so clammy that he feared he might drop his weapon. He slid a foot into the foyer and followed it with the other. Nathan raised a hand for him to stop, but the soldier took another step closer to Stumpp.

The faint reverberation continued. It was definitely a pattern of some kind, but it was still indiscernible.

The frightened soldier wanted to obey his leader, but he also wanted to get out of reaching distance should the werewolf yet live. Nathan didn't realize the man was refusing to comply; his focus was completely on Stumpp.

The noise got louder and more horrifyingly familiar.

Looking at the werewolf's throat, Nathan saw movement in the larynx. The impudence of the man came through even in his animal form, and Nathan recognized what everyone was hearing. Stumpp was laughing at them!

The soldier decided it was now or never and attempted a dash to safety.

"No, you fool! Stay where you are!" Nathan shouted.

Stumpp's enormous arm whipped around with lightning speed and grabbed the soldier by his leg. With his other arm, he lashed out at Nathan, and massive knuckles connected with his chest. Nathan rolled with the strike, but the force was such that it caused him to sail across the room into an undamaged piece of furniture. The werewolf moved faster than the mind could comprehend and was on his feet in no time, holding the soldier he'd snatched as a shield in front of him. The man barely covered the lycanthrope's chest, but none of the Lunar Guardians wanted to be responsible for taking the life of one of their own.

Mako didn't have the same reservations, although murdering an innocent wasn't on his agenda. He made his presence known from inside the dining room, throwing the doors open. "Put the man down, and step away from him now!"

Looking past his human shield, Stumpp's enlarged pupils dilated further, spying the detective aiming a pistol at his head.

"You!" he spat out furiously. "If you're here, that can only mean Jacob is …" He stopped himself, surmising his progeny's fate.

"As a fuckin' doornail." Mako sounded proud. "I told you I'd find a way to end this, only now I don't have to worry about bringing you in alive."

Stumpp snarled vehemently.

Continuing to goad the monster, Mako hoped to divert Stumpp's attention from his captive. "What's the matter? Can't think of anyone to quote for this occasion?"

The next motion, whether conscious or unconscious, showed an unbridled savagery only a madman could possess. Stumpp tightened his grip around the upper and lower parts of his prisoner's body and ripped the man in half, pushing his head through the spraying blood and guts, roaring at the person who drove him to the point of lunacy.

"No!" Mako shouted, but it was too late. The soldier was dead. Mako raised his weapon-arm a bit higher, lining up a shot between the werewolf's eyes, but Stumpp charged. With his aim ruined, afraid he'd end up like the trooper who now lay in two pieces, Mako ran to the rear of the room, searching for an escape.

Stumpp's footsteps caused mini-tremors, and the tableware shook with every stomp.

Mako's focus shifted to the large rectangular dining room table when a candelabra centerpiece toppled. He formulated a plan he'd only get one chance to execute. If it didn't work, he'd be a goner for sure.

The werewolf lunged for the detective.

Dropping his cellphone to his side so he could grip his gun tighter, using both hands, Mako took two steps before diving into the air toward Stumpp, twisting his body and slamming his back down onto the hard slick wood of the tabletop. The impact shocked his damaged ribs, forcing the air out of his lungs, and Mako was momentarily winded. The long handmade doily covering the table acted as a slide, quickly getting him from one side of the table to the other as the bloodthirsty lycanthrope sailed overhead. The detective wasn't one to waste an opportunity, so he fired three shots into the werewolf's body as they crossed each other. Much of the priceless china spilt over the sides of the table and was sacrificed. Mako then fell off the far end and rolled backwards into a crouching position, facing into the dining room to successfully complete his maneuver.

Stumpp's jaunt concluded similarly when he crashed down into the chair at the head of the table, completely demolishing it, and then swung around with every intention of renewing his attack. Both individuals stared at each other, each with weapons at the ready. "Impressive, Detective. Your fear motivated you to perform spectacularly."

"Who said I'm afraid?" Mako tried to steady his hands.

The beast laughed. "Please. The acrid stench of fear is oozing from your every pore." Stumpp moved a step to his left, leaving fewer obstacles between him and his prey. "It reminds me of Robert Mane right before I tore him to pieces."

Mako was reminded of the real reason he wanted Stumpp. "Why kill him and not Jacob?"

"Ever the detective. Mane was a pawn of my true enemy. To let him live would challenge my dominance. Jacob could have been a useful slave if he wasn't so terrified of his own power."

"And Mane's head?"

The werewolf formed an expression suggestive of a smile. "Haven't you heard? I've developed a taste for brains."

Mako recalled the rumor of how the Werewolf of Bedburg murdered his infant son. "You're going to die tonight," he stated confidently.

"You're so naïve, Detective. You can't kill me. I have a secret weapon at my disposal."

Unexpectedly, a voice called out from the second floor, "I've found it! I have the Heart of Lycaon!"

Now it was Mako's turn to beam. "That secret weapon?"

Stumpp growled wildly, "I'll kill all of you!"

The Guardians assembled outside the dining hall, behind the detective, and took aim at the creature at the far end of the room.

Mako called the monster's bluff. "I'm betting you can't deliver on that promise."

"You dare challenge me?" Stumpp roared.

"For all the protection the Silver Heart provides you, I'm guessing you're still vulnerable to massive injuries that would leave any ordinary lycanthrope catatonic—that is, until your body can heal. This shouldn't pose a threat to you except for the fact that you're surrounded by a bunch of men who would love to restrain you long enough to get you to their labs for study. And think about this: how unbelievable a find would it be to experiment on a live subject that could never die? It's every scientist's wet dream!"

Stumpp wanted to rip the detective's throat out, but his words rang true. There were too many foes opposing him, and he could be incapacitated long enough to become a prisoner or worse. While contemplating his next move, luck shone upon him.

"Johnny? Are you there?" the voice emanated from the cellphone lying on the floor. Jacquie was too stubborn to hang up before she was told what was going on.

The tables had turned once again, and Mako realized this could lead to a disastrous situation. "Jacquie, dammit, hang up the phone now!"

"What?" she shouted. "I can't hear you. Listen. Meet me back at your place. I want to help you put this freak in the ground!" She disconnected the call without comprehending the danger she'd put herself in.

Stumpp relaxed and adjusted his attention from the phone to the detective.

"I'll never let you get to her," Mako promised.

"You can't stop me."

"You won't reach the front door."

The werewolf swiveled his head slightly to the side and shot his arm outward, digging his claws into the wood paneling on the lower half of the wall next to him. "I won't have to." Stumpp heaved a chunk of wood away from the wall, revealing a secret passage.

Tired of wasting his breath, especially when none of his words could dissuade Stumpp from pursuing his murderous ways, Mako's finger tightened around the trigger. But Mako's aim was spoiled a second time when the wooden panel was hurled at him like a Frisbee at high speed, forcing him to dodge it before it sliced his head off. The bullet ejected from the gun, but it lodged in the wall, nowhere near its intended target.

The secret panel flew over the detective's head and served to scatter the men standing behind him before soaring out the front door. By the time they regained their composure, Stumpp was gone.

Mako holstered his weapon and said to Nathan, "Come on, we have to go."

"I don't think so. We have what we came for. Mission accomplished."

"But Jacquie—"

"Is not my problem. You want to save her, you do it alone. I've lost enough men."

"I thought you wanted to kill the Werewolf of Bedburg. And now that you've found him, you won't follow through?"

"You heard him. He can't be killed, at least not until we find out how to break his bond with the Heart. And that is our new priority."

"You knew, didn't you?" Mako played a hunch.

"I tried to tell you there is more history here than you will ever know."

"You knew Stumpp was Stubbe this whole time, and you didn't even have the decency to warn me."

"I owe you nothing, detective."

Jogging to the exit, he left Nathan with a thought: "I won't forget this, Williams." Outside, he cupped his hands, placing one on each side of his mouth, and cried out, "Brody! Brody! Where are you? I need your help!" The silence suggested that had Stumpp scared him away.

Mako needed to get back to his apartment fast. He was tempted to steal one of the Hummers, but those vehicles weren't built for the kind of speed he needed right now. Fortunately, his concerns were answered in the form of a Mercedes McLaren SLR sitting in the driveway. "Nice," he said. He hopped in the driver's seat, checked the visor for keys, and raced away to save Jacquie's life.

FORTY-NINE

The vehicle rolled to a stop in a fairly deserted area, and the driver got out. His body was weary from the night's activities, but a few small items remained on the agenda. "Show me," Nathan said, addressing his second-in-command.

Bronson opened the rear door of his Hummer. Lying next to one another in black body bags were the three fallen Lunar Guardians who had been slain in battle against their lycanthrope enemies.

"That makes four."

"Four?"

Nathan directed his attention to one of the other trucks. "Stumpp got one more of us while we were trying to secure the Heart."

"Did our man die in vain?"

Nathan snapped his fingers at one of the soldiers, who held a dark-colored duffle bag. He had the man unzip and hold it at the appropriate angle for Bronson to see its contents. The light from the streetlamp reflected off the Heart of Lycaon, much to everyone's satisfaction.

"And Stumpp?" Bronson trusted he'd been dealt with severely.

"We let him go. We had the Heart and had suffered too many losses already. The detective and his female partner decided they were going to deal with him. Imbeciles."

"It's not their responsibility. They're not equipped to handle him."

Nathan didn't like to be questioned by anyone, even those he respected. His manner became sterner, and his response emphasized his point. "Peter Stumpp continues to be protected by this relic. I will not sacrifice any more of my men until we discern how to make him as vulnerable as any ordinary lycanthrope."

"But sacrificing two more humans is okay with you?" Bronson recognized Nathan as his superior; but Bronson was also put in a position of authority, and it wasn't because he backed down easily from confrontation.

Unwilling to cause a scene in front of the rest of his men, Nathan proposed a solution: "If the two of them prove their tenacity and survive their clash with Stumpp, you can ask them to join our cause." He was relatively sure the detective and his partner would be brutally mutilated, and then he'd deal with Bronson's insubordination.

"They'll die without our help."

"Then I guess they won't be joining us after all." Shifting gears, Nathan had one more concern to attend to. "Now. Where's the boy?"

Although he was not pleased with how the conversation ended, Bronson went to the side of his vehicle and slid open the modified back passenger door, making sure to remain at a safe distance.

A hairy arm thrust forward, attempting to grab the nearest person; but the huge paw was kept in check as the werewolf's shoulder slammed against the metal bars of its cage, preventing him from stretching any farther. Louis Falcone was awake, angry, and ready to make a meal of his captors. He was visibly uncomfortable in the cramped quarters of his prison, but his discomfort and awkwardness ensured the Guardians' safety.

Nathan found these creatures so contemptuous that he didn't even regard them as human anymore. All he saw were rabid animals that needed to be extinguished. Their mere existence was an offense to him and his family's legacy. Reaching his hand out, he ordered, "Weapon." When no one complied, he turned to the man closest to him and repeated, "Give me a weapon, Soldier."

Bronson hesitated to obey the command because of a promise made earlier in the night. "Wasn't this one's life supposed to be spared?"

Nathan's nostrils flared at the notion of being questioned yet again. "I gave no such order."

"You told Mako—"

"I told Mako what he needed to hear at the moment!" Nathan said sharply.

Bronson noted that Nathan still had his pistols holstered on his belt. The command was simply a display of power, and he ultimately knew whom the majority of the men would side with. Bronson opened the front passenger side of his Hummer, retrieved the gun on the front seat, and placed it in Nathan's palm. But he didn't relinquish it right away, even after Nathan took a firm hold of it. The two had a slight tug-of-war, ending with Bronson reminding his commanding officer, "Mako gave his word to this man that he would not be harmed."

Nathan stared deeply into Bronson's eyes. "Mako did. I did not." Jerking the gun free, he pointed it at Louis and fired.

FIFTY

Flipping a few bills into the cab's driver's side window, Jacquie hurried up the porch steps to Mako's apartment, tore through the flimsy police crime scene tape across the broken front entrance, and raced up the stairs. The house was in shambles, and for a brief moment, she hoped the forensics team had properly collected evidence from the wreckage.

She dashed into the bedroom, grabbed her suitcase at the foot of the bed, and tossed it onto the mattress. Sifting through its contents, she withdrew a small gun box from under her clothing, entered the lock's combination, and retrieved a revolver with six bullets. A specific area on each of the projectiles was transparent, revealing a silver-colored liquid inside.

Loading the gun as she darted back through the living room, her clumsy movements made it difficult to easily fit each slug into its individual compartment. One slug slipped from her grasp and fell to the floor. Bending over to reach for it outside the unlit bathroom, she failed to notice Peter Stumpp, again in human form, observing her from the darkness. She slid the last shot into place and headed out.

At the top of the staircase, her cellphone rang with an unfamiliar number, but she answered it anyway. "Hello," she said cautiously.

"Jacquie," Mako's voice came through loud and clear. "Are you okay?"

"What number are you calling from?"

"The phone in Stumpp's Mercedes."

"You stole his car?" she asked, surprised he would do something like that.

"Of course not. He let me borrow it," he said sarcastically. "Yeah, I stole his car! How else was I supposed to get to you? Judge me later."

"Still, you stole a car for me?" She got teary-eyed. "You really do care. I knew it."

"Where are you?" he asked, rolling his eyes in disbelief of her reaction.

"At your apartment, or what's left of it anyway."

"I'll be there in a few minutes. Lock yourself away. I think Stumpp is on his way there too, and I don't know how fast he can travel on foot."

"I'm not worried," she said. "But it's cute that you are."

"This is not a game." He was not in the mood for flirtatious behavior. "Watch your ass. I'm on my way."

Jacquie couldn't resist. "When you get here, you can watch it for me."

"Don't make me turn this car around."

Disappointed at his refusal to flirt back, she commented, "You're no fun."

"Maybe later," he teased.

"Really?"

"No."

"You're a jerk," she said coldly.

"Just be careful. See you soon."

"Bye." Raising the pistol near her face, she thought out loud, "I've got something that'll take care of Stumpp, if he gets here first."

Without warning, powerful hands came from behind and grabbed her underneath the jaw and around her wrist, incapacitating her weapon and her tongue. "Are you sure about that, Ms. Dale?"

She managed to squeeze a string of words together through her clenched jaw. "Give me the chance to show you, and you'll get your answer."

He tightened his grip around her face until she whimpered in pain. "You are hardly in a position to threaten anyone. Don't you agree?" The question was purely rhetorical since he was applying enough pressure to make it impossible for her to speak.

Trying her best to break free, Jacquie knew she could not match her attacker's strength. Perhaps she could take him by surprise. A swift mule kick to his groin confirmed it.

Even with the immense strength of a supernatural creature of legend, Stumpp was nonetheless a man, vulnerable to some of the same weaknesses. The sensation startled him, and he lost hold of his captive.

Wriggling free, she ran down the steps and onto the street.

Stumpp leapt forward, taking seven steps in one jump, and landed on the first floor as Jacquie darted out of the building. He sprinted after her, wearing only a pair of black boxer briefs. She staggered him a second time by spinning around and firing a single shot from her firearm. The bullet penetrated his chest, and the transparent glass tube encased within the metal slug exploded when it hit his sternum, releasing the silver liquid into his body. Stumpp stopped in his tracks and clutched at his heart as if he'd gone into cardiac arrest.

She stopped too, wanting to see if she'd done him in.

He grunted irately.

She contemplated shooting him a few more times for good measure, but her police training overrode that compulsion. "Get down on the ground," she commanded, taking aim once again. "You're finished!"

Agonizing groans escaped his lips, but Peter Stumpp was far from finished. Throughout his life he'd suffered many torments, the worst of which had been in his hometown of Bedburg after he'd been convicted of the terrible crimes he'd committed. He'd been sentenced to the most cruel torture device in the history of man: the Wheel. Flesh had been torn from his body with red-hot pincers, limbs had been broken with the blunt side of an axe—a measure used to prevent the damned from climbing out of their graves—and finally, he'd been beheaded and burned on a pyre. For this insolent mortal to think she could end his life with a single bullet was laughable.

She shouted at him again, "Get down on the ground now, or I'll be forced to fire agai—"

In a fraction of a second Stumpp lunged at her, worked his way behind, and grabbed her by the throat with a hand now resembling a monster's inhuman appendage, preventing her from finishing her thought. "I don't know what's in that weapon of yours, but it packs quite a punch," he said, almost complimentary. "However, I have survived much worse; and you will not be given a second chance to use it." He snapped her wrist in one smooth motion, fracturing, if not breaking, the bones under the skin and forcing her to drop the gun.

"How—" She barely got the word out through the pain.

Curiosity got the better of him, and he hesitated in killing her. "How what?" he asked. "How come I'm not dead? How come no one is here to save you?"

"No," she said through gritted teeth.

"Enlighten me, then."

"How could I get so close to avenging my parents' deaths, only to become a victim of their murderer?" The tears trickled out, despite her best efforts to keep them at bay.

The fiend chuckled. "You think I killed your parents?"

"Didn't you?"

"No, I did not have the pleasure. But I know who did."

"Tell me."

"Now, where would the fun be in that?" A wicked smile formed on his lips. "I can give you a hint though. It was someone very close to you."

"You're lying."

"I assure you," the madman replied, "I'm not. Lying wouldn't cause you the misery I thrive on, and I want to see you suffer before you die."

Her jaw stiffened with rage. "I'll kill you."

"I highly doubt that, my dear." Stumpp tilted his head back and opened his mouth wide, revealing the razor-sharp fangs forming inside. Thrusting forward with a growl, he was intent on biting her head off. But a shot rang out and a silver slug ripped through his neck. The shock of the bullet tearing through his flesh stunned the werewolf, and he let go of his hostage to wrap his fingers around the wound and impede the bleeding. A second projectile and then a third, strategically shot into his shoulder and stomach, drew more blood. Stumpp roared and snapped his head forward to gaze upon his attacker.

Mako stood outside the stolen Mercedes McLaren SLR. The barrel of his gun was hot to the touch and aimed at the monster. He stretched his other arm outward in Jacquie's direction.

She scrambled over to him, but not before picking up her revolver. "So, you do care," she whispered.

"Don't trust me with your life anymore, huh?" he whispered back.

"Yeah, sorry about that. I was angry."

Steadying her next to him, Mako focused on the man in front of him, and said, "It's over, Stumpp. Your reign of terror ends tonight."

"You know, Detective," Stumpp replied, the hole in his neck almost completely healed, "I have to agree with Mark Twain when he said, 'Few things are harder to put up with than the annoyance of a good example.'"

"Let us not become weary in doing good, for at the proper time we will reap a harvest if we do not give up," Jacquie returned.

"Galatians 6:9?" Stumpp noted as another dented slug was dislodged from his body. "Am I correct?"

"You are," she answered.

"I take it she's the brains of your duo, eh, Detective?"

Mako racked his mind for an appropriate response, and when he believed he'd found one, he responded, "Maybe, but I do have one thing going for me."

"And what would that be?"

Furrowing his brow as he looked squarely at the man he'd come to loathe, he said, "I'm an excellent shot!" The detective brandished his gun for a split second before gunfire echoed through the quiet neighborhood.

Not expecting an attack at that precise moment, Stumpp did not react as quickly as he normally would. He was assaulted by a hail of bullets.

Squeezing off shot after shot, Mako refused to let up. With every explosion, a feeling of joy surged through his body. With every grunt of pain, he experienced a sense of elation from giving the beast a taste of its own medicine.

Jacquie watched the onslaught, unsure of what she should be feeling. She was glad to see the malicious Stumpp get what he deserved, but at the same time, she was frightened for Mako, who seemed a little too happy to dish out the punishment. She hadn't had much time to ruminate on the subject, however, when she noticed the silver bullets were losing their desired effect.

Shaking off the attacks easier now and regaining his footing, Stumpp lurched forward with hate in his eyes.

She didn't want to take any chances, so she fired off three bullets with her mini-cannon. The reaction to her special ammunition was even more astounding than before.

Stumpp clutched his chest again and howled in anguish. The pain was so severe it forced him to one knee, and for a moment he believed this was the end.

No, he thought.

I cannot lose.

I will not be defeated by lesser beings.

Using the monster within to conquer his pain, his breathing slowed as he concentrated on healing. He would suffer no more by their hands.

In mere seconds Peter Stumpp ripped out of what little clothing he had on and fully transformed into the wolf, roaring furiously. He was not more than ten feet away from his enemies. But a familiar voice that hadn't reached his ears in centuries halted his movement.

"Hello, Father."

The werewolf frantically searched for his son, twisting his body from side to side, trying to locate the source of the whisper that was heard only by him. He found what he was looking for nearly one thousand yards away, lying prone on a rooftop. He reverted back to human form. "Carl," Stumpp whispered back, prior to noticing the high-powered sniper rifle at his son's side.

Then he heard the explosion of a bullet already fired from the rifle, and in the moment before it hit him, he smiled at his son's treachery. The giant slug slammed him right between the eyes, penetrating the skull and embedding itself in Stumpp's brain. His head snapped back and he collapsed instantly, his final expression frozen on his face.

The mystified couple approached carefully, and some of their unspoken questions were answered upon seeing the hole in Stumpp's forehead. The rest of the mystery was solved when they spotted Jason walking down the street toward them.

"Nice to see you," Mako said sincerely. "I thought I lost you back at the house."

"I heard everything from my position. And when I knew he was coming here, and that Nathan refused to help, I couldn't leave you in good conscience." He made sure to keep his distance from the body.

"How long were you watching?" Jacquie asked.

"Almost the whole time."

Mako didn't want to sound ungrateful, but he had to ask, "And you waited until now to act?"

"It took some time to build up the courage to face him again."

"You were right on time," said Jacquie. She wanted Jason to be proud of his bravery.

"Yeah, thanks, kid," Mako went to shake hands. "I thought we were goners."

"From what I saw, you two were managing just fine. If he wasn't protected by the Silver Heart, you would have definitely finished him off."

"But he's dead now, right?" Jacquie asked, looking at the seemingly lifeless form at her feet.

"Because of the Heart, there is nothing on earth that can kill him," Jason answered dejectedly. "Its power protects him even now, but he's still subject to the weaknesses of all lycanthropes."

"So, he's in a coma until his body heals?" Mako chimed in.

"Precisely."

"How long do we have?"

"I really don't know. All lycanthropes are different."

"What I don't get is how you fired that shot off without him knowing."

"Once I got the nerve up, I called to my father to keep him from moving out of position; then I took the shot. Sound travels at approximately 680 feet per second. The bullet fired from my gun moves around 800 feet per second, give or take. By the time he heard it, it was too late to do anything about it."

"Pretty sneaky." Jacquie was impressed. "What do we do with him now?"

"I'll call Nathan. He and the Lunar Guardians can collect him."

"That would be best," Mako agreed. "The NCPD can't handle Falcone and Stumpp too."

"Mako," Jason said with trepidation, "with all due respect, the NCPD won't have Falcone in custody for long."

"What do you mean?"

"Nathan won't allow it. First chance he gets, he'll take the boy, just as he'll take the bodies of his fallen colleagues from the morgue. It's probably done already."

"What? I knew that asshole was up to something." A hint of anger surfaced. "Why didn't you tell me?"

"I had no choice. If I told you earlier, you would have tried to stop them, and you might've been killed." Jason let the thought sink in for a moment before adding, "It wasn't worth the risk."

"But Mullins—"

Jason interrupted him before the detective's thoughts ran rampant. "He'll be fine. Since he doesn't know too much, and probably won't offer any resistance, Nathan's men will go easy on him, I'm sure."

Figuring there wasn't much he could do about it, he stored the incident in his memory. "So, what do I call you now? Carl? Jason? Mr. Stumpp?"

"Wait a minute!" Jacquie spoke up. "You're Peter Stumpp's son? The one from the legend?"

"Yes. I was born Carl Stubbe, in the fifteenth century. My father cannot sire any more children in the traditional sense, not since his transformation. All lycanthropes are rendered sterile once the curse takes over. The only way they can reproduce is to bite another being and transfer the disease to them."

"Shouldn't you be dead?" she asked, remembering the story.

Jason nodded in agreement. "Only if fate wanted to treat me kindly. As you know, my father was a cruel and twisted man. I was born before he became an actual werewolf, but shortly thereafter, he decided to experiment on me. Rather than bite me and remake me in his image, he fed me some of his blood to see what would happen. I received all the benefits of the lycanthrope, but my body never underwent a transformation. My strengths are limited because of my human form, but it gives me distinct advantages over others.

"The torture began once he wanted to test the limits of my regenerative powers. The recorded tale of him eating my brains is true, but there was so much more done to me after they allegedly put him to death. The Heart has protected him almost the whole time he's been a lycanthrope; and even after all the horrors he was put through, he was able to regenerate back to human form. He sought me out for I was the only one who knew of his rebirth. It took years for him to heal and find me again, but he more than made up for it in the end. If it wasn't for Nathan's great-great-grandfather, I might still be his experiment today."

Jacquie's eyes welled up. "I'm so sorry."

"Thank you, but I've had centuries to come to terms with my pain."

"Now I understand why you wouldn't want to see your father again, or tell me who you really were initially," Mako said. "If I would've known—"

"How could you?" Jason interjected. "It was only a week ago that you discovered a new type of evil existed in the world."

"And that knife your father gave you?" Mako referred to the dagger Jason had used to lure him to the temporary headquarters of the Lunar Guardians in the Marriott Hotel.

"Yes." Jason knew where the detective was going with his inquiry. "It was the one he 'killed' me with time and again."

"Why keep it?"

"When I feel too weak to go on, it reminds me of how much I have overcome."

"Well, it looks like you didn't need me at all. You stopped him all by yourself. You should be proud."

"I guess I am, but I did need your help in getting here. Thank you."

Sirens resonated in the distance.

Jason became nervous. "I should leave. I'm not a big fan of the authorities." Then he remembered his associates were part of that vocation. "Present company excluded, of course."

"Go," Mako said, tossing him a set of car keys. "Your van is around the block. Get out of here ... Carl."

"Thank you, but I think I'll stick with Jason. Carl has too many bad memories."

Jacquie spontaneously hugged him. "We owe you our lives."

He awkwardly hugged back. "I really should go." The sirens were making him uncomfortable. Not taking it personally, she backed off. And Jason ran off into the night and out of view in seconds.

An ambulance pulled up to the curb where Stumpp's body lay, and two bald men jumped out and retrieved a stretcher from the back. They moved swiftly in securing Stumpp to the gurney. Then they placed him inside the rescue vehicle.

Mako flashed his badge. "I'm a detective in the Second. Get this man to lock-up immed—"

One of the bald technicians shoved him aside and returned to the vehicle's cab. Mako wanted to say something, but as the ambulance raced away from the area, he swore two glowing red eyes stared back through the rear windows.

"What was that all about?" Jacquie was not sure what she'd witnessed.

"Assholes," Mako explained. He looked around at his neighbor's house for any sign of activity. "I wonder who called nine-one-one?"

A block away, a faded light blue Camaro pulled away from the curb undetected.

Mako put his arm around Jacquie, thinking about how she'd handled herself during the fight, and silently commended her bravery. But there was one question he wanted answered. "What kind of heat are you packing? They seemed to work much better than these silver bullets."

"You want the long version or the short version?"

"Give me the version I'll understand."

She giggled. "Okay," she said, leaning against the Mercedes. "You know I believe in the supernatural, but that doesn't mean

I discount science. Werewolf legends say they were vulnerable to items made of silver, but there might be a small loophole in that thinking. When these tales were written, the metal mercury was thought of as a kind of silver. It was even called 'quicksilver.' Mercury, although it looks the same, is completely unrelated to silver; but it can be used as a substitute in certain applications. Alchemists often thought of mercury as the first matter from which all metals were formed. So I figured there could be a mistake in the translation that only silver could kill werewolves, and that it could actually be mercury that was first used to defeat them. The bullets I have in this gun are filled with liquid mercury in a glass casing. When the glass shatters, the mercury is spilled throughout the monster's insides, and the rest is history."

"Wow," Mako said, even more awed. "I guess you really are the smart one in this partnership, especially since you thought ahead to bring them."

"Well, after you sent me those … unusual blood samples, I wanted to be prepared to test my mercury bullet theory."

"At least you can rest easier now that you've avenged your parents."

She shook her head. "It wasn't Stumpp."

"What do you mean?"

"Stumpp told me he didn't kill them. He said it was someone close to me at that time."

"And you believe him? He had to be lying!"

"If he was responsible, he wouldn't pass the credit on to someone else. He would've wanted me to know. He thought he was going to kill me, remember?"

"So, what are you going to do?" Mako asked, already knowing the answer.

"Reopen my investigation, of course."

"Can I ask you another question?"

"Sure."

"Was Stumpp wearing a pair of my underwear?"

Jacquie chuckled. "I think so."

More sirens were heard, and now police cars and a second ambulance were seen looming in the distance.

"That's strange," he thought out loud, gesturing to the vehicles. "Why didn't the bus that took Stumpp wait for the uniforms to show?"

Placing a hand down on the Mercedes' hood, she asked, "You're not going to let them take this, are you?"

Mako placed his previous concerns aside, and then held the car keys out to her. "You wanna park it around the block before they get here?"

She glanced down the block at the approaching cars, staring directly into one of the strobe lights fastened to the roof of a police cruiser. She was temporarily blinded. Before she knew it, Jacquie heard voices chattering all around her. But a bothersome after-image prevented her from fully focusing on anything in particular. Blinking rapidly, attempting to adjust her vision back to normal, she was startled when someone took her by the arm.

"Please come with us, Miss," a voice said. "We need to get a statement from you."

FIFTY-ONE

Jacquie winced as the doctor examined her damaged wrist. Even the slightest touch sent a shock wave up her arm. He studied the X-ray film, hemming with every other breath, and she sighed heavily, alerting the physician to her impatience.

The elderly doctor spun around on his stool, X-ray still in hand, and asked, "You say this injury happened two days ago?"

"Just about."

"How come you didn't come in then?"

"I'm not from here, and I figured it could wait until I got back home. Why?" She hoped she hadn't made it worse by not getting it checked sooner. "Does it matter? I had other issues to attend to." She recalled the hours upon hours of interrogation she and Mako had gone through after the events that occurred outside his home.

"No," the doctor said with a harrumph. "But if you'd come sooner, you wouldn't have had to live with the pain of a fractured wrist."

"It's okay," she reassured him. "I'm tougher than I look."

"Sure you are, dear," the physician said patronizingly.

Outside the examining room, Mako read a magazine, waiting patiently. His phone rang. He answered without looking, and then wished he hadn't.

"Mako!" the caller yelled into his ear. "Get your ass down to the station! This is the moment I've been waiting for, and I want to break the news before the Review Board does!" There was unusual delight in the tone of the caller's voice.

"Sure thing, Lieutenant. But I'm at the hospital right now, so it'll have to wait until I'm done here." He wasn't in any rush to hear what Grimes had to say. If the lieutenant was anxious to speak to him, then it could only mean bad news.

"Don't make me wait too long," he warned. "It'll only be worse for you." He slammed the phone down hard enough to cause his detective to cringe.

He was about to resume reading when the doctor's office door opened. Mako spied the extra weight Jacquie was carrying on her arm.

She thanked the physician and offered a sincere farewell before turning to Johnny and rolling her eyes. "Male chauvinism will never die."

"So, what's the verdict?"

"It's only a soft cast, so as to not restrict the movement of the joint. But I have to schedule an appointment with my doctor once I get back home. Either way, the fracture should heal in a few weeks, and I'll be as good as new."

"Glad to hear it."

"Do we have time to get something to eat before my flight?"

"When is it again?"

"One thirty."

Mako checked his watch. "I think all we have time for is drive-through."

On that note, her phone chimed. Flipping her hair to the side, she answered, "Hello, Max." She covered the phone and whispered, "It's Max," in case Mako was wondering.

"I heard," he whispered back.

She went back to her call. "What's up?"

"You wanted me to update you on the Jarvis case, right?"

"Yes," she responded nervously. "Is something wrong?"

Clearing his throat, Max contemplated how to proceed. "Everything was fine until yesterday. We thought it was a done deal even without the murder weapon, but ... uh ..."

"Just tell me."

"The body's gone."

She hesitated before asking, "Dave Jarvis fled?"

"No. Jesse Pasco is gone. His body went missing from the morgue yesterday."

"Do we have any idea who would have taken the body?"

"That's the thing. There was no sign of forced entry into the morgue, and according to the security cameras—oh jeez, I can't even believe I'm about to say this."

"Max," she said as if speaking to a child.

"According to the cameras," he resumed, "Pasco walked out on his own."

"What?"

Mako cut in. "Is everything all right?"

Jacquie waved him off so she could get back to what Max was telling her.

"I know. It's crazy, but it's all we've got to go on."

Putting her skepticism aside, she inhaled deeply. Then, to let him know that she didn't think he was crazy, she told him she would be back in the office that afternoon and together they would investigate further.

"Don't you want to relax from your trip?"

"Max, sweetie," she replied fondly. "A body walks out of my morgue on a case I was working on, and you think I'm not going to get right on that? For now, figure out how far he could have gotten since his time of departure and canvass the area with photos. Maybe someone has seen him. And have our contacts in the police department check in with their informants. Maybe they've seen or heard something too."

"You got it, Boss," he sounded energized. "Text me the flight information, so I can have a car waiting to pick you up at the airport."

"Thanks. You're the best." She ended the conversation, turned around, grabbed Mako by the arm, and rushed toward the exit. "Drive-through sounds great, but let's hurry. I can't miss my flight."

"Problems?"

"I'll tell you on the way."

Barely half an hour later, Mako maneuvered his car next to the curb in front of a NO PARKING sign outside the airport terminal. The light green Honda Civic he was driving made him realize how much he missed his own car. The repair shop he'd been going to for years couldn't fathom what had caused all the damage, and they recommended he total the car and get a new one. But Mako had a sentimental attachment to his Lancer, so he was mulling it over before coming to a final decision. A security officer shouted at him to move, but he flashed his detective's shield to buy time to say goodbye.

"Well," Jacquie said, "this is it."

"I guess so." Getting her bags from the trunk, he didn't know if he should hug her or not. She made the decision for him and held him tightly. "I couldn't have done this without you," he said.

"I know," she answered, trying to be funny. Truth was she didn't want to go.

"I owe you one." He gently pushed her back so he could look into her eyes. "I mean it. If you need anything, let me know."

"Thanks." She hugged him again. "I'll collect one day."

"I'm sure you will."

The two quietly embraced for a few moments until their peace was disturbed by the same security guard who'd scolded them only a few moments ago.

"Hey," Mako yelled back, "fuck off already! Why don't you go find a lost kid or something?"

The rent-a-cop gave a one-finger salute before shuffling off to harass another illegally parked driver.

Moving away from Mako, Jacquie realized she shouldn't put off the inevitable any longer. "I better go." She lifted her luggage off the curb.

"You need any help with your little problem?"

Knowing he was talking about her missing corpse, she said, "Probably, but you can't take off from work to help me on a case. It'd be nice if you could though."

" I'll see if I have any vacation time coming to me." Reluctant to upset her, he kept quiet about the lieutenant's call. "But taking off is always a bitch. Still, if you want me to run any names for you, it's the least I can do."

"I appreciate it."

The two of them stared at each other for a few moments before she started for the terminal entrance. He waited for her to enter safely. She almost made it the whole way without turning back, but one thing on her mind kept nagging at her. "Can I ask you something?"

"Always."

"How come we didn't work out? We make a pretty good team."

"People change. Lives move in different directions. I guess we're no different."

"Maybe you're right."

"Maybe?" he joked. Taking a more serious tone, he added, "Look, Jacquie, I want you to be happy. There's someone out there much more suited for you than me."

"You're probably right. You're too hard-headed." She smiled, ran back and kissed him on the cheek.

"All part of my charm. Now, go catch your plane." He smiled too, and waited for her to disappear within the crowded airport.

Thinking about his last words to Jacquie, Mako was almost home when his phone rang. Suspecting it might be his lieutenant calling to yell again, he checked the display first.

"S'up?"

"What's up, Matt?"

"Haven't heard from you in a few days. How's everything working out with Jacquie?"

"Long story, but she's on her way back to Georgia."

"How about that case you were working on? Everything okay?"

"Longer story."

Matt was curious about the short answers and no explanations. "Is everything okay now?"

"I just have a lot on my mind."

Matt wanted to pursue his line of questioning, but one of his kids started crying. "Listen, I gotta go check out what's going on."

"Okay."

"You wanna come over later and hang out?"

"Your wife going to be home?"

"Well, she's out now, so probably. Why?"

"We'll see. I might have some stuff to take care of."

"Copper'll be here." Matt used the one bargaining chip he had.

Mako was always a sucker for animals, especially Copper. "Maybe for a little while, then. I'll call you."

"Later," Matt offered his usual send-off and hung up, yelling at his kids for making a mess of their toys.

"If it wasn't for Copper …," Mako finished the thought to himself as he pulled up in front of the house he used to call home. With its current condition, and with a pending police investigation, he'd have to find a new place to live.

"Hey, neighbor," Rikki waved, already waiting outside.

Mako tossed the set of car keys over to him. "Thanks for letting me borrow your car." Recalling everything else Rikki had done for him, he added, "And for taking care of my animals."

"It's no problem. I like doing it."

Mako was always ill at ease confessing his inner feelings, but the overwhelming need to express something to his neighbor won out. "I want you to know that I realize you help me out a lot, even if I bust your chops from time to time."

Rikki looked at him strangely. "Time to time, huh?"

"All right. A lot of the time."

Knowing how difficult this must be for Mako, Rikki didn't want to make it any harder, chiefly because he realized the hard times Mako had ahead of him.

"I want you to know that I appreciate you."

Rikki's expression turned to one of amazement. "That must have hurt to say."

"Not as much as I thought it would," he teased.

"Come inside for a second, there are some recovering pets that miss their daddy."

Checking the time, Mako imagined the smoke spewing from Lieutenant Grimes' ears right about now, but his animals were more important to him. Besides, he figured whatever was coming couldn't get much worse than he imagined it to be.

Rikki's apartment looked relatively untouched besides a few spots around the living room where plaster dust had fallen on the floor and furniture. There was also a long crack in the ceiling where there wasn't one before, but all in all, the place was livable. A few dishes had been knocked onto the kitchen floor and shattered, but there was nothing that couldn't be replaced.

Limping out from the bedroom were two banged-up dogs, excited to see their master. Even in their bruised state, they found the strength to wag their tails energetically until Mako kneeled down to pet them.

"The vet said they should have the bandages off in a few weeks." Rikki tried to allay any worries. "After that, you won't even know they were in a fight."

"What about Booger?" Mako asked, not seeing his cat anywhere.

"His injuries were … a little more extensive."

"Where is he?"

The sound of his neighbor's voice indicated that he expected the worst, so Rikki quickly amended his statement. "Oh no, he's alive. He's just going to need more time to recover."

"Is he here?"

"No," said Rikki, feeling bad that he couldn't reunite the two. "He'll be at the vet a few more days for observation. His back was broken, and he had a punctured lung and heavy internal bleeding. The vet said he shouldn't be alive, but I guess whatever Jacquie did saved him."

"I owe her another one, then."

"I do have a surprise though." Rikki chippered up to brighten the mood. "Stay right there. I'll go get it." He disappeared into the bedroom, then he returned holding a pet carrier. The solid part of the case faced Mako, so he couldn't see inside. But he heard scratching. Holding the carrier chest-high, Rikki's brisk walk across the floor made it appear as if his butt cheeks were clenched tightly together.

"Is that who I think it is?"

"I told you Booger's at the hospital. This little girl was left there, abandoned by her owners, without a home. I fell in love at first sight and just had to bring her home."

"Are you going to show me, or do I have to guess what's in the box?"

Rikki spun the case around to give his guest a clear view of the new addition. Lying happily inside was a small tabby cat with big green eyes and tiger striping. "Isn't she adorable?" Rikki gushed. "I named her Toni."

"I thought you said it was a girl."

"What did Jacquie ever see in you?" Rikki thought out loud. "It's with an I, not a Y. I think it's cute."

Time kept moving, and Mako didn't want to press his luck any more than he had already. He had to get down to the precinct and face the music, no matter how dreadful the overture might sound. "I have to get going, but there's one more favor I have to ask. Can these guys stay with you until I find a new place to live? I'll try not to put you out too much."

Rikki understood the enormity of the situation. He knew it must be a strain for a man with so much pride to have to accept such losses and admit he was defeated, even if it was indirectly. "Sure. Sure," he consented, hoping to make things easier. "You know I think of them as my babies. They can stay as long as you need them to. I'll enjoy the company."

"Thanks. I really appreciate it." Mako ran his fingers through Chip's fur and scratched Bruno under his massive neck. "I have to get to work. But I'll be back later to see how things are, if that's okay with you."

"Of course." Rikki put the cat carrier down and walked Mako to the door. "You're always welcome here. Hey," he said, changing the subject, "you need to borrow the car again?"

"It's okay. You might need it. Besides, I don't know when I'll be back, but if it gets too late, I'll call and come by tomorrow." He dialed a cab service.

"You going to be okay, Johnny?"

Someone from the taxi company answered the phone, but he took a moment to reflect on the question. "I don't really have a choice, do I?"

Mako strode through the main entrance of the Second Precinct. The look he received from the desk officer was the kind of stare that let a person know exactly what was coming, and in the detective's case, it was nothing good.

"Hey," the officer called over to him. "You need to get up to Grimes' office right away. He's been waiting for you."

"That's why I'm here." He forced himself to reach the second floor, and then he checked the surrounding faces. Their eyes told a story he didn't want to hear, but he was about to, regardless.

"MAKO! I know you're out there! D.O. told me you were on the way up!" the lieutenant shouted from within his office.

Not needing another outburst to further humiliate him, Mako hurried in and closed the door. "You wanted to see me, sir," he said, affecting nonchalance.

"You're damn right. Sit down." Grimes forcefully pointed at a chair in front of his desk.

Defiant as always, the detective responded, "If it's all the same to you, I'll stand."

Normally the lieutenant would react hostilely to the insubordination, but not today. Today, he leaned back in his chair and smiled. "Suit yourself. This won't take long," he said with a hearty chuckle.

A suspicious-looking file sat on the lieutenant's desk. Mako had noticed it almost as soon as he entered the room, and now that he was closer to it, he could clearly read his name on the label. His stomach twisted, but he did not show his anger.

Grimes rubbed his hands together much like an old black and white movie villain. All he was missing was the trademark handlebar moustache to twirl. As he studied his subordinate's face, he supposed the anticipation was eating away at him. And although he wanted to let Mako linger in drawn-out suspense, he could hardly contain his own excitement. Leaning forward, the lieutenant pulled the file back toward him and went through the loose papers inside.

"You really fucked up this time." He stopped to read one of the sheets. "Besides the fact that you let a material witness get murdered under your protection, which I thought would be enough to shit-can you, I have more." The lieutenant was clueless to the fact that Louis Falcone had not died at the motel, but Mako wouldn't dare reveal the truth. "Let me start with some things you already know," continued Grimes. Removing a page, he placed it on the desk. "Here's the formal complaint against you made by Investigator Thomas Samms for allegedly removing evidence from his possession. Feel free to read it over. I found it exhilarating."

Mako didn't reach for the document and offered no rebuttal.

Grimes continued, "Next item. I told you to stay out of Homicide's way in the matter of Robert Mane's murder. You didn't listen, and you pissed off a lot of influential people, both in and out of the department." He placed a second piece of paper on the desk. "This grievance is for interrupting an interview with Mr. Ethan Walker, an exec over at Stumpp Industries, and coming on a little too strong. An interview, I might add, that was supposed to be conducted by Mullins."

The detective gritted his teeth.

"I haven't had a chance to meet Walker, but I'll make sure he will testify personally in any hearing against you." The lieutenant picked another sheet out of the folder but only summarized it instead of showing it. "What I have in my hand is a confidential statement from one of your colleagues. It says how you flagrantly disregard almost any order I issue, pertaining to this case or otherwise. Your fellow officer describes the times and dates when you interfered with a case you had no business being part of."

A list of suspects shot through the detective's mind.

Returning the page to the folder, Grimes said, "In the report it also says how you brought in help from outside the department—a Ms. Jacquie Dale, to be specific. And we're all familiar with her expertise. You still hittin' that, or did she figure out what a loser you are and move onto better feeding grounds?" Mako's jaw clenched, illustrating that the lieutenant's attempt to get a rise out of him was working to a certain degree. Grimes hoped Mako would do something stupid to guarantee his demise. "I think it's pretty fuckin' convenient that Dale is a forensics expert who could easily analyze Samms' stolen evidence. I'm sure others will agree. What do you think?"

He said nothing.

"Why you so quiet today?" The commanding officer paused for an answer. "You always have such a big fuckin' mouth. Why not today? Is it because you know you're finished, you miserable piece of shit? I told you I've been waiting for this day. But wait, it gets better." The lieutenant flipped a few photos from the detective's file on the desk. "You know these men?"

Glancing at the pictures, Mako immediately identified the people in the images: Nathan Williams, Jason Brody, and several members of the Lunar Guardians, most of them armed.

"I don't give a shit if you say anything or not because I already know the answer!" Grimes tossed a few more photos down. The new set showed the detective speaking with several of them in various locations. "We're looking into the identities of men who could be part of a known terrorist group, and here you are consorting with them! Those firearms alone are illegal, and you didn't bother to call this in. Want to know something else? Guess where most of these were taken? Ah, screw it! I'll tell you anyways. They came from the morgue, where surprisingly, two bodies were stolen! Do you believe that? They stole two bodies! Not only that, but they injured an officer of the law! Did you know that? Mullins was found unconscious at a murder scene! Of course, we don't know who was killed because that body was removed too, bringing the stolen corpse count up to three, but there was enough blood in the surrounding area that we should get a DNA match sometime in the next forty-eight hours. And you'd better hope we find Falcone's body by then too, because his parents are threatening to sue! But I'm sure you have no idea what happened to him either." The sarcasm served to indicate that he would believe nothing his subordinate told him from this point on.

Grimes was rambling off tons of information, but Mako didn't need a recap. He had been there, and he'd witnessed almost everything firsthand.

"You know what the kicker is? The morgue has so many holes in it, it looks like a block of Swiss cheese! You wouldn't happen to know how it got that way, would you? Not to mention the fact that when Mullins came to, the first thing he said was that you were trouble and we had to find you. Man, I gotta hand it to you. When you fuck up, you do it in a big way! This leads me to my next bit of incriminating evidence against you, the case of a missing person. Perhaps you've heard of Peter Stumpp? His Mercedes was found parked outside your shitty apartment, which we're still investigating due to your claim of an intruder, but there was no Stumpp. Any idea where he could have gone?"

Mako had kept quiet long enough. The other allegations were bad but disputable. But a kidnapping charge could lead to serious jail time, and one place a cop doesn't want to end up is locked away with the people he's arrested. After the verbal bashing he'd received, he threw professionalism out the window. "Don't dare try to pin that on me! I already gave a statement, and so did Jacquie, attesting to the fact that an ambulance picked his body up that night!"

"Right." The lieutenant's distrust was evident. "You stated that Stumpp came to continue an argument which previously began in his office. And that as the situation became heated, he attacked you two, leaving you no choice but to fire on him. And that he was taken down with a slug to his cranium. I've read the report. Still doesn't explain the enormous amount of bullet casings we found at the scene. But besides that, no one showed up at the hospital with Stumpp's body, and someone has to be held accountable for that."

"What is it with you? What do you have against me?" Mako's curiosity superseded his anger. "You've had it in for me ever since I got my detective's shield. What'd I ever do to you?"

The lieutenant stared squarely into his bright blue eyes and said, "I don't like you. You parachuted into your promotion, and I don't respect that."

"Parachuted?" he shouted. "You son of a bitch! I didn't ask for that promotion! I got it because I stopped an armed robbery and saved a man's life! I was doing my job!"

"You got lucky! Don't think you deserve anything for it! I have plenty of cops busting their asses every day trying to save lives, and they don't get shit for it!"

"Is that the real reason, or is it something else?"

"You're uncontrollable, too headstrong, and I don't like it! I've given you plenty of opportunities to get in line, but you think it's funnier to insult me and ignore commands! I don't have time for the likes of you!"

"I get it." Now it was Mako's turn to give some back. "You're afraid of me, or of people like me—people who have a brain, and don't get by just because of a big mouth and influential friends. You're afraid that if someone ever discovered the fact that you're dumber than wood, I might be sitting in that chair telling you what to do someday. You'd rather have an army of trained monkeys hanging on your every word than a number of thinking individuals out on the streets and more equipped to save lives!"

"There are plenty of lives to save out there! Even a trained monkey will get one right sooner or later! I don't think you're worth salvaging, and I have enough of a case here to burn you good!"

"How do you look at yourself in the mirror?"

"It's days like these I find it very easy." Grimes tapped a finger on his desk. "Turn in your shield and firearm. You're officially suspended without pay until such time as a hearing can be set to determine your eligibility to retain your position."

The detective had no choice but to comply.

"Unofficially," Grimes said as his detective was about to walk out of his office, "I'd start looking for work in the private sector, if I were you. I'm going to make sure you never set foot in a police precinct unless you're under arrest."

Knowing he couldn't make matters any worse than they already were, Mako relieved some of his tension. "Go fuck yourself."

"Hey," Grimes yelled, pointing at his underling. "I'm your boss as of right now, so you will address me with the proper respect."

"Fine," Mako corrected himself. "Go fuck yourself, sir!" He slammed the door as he left.

Off to the left was Mullins' desk. Mako had thought they'd parted as friends, but after what the lieutenant told him, he wasn't certain. Mullins was startled when Mako unexpectedly grabbed his neatly pressed collared shirt. "How could you stab me in the back like that?"

All in attendance paid close attention to the developing scene. Mullins couldn't have his clout questioned in front of so many, and he smacked Mako's arms off of him. "Get your hands off me, ya fuckin' mutt! I didn't do anything to you!"

"But Grimes said—"

"You believe everything that prick tells you?" He flattened his wrinkled shirt. "Don't let him fool you. Grimes don't like me either because he has to watch his ass around me while my father still has so much pull in the department."

"He said you gave an incriminating statement to officers who arrived at the morgue."

"That's true," Mullins admitted. "But what he didn't tell you is that the officers took it out of context. I was on the phone with Jacquie. She told me you were in a lot of trouble and we had to get to you. Before I could answer her, I got cold-cocked by those two morons who stayed behind. And when I came to, I must have been trying to repeat what she told me—only it didn't come out right. Even after I fully regained consciousness, they wouldn't let me amend my statement. Grimes must have gotten to them already."

Feeling guilty for accusing his fellow detective, Mako said, "Sorry, Jimmy. I'm just so pissed. How did he get all this evidence against me? He's got photos and statements and phone calls. Grimes even told me someone in the department ratted me out, and since he said your name, I assumed you'd handed him everything else too."

"Don't worry about it." Mullins brushed it off. "I tried to get you a temporary promotion to be my partner, until we could make it permanent. But Grimes wouldn't go for it. I even went to my dad, but with all the shit they got, my father couldn't go to bat for you. I'm sorry."

"Don't be. You stuck your neck out for me more than anyone else in this shithole has." Mako ran his hand through his hair. "I wish I could get my hands on whoever sold me out."

Mullins checked all around before divulging some information. "From what I hear," he whispered, "most of that proof came in today, and the guy who brought it is still in Interview Room Three. But you didn't hear that from me."

"Hear what?" Mako spoke softly and shook Mullins' hand. Making his way to the aforementioned room, he ensured that no one was present to stop him. Satisfied he'd be uninterrupted for an ample amount of time, he kicked the interrogation room's door open and rushed in. But he froze in place upon seeing the man inside. "You gotta be kiddin' me!"

Detective Fred Bailey stood on the opposite end of the room, just as shocked as his former partner, not expecting company in the form of the man whose career he'd helped end. Bailey wasn't a pushover and resorted to intimidation tactics. "You're not supposed to be here, Johnny!" His baritone voice echoed throughout. "Get the hell out of here before I have you thrown in a holding cell!"

"Throw me in a cell?" Mako couldn't believe his ears. "You mother fucker! You were supposed to be my partner!"

"I told you I wasn't going down for you."

"You're gonna go down all right!" Mako jumped at Bailey, but the timely arrival of Mullins and another officer proved sufficient to hold him back.

"Johnny," Mullins grunted. "Calm down! This won't help your case!"

"I don't care! He's supposed to be my partner!" Mako was able to get some forward momentum and dragged the two officers a few inches with pure adrenaline. But two more officers provided backup, and all four men removed him from the room.

The lieutenant was waiting outside with a big grin on his face. "Ain't that a bitch, Mako? You can't even trust your own partner. I guess you rub everyone the wrong way."

"Go to hell," he said, still restrained by the others.

"Get'im outta here!" Grimes watched as Mako was forcibly escorted off the second floor.

Once in the lobby, Mullins walked his colleague out the front door. The other three stood ready in case the former detective needed to be controlled again.

"I could kill him," Mako blurted out in a fit of rage.

"Careful what you say," Mullins said, reminding him other people were listening. "I could be ordered to arrest you for threatening his life, and you know that."

"I can't believe it!"

"Well, get over it. You can't do anything about it now."

"I can do one thing," Mako said. "I can find out who took Stumpp's body."

"How you gonna do that?"

"Can you find me an address?"

Ethan Walker rested in front of the shrine he'd erected to his family's memory, slowly and calmly snuffing each candle between his thumb and index finger. He overheard an argument his secretary was having with someone who was determined to gain entrance to his office, and he waited patiently for the dispute to reach its conclusion.

The door was violently thrown open, and Mako angrily marched in. "What did you do you with Stumpp's body?" He whipped out his reserve gun and aimed it at Ethan's back.

"I'm so sorry, Mr. Walker," the frightened woman apologized. "I'll call the police."

"Don't bother." Ethan unhurriedly turned around. "I can handle it from here."

"As you wish, sir." The secretary left.

Ethan moved across the floor to his comfortable high back executive's chair. "That really isn't necessary, Detective." He referred to the pistol pointed at him.

"I'll take that under advisement." Mako had no intention of putting the gun away. "Now, answer the question!"

"How did you find me? I have several offices throughout the tri-state area."

"This is the fourth one I checked, and I had more to go, if you weren't here," he said, pulling out a small list as proof. "Quit stalling, and tell me where your boss is."

Gesturing to his private bar off in a corner of the office, Ethan asked, "Care for a drink? I am unable to feel the effects of alcohol any longer, but I do enjoy the taste of it."

"You don't know, do you?"

"Nor do I care. May I?" He asked permission to leave his seat so the detective wouldn't perceive any movement as a potential attack. Ascertaining that there was no direct threat to him, Mako responded by holstering his firearm. Ethan went to the bar and poured himself a Johnnie Walker Blue Label. "Thank you." He lifted the bottle higher in a second attempt to offer Mako a drink, but Mako declined.

"What's your deal anyway? You work for Stumpp, but you have secret meetings behind his back with his son, who claims you have an agenda all your own."

"Vendetta is more like it." After sipping the fine scotch, he pointed with his glass at the pictures on the opposite wall. "See those people, Detective? A long time ago I had a family whom I loved more than life itself. Peter came to me at a time when I was struggling to make ends meet, and he offered me a job, paying more money than I could ever hope for. I had to provide for my family, and I knew this would allow them to live comfortably for years to come. Obviously, I jumped at the chance and became Peter's assistant. He entrusted me with the inner workings of his empire, and soon after, I wished he hadn't.

"I was working late one night, and as I did every night before I left, I made my rounds through the building to ensure that everything was secure. I was on a catwalk inside one of our warehouses when I found a vagrant stumbling around below. I was about to rectify the problem, but instead I saw the most fearsome thing I'd ever witnessed: a giant wolf emerged from the darkness and butchered the man right in front of my eyes. Then it turned its massive head and looked at me.

"It jumped straight up, at least twenty feet high, and was on the catwalk with me before I could scream. I thought I was a dead man, but then the strangest thing happened. The beast spoke to me, right before it transformed into my employer, Peter Stumpp. He explained what he was and why he did what he did. He asked me not to divulge his secret to anyone. I imagine the only reason he didn't kill me right there was because he needed me to take care of his business while he engaged in activities that prevented him from frequently being seen.

"Either way, I kept my word and didn't tell a soul. I pretended none of it happened, even on the late night shifts when I could hear men, women, and sometimes children begging for their lives to the giant wolf who would devour them. I understood he was evil, but I also realized I was powerless to stop him. All I could do was keep my family safe, but even that didn't last very long. Maybe he thought I would break my promise, or maybe he noticed how repulsed I was to be in his presence, but one evening those pleas to the giant wolf came from me.

"He stalked me throughout the compound. Taunted me. Made me fear him as I feared no one else. And then he pounced. As you know, he spared my life. But he left me with a scar that would never heal, and I'm not speaking of the wound where his fangs sank into my skin. During the first week of my transformations into the monster I had become, Peter kept me in isolation. Starved me. The last night of that same week, he brought my family to visit. He locked them in a chamber with me for the whole day, so I could cherish my last moments with them.

"They didn't know what was in store for them as the sun was replaced by the moon—but I did, and I implored Peter to release them. He laughed. As I started to turn, their screams echoed throughout the room. It must have been like music to his ears. If I had been more in control of the creature, as I am now, I would have never succumbed to my baser instincts. As it was, I was starving, and the pure unfettered fury of the animal came out. In the morning, I had become myself again, and all that remained of my family was tattered clothing and some chewed up bits scattered about the room. I was happy to not remember the incident fully, but I have continued to grieve for them every day of my long and miserable existence."

Mako was appalled by the gruesome tale. "I'm sorry. I can't even imagine—"

"No," Ethan interrupted. "You can't." He finished his drink in one gulp. "I know you must be asking yourself why I didn't try to kill him then for what he had made me do, but I couldn't. I had thought about it, believe me. But when I say I couldn't, I mean it was impossible. Peter had shown me the Heart of Lycaon and explained how it made him immortal so that no weapon on earth could destroy him. I knew any attempt I made would be futile, and he would only kill me in return. I decided to stay in his employ, so that one day I could uncover the secrets of the Heart, break Peter's bond with it, and finally avenge the lives of my loved ones. I have lived for over two hundred years waiting for that moment. And now, thanks to you, my wait is over."

"But I didn't kill him."

"True, but you put him down long enough for him to be dealt with."

"So, you do know where he is."

"Not exactly, Detective, but I can guess who took him. And they are no friends of mine."

"Do me a favor." Mako wanted to clear one thing up before he allowed Ethan to continue. "Stop calling me Detective. Partially thanks to your complaints, I won't be one for long."

"Complaints?" Ethan sounded genuinely surprised. "I can assure you I am not a man to complain to others about his problems. I take care of them myself, although I am glad I decided to let you live."

"Anyway," Mako said, letting that subject slide for the moment, assuming it'd been Bailey who filed the grievance, "let's get back to who took Stumpp's body."

"If I tell you, would you kindly take your leave afterward?"

Exiting Ethan's office building, Mako tried to process all the information swimming through his head. Preoccupied with the idea of a new threat looming on the horizon, it was no wonder that Mako was unable to detect his former partner standing a block away, leaning on a faded light blue Chevy Camaro.

Bailey wondered what thoughts were running through Mako's mind. But his own were interrupted by a whisper from the dark alley, a few feet from his position.

"Detective." The man known as Harris stepped into the daylight. "Please, join me." When it appeared that Bailey was hesitant, Harris persuaded him with a pistol held discreetly at his side, his finger on the trigger. "Now."

"What do you want? I did your dirty work. Now, leave me and my family alone!"

Bailey could intimidate pretty much anyone he came into contact with, but Harris wasn't like anyone else. "You aren't in a position to bark orders at me."

From behind the detective, a large figure moved in the part of the alley that was completely devoid of sunlight, maneuvering its position to the detective's left. Bailey knew it was there and was too petrified to move as a large, emaciated hand, with enormous, threatening claws on each bony finger, lightly curled around his shoulder. The massive figure lowered itself to stare directly into Bailey's eyes. The giant creature was covered in black fur and had the head of a wolf with glowing red eyes. It opened its mouth, and Bailey saw the saliva dripping off its sharp fangs.

"We aren't done with you yet," Harris said. "You did such a good job with your former partner that we want to keep you around for a while longer."

"You're lucky you have your pet with you, Harris, or I'd—"

"Be cautious of the tone you take with us, human!" Harris cut the detective off. But now his voice was lower and throatier. His eyes rolled back into his head and his body stiffened up like something else took control of him. "You apparently do not know who is the pet and who is the master, but I would advise you not to insult us again—not unless you want that tasty morsel of a sister to suffer for your sins! Ah, what we would do to her."

"All right." Bailey had heard enough. "You win. I'll work for you. Don't touch my sister or anyone else close to me."

"Good boy," Harris commented from his trance-like state.

"What do you want me to do to Mako next?"

"Don't worry about that. We've got plans of our own for him."

"Who do you want me to take care of then?" he asked anxiously. "Brody, Williams, Stumpp?"

"So eager," Harris replied. "Brody and Williams can wait, and as for our hated enemy, he's been taken care of already." Harris and the wolf creature laughed simultaneously with possibly the most disturbing cachinnation Bailey had ever heard.

Peter Stumpp lay on his back, still as a corpse. The large bullet that had lodged in his brain a few days prior was pushed out by his amazing regenerative powers, and the slug rolled off his face and onto the soft fabric beneath him.

His eyes opened gradually as if awakening from a deep sleep. Stretching the muscles in his neck, he twisted it from side to side. His arms widened a few inches and came into contact with a hard surface that burned his skin. The sensation immediately jolted him awake, but with every move he made, Stumpp's naked body hit into something that set his skin on fire.

Blinking rapidly to clear his vision, he realized there was nothing wrong with his sight; rather, the problem was with his surroundings. He was sealed shut in a tightly packed space, but what exactly was burning his skin remained a mystery. In a desperate attempt to free himself, he pushed both palms against the top plane, using all his strength. A few agonizing moments was all he could stand before giving up. He wondered why his underside wasn't experiencing the same sensation, but then he observed that he was lying on cushy material. If he remained motionless, nothing could harm him, but he would certainly linger in captivity.

Then he felt something small resting under his right thigh. He gently took it and slid his arm up onto his chest, careful not to touch the sides of his prison. With his acute vision, he determined it was a cigarette lighter. He ignited it, hoping to acquire a better idea of where he was, and the picture became apparent. Directly in his line of sight was a small, engraved plaque that read, "Rest in Peace. Your friend, Harris."

Stumpp seethed, now understanding what was holding him prisoner and why it was painful to the touch. He'd been sealed in a coffin made of pure silver! Although he tried to work out an escape plan, nothing came to him. He howled in rage, but there was no one around to hear.

Mako wandered down an unfamiliar street in an unfamiliar neighborhood, taking inventory of his current situation. He'd lost his car and his home, and he was going to lose his job and his steady paycheck—it was only a matter of when. His pets and friends had almost died because of his involvement in a case he could have easily let go, but his stubbornness had told him he had something to prove. Not only physically spent, he was mentally and emotionally lost too. And he didn't even know where he'd be sleeping that night.

A vehicle rolled up next to him, and the passenger side window slid down. "Excuse me. Can I have a moment of your time?" The car came to a standstill, and Mark Bronson, deputy leader of the Lunar Guardians, exited.

Not pleased to see him, Mako said, "I thought you guys went back to your secret clubhouse."

Bronson understood the attitude, so he got right to the point of his visit. "We did. But I have a specific reason for returning, and it concerns what happened the night we encountered Peter Stumpp."

"Let's get one thing straight." Mako's agitation level was rising rapidly. "You didn't do a damn thing except assault a police officer and take off with a key witness in a murder trial—a witness who could have saved my job!"

"Yes. I did hear of your unfortunate circumstances with the police department."

"How could you? I only found out today."

"We do our homework, Mr. Mako."

"And cut that 'Mr. Mako' shit out! You suddenly want to show me some respect?"

"That wasn't my fault. Nathan is my superior, and out in the field, it would be improper to challenge his command."

"Speaking of Mr. Wonderful, where's your backup? Got another wolf to catch?"

"No. I came alone, and I came for you." Bronson was not playing games. "I want to offer you a place within the Lunar Guardians. You have shown tremendous resolve in the face of danger. You stood up to the most dangerous lycanthrope to ever live and you survived. Not many can say the same."

Bronson continued, "You would have shelter, food, and earn a weekly stipend for your services. Your pets could stay at the compound with you, if you so chose. And you would receive ample training and be permitted access to our stockpile of weaponry for hunting the beasts."

Mako weighed the pros and cons, unsure if he should sincerely consider the offer.

"I don't believe you have many options at this time," Bronson said, placing his last card on the table and allowing his companion to contemplate his current circumstances for a few more seconds. And then, reaching out a hand to seal the deal, he asked, "So, Mako, what's it gonna be?"

ACKNOWLEDGMENTS

This book has taken several years to complete, and I would like to take a moment to thank everyone who has assisted me in this endeavor. First and foremost, I would like to thank God for helping me through this process and all its complexities—including finding the right people, like Denise Adamo, who would help me achieve success. Denise initially proofread my book and significantly improved some of my technical skills when revising it. I would also like to thank Carl Graves of Extended Imagery for his creative genius to design such a fantastic cover. He took what I envisioned in my mind and made it numerous times better on paper. By extension, I have to thank author J. A. Konrath for his blog because it was through it that I found Carl. I must also thank my co-worker, Helene, who pointed out a critical color detail I somehow missed in the cover art. I want to thank James M. Loeffler and Thomas Rosselli, who copyrighted my manuscript to ensure I didn't goof up trying to do it on my own. I would also like to thank Carol Webb of Bella Media Management for all the formatting and design work she contributed to this book. Thank you to Linda H. Dolan of Write to Sell Your Book for meticulously copy-editing my manuscript, correcting all the small details I missed and helping me tie all the loose ends together. And many thanks to Diane O'Connell of Write to Sell Your Book for her eye to detail and great insight as an editor, and for her integral role in the publishing process; without her knowledge and expertise I do not think I would have been able to handle this massive undertaking on my own. I want to thank my friends and family who supported me, even if it was to simply hound me to get it done. And I especially thank my Aunt Bernadette whose advice to me a long time ago was, "Write what you know, and people will read it." Here's to hoping she was right. And last, but definitely not least, I thank all of you who took a chance on someone new to the publishing industry and read this book.

Thank you.

www.ingramcontent.com/pod-product-compliance
Lightning Source LLC
Chambersburg PA
CBHW070346260626
47161CB00001B/42